CHAPTER 1

The man wielded a pair of dueling wands like he knew how to use them.

I didn't have a chance to ask him who he was or what he wanted before he gave me a demonstration of his skill. Energy whipped from the tip of his left-hand wand, but it was just a feint. Those untrained in dueling would have defended against the attack, leaving them open to the deathblow from the right-hand wand. I drew my wands on sheer reflex, parried the feint with one hand, and shielded the critical strike with the other.

"What the hell?" I shouted. "I'm just trying to get a drink!"

It all happened so fast it took a moment for the other patrons in the crowded bar to realize lethal force was in play nearby. Predictably, they panicked, scattering like wild gazelle before a pride of lions. Shouting patrons knocked over tables and chairs. Glasses shattered on the concrete floor, contents spreading like spilled blood.

I parried another blow and responded with an attack of my own. The whirling orb smacked against a support beam, leaving a black, smoking crater in the wood. The attacker snarled and unleashed volleys from both wands. I rolled to the side and the attack smashed into the top shelf behind the bar, boiling expensive liquor to steam.

I flung a shield between me and the other man. "What do you want?" The guy was of medium build with brown hair and olive skin. I'd never seen him before, but it wasn't the first time a stranger had tried to kill me. I could count the number of friends I had on two fingers. More advanced math was required to calculate the number of enemies and haters.

The man shouted, face contorted with rage, but the noise emanating from his mouth was pure gibberish. I strained to make sense of it but couldn't understand a word. He nodded in satisfaction and glared at me when he finished his indecipherable rant then rushed me from across the room.

I decided to take him alive. Though a lot of people wanted me dead, very few came after me themselves. This guy was probably a hired gun, and I wanted to know who he worked for. There was a public bounty on me, but it was only worth fifty grand. Not many people were willing to risk their lives for so little against someone who used to guard the high fae.

I focused on the space behind him and prepared to ghostwalk. The hairs on my neck prickled. I dodged to the side as a white-hot orb flashed past me and bored a hole the size of a golf ball through the would-be assassin's chest. He dropped dead without a sound, heart charred to a crisp.

I glared at the fat man behind the bar. He held a pump-action staff, the kind used by supers who weren't adept at magic. "Were you trying to shoot me or him?"

His beady eyes narrowed. "Didn't matter to me either way."

I whirled my dueling wands and holstered them without looking away from him. "Perhaps I'll make it matter." The other patrons went deathly quiet and still as I stalked toward the bar. Keeping my voice calm but frosty, I said, "Perhaps you don't know who I am."

The bartender gulped audibly. He dropped the weapon and held up his hands. "I was aiming at him."

"At him, *sir*." I stopped in front of him.

Sweat beaded on the man's head. "I was aiming at him, sir."

I looked around the room at the other patrons. "Anyone else feeling lucky tonight?"

No one made a peep.

"Good." I tapped on the bar. "I'd like a Malibu Mangorita, please. Frozen, no salt."

"At once, sir." The bartender moved so fast he could've outrun a werewolf.

I turned back to the rest of the crowd. "I need information, and I'm willing to pay. If anyone has information about how to break a bargain with a god, come forward and I'll make it well worth your while."

The crowd began to murmur, and several people looked at me like I was crazy. They probably weren't too far from the truth.

A pair of servers came from behind the bar and began cleaning up the broken glass and spilled alcohol all while ignoring the dead assassin. Since no one came forward, I went to the assassin's body and frisked it. There was nothing, no ID, not even a spare penny lurking in the folds of his plain gray robe. I loosened the robe and examined his body for tattoos or other identifying marks.

Aside from a cluster of freckles on his neck a scar on his left rib, there wasn't anything that'd make it easier to discover his identity. I took pictures of him with my phone, though I wasn't sure what I'd do with them. Without the resources of Eclipse, the assassination and bounty hunting agency I'd once worked for, I'd have to rely on non-magical means of facial recognition.

Once again, I turned to the room. "Does anyone recognize this man?"

I received stares, glares, and glances, but no answers.

The barkeep returned with a frosty orange beverage. "One Malibu Mangorita."

I took the dead man's wands and left the body on the floor. It wasn't my problem anymore. I examined the drink and frowned. "Where's the plastic pirate sword and the toothpick umbrella in a slice of pineapple?"

The bartender trembled. "Sir, we don't have fresh pineapple or plastic swords."

"Or toothpick umbrellas?" I sighed. "And yet you have the ingredients for a mangorita?"

"I had to use a powdered mix," he said.

I took a sip through the straw and grimaced. "Gods almighty. What is this abomination?"

"We're not really equipped to make frozen drinks or anything—uh—"

"Girly?" I said.

He nodded. "If you say so."

I shrugged. "I love girly drinks." The dull roar of conversation had resumed, but I turned to the rest of the bar and silenced it with a loud question. "Who here loves girly drinks?"

A table of witches hesitantly raised their hands. The warlocks sitting with them joined their ranks, but most likely because they wanted to get laid. A pair of male elves also showed their hands.

"Where is the best super-friendly place to get such drinks?" I said.

One of the witches answered. "Voltaire's?"

I groaned. "Besides there."

"Shipwreck," a male voice shouted back.

I hadn't been there before, but I'd heard of it. I switched subjects while I had their attention. "I'll ask you once more. Does anyone here have information about breaking covenant with a god?"

"Oh, I could tell you plenty." The voice came from the open door of the pub. A middle-aged woman waltzed inside like she owned the place, detouring around the assassin's body without even looking at it.

The patrons remained silent, as if everyone wanted to hear the secret, but the longer she remained quiet, the more restless the crowd became. By the time she reached the bar, the noise level was back to normal.

The woman tapped the bar. "I'll have an Original Sinrise, please."

The barkeep frowned, eyes flicking from her to me, then he got busy.

"Hey, wait," I called.

He turned around. "Yes, sir?"

"Do you make those better than your mangoritas?"

"Yes, sir."

"Then I'll have one." I shoved the awful orange concoction away from me and turned to the woman. "And you are?"

"Susan." She climbed onto the barstool and let her legs dangle. "You've been asking an awful lot of questions around town, Cain."

Most people would've been surprised by such familiarity from a stranger, but I'd grown accustomed to my infamy. "That's usually the way to get an awful lot of answers."

"Unless it's about breaking bargains with gods," she said dryly.

I wanted to summon my oblivion staff for a look at this woman through the true-sight scope, but it seemed overly rude, even for me. She looked like someone's kindergarten teacher, but looks were deceiving. Mages could hide behind illusion. Shapeshifters could assume the shape of almost anyone or anything. Fae glamour could fool even the most discerning gaze.

I didn't notice any flickers, uneven lines, or bad color blends that usually gave away an illusion. Without my scope, I wouldn't know what kind of super she might be. So, I took the lazy route and just asked. "What kind of super are you?"

Susan smirked. "Humans have such quaint terms."

That comment gave me pause. She wasn't an elf, and she didn't give off a fae vibe. Then again, she might just be trying to throw me off her scent by making such a strange comment.

"Yeah, humans sure do." I pursed my lips and stared at her, waiting for an answer.

"Look, Cain, I'm just here to enjoy a drink and to tell you to stop asking questions and mind your own business, okay?" She leaned an elbow on the bar. "Do you think if there were a way to break a Faustian bargain with a god, the gods would want that information known?"

"Is Cthulhu even a god?" I said.

"Close enough." Susan's gaze wandered to the bartender and back to me. "You're attracting a lot of attention and rousing the ire of some beings who have been content to sit back and enjoy life for the past couple of thousand years. Do you really want to stir them up?"

"Are you a minion of Cthulhu?" I asked.

"No."

"Are you a member of one of the factions trying to control the demis?" I said. "The Pandora Combine? The Divine Council? The Underlords? The Enders?" I felt certain she wasn't with the Firsters. That racist bunch was too stupid to have the information she did.

"No, no, and no again."

"You're two *no*s short," I said.

"Technically, a single no to your first question would've sufficed." Susan glared at the barkeep. "I wish you hadn't gotten yourself banned from Voltaire's. I'd prefer to get a drink there far more than this hole in the wall."

"Me too." My mood soured. I'd been banned because apparently, I caused too much trouble and destruction even though it had been Sigma, not me, who blasted the parking lot to bubbling tar and nearly created a major incident with the nub police.

It was also where Aura worked.

I was still pissed at her for betraying me. For lying to me. For making me like her and then revealing she'd been using me all along. And yet, I wanted to see her.

The bartender placed our drinks before us, then beat a hasty retreat before we had a chance to say anything. A tiny red apple bobbed in the glowing white liquid. Susan pulled the apple out by its stem, took a bite, and dropped it back in. The liquid clouded black as night.

She took a sip and sighed contentedly. "Mm. Tastes like sin."

I tested the drink. The white liquid was bland and watery. "This is awful."

Susan rolled her eyes. "Because goodness tastes like shit. Bite the apple."

I did so and dropped it back into the glass. Darkness rippled through the liquid. I took a sip. It was sweet and sticky. It went down my throat smoothly, warming me from the inside out. A moment later, a bad aftertaste soured my taste buds. I took another sip and it banished the aftertaste, but only for a moment.

"Just like real sin," I said. "Feels good going down but leaves a bad taste in your mouth."

"So, you sin some more." Susan held up her glass and clinked it against mine. "To all the sin that makes life so sweet."

I clinked her glass back and took another drink. "To the good people who make it possible."

Susan raised an eyebrow. "You're going to ignore my request, aren't you?"

I nodded. "Cthulhu forced someone I care about to make a bargain."

"A rarity in your life," she said dryly.

"Exactly." I set down the drink. "Which is why it's important to me."

"You don't have to care," Susan said. "Just go back to being your old self, Cain."

I shook my head. "Life is meaningless enough already. I'd prefer to share my misery with a friend."

Susan tossed back the remains of her drink, apple and all as easily as water. "I'm just a friendly messenger. You don't want to anger the beings I work for."

It seemed pretty clear who that was. "Who, Lucifer?"

Susan shrugged. "Agree to walk away from this and I'll tell you."

I leaned over and sniffed her. "I haven't met many demons. Can you hide the brimstone odor?"

She leaned back and folded her arms across her chest. "Decide, Cain. Once I leave, there will be no more offers of amnesty."

"Amnesty?" I took the apple from the drink and nibbled at it. "I was unlawfully tricked into using a magic relic that bound me to Cthulhu. When I refused to serve him, he tricked a young girl into taking my place."

"I'll take that as a no." Susan dropped off the stool and waved an arm at the room. "You and that girl are no better than all these people in the one way that matters—you're human. Gods make the rules and humans abide by them."

"Hannah is a demigod," I said. "She's not entirely human."

"Doesn't matter." Susan pushed the stool under the bar. "She doesn't have the power to change things and neither do you. I suggest you use the cards you were dealt and leave the gods well enough alone."

I resisted the urge to grip her by the throat and lift her short frame off the ground. Instead, I stood and glared down at her. "Don't make me ask who you work for again, Susan. There's no fae safe zone here. I can take you any time I please."

"Can you, though?" She raised an eyebrow. "I'd almost like to see you try except I'm running late to another appointment."

That was when I put two and two together. *Messenger. Running.* I summoned my staff and peered through the scope at her. Nothing changed. It wasn't because she wasn't using illusion, but because the magic behind the disguise was too powerful for even the scope to penetrate.

"Rude!" She slapped the end of the staff out of her face. "And completely useless. Hephaestus forged these silly staffs. Do you really think he'd allow them to be used against—" Susan broke off abruptly, as if realizing her next words would be a giveaway.

"Against a god?" I grinned. "Hello, Hermes."

CHAPTER 2

Susan's lips pursed and then flattened into a thin line.

"Don't deny it," I said. "You dropped all the hints, whether purposefully or not."

"Oh, I'm not denying it." She shook her head. "I'm just surprised you're not even the least bit awed to be in the presence of a god."

I wasn't so much awed as scared shitless. Even the least of the gods could kill me without breaking a sweat. Up until a few months ago, I'd thought they were all dead only to discover most of them were hiding out among the populace, pumping out demigods with humans, or leading a conspiracy to kill all the demigods.

But I hadn't earned a spot in the Oblivion Guard by showing fear. I shrugged. "I've met Cthulhu, so meeting a Greek god isn't that big of a deal."

"Outside, now." Susan stalked to the door, ignoring the eyes following us.

It was probably a terrible idea, but I followed her outside and into a filthy alley on the left side of the building. Susan's visage shimmered away, revealing a young male with curly brown hair. He wore modern athletic gear. Even his famed winged shoes were modern high-top tennis shoes with a familiar logo on the side. While his torso was well-muscled, it was the massive muscles on his legs that made my jaw drop.

I whistled. "Gods, you work out, don't you?"

"Not really." He flexed a quad and grinned. "Being a god has its benefits."

His boast brought me back to reality. I was in a dirty alley with a being who could crush my head like a tin can between his meaty legs. "Did Hera send you?" I asked.

Hermes clapped me on the shoulder in a friendly but condescending manner. "Look, Cain, I kind of like you. You made waves in the community when you took out the Firster leaders. But you also made some serious enemies. I personally won't take part in this, but I will be the messenger."

I grunted. "So you won't kill me, but Hera will."

"Pro tip, Cain—just like the fae can't take direct action against a human, neither can the gods. That's why they have minions do their dirty work. But there is one major exception to the rule."

"If I take direct action against a fae or a god, then they can do likewise to me," I said.

Hermes' eyebrows arched. "Not many know that rule. Guess your time with the fae taught you a few things."

"As if I had a choice." I shrugged. "They adopted me and tried to make me one of their own, for some reason."

"Ah, yeah." Hermes tsked. "I get it. Last of your tribe and all that."

I blinked. "Say what?"

He patted my shoulder again. "Let's spar sometime. It won't count as you taking direct action against me, so unless things get out of hand, it'd be harmless."

"Go back to that part about last of my tribe," I said.

There was a rush of air and a blur and Hermes was gone.

I raised a fist. "You said that on purpose and left me hanging!"

Laughter echoed on the wind and faded away.

Hermes might be the messenger of the gods, but he was also known as a trickster. What he'd said might have been a lie or misdirection. Or it could have been a sliver of truth left to torment me. I'd pondered the fate of my parents off and on over the years. The only thing my adoptive fae parents would tell me was that they'd died in a terrible battle. They'd never said who, what, or why, and I'd never found any answers. The tremendous pressure of training like a fae had also taken up most of my free time. I'd been a mere human trying to prove I could do whatever elves and other non-humans could do.

Now that I had more free time than I knew what to do with, maybe it was time to add another investigation to my agenda. Or perhaps that comment was a seed of misdirection intentionally planted by Hermes to divert me from freeing Hannah from her servitude.

A napkin trapped by the tip of my shoe fluttered in the breeze. Despite the filth on the alley ground, the napkin looked practically new. It was a small, square napkin, the kind used as a coaster by restaurants. Something was printed in the center of the napkin, and it wasn't the name of this place.

Oddly enough, the word printed in the center was *Shipwreck*, the name of the bar someone had answered in response to my query. It was too strange to be coincidence. I wondered if, despite Hermes' warning, he'd left this beneath my foot when he left.

I probably should have been concerned, but the desire for a real mangorita splashing across my tongue was too strong to ignore. Plus, there'd be a fresh crowd I could interrogate, and the bartender there might actually have real skills. But as I reached the parking lot in the back, I saw something that made me so furious, I nearly lost my cool.

Three men in tight burgundy robes glared at me. Sirs Colin, Henry, and Francis, knights of Mage Guild, had wanted to take me into custody for some time. They'd threatened me, spread mostly untrue rumors about me, and ruined many an evening at Voltaire's. It was obvious they'd heard I was here and come to ruin yet another bar for me.

But that wasn't what infuriated me.

What made my blood boil was the casual way in which they leaned against Dolores, my nineteen-seventy Dodge Corona Super Bee.

It took everything I had not to ghostwalk across the parking lot and part their heads from their bodies in one slash of my staff. "Get off my car!" I didn't even know how they knew Dolores was mine, unless someone here had seen my arrival and told them.

Colin smirked and bared his nasty corn-yellow teeth through a bushy black beard. "At last we find you outside the protection of a safe zone, traitor. You will finally be brought to justice."

I showed him my teeth and briefly wondered if drinking all that sin had blackened them. "Were you so drunk last time that you forgot I let you have at me outside of the safe zone? Or are you just that stupid?"

"The stupidity is yours!" Sir Henry brandished his sword. "And I will cut out your tongue for the insult."

Colin put his hand over Henry's wrist and made him lower his sword. "The tongue cutting can come later, Henry." Colin puffed out his chest. "Cain Sthyldor, you are charged with treason, murder, and too many other offenses to list. I hereby place you under arrest."

I held out my wrists. "Ooh, kinky, Colin. I like your foreplay."

"I will kill him!" Henry roared.

Sir Francis held him back by the shoulders. Henry was short and stocky, whereas Francis was the tallest of the group by far.

I snorted. "It's like watching a German Shepherd hold back a Chihuahua."

"Mock all you desire," Francis said, "but there is no escape for you this time."

The hair on the back of my neck prickled and I realized the knights had brought back-up this time. Silhouettes appeared on the rooftops bordering the parking lot, and I knew without looking there were more on the bar behind me. We might be in downtown Atlanta, but this was the perfect place to get away with murder.

The only way to the parking lot was through two narrow alleys just wide enough for a car. The buildings on all sides were owned by supers. The surrounding area was peppered with avoidance wards that kept normal humans, nubs, from coming anywhere close. So the knights could get away with pretty much anything back here.

Then again, so could I.

My car wasn't blocked in. I considered ghostwalking behind the trio, kicking them away, and driving off before anyone could stop me, but I hesitated to use my ace in the hole. Few people knew ghostwalking existed, and even fewer knew I had the power.

I flicked my fingers through a pattern and cast a small spell to help me sense everyone nearby. It drifted across the parking lot, a barely visible vapor, touching warm bodies and giving me their locations.

I counted eighteen men and twelve women, armed with swords and staffs. Mage knights usually relied on magic-enhanced blades to fight since most of them weren't very adept at using magic. Then again, that went for the bulk of mages I'd met.

Despite their lack of skills, if it came down to a fight, I couldn't take on thirty people at the same time.

The spell sensed those on the rooftops powering spells, the magic equivalent of training guns on me. It seemed they weren't taking any chances. In a moment, ghostwalking would be the only choice left to me.

"Do you want people to die?" I said. "Because this is how people die."

Colin smirked. "With thirty of the finest knights in Atlanta prepared to take you down, I don't think we need to worry about you hurting anyone."

Even though using it had given me deadly magic cancer and bound me to Cthulhu, I almost wished I still had the pearl dangling around my neck. It greatly amplified my power and had rescued me from too many sticky situations to remember.

I could simply ghostwalk out of there, but it would mean leaving Dolores behind. Her magical protections wouldn't prevent the mage knights from trashing her out of anger once I escaped their clutches.

And even if I abandoned my precious to these louts, what would stop them from tracking me to the next location and the next? They might be morons, but they had eyes everywhere. I'd soon have no safe place to get a mangorita if I didn't teach them a valuable lesson.

All things considered, it seemed best if I put my training to good use and convinced these assholes to leave me alone. It meant I'd have to let the rabbit out of the hat and ghostwalk, but at least I'd have the satisfaction of seeing Sir Colin shit his pants.

I steeled myself. Straightened my shoulders and took a deep breath. "Fine. Don't say I didn't warn you." I sensed pinpricks of heat all along my back as the mages on the roofs prepared to unleash their spells. I reached over my back and summoned my oblivion staff. The hilt found my hand and it slid from the pocket dimension where I sheathed it.

The brightblade blazed to life. The pinpricks on my back grew hotter as the mages fired. I twisted around, spun the brightblade, and parried four sizzling beams of energy. They ricocheted back at the rooftops with flicks of my hand. Brick and mortar exploded. Mages shouted in pain and surprise. Arms flailed and the attackers leapt back out of view.

Another volley came from the roof to the left of the bar. I swept the brightblade in a blur, intercepting each bolt inches from hitting me and sent most of them back at the roof. A few of them bounced randomly and exploded against the building. Windows shattered and glass clinked to the asphalt.

The mages on the roof to the right of the bar fired almost at the same time as those on the left, but I was farther from them, affording me almost an entire extra second to spin and bat the spells back at their casters. Destructive energy soared high off the mark, lighting the night sky like fireworks.

Before they could unleash another volley, I powered the sigils tattooed on my body for a burst of strength and speed and dashed toward Colin and his butt-buddies. Henry's eyes blazed with fury. He roared and charged.

I wanted to kill him so badly, I could taste it. But killing wasn't the lesson I wanted to teach. It would be akin to killing an on-duty cop. Knights from other cities would rally behind their brethren, unleashing a manhunt that would only end with me being captured or killed if I didn't go into deep hiding.

The swords of mage knights were enchanted to resist magic attacks. Otherwise, my brightblade would have sliced right through Henry's steel. I met his attack. Metal clanged and the brightblade crackled and hummed. He swung his sword wildly, abandoning skill to unleash blind rage. I stifled a yawn and met every attack with ease, especially since those on the rooftops wouldn't fire with one of their brethren in such close proximity.

I forced him back toward Colin and Francis who hadn't moved to help him due to the limited space between parked cars. When I was closer to Dolores, I shifted tactics and met Henry's attacks with greater force. His enchanted blade was indestructible by most magical means, but it couldn't hold up to a weapon forged by the blacksmith of the gods.

"Die!" Henry roared and swung his one-handed sword with both hands down at my head.

If successful, the blow would have cut me in half from crown to crotch. But it had no chance of success. I swung my brightblade against the flat side of his blade. The metal was already cracked from all the blows I'd dealt it, and this one proved to be its last.

It shattered like a souvenir from a renaissance fair. Fragments clattered against a nearby car, breaking windows and scratching paint. Colin and Francis gasped. Henry held the hilt and stared at the jagged remains of his sword. I really wanted to make a smart remark and rub it in, but the situation mandated that I finish him off quickly and get out of here as soon as possible.

I gripped the stunned knight's other wrist, twisted him around, and slammed his head into a car hard enough to make it ring like a bell. He went down in a boneless heap. Before Francis could react, I slid across the hood of the car between us and landed between him and Colin. Francis went for his sword. I knocked his hand away from the hilt, braced my left foot on the ground, and delivered a magically enhanced kick with my right.

Aided by the power from my tattoos, I sent him stumbling back ten feet before he hit the side mirror on a car and fell down.

Metal sang behind me as Colin drew his sword. I didn't feel like another sword fight, so I reversed my stance and donkey-kicked him, thrusting my left foot straight back. It cracked against his wrist and the blade clattered on the asphalt. Before the knight could recover, I kneed him in the balls.

"That's for touching Dolores," I hissed. I wrapped an arm around his neck and used him as a meat shield from his comrades. I raised my voice to address the small army on the rooftops. "I could have killed you all tonight," I lied. "I could have brought down those buildings and buried you in rubble. Instead, I've shown mercy. I am not evil because I once served the fae. I'm not even a bad guy. In fact, I'm kind of nice once you get to know me."

"Cease your lies," Colin gasped as he vainly tried to free himself from the chokehold. "I will kill you myself."

I squeezed a little harder to deprive him of oxygen. "Leave me be or the next time, there will be blood. *Comprende?*"

No one answered, but I hadn't really expected them to. I powered the sigil on Dolores's door handle, and the door popped open behind me. I released Colin and gave him a good boot in the ass to get him out of the way, then slid inside the car and hit the accelerator.

Spells rained down, rattling on the rooftop like hailstones. I screeched into the alley, narrowly avoiding scraping the brick. Dolores's enchanted paint would protect her against normal collisions, but I suspected she'd have some nasty scars from this battle. I still hadn't repaired the handprint-shaped dents in the hood left by Sigma during our first encounter.

That kind of damage didn't just buff out.

I made a hard right on the street, avoiding oversteering so I didn't fishtail, and then jetted down the avenue a couple of blocks before slowing down so a random cop didn't stop me for speeding.

I'd encountered an assassin, a god, and now an army of knights, and it wasn't even ten o'clock yet.

I was doing something very right, or incredibly wrong.

CHAPTER 3

I almost went home.

The assassin's attack alone should've been enough to make me consider that option, but I'd been through too much in my nearly forty years to let something like that faze me. The visit from Hermes should've been my second clue that tonight just wasn't my night. Then again, that encounter hadn't been entirely negative.

Then there was the matter of the mage knights. That situation could have easily gone against me if not for their poor positioning and strategy. If they'd surrounded me in the parking lot instead of ambushing from the rooftops like cowards in an old western, they probably could have overpowered me.

Not that I was complaining.

The question at this point was, did I go home or did I check out Shipwreck? I'd spent the past few months hunting for someone, anyone, who might know how to break a bargain with a god, so the fact that I'd resorted to asking random strangers in bars really smacked of desperation.

If Hermes had intentionally left behind that napkin, then how could I not investigate?

It didn't matter where I went, I'd encounter outright hostility from other supers. They looked upon me as a traitor to the human race since I'd served the fae during the Human-Fae War. The fae and their allies also considered me a traitor since I'd abandoned my position as a member of the Oblivion Guard and nearly started another war in the process.

On the upside, my inquiries must have stirred the pot enough that some gods were getting worried, or at least one in particular—Hera. Either it meant she was sick of my shit, or maybe, just maybe, I was creeping closer to finding answers. As long as there was hope of freeing Hannah, I had to keep going.

So I drove far north of the perimeter and found a large stone lodge on the shores of the Chattahoochee River. Shipwreck looked much better than the other holes in the wall I'd been to. It wasn't far from a Feary portal and was inside a designated fae safe zone like Voltaire's. The only reason it wasn't as popular as its in-town rival was because Faevalorn, the unified capital of the summer and winter fae, wasn't on the other side of the portal.

Voltaire's sat right smack dab in the middle of Faevalorn, just on the other side of a portal. It was a major hub of supernatural commerce, and the fae preferred to keep it that way. Having grown up in Feary, I knew that a few small villages lay on the other side of the closest Feary portal in this area. There was just enough traffic between the worlds that the fae granted its neutral designation.

A silver disc engraved with a tree that grew above and below ground marked the safe zone perimeter. Another disc was embedded in the ground half a furlong distant, and another after that. A thin line connected the discs, outlining the circular perimeter.

If I'd employed any illusions to hide my true countenance, they would have vanished the moment I stepped across the line. Ever since being cured of the black veins and blight from Cthulhu's curse, I'd gone around as plain old me. It was nice not scaring kids with my real face anymore. Even nicer, I didn't have constant chest pains and shortness of breath.

The front door to Shipwreck was ten feet of dark-stained hardwood with black iron banding and a speak-easy door. I knocked on it and a pair of beady red eyes appeared.

I used the same password that worked at Voltaire's. "Feary."

The speakeasy door shut and the main door opened, revealing a hulking ogre on the other side. He bared thick yellowed teeth. "Cain the betrayer. You steal our gryphons. Make Targ have to work in Gaia!"

After my resignation from the guard, I'd done a few good deeds by necessity. One of those had been freeing sentient beings from servitude and using them as a small army to win my true freedom from the fae. Ogres, dark elves, and goblins, to name a few, had enslaved gryphons, cecrops, and other sentient beings. While I was popular among the freed slaves, I was hated and despised by those who'd profited from the slave trade.

I spread my hands. "Cain sorry, Targ. Me no like slavery. Ogres real shit lords for doing it."

He growled and raised a fist. "Pound you to blood butter, little man."

I flashed a grin. "Try it." As long as I dodged his attacks and didn't fight back, I wouldn't trigger the safe zone protections. Targ, on the other hand, would probably lose his hand. I was a little disappointed when a female ogre rushed from out of nowhere and gripped his wrist.

"Targ, no!" She was only about six feet tall compared to his ten feet, and proportionately a lot closer to a human female than her male counterpart. Female ogres resembled hearty Viking women with green skin, and anyone in their right mind would fear crossing them.

Targ's green face reddened as he strained but failed to overpower the ogress. "Go, Norna. Let Targ go!"

She blew out a long sigh. "You want the fae to cut off your hands, Targ? Because they will if you raise a hand against this man."

"But it Cain!" he bellowed.

Norna bared her teeth. "Don't make me take you outside, Targ. I will drag you outside the safe zone and beat you within an inch of your life."

Targ's face paled considerably. "Sorry, Norna." His shoulders slumped and he settled down on a massive stool custom built to support his big frame. "I hates Cain."

She patted his hand. "I know, I know. But what's done is done, and you need this job."

He nodded. "Yes. Targ needs."

Norna turned to me and held out a hand. "Welcome to my humble establishment, Cain. Please forgive Targ."

I took her hand and shook it. I could tell she went easy on me, because she probably could've crushed my hand with her grip. "The pleasure is all mine, Norna. You're the first female ogre I've seen on this side of the wall." The wall was a colloquial term used to describe the interdimensional barrier that separated Feary, Gaia, and the other worlds from each other.

"It's because ogresses are too busy running the ogre nations these days." She released my hand and motioned to the bar. "What can I get you?"

With the brief altercation over, I realized why she was being so friendly. The bar was virtually empty. An old wizard with a white beard and long pointy hat slumbered in a booth. Three empty pitchers sat on the table between him and a dwarf who was reading something on his smartphone and drinking out of a thick wooden mug.

"Bad night for business?" I asked.

Her smile faltered. "That would describe every night." She waved a hand at the wizard and his companion. "Old Bisbee and Dwight come here most nights and drink mead 'til they pass out. Our other regulars aren't quite regular enough."

I nodded. "Well, that explains why you're being nice to me." The interior was beautifully rustic. Thick wooden beams ran from the floor, meeting stained joists and beaded wood on the peaked ceiling. Old-school bronze chandeliers with mana globes hung from the beams above. The tables and booths also boasted stained wood and chairs upholstered with dark red leather. "You must have spent a pretty penny on this place."

"Let's just say it was everything I owned." Norna mustered another smile. "May I pour you a drink?"

"Can you make a mangorita?" I said.

She rubbed her hands together. "Absolutely! We're fully stocked." Norna hurried through the swinging bar door and began concocting the drink.

I sat on one of the cushy barstools and rubbed the leather. "You're the owner and bartender?"

"And cook, and cleaner, and dish washer." Norna somehow kept her smile. "Can't afford more help."

"Get Targ to do some cleaning." I turned to look at him and saw him staring at the screen of a tablet. "Not like he's doing much else."

"There's only so much I can make my brother do," she said. "He used to make quite a killing as a slaver, but you put an end to that."

I grimaced. "Sorry, not sorry?"

Norna chuckled. "Don't tell him this, but there were a lot of us who despised slave trading. They did awful things to gryphons and cecrops. I mean, it's forty-eight nine seventy-two, for gods' sake. The fae should've outlawed it long ago."

The fae calendar was on the year forty-eight thousand, nine hundred and seventy-two, but almost no one, not even the fae, went around spouting off the ridiculous year number. I couldn't stifle a laugh. "Keeping track with the fae calendar, I see."

"I think it's hilarious to throw around weird shit like that," Norna said. "Makes people cross their eyes in confusion."

"Maybe you should've done standup instead of buying a bar," I said.

She shrugged. "Kind of hard for an ogress to make it in a human world."

"True." I pursed my lips. "Though, by today's standards, a woman with green skin wouldn't really stick out."

She snorted. "You might be right." Norna vanished behind the liquor shelves and started a blender. I turned in my seat to look at Dwight the dwarf and the Wizard Bisbee. They were certainly an odd pair. At one time, dwarves had come to Gaia in droves because there was such a huge market for souvenir and jewelry metalworking, but the fae had put a clamp on immigration since the surge in population of little people had drawn undue attention from nubs.

Dwarves, like most Feary natives, didn't associate with human supers very often as emotions were still raw, even a decade after the end of the war. The feeling was mutual. Seeing a human mage with a dwarf drinking buddy wasn't unheard of, but it was enough to cause a blip on my radar.

Norna returned with a tall curved glass of frosty mango lusciousness, complete with plastic pirate sword and toothpick umbrella. "Here you go, sir."

"Don't call me sir," I said. "Cain will do."

"Here you go, Cain."

I took the straw and tried a taste. It was nearly as good as Aura's. "I have to deduct a point for the non-curvy straw, but this is almost perfect."

Norna reached beneath the counter and grabbed something, then plucked the plain straw out and replaced it with a straw that spiraled, looped, and curved like a miniature roller coaster. "Full marks now?"

I grinned. "Perfection." I took a long draw and let it slide down my throat. "It's a bit of a drive, but Shipwreck is my new favorite place."

She picked up a rag and wiped down the bar even though it was perfectly clean. "I heard you were banned from Voltaire's. That's quite an accomplishment since it's a fae peace zone and you can't really do anything ban-worthy without the fae cutting off your hand or killing you."

I shrugged. "I couldn't help that a demigod decided to attack me there."

Norna froze. "So, it's true? It was a demigod?"

"Yep." I raised an eyebrow. "What have you heard?"

"Everything from a super-powered mage to a new god no one had heard of." She leaned on the bar. "How does a demigod exist these days? I thought all the gods were dead."

"They're not." I sipped the mangorita. "Most are still alive and apparently impregnating a lot of mortal women."

"My gods, I can't believe it." Norna tilted her head and looked at me as if trying to discern if I was lying. "So the person who blew up the cars in Voltaire's parking lot and completely disregarded safe zone rules was a demigod?"

I nodded. "His name was Sigma."

"Was?"

I nodded again. "I killed him."

Norna's mouth dropped open. "You killed a demigod? I thought they were nearly indestructible."

"They don't make 'em like they used to," I said.

Her eyebrow quirked. "He was no Hercules?"

"No, more like a mini-Zeus." I shrugged. "Still really damned deadly, though."

"I hear you're searching for a weapon to defeat the gods," an elderly voice said from behind me.

Norna flinched as if she'd seen a ghost. I spun around because I hadn't sensed anyone approaching and met the gaze of Bisbee the wizard.

"How in the hell?" I looked at the table where Dwight still sat across from the snoozing wizard. "How are you here and there at the same time?"

Bisbee frowned and looked at the table. "Oh, my goodness. I left my body behind again, didn't I?" He sighed. "Too much mead, I'm afraid."

"Again?" Norna shook her head. "I've never seen you do this."

"I usually do it at home," Bisbee said. "Apparently, Cain's presence intrigued me so much I decided to join the conversation."

I reached for his shoulder, but my hand passed through it. "Astral projection?"

He shook his head. "No. I often drink to quiet my mind so I can think straight. Even when unconscious, I'm able to project my consciousness through an illusion."

"That's impressive." I picked up my drink and took a sip. "I didn't realize that was possible."

"It's a lost art," Bisbee said. "Wizards of yore used such tactics frequently to frighten villagers and control kings. The practice was frowned upon in later ages as the normal humans turned on our kind."

Norna shook her head slowly. "It's amazing."

"You've caused quite a disturbance in the community lately, Cain."

Bisbee's sharp blue eyes watched me closely. "You seek a method to break a god's hold on a mortal, do you not?"

I chose my phrasing carefully. "My ward accepted a bargain from Cthulhu to protect me. Now she's his minion and I wish to undo that."

"Cthulhu?" The wizard's eyes widened.

Norna frowned. "I thought he was legend."

"Definitely not," I said. "And I need to break a bargain with him."

"Ah," Bisbee leaned on the bar and stumbled sideways as he passed right through it. He caught his balance and stepped back to where he'd been. "I forget I'm not solid."

I raised my eyebrows. "Have any useful advice?"

"Some gods deal in bargains while others create bonds," Bisbee said. "What your ward did was accept a bond." He held out his hand and traced a pattern on it. "Lore has it that Cthulhu brands his minions on the top of their hands, thus granting them access to his powers and securing their loyalty. Should they act against him or his interests, the brand can cripple or even kill."

I pursed my lips. "Can it be removed?"

"Certainly, provided you defeat Cthulhu in trial by combat, or kill him in some other way."

I scoffed. "How in the hell am I supposed to kill an immortal?"

"Immortality is simply another way of saying someone is extremely hard to kill," Bisbee said. "Fortunately for you, there is another way."

I blinked. "Another way?"

He smiled. "Yes, another way to save your ward."

CHAPTER 4

Bisbee had my attention. I set down my drink. "Explain."

"You've heard of the Pandora Combine?" he said.

I nodded. "They're a splinter group that broke off from the Enders. They want to enslave the gods."

"I see you know quite a lot about the secret war," Bisbee said. "And you know of the prophecy as well?"

I nodded. "The Oblivion Codex."

"Well, it seems you're one of the few graced or cursed with the knowledge." He put a hand to his chin. "Such knowledge is very dangerous when gods will do anything to keep it secret."

"What's this other way you spoke of?" I said.

"The Pandora Combine is run by a brilliant man. Though most beings believed the gods to be dead, he knew it was a lie and worked tirelessly to find a way to give humans the upper hand and put them in charge." Bisbee almost leaned on the counter again but caught himself in time. "He discovered gods living among us, many of them mating and producing superhuman offspring while others made bargains with mortals that indentured them for a lifetime."

Norna scowled. "Gods be damned."

"Aye," Bisbee said. "He despised the gods and sought ways to break these bonds. But he lacked ancient knowledge and sought help. He joined the Enders for a time because he believed their goals aligned. But eventually, it became clear that they only wanted to spread chaos—to end the world as we know it so a new world order would arise. Horatio believed it was important that he controlled the chaos so he could create the new world order instead of leaving it to chance."

I raised an eyebrow. "Horatio is the one who founded the Pandora Combine?" Aura, a member of the Enders, had mentioned them, but I hadn't dug too deep into the details.

"Yes," Bisbee said.

"Where'd you get this information?" I said.

Bisbee sighed. "The man I speak of is my younger brother, Horatio."

"He's also a wizard?" I said.

"His skillset is not in magic." Bisbee sighed. "Despite Horatio's hatred of most gods, he is a member of an order that reveres Hephaestus."

My thought process nearly jumped the tracks making the connection. "He's a mechanist."

"Precisely," Bisbee said. "He seeks perfection in clockwork machines."

I frowned. "They're a reclusive order. Are they the only ones in the Pandora Combine?"

"No," Bisbee said. "Surprising as it sounds, they are allied with other supers."

I grunted. "Well, they've got an uphill battle if they want to defeat the gods."

Bisbee's lips pressed into a flat line "He believes he has a way to tip the balance of power in his favor."

Aura had already told me how the Combine planned to defeat the gods, but I kept that to myself in case Bisbee was talking about something entirely different.

"What drove him to such an extreme?" Norna asked. "Surely he didn't simply wake up one day and decide to kill the gods."

"You're right, of course." Bisbee shrugged. "Horatio was a cheerful and fun-loving young man. He married and had a child by the time he was twenty. While on vacation in Greece, he rented a boat to take his family to Delos. On the way there, a great storm came from nowhere. He tried to turn around, but the tide drew him inexorably toward a dark funnel of water and air. The boat was tossed about and crashed against rocks. The anchor chain tangled in the rocks and trapped him in place, saving him from being sucked into the water. Before he lost consciousness, he saw two men battling above the waves. One brandished a triton, and the other a great red sword."

"My gods," Norna breathed. "Poseidon and Ares?"

"Yes," Bisbee said. "Horatio awoke to the sound of booming laughter and conversation in Greek. He knew enough to understand that destroying the boat amused them because they were simply sparring, and the boat was caught in the crossfire."

"It's enough to drive a man mad," I said.

"At the time, Horatio was an acolyte with the mechanists. The armory of Hephaestus is a holy grail to them, rumored to hold some of his greatest creations." Bisbee sighed. "Horatio, however, knew that it also contained great weapons that could make a man into a god. So he began his quest to kill the Olympians, save Hephaestus."

"Why not him as well?" I said.

"Because the blacksmith of the gods was cast out. He is deformed and looked down upon by the other gods."

I grunted. "So he's not really one of them."

Bisbee nodded. "Precisely. But Horatio would gladly kill all the gods if possible."

"With all the enemies the Olympians made over the millennia, you'd think someone would have killed at least one." I pursed my lips. "Even the fae failed. Why does Horatio think he'll be any more successful?"

"The simple answer is Hephaestus," Bisbee said. "Horatio told me very little, but he did say the Olympians considered their former blacksmith a threat and tried to kill him many centuries ago."

That was news to me. "Why would they kill him? He's the one who made all their weapons."

Bisbee nodded. "All of this is rumor and legend, so it may be wrong, but Ares convinced Hephaestus to arm demigods because he wished for the final battle to begin. That was around the time the Oblivion Codex was prophesied. As a result, Hera formed the Divine Council and began executing demigods."

"Yeah, I can see how Hera would be concerned." It was hard to believe the old gods were still around even though I'd met Hermes only a little while ago.

Bisbee continued his story. "Using one of the eyes of Argus, Artemis found Hephaestus and fired one of her arrows at him. But the blacksmith wore special armor beneath his clothing. The arrow still almost killed him, but he fled into hiding and has been unheard of ever since."

"That's quite a bit of detail for rumor," I said.

"Horatio came into possession of the arrow and wished to turn it against the gods. The Ender faction didn't agree." Bisbee sighed. "That was when he left and created a splinter group, intent to find a way to use the arrow against the gods."

"What good would a single arrow do?" I said.

Bisbee raised an eyebrow. "Because it is a divine weapon, capable of killing a god, unlike mortal weapons."

"Interesting," I said. "The gods wouldn't have any super-powered weapons without Hephaestus and Cyclops." I summoned my oblivion staff and tapped the end gently against the granite bar top.

Bisbee and Norna gasped. Bisbee tried to touch the staff but failed since he was just an illusion.

Norna regarded it with wide eyes. "It's beautiful. I've heard about oblivion staffs but have never seen one before."

"It's usually bad news if you see one," I said. "Because it means a guardian is about to do something nasty." I sheathed it back in its pocket dimension. "Are you suggesting we steal the arrow and use it to kill Cthulhu?"

"I'm getting to that." Bisbee held up a hand palm toward me. "As an Oblivion Guard—"

"Former," I said.

He nodded and continued. "Your staff gives you the ability to planeswalk. You can travel to Oblivion. The arrow gave Horatio an idea —to find the lost armory of Hephaestus and use the weapons within to give humans power over the gods. The armory is supposedly in Oblivion, left there when the gods moved to Olympus."

"I've been to Oblivion," I said. "The guardians train there because the environment is so harsh, it could kill most mortals. Going there is no picnic."

"So I've heard," Bisbee said. "This is why you're the perfect man for the job."

I shook my head. "If such weapons exist, they'll be heavily guarded. If not by creatures, then by booby traps. What you're asking is impossible."

"Perhaps," Bisbee said, "but if you found a god-killing weapon, you could trade it for your ward."

I grunted. "Why hasn't the Combine tried to raid the armory yet?"

"Word is they're actually very close to finding it," Bisbee said.

I blinked. "But they'd need to reach Oblivion first, and there aren't any portals leading there. Only gods and the fae have that power."

"And those with oblivions staffs," Bisbee said.

I scoffed. "I wouldn't even know where to look for the original forge. Oblivion isn't a safe place for humans, or anyone, for that matter, so I can't simply go there and ask around. The few creatures that live there aren't exactly the friendly sort."

"That's where Horatio comes in." Bisbee waved a hand as if producing something. "He has a map with the location of the original Mount Olympus in Oblivion. The original forge of Hephaestus is beneath the mountain."

I frowned. "I thought the forge was beneath Mount Aetna, at least here in Gaia."

Norna poured herself a tall shot of slimy green rot juice—the favorite alcohol of ogres—and downed it. "This is unbelievable. I thought Oblivion was a myth."

"Fae propaganda," I said. "They spread misinformation to outsiders and keep the truth only for themselves. It was quite a surprise when I was taken there for survival training."

"The fae are masters of manipulation," Bisbee said. "Information is costly and they control as much as possible."

I took a sip of my mangorita and gave the proposition some thought. "Bisbee, I'd like to know how you know so much about Horatio's plans if you lost contact with him."

"I planted an enchanted amulet among his things when he was packing to leave." Bisbee summoned a sheepish grin. "I was concerned for his wellbeing and wanted a way to check in on him from time to time."

"Spying on your own brother?" Norna shook her head. "I suppose it's understandable given the circumstances."

"The amulet is in his living quarters which he seldom visits except to sleep." Bisbee sighed. "I've gleaned what little information I have because he talks to himself incessantly when he's alone. I believe his mind teeters on the brink of insanity."

"Probably." I watched Bisbee closely, divining if he spoke the truth. His story didn't sound too outlandish, and it seemed somewhat plausible that he'd bug his own brother out of concern. But I was skeptical by nature and my skepticism had saved my life on more than a few occasions. I didn't know Bisbee from Adam and trusting someone I'd just met would be madness.

"Why would you help me?" I said. "You don't know me."

"Because our interests align," Bisbee said. "If I help you, then you'll help my brother. You might be able to rescue him from this reckless path."

"Except by handing over a god-killer weapon to Cthulhu, I'll be making enemies of all the Olympians, not to mention the other gods." I shook my head. "There's got to be a better way."

"It sounds like a terrible risk," Norna said. "Perhaps there's some other trade Cthulhu would be willing to make."

"Doubtful," I said. "A demigod is too powerful a weapon for him to give up without receiving something or someone of greater value."

Bisbee frowned at Norna. "I'm afraid there's little else Cthulhu wants. He has a score to settle with the Olympians."

"Yeah, well what about the other pantheons?" I said. "Are Thor and the other Norse gods still around? What about Ra and the Egyptian gods? Which ones are real and which ones are myth?"

"That's an excellent question," Bisbee said. "So far, I've only seen proof of Greek and Norse gods."

"What about Roman gods?" Norna said.

"They're one and the same as the Greek gods." Bisbee clasped his hands at his waist. "I wondered myself if they were separate entities but have found no proof supporting that hypothesis. I have seen evidence of other minor deities, but my research is far from conclusive."

This guy had way too much information to be an ordinary wizard. I summoned my staff and gazed at his sleeping body through the scope, not caring if it was rude or not. His vitals and body temperature read slightly above normal for a human, but that was common in mages. They tended to have a longer lifespan than nubs, depending on their power. His soul bore the faint glow of a mage and he wasn't using illusion to hide anything.

Despite my misgivings, this was the closest I'd come to finding a way to free Hannah. I couldn't just walk away even though my gut instinct told me something wasn't right about this situation. I waited for the ghosts to whisper their opinions and remembered they were gone, thanks to Thanatos. As much as I enjoyed being alone in my head, sometimes it felt awfully lonely.

"I don't know how much I can trust you, Bisbee, but I'm willing to hear you out." I slurped down the rest of my drink. "Norna, may I have another, please?"

"You're polite for an assassin." She downed another shot of rot juice and started making another drink for me.

I nodded at the table where the wizard's body slept. "I'd like to speak to you and your associate while you're awake."

"Dwight doesn't much like humans," Bisbee said. "I'll have to convince him."

"How are you and a dwarf even a thing?" I said.

"That is a story best saved for another time," he said with a smile.

I leaned against the bar. "Well, wake up and convince him."

Bisbee flickered and vanished. A moment later, his body stirred and moaned like a dying whale.

"Oh, goodness." Bisbee sat up and rubbed his eyes. "I don't feel well."

Dwight turned in his seat and narrowed his eyes at me, then turned to Bisbee and muttered something.

The wizard nodded and slid to the edge of the booth seat. Using a long, wooden staff, he pulled himself to his feet and hobbled toward me. "Dwight overheard our conversation and has decided to talk to you."

I raised my eyebrows. "Well, that's nice."

"Isn't it, though?" Bisbee put a hand on the bar. "Water, please, my dear."

Norna set a cup down in front of him. He produced a vial of cloudy blue liquid from his robes and drank it, then guzzled the water. Bisbee put a hand to his forehead and groaned.

I shook my head. "Maybe you should take it easy on the mead."

"It helps calm the nerves." Bisbee waved me toward the booth where Dwight still sat. "Come, now. Let us assuage your concerns." He slid into the booth on the dwarf's side.

I took the seat across from them so I could study their expressions as we talked.

Dwight studied my face. "You look different than the last time I saw you."

Like most of his kind, Dwight was under five feet tall and stocky. Unlike most of his kind, he was clean-shaven and wore his hair short. He was the most metrosexual dwarf I'd ever seen. "When did you last see me?" I asked.

"Voltaire's a few months ago." He pursed his lips. "The side of your face was covered in dark veins and you looked much older."

"Curse of Cthulhu." I shrugged. "If you overheard our conversation, then you know why I'm here. Got anything to add?"

"Plenty." Dwight rapped his oddly long fingers on the table. "Bisbee has obsessed about helping Horatio for years. You're not the first person he's talked to about this mad plan of his. I think you shouldn't do it."

Bisbee sighed. "If anyone can pull this off it would be Cain."

"Let me lay it out for you, assassin." Dwight reached into his sweater vest and removed a folded piece of leather. He flattened it on the table to reveal a hand-drawn map that looked like something torn from an epic fantasy novel.

"Did you make this yourself?" I asked.

"Of course." Dwight lifted his mug and sipped the mead. "Anything is better than those infernal contraptions humans use."

I frowned, unable to make heads or tails of it. "What am I looking at?"

"This is Deepvale, the headquarters for the Pandora Combine." Dwight turned the map toward me and tapped a finger on the left side. "It's a castle hidden in the mountains of Romania."

Though Dwight obviously had artistic talent, the map was severely lacking in accurate cartographic details that were essential for any kind of planning. It looked as if the castle sat on the edge of a lake in a valley surrounded by mountains.

"Is this map usable?" I asked.

Dwight scowled. "Do you know anything about dwarf craftsmanship?"

"Jewelry and metalworking, yes. Cartography, no."

"It's as perfect as it gets without me physically going there and measuring everything." He rolled it up and stuffed it back in his vest. "As you can see, it's nearly impossible to get close to the castle without traveling through rugged terrain on foot."

I'd been to Romania during the war so the fae could talk peace with the vampire leadership. It didn't have the population of vampires it once had, but I still avoided it like the plague. Vlad Tepes, or Dracula, as most of the world knew him, would like nothing more than to mount my head on a pike.

Though Dwight's map lacked context, I could infer plenty just from the location. "Is Tepes financing the Combine?"

Dwight exchanged a look with Bisbee. "Highly likely."

I grunted. "So, in addition to mechanists, the castle is probably guarded by vampires too."

"But no werewolves," Bisbee said. "Their alliance with the others was always fragile at best."

"Any mages?" I said. Mechanists were notoriously xenophobic, but if they were allied with vampires, then anything was possible.

Bisbee nodded. "The Combine boasts an erratic assortment of supers."

Mechanists usually didn't like mages, even though they used magical means to power their contraptions.

I tapped a finger on my chin. "How many ways are there into the castle?"

"That depends on the approach," Dwight said.

I shook my head. "No offense, but I'm going to need a lot more than a hand-drawn map."

Dwight looked offended. "None taken." He leaned back in his chair and studied me. "I'm curious how you became entangled with Cthulhu."

"Long story," I said.

The dwarf lifted an eyebrow. "We have time."

I glanced at the bar and hoped Norna was almost finished making my mangorita. "I was tricked into accepting a cursed object that was supposed to bind me to him. Instead, it just gave me magic cancer. Cthulhu told me the only way to cure it was by accepting the bond. Resisting it was killing me slowly but surely."

Dwight put his elbows on the table and regarded me intently. "Fascinating. You've actually spoken to him?"

"A few times." I shrugged. "After everything that happened, I read all the history I could find on him."

"Legend says Cthulhu is trapped in eternal slumber in the sunken city of R'lyeh," Bisbee said.

I nodded. "When I talk to him, it's in a dream state. I'm not actually there."

"Did you see him?" Bisbee asked.

"I saw the dream version of him, a giant with the head of an octopus." I scoffed. "For all I know he might really be a jellyfish." I waved off any other questions. "Let's get back to the mountain castle. Where exactly is it, and do you have a detailed layout?"

"The amulet has pinpointed the location," Bisbee said, "but we don't know the layout."

"The castle sits in an enclosed valley surrounded on all sides by sheer mountain cliffs. The only way in seems to be by air." Dwight idly turned his mug on the table. "I can't provide you much more information, I'm afraid."

I scoffed. "You make it sound so easy."

"Just setting expectations," Dwight said.

"Let me get this straight. I have to scale a mountain, infiltrate a vampire-infested castle, find a map somewhere within the unknown confines of said castle, take a picture or steal the map, and then escape." I tried not to laugh at the absurdity of the plan. "Provided I survive that mission, I have to go to Oblivion, survive the harsh terrain and environment, penetrate a hidden armory, and steal a god-killer weapon that won't also end the world."

There was no way in hell I could pull this off.

CHAPTER 5

Bisbee raised a hand. "You'll need to procure two weapons. One to trade Cthulhu for your ward, and the other for Horatio."

"It's an impossible mission," Dwight said. "I've told Bisbee time and time again that it's hopeless."

I looked at Bisbee and back to Dwight. "Are you using reverse psychology?"

"No," Dwight said, "I'm telling you that the odds of success are tiny, even for someone like yourself." He turned to Bisbee as if expecting the wizard to interject, but the old man just shrugged. Dwight turned back to me. "Giving Cthulhu a god-killer weapon of any kind is asking for the apocalypse."

"Depends," I said. "I'll just have to be careful what I pick from the armory." I paused to consider what I'd just said, because it sounded like I was talking myself into undertaking this venture instead of finding reasons to avoid it.

Bisbee's eyes brightened. "So, you'll do it?"

Norna set my drink down and raised an eyebrow. "What did I miss?"

Dwight shook his head. "Norna, as much as I like you, this is none of your concern."

"Then Bisbee shouldn't run his mouth so much," she shot back.

The dwarf groaned. "He's impossible."

I took a long draw of the mangorita and sighed in contentment. "Unless and until you connect a few dots, there is no mission." I set down the drink. "I'm not going into that castle blind."

Dwight made a shooing motion at Norna. "Leave us."

She shook her head and slid into the booth next to me, pressing her thigh against mine. "If you didn't want me knowing anything, Bisbee could've taken Cain somewhere else to talk. I want to hear more."

Now that this was rapidly turning into a real thing, I worried about too many ears. "I had a visitor earlier today who warned me to stop asking questions about the gods."

Bisbee's eyebrows rose. "Who would dare order you about?"

"Just a little guy named Hermes."

Their mouths dropped open.

I shrugged. "He was nice about it, but I suspect things could get ugly really fast if he or Hera find out about this mission." I turned to Norna. "Which is why no one at this table will say a word about it if we decided to do it."

"We?" Dwight shook his head. "I'll have nothing to do with it."

"Yes, we." I turned to Bisbee. "I'll have a blood oath from everyone here before I commit."

"A blood oath?" Norna scoffed. "Can't you just trust us?"

"Hell no." I scoffed back. "I have enough trouble trusting people I know, much less people I just met. Bisbee, I need a blood oath from everyone at this table before I'll agree to your mission."

"I'll do it," Bisbee said.

Dwight crossed his arms. "I won't be a party to this insanity."

"If the oath is properly framed, I'd be willing to take it," Norna said.

"Well, that leaves Dwight." I stretched and slid across the booth seat toward Norna. "I need to use the bathroom."

She slid out of the way and I got up.

"I want a yes or no by the time I get back." I started walking, stopped, and turned back. "By the way, I'm just going number one, so it won't take long."

Norna laughed.

I went to the bathroom, took a piss, and then took a moment to consider the situation. It was a setup, plain and simple. What were the odds I'd find a nice bar like this occupied only by a wizard, a dwarf, and two ogres? What were the odds that I'd happen upon the one wizard with the perfect way for me to free Hannah? What were the odds not a single other person had entered the bar since I'd arrived?

I'd made enough noise about my quest around town to get the attention of Hera, so it made sense that I'd attract the attention of other groups too. Finding the napkin from Shipwreck was far too much of a coincidence. Hermes might not have left it under my foot, but that didn't mean someone couldn't have conjured it there.

Were Dwight, Norna, and Bisbee with a faction or were they freelancers? Was Bisbee even related to Horatio?

It was impossible to know without going through the trouble of questioning them or digging into their backgrounds. That was a lot of work for little reward.

Did I go with the flow or just get it over with and tell them I knew this was a setup?

The job itself was certainly real, of that I had little doubt. They saw my need as an opportunity to help them find the legendary armory of Hephaestus. The weapons cache inside would make the seller rich beyond their wildest dreams.

It also seemed likely that they'd want to participate in pulling off the job, or at least the part involving Oblivion. That was when they'd either convince me to let them walk out with as many valuables as they could carry, or they'd try to double cross me.

Maybe I could let them double-cross me and then triple-cross them right back.

While it might be amusing, it would also be risky. I didn't know what these people were capable of. They had muscle, magic, and brains. I might have been a guardian, but I certainly wasn't infallible or unkillable.

When it came down to it, I needed to do this job because after months of searching, it seemed the only way to get Hannah back.

Dealing with Bisbee and crew was only the first dilemma. The second was hoping Cthulhu would be willing to trade Hannah provided I found the weapons. I considered asking him if he'd be willing to trade, but if he found out about the map, it was likely he'd send his own minions to take it from Horatio. Then Cthulhu would have access to the entire armory.

I couldn't let that happen.

There was also the mystery of what Bisbee and crew had to gain from this. Were they simply after money? Did they want weapons to use for themselves? They might even be with the Combine for all I knew. If they allowed me to find the map, I'd unwittingly give them access to Oblivion and the armory.

There were too many possibilities for me to consider. There was a thin line between being skeptical and being paranoid. I knew where to stop myself before spiraling into the realm of infinite scenarios. I couldn't hope to outwit a god who'd been around thousands of years, but I could certainly outwit their human minions.

So, back to the matter at hand—did I confront Bisbee with the truth now, or should I wait for betrayal and plan accordingly?

It wasn't an easy decision. They could deny, deny, deny, and put me in an even more untenable situation because I'd lose the element of surprise. The other option was framing the blood oath so they couldn't betray me. I suspected they'd try to wriggle out of doing the oath one way or the other. I was prepared to let them do so because I could plan around it.

It seemed best to hold my cards close and not let them know I knew this was a setup. I washed my hands and stepped out of the bathroom, pausing to examine the rafters above. I took a moment to add some insurance to my plan and then went back to the booth. Before Norna could get up to let me in, I slid in next to her.

"So?" I steepled my fingers and raised my eyebrows.

Dwight huffed and puffed convincingly. "I'll help, but no blood oath."

"You need muscle," Norna said. "Targ and I can help, but I know he won't commit to a blood oath."

"A blood oath is dangerous," Bisbee said. "I think we can trust each other enough to cooperate, yes?"

"You're going to let a bartender and bouncer in on this job?" I feigned surprise and looked at Norna. "Besides making a great mangorita, what other qualifications do you have?"

"You'll need help carrying out whatever is in the armory," Norna said. "Targ and I can carry a lot."

"Whoa." I shook my head. "Looting the armory of everything isn't in the cards. There's no telling what kind of deadly shit Hephaestus locked up in there. We don't want to end the world by accident."

Bisbee nodded. "I agree. It would be foolish to carry out everything. But Norna and Targ would be valuable, especially in the hostile plane of Oblivion."

"True." I put a hand on my chin and pretended to think it over. "I've got one more team member to add and we'll be good."

"The last thing we need is another person," Dwight said. "The four of us are more than enough."

I shook my head. "Look, you all know each other in one way or another. Today is my first time meeting you. No offense, but I want someone I know on the team too."

"Perfectly fine," Bisbee said in a reassuring tone. "When shall we have our first planning session?"

"Tomorrow works," I said. "Meet back here at noon?"

Norna nodded. "I have private rooms in case we ever get any other patrons."

I had a feeling the place would be teeming with patrons now that this "chance" meeting had occurred. I slapped a hand on the table. "Then it's settled. Tomorrow at noon we'll meet here." I finished off my drink and stood. Norna exchanged a look with Bisbee that was hard to miss. These folks were trying hard, but they weren't pros. What came next was as obvious as Norna's green skin.

And I wasn't really opposed to it.

I turned for the door. "Until tomorrow."

Targo scowled at me but opened the door without threatening me again. I had a feeling his earlier reaction hadn't been an act. Male ogres weren't renowned for their intelligence. If not for the females, they probably would've gone extinct ages ago. When I stepped outside, I sensed the presence I expected.

"Cain, wait." Norna put a hand on my shoulder.

I turned around. "Yeah?" She stood about half a head taller than me. Female ogres were strong, but they weren't bulky looking like the males. Even so, she could break even the buffest human male over her knee if she wanted to.

But if my suspicions were correct, this was going to be more about her bending over.

"I-I really enjoyed meeting you. You're not as bad as all the rumors." She smiled, revealing nice white teeth. "Maybe we could get to know each other a little better?"

I reached out and took her hand. "I'd like that."

She blinked and her smiled widened. "Oh, really?"

"Anyone who makes mangoritas that tasty is worth knowing." I reached up and put my hand on her neck, then pulled her face down for a kiss. Her lips were soft, and she smelled of rum and coconuts. "I'll see you soon, okay?"

She shivered. "I hope so."

I watched her go inside, and then took out my phone while heading toward my car. I opened the camera app and accessed the mini-cam I'd installed on a rafter near the bathroom. It offered a wide view of the interior.

Norna walked toward Dwight and Bisbee, a big grin on her face. "I think he's ours."

"Did you seduce him?" Bisbee said.

"I didn't even have to," she said. "It was super easy, barely an inconvenience."

Dwight scoffed. His back was to the camera, but he probably rolled his eyes too. "Human males are easy to sexually manipulate."

Bisbee nodded. "I know it's a great deal to ask, but you might have to sleep with him, Norna."

"You don't have to ask," she said. "I like the guy. He's not at all the evil bastard you made him out to be." Her eye twitched noticeably when she said that. She was probably lying, trying to appear eager to do her duty.

"Perhaps." Dwight stood and paced. "But there is no telling what he might do if he discovers our deception."

"He's an assassin, a thug." Bisbee swatted the air. "He might be suspicious of everything, but that doesn't mean he's perceptive enough to realize we're using him."

"It's for a good cause." Norna picked up the glass I'd left and took it to the bar. "Maybe we should have told him."

"Absolutely not." Bisbee glared at her. "He's using us, and we're using him."

"Precisely." Dwight gripped a mug of mead. "Stick to the plan." He yawned. "I'm going to bed."

Norna sighed. "I hope this works."

Bisbee patted her hand. "Cain was the final piece of the puzzle. With him, the odds are in our favor."

"What if he discovers Horatio isn't your brother?" Norna said.

"Why should he bother checking?" Bisbee replied. "The objective will be to get in and out of the castle without being detected. I doubt he'll stop to chitchat with anyone."

She sighed. "True."

"Wrap Cain around your little finger, dear." Bisbee leaned on the bar. "Make him yours so he'll be too distracted to ask such questions." He stretched and wandered out of sight.

Norna looked toward the front door which was just out of sight behind a beam. "Targ, you can lock up and go to bed, okay?"

"Targ go night-night." The big lug lumbered into view and vanished off camera.

Norna cleaned the pitcher and mugs, then shut off the lights and left. I looked up from my phone screen at the building. Lights blinked on in a room on the second story of the tavern. Like Voltaire's, Shipwreck was a pub and an inn. Apparently, Bisbee's crew lived there.

I was disappointed they hadn't mentioned their endgame. It didn't sound like they were in it for the money, or at least Norna wasn't. What was their good cause she'd mentioned? And how did they all know each other?

I sent a text to my potential crewmember and prayed she'd come through for me. Then I shifted Dolores into gear and headed home. It had been a long day and an even longer night, but it felt great to finally be on a course that might help me free Hannah. All I had to do was avoid the double-cross and I'd be home free.

But if I didn't, I'd likely end up dead.

CHAPTER 6

My home was south, but I went to the highway and drove north a mile, then turned into a busy area near a mall and restaurants, keeping an eye on the rearview mirror. I didn't see anyone following me, but there was no sense taking chances. I drove through a parking deck and powered the illusion sigils on Dolores, changing her from a black station wagon to a white minivan. To anyone on the outside, I'd look like a middle-aged soccer mom instead of a middle-aged assassin.

After a few more twists, turns, and illusion changes, I got back on the highway and headed south. Traffic was light enough that spotting a tail would be easier. Unless they were invisible, no one was behind me, so I headed straight home.

My house had long ago been a church run by a cult. It sat in the middle of eight acres that had once been farmland and was now surrounded by suburbia. Aversion wards, illusion, and a dome of fae magic kept everyone away and made it invisible from the air. The land near the church was consecrated and ringed by silver to keep out vampires, werewolves, and any other undead who somehow made it past the deadly wards protecting the perimeter.

Only four people, including myself, knew where it was, which was why I cursed in surprise as I turned onto the private road leading to the church. A lone figure sitting on the side of the road jumped up and waved me down. I summoned my staff and peered at the figure with my scope. Aside from an oily fringe to the soul aura, this person was the real deal.

Under ordinary circumstances, I would've leapt out of the car with a weapon drawn. This time, I leapt out, arms wide. "Hannah!"

"Cain!" She ran into my arms and hugged me as if she never wanted to let go. "How's my big bro?"

"My gods, Hannah, I haven't seen you in months." I held her out from me and looked her up and down. Her face was gaunt. Bones pressed against her skin. She'd lost an unhealthy amount of weight and her light brown skin looked pale and sallow. She wore torn jeans and a dirty sweatshirt at least two sizes too large. "What in the hell happened to you?"

A large tear pooled in her eye. "I haven't been doing very well. The place where I live is damp and stinks like fish all the time. There are mostly humans there, but also other awful looking creatures."

The cloying odor of dead fish clung to her hair and clothes, but I didn't care how bad she smelled. I opened the passenger door. "Get in. I'm taking you home."

She wiped her eyes. "You don't know how long I've wanted to hear that."

I got in the driver side. Hannah slid across the bench seat and leaned against me. "It's good to be home, Cain."

I mussed her hair. "Yeah it is."

I drove down the road to a gate, slowing so I could disable the ward protecting it. It slid open and closed behind us once I'd driven through. The road seemingly ended in a wall of trees, but I drove straight on through. There was a brief flicker as I passed through the illusion and then the road reappeared.

The silhouette of a burnt-out farmhouse rose ahead, made visible by the high beams on the car. Vines and vegetation covered other nearby outbuildings and the fields were overgrown with saplings and bushes. I continued onward to the heart of the eight acres where I reached a clearing of old stumps and clumps of grass in hard-packed earth.

Faded tombstones jutted at various angles from the ground on the left and right of the road. There were three-hundred and thirty-three marked graves distributed almost evenly on each side of the road, all former cult members, most of them belonging to the same family whose bloodline ended with the passing of the farmer who'd bequeathed me this place.

The church sat beyond the gravestones. It was octagonal with a sturdy granite foundation and framed by thick stained timbers. An octagonal tower rose from the center of the peaked roof and rose thirty feet. It was a strangely beautiful place that, despite its questionable history, I was happy to call home.

I parked Dolores in a wooden outbuilding I'd converted into a garage and went to the front door of the church. I disabled the ward, stepped into the foyer, and did the same to the ward protecting the inner door. There were other ways in and out, but I was the only one who knew about them.

The den and kitchen space were on the other side of the inner door. My bedroom was on the left, and the guest rooms on the right. A pool of dark water occupied the right corner just past the entrance. It was ten feet square and thirty feet deep—a massive aquarium for a single occupant.

Hannah laughed and looked down at four rat corpses neatly arranged on the area rug in the den. Their noses touched and their tails pointed straight out to form a cross. "Fred's up to his usual tricks."

I sighed. "Two days ago, I found three sparrows. I still don't know how or why he does it."

She went to the pool and investigated the dark waters. "Where is he?"

"Hell, if I know." I went to the kitchen and started making a sandwich with homemade bread. "What I do know is that you need about a dozen sandwiches. You're nothing but skin and bones."

"It's hard to eat where they keep me." Hannah shuddered. "It stinks and the food is squirmy. I don't think Cthulhu knows how to treat human guests."

"You're not a guest, you're his minion." I deftly sliced lettuce and tomatoes, topping them with lightly salted ham. "Don't think I'm not happy to have you here, but why are you here?"

"Reasons." She dropped onto the couch and moaned in pleasure. "This is amazing."

I poured a glass of milk and delivered it and the sandwich to Hannah, then sat down next to her. "Eat first, explain later."

She took a big bite of the sandwich and moaned, then gobbled it down so fast, she nearly choked. Hannah gulped the milk and sighed. "Real food is so amazing." When she put the plate on the coffee table, the sleeves of her sweatshirt slid up, revealing green bruises all along her forearm.

I sucked a breath between my teeth and gently took her arm, slid up the sleeve. In addition to old bruises, her arm was covered in puncture wounds and bitemarks. Holding back the boiling rage, I said, "What in the fuck did they do to you, Hannah?"

"I can't use my powers at will, so they tried putting me in danger to see if that worked. Then they tried beating me." Hannah looked down and bit her lower lip. "I can't control my abilities at will."

"I'll kill Cthulhu myself!" I roared and jumped to my feet. "Fred!" I went to his pool and shouted at the water. "Fred, get up here!"

A tentacle dangled from above. I looked up and saw Fred dangling off a rafter, his tentacles stretching so abnormally long that he reached the ground without falling. I used to consider him my pet octopus, but he was a spy—a familiar of Cthulhu. Unfortunately, I couldn't get rid of him or Cthulhu would kill him. It wasn't Fred's fault he was a slave.

Fred crawled across the floor backwards, watching me with his golden eyes.

"Don't you run away from me," I warned.

He slipped into the water, rubbing himself with his tentacles as if to moisten his skin, and then climbed onto the edge. A single tentacle reached for me. I sat down and held out my palm, taking the slippery limb into my hand.

Sorrow.

It seemed to be his way of apologizing, but sometimes he said it in such a way I wasn't sure if it meant something else entirely. Oily black clouded his eyes until they turned dark as pitch. The world flickered and suddenly I stood atop a rocky outcropping before a vast underground sea. A monstrous creature towered over me. His head was that of an octopus, the tentacles writhing around a scowling maw. His body was humanoid, but scaly like a fish. His hands bore claws and were webbed between the fingers.

Cthulhu was a scary looking guy, but I wondered if that was what he looked like in real life. According to legend, he was trapped in the underwater city of R'lyeh, asleep and dreaming. The dream version of him might be a false projection, an overly monstrous avatar controlled by a baby shark, doo, doo, doo, doo, doo.

Though it was a dream state, the air felt damp against my skin. I tasted salt in the air, smelled seawater and fish. It felt as if I were here in the flesh even though my body was sitting on the floor next to Fred.

The Great Old One spoked in a guttural, foreign tongue, but English echoed in my head. *You will train the girl and return her to me within a month.*

I held up a fist, puny though it seemed in the face of the ancient one. "You starve and abuse Hannah and then come to me with demands? I'll come to R'lyeh and kill you in your sleep!"

A deep laugh boomed through the vast cavern. *Brave little man. You are but a speck. Do as I command, or the girl will be of no use to me.*

I had no doubt what he'd do to Hannah if he couldn't use her. "You need to treat her like a human, not one of your fishy minions. She can't learn if you don't feed her properly and keep her somewhere warm and dry."

Suffering brings strength in mind and body. She must be molded and hardened into a weapon.

My hands trembled with rage, but there was nothing I could do even if the sleeping giant lay before me. I didn't hide my rage, but I kept my thoughts shielded in case he could read them in this dream state. "I'll train her, but I want visitation rights. I want you to promise that she can come visit me every other weekend without your interference."

It is agreed.

"And I want you to leave her alone completely while she's with me." I folded my arms over my chest. "I need her mind clear of your influence or it'll be much harder."

Just because I am not in her mind does not mean I cannot find her, Cthulhu said. *The bond cannot be severed.*

I decided to test the waters with another offer. "Will you accept me into your service instead of her?"

No. A demigod is worth ten of you.

"In case you didn't know, I killed the demigod, Sigma."

I know everything you and the girl did to survive. I know the training you gave her in a few days progressed her abilities more than anything else in the past six months. I will add you to my ranks, but I will not trade her for you.

"What if I brought you another demigod?" I said. "One that already has her powers?" I was thinking of Daphne, the solar-powered demigod controlled by the Humans First faction.

I would consider the sun goddess a fair trade for this useless girl.

I shouldn't have been surprised he knew about her, but I was. "I assume Hannah told you about her as well?"

She told me all. Cthulhu stepped forward, his giant feet sending massive waves crashing against the rocks. *Train her or bring me another demigod of great powers. If she is not ready by month's end, or you have not found a suitable replacement, the girl's life will be forfeit.* He raised a giant fist and brought it down toward my head.

I braced myself and held my ground. "I'll kill you before I let that happen!" The fist crashed against the rocks. The pedestal broke apart and plunged into the sea. Strong currents dragged me underwater. I swam desperately for the surface, lungs burning for oxygen. Something green and scaly darted toward me. A gaping maw swallowed me whole.

The world flickered and I was back in my house, gasping for breath.

"Cain!" Hannah knelt next to me hands pressed to my face. "What did he do to you?"

Sorrow. Fred withdrew his tentacle and slipped back into his pool, vanishing beneath the surface.

I told her everything. "He'll kill you if I don't train you or find a replacement."

Tears trickled down her cheeks. "I won't let you do it, Cain."

"Train you?" I gripped her hand. "I won't let him kill you!"

"No, I won't let you find a replacement." Hannah wiped her face.

"Training is fine, but I wouldn't wish this on my worst enemy—not even Sigma if he was still alive."

"I'd trade someone else in a heartbeat," I said. "Especially Sigma."

"I don't think you would." She smiled. "You wouldn't even eat a unicorn heart to save your life."

"I would have if I realized you'd offer yourself to Cthulhu to save my life." I stood and helped Hannah to her feet. "Did he brand you?"

She shook her head. "No, that comes once I've proven myself. Until then, I'm just a bonded minion."

"Can he see what you see? Spy on you in real time?" I examined her eyes as if I might spot another consciousness lurking inside.

"That's not how it works," she said. "Cthulhu can't read minds through the bond, but he can take control and then see everything."

I hissed. "He can remote control you?"

"When I'm branded, yes." Hannah tugged down the sleeves of her shirt. "Sentient minds are harder to control through just a bond."

"Why hasn't he branded you then?" I shook my head. "Doesn't make sense."

"Because a brand creates two-way communication," she said. "It allows me access to his power and his plane. It means I could contact him almost anytime."

I nodded. "So, he can't spy on you willy-nilly with just the bond, and if he tries, then we'll know."

Hannah nodded back.

"How does he control Fred?" I glanced at the pool. "I don't see a brand on him, and he seems sentient."

"Fred is a creature of the deep. Cthulhu shares a natural connection with many of them already, especially cephalopods."

I grimaced. "Like evil Aquaman?"

"Exactly like that, but nowhere near as cute."

I grinned and mussed her already messy hair. "Let's get you cleaned up. You stink like a busy wharf." I nodded toward the guest room where she'd stayed last time. "All your clothes are still in there since you left without packing."

"I didn't really have time to take anything." Hannah looked down. "It all happened so fast, and you were unconscious. I hated leaving without saying goodbye."

"Me too." I swallowed a lump in my throat. "Get some rest. We've got a lot to talk about in the morning over a huge breakfast, okay?"

She bit her bottom lip. "I could eat another sandwich before going to sleep."

"I'll have one ready when you get out of the shower." I kissed her forehead, pulled back and wrinkled my nose. "Go wash up, you stinker."

Hannah laughed and went into the hallway with her guest room. I made her two more sandwiches along with a couple for me since I hadn't eaten dinner yet. Then I did some serious thinking while I ate.

There was a lot to be suspicious about with her sudden appearance after I'd just made a deal to infiltrate the Pandora Combine. Yet, it seemed impossible for Cthulhu to know about something that had only happened hours ago. Maybe it was just good timing, or maybe the Great Old One knew all.

It was yet another twist that could completely derail my plans to save Hannah.

CHAPTER 7

Nothing I'd read suggested Cthulhu was omniscient, and I'd seen no signs that Bisbee and pals were connected to the ancient one. While the timing of Hannah's appearance was suspicious, it probably had nothing to do with the job. I imagined Cthulhu throwing up his hands and tentacles in frustration after Hannah repeatedly failed to control her abilities and ordering her to go to me for help.

I planned to send her back as well trained as possible. If Cthulhu refused to trade her for a weapon from the armory, then I'd get her to help me kill him.

I finished my sandwiches by the time she emerged from her room, all shiny and clean. She wore pink pjs with cats on them, and her hair was tied back in a wet ponytail. Hannah beamed and practically skipped across the room toward me.

"I'm so happy to be home." She hugged me and then backed up. "There's also something else I didn't tell you."

And here it is. "What's that?"

"My birthday is next week."

I certainly hadn't expected that to be the next thing she said. "You'll be seventeen?"

Hannah nodded. "I begged Cthulhu to send me to you for training, but I didn't tell him it was really because I wanted to be with you on my birthday."

"Have you intentionally not learned how to control your powers?" I asked.

She shook her head. "It's not the same as when I was with you. I could reach out and touch the power, but now it's distant. I can't even meditate in that awful place."

"Anxiety is the mind killer." I smiled. "We'll work on it. For now, let's get some rest, okay?"

Hannah wiped away a tear and nodded. "Okay." She turned for her room, hesitated, and looked back. "Thanks again, Cain."

I cleared the lump from my throat. "You're welcome." Then I hurried to my room before things got too sentimental. I just wasn't cut out for it.

Despite the busy day, my mind was too restless to let me sleep. I considered going back to Shipwreck, infiltrating the tavern, and planting more cameras. I suspected the bar would have more patrons tomorrow and keeping the camera in its current location would be less than ideal.

It was ordinary nub tech, and most mages were too busy looking for magical spying wards to think about scanning for wireless signals. That meant I could probably put that camera and others like it just about anywhere. They connected via a cell signal so I could login remotely with an internet connection.

I must have drifted off to sleep because the vibrations of my phone on my chest jerked me awake. Clearing my bleary eyes, I looked at the screen and saw a message from the person I'd asked to be part of my crew.

You're useless without me, aren't you? Layla Blade hadn't lost a bit of her sweetness or charm since I'd last seen her.

I sent a message. *I can't even tie my shoes without you.*

Fine. Pick me up from the W Buckhead in the morning, Layla texted back.

She rarely agreed to anything so quickly, but it was almost three in the morning, so she was probably about to go to sleep after a long night of drinking and partying. Her being at the W Hotel only confirmed that.

Sure, I'll be your Uber driver, I sent back.

Don't get ahead of yourself. You're more like my chauffeur.

I put my phone on the nightstand, stripped down to my underwear, and crawled under the covers. It didn't take long to fall asleep.

I WOKE up early the next morning and made pancakes, bacon, eggs, and homemade biscuits.

Hannah dragged herself out of bed, eyes half-closed, her nose angled up as if it were leading her to the table. "It smells so good." She wore a panda onesie I'd bought her from Goodwill months ago.

I frowned. "Weren't you wearing pink pjs last night?"

"I really wanted to wear this one too!" She whirled in a circle.

She looked adorable, but I kept that opinion to myself. I'd definitely lose my assassin creds if I started throwing around words like cute and adorable.

"Okay, panda girl." I piled some pancakes on my plate and started eating.

Hannah stared at me as if seeing me for the first time. "I was so exhausted yesterday I didn't even realize how much younger and better you look now." She shook her head. "You looked so old with the curse."

I shrugged. "It really did a number on me." I sighed. "Thanks for saving me, but gods damn it, I hate what you're going through now."

"I'd do it all over again to save you, Cain." Hannah bit into a slice of bacon. "We saved each other."

I felt like she'd done a lot more saving than I had. I might have taken her from a hellish life as a foster kid, but now her life truly was a living hell. She should've let me die, but I didn't want to take away what little joy she had.

"Yeah, we did." I stuffed my mouth with eggs, so I didn't say anything else.

Naturally, Layla texted before I finished eating. *I'm ready. Penthouse level. Just come in.*

I sighed. "I've got to go get Layla." I got up and poured some coffee into my to-go mug. "We've got a lot to talk about when I get back."

"Can I go?" Hannah asked.

"Better if you wait here." I pulled on my boots and headed for the door. "Be back soon."

It took twenty minutes with traffic to get to the hotel. I dropped Dolores with the valet and told him I was just running up to get someone. The elevator required a keycard to go to the penthouse, so I took it to the highest floor I could, and then picked the lock to the stairwell with a spell.

It felt great being able to take several flights of stairs without winding myself. It had taken me months to regain muscle and stamina after Cthulhu removed the curse. When I still had the curse, this many flights of stairs would have damn near given me a heart attack.

A rolled-up magazine held open the penthouse door. I pushed it open and went inside. Empty champagne and liquor bottles littered the kitchen counter. A long table held the remains of a feast. The odor of stale alcohol lingered in the air. Past the kitchen, a new odor took hold.

Clothes were scattered all over the floor—far too many to belong to two or even three people.

Naked people slumbered on the couch, the floor, and on blow-up mattresses. Some huddled together for warmth and others had been lucky enough to score blankets. The smell of sex, old sweat, and body odor filled my nostrils.

A young man pushed himself up from beneath three slumbering women. He smiled with wine-stained lips. "Well, aren't you a sight?" He gripped a decanter from the coffee table and took a long draw from it. "You look like a man on a mission, Cain."

I blinked and narrowed my eyes. "Is that you again, Hermes?"

The man giggled drunkenly. "Heavens no. He doesn't like to party."

"Layla told you about me?" I said.

He pursed his lips. "Your girl likes to party, Cain. Perhaps it was chance that met her, or perhaps some other divine force. Because I really had no idea you'd show up here."

I got straight to the point. "Who are you?"

He smacked one of the naked girls on the ass and pushed himself up. "Simply a lover of life, my grim-faced darling." He leaned over and kissed a dozing man on the lips. "Let go of your worries and taste the sweet nectar of life for once."

I sighed. "I don't have time for this." I didn't see Layla in the vicinity, so I headed toward the bedroom.

The man suddenly stood in front of me without seeming to have moved. He put a hand on my chest. "Bow to me, Cain, and I will make your life worth living."

"Gods be damned." I backed up a step and looked at him in a new light. The wine-stained lips. The debauchery and partying. "You're Dionysus."

He grimaced. "Oh, Bacchus, please. I had someone call me Dion once, and it just killed me."

"I go my whole life thinking the gods are dead, and now I've met two within twenty-four hours. What the hell is going on?"

"You're ensnared by fate, or chosen, it seems." Bacchus traced a finger down my chest. "And you look deliciously upset about it."

I wasn't sure if grabbing his finger was considered taking direct action against a god, so I simply backed up a step. "Look, I'm here for a friend. Do you mind?"

He tutted. "Oh, Cain, you haven't enjoyed a good fucking in a while, have you?"

"Not that it's any of your business—"

"Oh, it's certainly my business," he interjected. Bacchus produced a glass of wine seemingly from nowhere, but this one was filled with amber liquid. "Take a sip, friend, and let go."

Moans of pleasure rose from behind me. I looked back at the couch and saw the men and women rousing from slumber, hands grasping greedily at whatever was there, mouths and tongues tracing paths of pleasure down naked flesh.

I ghostwalked to the bedroom door to get myself out of there.

Bacchus sighed. "Another time, perhaps." He blew me a kiss and downed his drink, then went back to the couch and joined in the fresh festivities. I opened the bedroom door and stepped inside.

Four people shared the bed, but Layla wasn't among them. "Son of a bitch," I muttered. A hair dryer hummed to life behind a closed bathroom door. I opened it and steam drifted out. When it cleared a little, I found Layla drying her hair.

"Gods damn it, you're not even dressed yet?" I said.

She grabbed a dry towel and turned her naked backside to me. "Help a girl out?"

Her muscular legs and ass were something to behold, but I knew better than to express interest. Layla wasn't into me. I snatched the towel and patted down her scarred back. I hadn't asked her how she'd gotten the crisscrossing marks, but it was obvious she'd been badly flogged and whipped long ago. I finished drying her back while she squeezed her hair in the other towel.

"Get between the cheeks too, Cain."

"Fuck off." I resisted the urge to crack the towel against her bare ass. "Guess I missed the orgy, huh?"

"It was great." She took the towel from me, grinned lasciviously, and flossed it between her legs. "You could probably get sloppy thirds or fourths from someone out there."

"Yeah, Bacchus already tried that on me." I shuddered at how much body fluids covered the people and that couch.

Layla paused a moment. "Who?"

"The god of wine and debauchery." I rolled my eyes. "You didn't realize you've been partying with a god lately?"

"Gods be damned." She laughed. "I knew there was something special about that man."

A strange feeling knotted my guts for an instant, but I pushed it aside. "Yeah, because he's no man."

"I met a god." Layla laughed again and thrust out her hips. "Suck it, Cain."

I sighed. "You're so sweet and refined."

Layla finished drying and slid into a tight-fitting leather skirt and top, examined herself in the mirror, and nodded. "Good to go."

I noted the faint outlines of throwing daggers hidden in the hem of her skirt. She opened a closet outside the bathroom and removed a long black backpack that presumably held her bow and arrows.

Foul body odor assaulted my nostrils again when I left the bathroom. Layla stopped by the bed to kiss a woman and man who were still asleep, then followed me out with a skip in her step.

"New girlfriend and boyfriend?" I asked.

"Gods no." She scoffed. "Serious relationships are too much maintenance. I like to whore it up and enjoy life, not tie myself down." She used a keycard to call the elevator and then tossed it back into the room. "Are you still pining over Aura?"

"I'm not pining over anyone." I gave her a sideways look. "Why, have you seen her lately?"

Layla snorted. "She's still bartending at Voltaire's. Not that you'd know, Mr. Persona Non Grata."

"I still don't understand why I was banned." The elevator doors slid open and I stepped inside. "Who even has the authority to do that?"

"Gods you're stupid." Layla pressed the lobby button and glared at me. "The owner did it."

I'd never investigated who owned Voltaire's because it never seemed that important. I really didn't want to admit that to Layla but gave in after a moment of silence. "And that is?"

She burst into laughter, slapping my back hard enough to leave a mark. "You're going to love this, Cain. I can't wait to see the look on your stupid face when I tell you."

She didn't even have to say the name, because I knew right then and there who it was. Keeping my face as stony as possible, I said, "You've got to be fucking kidding me. Aura owns Voltaire's?"

"Lock, stock, and barrel, baby." Layla doubled over with laughter. "Oh, gods, this is priceless. I wish I'd taken a picture of your face."

"No wonder she's been there so long." I didn't understand why Layla thought it was so funny. "Why would she ban me?"

"Because Hannah is gone, and you're blacklisted by Eclipse." Layla punched my shoulder. "You're useless to her, Cain. Game over."

I didn't want to admit that it hurt. I'd known Aura for years and had developed feelings for her without meaning to. Then I'd found out she'd been using me to help the Enders get their very own demi. She'd fucked me both literally and figuratively to get what she wanted.

"Aw, you look sad." Layla patted my shoulder. "Maybe I should put you out of your misery and collect that ten-mil bounty on your worthless hide."

"Frankly, I'm surprised Torvin hasn't sent every assassin in Eclipse to do that yet." My old commander from the Oblivion Guard had special reason to hate me. He used power like a blunt weapon, destroying anything in his way.

"Aura must not have told him where you live," Layla said. "Maybe it's a kindness she banned you from Voltaire's. He probably would have found you by now if you continued visiting your old watering hole."

The doors slid open and we entered the lobby.

Men and women alike paused in their routine to watch Layla pass. From their perspective she must look very imposing. Layla's torso and shoulders were deceptively petite. Her lower body was thick and muscular with legs that looked like they could deadlift a small car. A thin scar running from the corner of her left eye, across her cheek, and stopping at the corner of her mouth accentuated an already fierce resting bitch face.

Her pupils weren't quite round, almost vertical like a feline's, adding a predatory gaze to her bright hazel eyes. She'd shaven the left side of her head and wore the rest of her long black hair in a high ponytail, leaving her slightly pointed ears visible to everyone. With her tight leather outfit, she could pass for a cosplayer. That only made her stand out more from the human crowd.

Layla Blade was half fae, an abomination in the eyes of the fae, but pretty awesome by most human standards. Either way, she didn't really care what anyone thought of her, and barely glanced at the nubs watching her pass.

We went outside and the valet brought Dolores to me. I usually hated it when anyone except me drove her, but for some reason, valets didn't faze me.

I'd expected Layla to dig at me constantly about Aura on the drive home, but instead, she folded the seat back and dozed. It should have been a mercy, but I hadn't seen or talked with her in quite some time, and it made me feel a little lonely. I looked down at her and tried not to admit I kind of liked having her around.

When we reached the church, I parked Dolores in the garage, and we headed outside to the front door of the church. A faint whisper in the air was my only warning. I dove, tumbled, and bounced up on my feet, narrowly dodging the blade Layla thrust at my back. Without hesitation, she threw it at me. I cast a shield and the blade bounced off.

Layla's bow appeared in her hand almost as if by magic. A quick snap unfolded it, and a flap on her backpack flipped up to reveal dozens of arrows. Before I could utter a word, her hand blurred, drawing an arrow, nocking, and releasing it within a second.

I summoned my staff and the brightblade crackled to life. I blocked the first arrow inches from my face, the next one inches from my heart, and the third uncomfortably close to my crotch. Arrows sang through the air. Using a focusing spell to aid my eyes, I intercepted each one, splintering them to dust.

A faint glow from one arrow caught my attention. Rather than intercept it, I dodged to the side and let it pass. It struck a tree and exploded. Layla loosed three more of the explosive arrows at the same time. I spun my staff and cast a turbulence spell. The arrows flew erratically, missing me and detonating in the air.

One explosion threw Layla back, but she landed solidly on her feet, dropped her bow and flung razor-sharp daggers. An instant after throwing them, she charged me. Eyes narrowed, a short blade in each hand, Layla shot across the ground at superhuman speed. I swung my staff and deflected the blades back at her. She swatted them contemptuously with her short swords. I powered the tattooed sigils on my body and stepped forward to meet the charge.

Layla's blade pinged against the brightblade. Sparks flew and energy crackled.

"You wouldn't be shit without that staff." She pressed harder against it, her fae heritage granting her far more strength than my magically assisted muscles.

I smirked and threw it back in her face. "All that fae strength, and you're still not shit." I stepped back the instant her face reddened in anger, gripped her wrist, and used her strength to propel her past me. I twisted her arm and turned, flipping her onto her back—or tried to.

Layla flipped, but landed lightly on her feet, then swung her leg and donkey-kicked me. I barely blocked the blow in time. I avoided cracked ribs but couldn't hold my ground. I flew backward through the air about five feet and stumbled to stay upright. Before I could recover, Layla blurred toward me.

Lips peeled back in a snarl, I could tell she wanted to kill me for real this time.

CHAPTER 8

I sheathed my staff in its pocket dimension. As her blade swung toward my face, I sidestepped and tapped two fingers against the inside of her wrist, releasing a spell that shocked the nerves. The short sword dropped to the ground. Layla's fist came out of nowhere and slammed into my temple. The world blinked out for an instant and came back just in time for her to land a blow against my chest.

I stumbled back, threw up a shield, and blocked a vicious knee that would've sent my balls into Neverland. Layla cried out in pain as her knee cracked against the invisible barrier. I dissolved the shield, sent more power into my sigil tattoos, and slammed my fist against her cheek. Without pause, I punched her in the gut, grabbed her by the neck and slammed her to the ground.

Dirt and leaves exploded into the air.

"I'll fucking kill you!" Layla's legs kicked up behind me, looped around my neck and slammed me onto the ground.

Somehow, I squirmed loose before she had a chance to crush my skull. I zapped the inside of her thighs with another shock spell.

Her body convulsed. "That was my fucking twat!"

I leapt back atop her and punched her three times in the face. Layla blocked my fourth blow, grabbed my neck and shifted, rolling me onto the ground. I blocked her blows with a shield, then used a burst of magic to propel us up into the air.

I landed on my feet. Layla rolled away and lashed out with a foot.

I caught her foot, but she jumped and swung her other foot, knocking me off my feet. I held onto her foot and yanked even as I fell. Without a foot on the ground, she slammed to earth beside me. She rolled atop me, gripped my neck and cocked her fist.

Another shield gripped her fist and held it in place. "Have you made your point yet?" I wheezed from my constricted airway.

Layla scowled and nodded. "Yeah. You passed." She leaned down and pecked a kiss on my forehead. "You're almost impressive, Cain."

I knocked her hand from my throat. "Gee, thanks."

She stood and then offered a hand to help me up.

I didn't trust the gesture and got up on my own. Grass and dirt stained her clothes and mine, and her hair was all over the place. Blood trickled from her nose, mouth, and a cut on her forehead. "You just took a shower, dummy. Now look at us."

Layla laughed. "Gods, it was fun, though. Been a while since I fought anyone who could even come close to holding their own against me."

"Close?" I scoffed. "I beat you."

She shook her head. "Not even close. And you zapped my pussy."

"You went for my balls, so let's call it even."

She snorted.

I rolled my eyes. "Gods damn it, I hate this."

Layla raised an eyebrow. "Why?"

"Because fighting you gave me an awkward boner."

She grinned. "I've got a nice lady boner myself, but you'll never taste my sweet meat."

I wiped my mouth and looked at the blood on my hands, unable to tell if it came from me or her. "Let's go inside. There's a lot to talk about."

"What in the hell happened?" Hannah waited just inside the door with wide eyes when we entered. "I heard explosions, but I couldn't get past your wards to look outside."

"Just Layla being Layla," I said.

Layla's mouth dropped open. "What the fuck is she doing here?"

"I'll tell you when I get back." I left them in the den and went into my room to wash the blood off my face and hands. My face didn't look much better than Layla's, and my clothes were trashed. I grabbed a bottle of bandage potion and dabbed it on my wounds to stop the bleeding, then got a damp rag and went to the den.

Layla sat on the couch, not even the least bit concerned about staining it with dirt and blood.

"Get up, you filthy woman!" I tugged her off the couch. "You're the worst guest ever."

"Layla being Layla," Hannah said.

I dabbed at the wounds on Layla's face.

She smirked at me. "Good work, servant." Her eyes went to Hannah. "He's such a good boy. Did you know he dried my ass crack at the hotel?"

Hannah giggled. "Are you kidding me?"

I grunted. "You don't want to know how many dingle berries she had."

Hannah laughed even harder.

"Just like old times, huh?" Layla didn't even wince as I applied bandage potion to her cuts. "We're only missing Aura."

"Better off without her," Hannah said.

I backed away and inspected Layla. She was dirty, but at least she wasn't bleeding. I got a thick blanket and spread it over the couch so we could sit without soiling the leather. Then I got my laptop and copied the video from the camera at Shipwreck to it.

"So, Cain." Layla crossed her legs. "Make me a sammich and tell me why I'm here."

"I'll do both at the same time." I told them everything about last night—the assassin, my encounter with Hermes, the mage knights, and most importantly, the staged encounter with Bisbee. Then I played them the video from the camera.

"This is why you asked if Cthulhu could spy on me," Hannah said. "You wanted to make sure he didn't know about this plan of yours."

I nodded. "It's vital he doesn't know about the armory. If he or another faction found it, they could slaughter their enemies."

"You think Bisbee is with the Pandora Combine?" Layla took a bite of her second sandwich. "By taking this mission, you'll be giving them the key to the kingdom."

"I don't think so," I said. "They seem to have reasons of their own, but I don't know what they are yet."

"Am I officially in on this?" Hannah asked.

I shook my head. "No, but you're coming along anyway. I don't know how long this heist will take and I want you close so I can train you when I have free time."

She beamed. "I'm totally in!"

"You still have those dossiers about the factions?" Layla asked.

I nodded. "Yeah, but they don't have much of anything on the Combine."

Layla pursed her lips. "How liquid are you right now?"

"Money isn't a problem." I tilted my head to the side. "Why?"

"It'd be wise to have all the info we can on your new friends before jumping into bed with them." Layla wiped mustard from her face with the back of her hand and then wiped it on the blanket covering the couch. "And a full workup of Horatio and known accomplices would be a good idea too."

"That'd take weeks," I said. "I've been out of the game for months. I don't even have contacts with that kind of skillset."

"Well, there's one, but you'd better let me do the asking." Layla smirked. "She might not want to help if she knows it's you."

"Are you serious?" I scoffed. "I'm not giving Aura money for anything, even if she has magic wand that'd take me to the armory right now."

Layla held out her hands helplessly. "I'm just saying, if you want to go into this eyes-wide-open we're going to need intel. You already know you can't trust Bisbee, so let's find out why we can't trust him."

Hannah nodded. "I hate to say it, Cain, but I think she's right."

Of course, she's right, I thought. I just hated the idea of paying Aura for information. "Is Aura still working for Eclipse?"

Layla nodded. "She brings it up sometimes. If it makes you feel any better, she hates her current assets. Says all of them combined don't add up to one Cain."

I narrowed my eyes. "First of all, you'd never tell me if someone complimented me. Second of all, you're trying to butter me up so I'll be okay recruiting Aura."

Layla held up a hand like someone taking a pledge. "I'm not lying, Cain.

You might be average compared to me, but you're head and shoulders above the morons she's dealing with now. I should know—she won't shut up about how shitty they are."

I frowned. "She just tells you all this while you're at the bar?"

"Yeah, mostly." Layla took another bite of her sandwich.

My heart skipped a beat. "Did you sleep with her?"

She rolled her eyes and spoke while her mouth was still full. "No, I didn't fuck her, Cain. Gods know I tried to get her in bed, mainly just to rub it in your face, but I'm not her type."

I didn't like the surge of jealousy at the thought of her and Layla getting it on. I also didn't like that it kind of aroused me too. If anything, I wished I could just purge myself of all emotion regarding Aura. I didn't like being used or betrayed, and she'd done all of the above. It took a major effort on my part, but I kept my face neutral.

"Layla, you're such a bitch." Hannah's eyes glowed. "I just want to beat the shit out of you sometimes."

I snorted. "Looks like all Cthulhu needs to do is have Layla come visit you every once in a while."

Hanna held a hand next to her eye as if feeling the warmth. "Wow, I haven't done this in months. I guess Layla is good for something."

Layla opened her mouth, but I waved off her response and talked over her. "Find out how much it'll cost for dossiers on Bisbee and gang, and Horatio and the Combine. Just don't let her know it's about the lost armory. We definitely don't want Eclipse getting wind of this, because divine weapons are the kind of things that makes Torvin Rayne jizz in his pants." Not to mention he had direct ties to the Divine Council. The last thing I wanted to do was give Hera more powerful weapons than the demis she already used.

"I'll go take another shower and we can go to Voltaire's." Layla polished off her sandwich and stood.

"It's not even noon yet," I said. "Why go there now?"

Layla sighed. "Because Aura's home office is there."

I quirked an eyebrow. "You can just walk in?"

She nodded. "She showed me around. Told me how the agency works. I think she was trying to recruit me, but I told her I strictly freelance."

"I'll drive you there, but I can't go inside," I said.

"Duh." Layla scoffed. "Just stay in the car."

Hannah gave me a hopeful look. "Can I come?"

"Yep." I looked her up and down. "Better change out of the panda onesie though."

"But it's adorable," she said. "And warm."

"Should I get you a onesie too, Layla?" I smirked in her general direction.

"Could come in handy." Layla smirked back. "Last thing someone expects is getting stabbed in the guts by someone in a onesie."

Hannah shuddered. "Is nothing sacred to you?"

Layla nodded. "My workout regimen." She looked at her bloodied skirt and top. The leather was torn just above the shoulder. "Looks like I'll need to borrow something to wear until Cain pays to have my clothes repaired and cleaned."

I pshawed. "Why the hell should I pay? You attacked me."

"Because I'm your guest, Cain." Layla rolled her eyes. "Girl, get me something to wear while I shower."

Hannah crossed her arms. "Not unless you say my name and please."

A poisonous smile crossed Layla's lips. "Dear sweet Hannah, may I please borrow some clothes?"

"Aww, how sweet." Hannah reached out and patted her hand. "Of course you can, dear sweet Layla."

Layla stalked toward the guest room she and Aura stayed in last time. It was hard to believe I'd played host to three people at one time when before I'd never had a single guest. Once again, it was practically a full house—two assassins and a demigod. All that was missing was the elf.

I went to my room, showered, and changed clothes since I looked no better than Layla. When I came out, Hannah was waiting in a t-shirt and jeans.

"Did you really dry out Layla's ass crack?" she asked.

"Just her back," I said.

She sighed. "Can't you find better friends? Layla is such a bitch."

"We're not friends." I sat on the back of the couch. "She's a mercenary and she's damned good at her job."

"You're paying her to help?"

"She hasn't brought that up," I said. "Last time she helped because she wanted to see a unicorn. I'm not sure what she wants this time." I caught movement in the corner of my eye and turned to see Layla wearing a plain blue dress that barely reached her knees.

"You know what I want, Cain." Layla twirled in the dress. "I want a pretty weapon from the armory to go with my dress."

"I thought you were smarter than that," I said. "Gods know what kind of havoc those weapons could wreak."

"I certainly won't take a world-killer or plague dealer," she said. "I mean, you got a lovely dagger from the unicorn. I'd like my own mythical weapon."

Shraya, one of the last original unicorns, had offered her beating heart as a prize should I assassinate high-priority targets that threatened to exterminate what remained of her herd. She'd given me Carnwennan, the legendary dagger of King Arthur, to do the deed since it would cut through her magically tough hide where a normal dagger wouldn't. When I decided not to kill her, I opted for the dagger as a gift instead and used it to kill the demigod, Sigma, who'd been trying to kill Hannah.

I hadn't used it since then but kept it close in case I needed it against another demigod. "I'll give you Carnwennan if we don't find anything suitable in the armory."

Layla shook her head. "You're too soft, Cain. The girl made a choice. Let her live with it."

I ignored her dig. "Is it a deal?"

She pursed her lips. "Conditionally, yes. If there's nothing I like in the armory, I'll take your dagger."

"That leaves too much wiggle room," I said. "I want assurances you won't take a weapon that's too dangerous to be out and about."

She raised an eyebrow. "Do you want my help or not?"

Considering she was the only competent backup I trusted, I couldn't exactly turn her away. And if she could secure valuable information from Aura, that made her doubly valuable to me. But did I really want to risk giving Layla the chance to walk out of the armory with something that could blow up a city?

"I think I broke him," Layla said to Hannah. "He's so torn between letting me have a powerful weapon and saving you that he can't talk."

"I don't blame him," Hannah said. "If it comes down to you being able to end the world and me getting free of Cthulhu, then I'll stick with octo-face."

"Cute nickname." Layla smirked.

"Fine," I said at last. "Just don't disappoint me, Layla."

She blinked, as if caught by surprise, but quickly recovered. "You're not my father."

"No, but I'm the closest thing you have to a friend," I said. "So whether you want to admit it or not, my opinion matters to you."

Layla huffed. "Can we get going before Cain starts crying?"

Hannah snorted. "That'd be the day."

We piled into Dolores and headed to Voltaire's. I found a parking spot just outside the safe zone and got out of the car.

"Hannah and I will be over there." I pointed to a nub pub just down the block.

Hannah looked across the street from us. "Do you mind if I look in the thrift store?"

"Sure, go ahead." I turned to Layla. "Good luck."

"I don't need luck when money talks." She turned to go. "I'll be back soon." Layla headed across the parking lot leading to Voltaire's speakeasy entrance about a hundred yards away.

The asphalt looked to have been recently repaved, repairing the damage done by Sigma when he'd tried to charbroil Hannah and me. I'd killed him in a park not far from here and nearly died from magic cancer and my wounds not long after. During my long recovery, Layla had buried Sigma in a plot outside the church. Taking the body from the scene had been the right move since she couldn't call on ghouls to devour the body in broad daylight.

I wondered if Hera even knew what had happened to her boy assassin. Hermes hadn't mentioned it, so it was possible they didn't know I'd killed him. Or maybe Hera didn't care. She probably had other demis in the stable she could brainwash and train to wipe out others of their kind.

I headed into the pub down the block and was disappointed to learn they couldn't make mangoritas, or 'ritas of any kind. I ordered a stout beer for a change and nursed it for twenty minutes or so. Layla hadn't texted yet, but that wasn't unexpected. If Aura was working, she might not have time to talk right away, or they might be in intense negotiations. I ordered another beer and was halfway through it when Layla texted.

Meet back at the car.

Good news? I sent back.

You're going to love it.

I didn't like the sound of that at all. I took a moment to polish off the beer and pay, then I went back toward the car. Hannah was probably still shopping, but I could get her after I heard what Layla had to say.

My hackles rose the moment I reached Dolores, but I didn't know why. Aversion wards kept most nubs away from the area, so foot traffic was light. A pair of mages walked parallel to my position, but I saw no danger.

Then I noticed a smudge in the air rapidly closing the distance between us. Someone was hiding behind a camouflage illusion and I doubted it was Layla. I didn't want to make too big a scene, so I drew my dueling wands and readied a shield. The smudge crossed the safe zone line and the camouflage blind vanished.

A man brandishing dueling wands thrust them toward me. Power crackled from the tips. I parried the blow, intercepting it with power of my own. I spun, kicked the man in the ribs. He grunted and stumbled back. Bared his teeth and came for me.

That was when I realized that I recognized the man. It was the same person I'd killed yesterday.

CHAPTER 9

"Who the hell are you?" I shouted.

He shouted back in a garbled tongue. As with yesterday, he wasn't speaking another language, but nonsense. The expression on his face made it seem as if he thought he was talking normally. I'd heard of aphasia, but this was something different. Before I could ask another question, he came at me with the wands again.

This time, he went old-school and thrust his wand point-blank at my chest. I slapped it aside with a wand, blocked a second blow, and zapped him on the wrist with my left wand. I delivered an elbow to his chin, spun, and nailed him with my other elbow. He fell flat on his back, stunned. Before he could recover, I jammed two fingers into his neck and sent a jolt of power into the nerve.

His body convulsed and he went still.

"Gods damn it, Cain. Can't you go a minute without raising hell?"

I looked up at the familiar voice and saw Aura walking alongside Layla. Her red hair had grown down past her shoulders and her eyes gleamed like emeralds. It felt so good to see her again that I forgot an unconscious body lay at my feet.

"Gaia to Cain." Layla snapped her fingers. "Wake up, Cain."

I snapped out of my daze. Without responding to them, I powered a sigil on Dolores's rear door, and it popped open. I dumped the unconscious assassin inside and frisked him for weapons or identification.

"This can't be the same guy," I muttered. "No one survives a hole in the chest." Like the guy yesterday, he had nothing but the dueling wands on him. I slashed open his robe and looked for hidden pockets. There weren't any. But there was something different. Where the guy yesterday had a scar on his rib, this guy had two identical scars side-by-side. I examined them more closely to make sure they weren't tattoos. I was no expert, but they seemed like real scars.

I bound him with straps I used for just such occasions and covered him with a blanket, then closed the rear door.

"Cain?" Aura watched me, hands on hips. "Who was that and why were you fighting him?"

I glared at Layla. "What's she doing here?"

Layla looked almost ashamed. "She saw through my ruse. Figured the only reason I'd ask for info about the Combine was because of you."

"Cain, I want an explanation right now." Aura stepped closer. "Who's that man and why are you asking questions about the Pandora Combine?"

"A man tried to kill me yesterday at Drigger's Bay." I said.

She wrinkled her nose. "That nasty dump?" She took another step closer. "What else?"

"This guy was apparently his twin brother." I considered the scar. "Maybe even Siamese twins, separated at birth."

Layla snorted. "Just when I think you can't get any more bizarre, you go and say something like that."

"The guy came out of nowhere and tried to kill me," I said. I stared back at Aura. "What did Layla tell you?"

"Not much. She said I'd have to ask you."

I sighed. "Fine. Can we talk about it inside?"

Aura shook her head and jabbed a finger at the back of the car. "You're not welcome in Voltaire's because of shit like this, Cain. You killed Sigma right down the block from here, and if Layla hadn't covered your ass, cops would have swarmed the place."

"Sigma's the one who fought the cops right outside your door," I said. "Not me."

"It's not personal, Cain." Aura crossed her arms. "Just business."

"I don't know," I said. "You made it pretty fucking personal when you tried to betray me."

"Oh my gods." Aura craned her neck to look straight up and huffed like a spoiled teenager. "Are you ever going to get over that? I was just doing my job."

"For a faction that wanted Hannah!" I slashed a hand through the air. "Look, if I offer you money, will you work up dossiers on the Pandora Combine, a mage named Horatio, and three other people?"

Aura frowned. "I want to know what this is about first."

"Are the Enders allied with the Combine?"

"Absolutely not," she said.

"Then why does it matter to you?" I shot back.

Aura stepped closer. If she hadn't been a head shorter, our noses might have touched. "In case you don't realize it, I hold the power to grant or deny you access to valuable information. So, either tell me everything, or go away."

She thought she had me over a barrel, but I wasn't about to give in to her demands. "I don't need it that badly. Goodbye." I turned and headed across the road to the thrift store to get Hannah.

Layla came up beside me and grabbed my upper arm. "For fuck's sake, just tell her. Good intel could save us some serious headaches."

I glanced back and saw Aura watching us. She hadn't moved, which meant she wanted to know what we were up to. Which meant I had a smidgen of power to negotiate. "You do understand that if I tell her and she blabs to her faction, they could come after the weapons too?"

Layla shrugged. "Yeah, so make a deal that keeps her mouth shut and her body close."

I stopped on the sidewalk across the road and gave it some thought. "I'll try one more time." First, I went inside the shop and found Hannah with an armload of clothes.

She beamed. "Look at all these great deals I found!"

"Awesome. We've got to go." I took the clothes from her and piled them in front of the cashier. It took the woman ten minutes to ring them up and bag everything. Visible through the window, Aura still waited across the street. If she was willing to wait this long, I had more power than I'd hoped.

Hannah saw Aura too. "What's she doing out there?"

"Negotiating," I said. I paid the cashier, hefted the bags, and headed for the door. "You got an entire wardrobe, didn't you?"

"It's not all for me," she said. "I got a few things for Layla so she's not trying to fit her thick frame into my petite clothes. If she wasn't small up top, there's no way she could even wear my dresses."

"I'm sure she'll appreciate the gesture," I said.

Hannah snorted. "Oh, she'll be giddy with joy."

I dumped the bags next to the unconscious assassin in the back of the station wagon.

Hannah's mouth dropped open. "Uh, who's that?"

"Good question." I pressed my lips into a flat line and stared at Aura a moment. "I'll tell you what this is about, but only if you promise not to tell anyone else about it, and to work up the dossiers."

Aura pursed her lips. "Fine."

"Promise me," I said.

"Cain, I promise not to tell anyone about whatever it is you're doing, and I'll do the dossiers for a fair price." She crossed her arms. "Good enough?"

"Probably not," I said, "but whatevs."

Hannah scoffed. "You need a blood oath to trust her."

"Not gonna happen," Aura said. "Too dangerous."

Blood oaths had a way of backfiring if they weren't precisely worded. Otherwise, I'd use them for everything. I walked to the driver door. "Let's talk inside."

Aura took shotgun while Layla and Hannah slid into the backseat. I told Aura what little I knew about those involved and laid out the stakes.

She remained quiet for a while after I finished and seemed to reach a conclusion. "Cthulhu's goals somewhat align with the Enders. I wouldn't be averse to giving him a leg up, provided he can't annihilate existence."

"Wonderful." I clapped my hands together. "How much for the dossiers?"

"Admission to the show," she said. "I want to be part of the heist."

I groaned. "The last thing I need is another team member, especially one who will try to screw us over when we least expect it."

"I always expect it," Layla said.

"I won't betray you or lie to you," Aura said. "But I would like to see what the armory has to offer."

I groaned. "I'm beginning to regret ever bringing in partners. Layla wants a weapon, and now you want one too. Why don't we just steal a nuke and get it over with?"

"Do you really think every weapon in the armory is that dangerous?" Aura said.

"I have no idea what's in there." I turned in my seat to look at the others. "Don't you think giving Cthulhu a weapon from there is bad enough? Hephaestus hid that shit in there for a reason. What if we take something that gives us magic cancer like Cthulhu's pearl did to me? What if we unleash a plague?"

"Cain, I'm aware of the dangers," Layla said, "so I'll be very careful if I choose to take anything."

"As will I," Aura said.

Hannah smiled brightly. "I'd like a nuke."

I groaned. I felt control of this project slipping further from my grasp. But if I wanted a higher chance to succeed, then I needed Aura and Layla. I also wasn't sure how Bisbee would respond if I showed up to our meeting with three additional team members.

"Fine, we'll see how badly this turns out." I turned back to Aura. "I need the info as soon as possible. For the time being, I'm only going to introduce Layla to the others. I don't want to spook them by bringing in a whole crew of my own."

"Smart move," Aura said.

I grunted. "So, am I still banned from Voltaire's?"

"Yep." She got out. "I'll text you when I have something." Then she closed the door and walked away.

Layla snorted. "Cold."

"What a bitch." Hannah patted my shoulder. "You can do better, bro."

"Doubtful." Rather than get out of the back door and use the passenger door like a human, Layla slid over the front seat, exposing her lack of underwear to everyone in the car. Her backside pressed against my shoulder as she wriggled across.

I put up my hands in defense. "Get your ass out of my face!"

Layla righted herself and guffawed. "Most men would enjoy a gift like that, Cain."

Hanna giggle-snorted. "Layla, I hate you most of the time, but that was pretty funny." She held up a hand and Layla high-fived her.

"Because she put her bare ass in my face?" I started driving. "Maybe you could avoid doing that when you meet Bisbee and the others."

Layla pursed her lips. "Maybe."

I headed home so I could secure the assassin in an underground cell. I hoped to figure out why he couldn't talk right and wring some information out of him. When we arrived at the church, I parked Dolores and opened the rear door. The assassin stared blankly back at me. Foamy spittle covered his lips and his skin was pale and cold.

Hannah gasped. "He's dead!"

I pried open his mouth with the tip of a dagger. "Poison capsule of some kind."

"Oh, well." Layla hoisted the body and headed toward the graveyard. "We can bury him next to Sigma."

"We don't have time right now." I showed her the clock on my phone. "We have to leave for Shipwreck right now."

Layla dumped the body on the ground. Her hand slipped beneath her dress and returned with a dagger. She thrust it through the assassin's heart, twisted, and removed it, wiping the blood on his robes. "Wanted to make sure he's dead and not just faking it."

I nodded. "Good idea."

"You're just going to leave him there?" Hannah grimaced. "I can bury him."

I shook my head. "I want you to practice with the golems."

"Dancing again?" she asked.

I nodded. "You need a refresher course." I disarmed the wards on the doors and let her in. "We'll be back in a few hours."

She gripped my hand. "Be careful."

"I will. I retrieved her shopping bags from the car and set them inside. Then Layla and I headed north to Shipwreck. We arrived a little after noon. The parking lot was a quarter full, and I wasn't surprised to find a decent crowd drinking and dining once Targ let us in. Two humans waited tables, and Norna was bartending. Bisbee and Dwight were nowhere to be seen.

Norna blinked when she looked up from mixing a drink and saw me and Layla. I offered a reassuring smile and sat down at the bar. "Ready?"

She nodded at Layla. "Who's that?"

Layla leaned on the bar. "Like what you see?"

Norna frowned. "Not really."

"Norna, meet Layla." I forced another reassuring smile. "She's the crewmember I mentioned bringing on board yesterday."

The ogress looked Layla up and down. "Does she always dress like that?"

I snorted. "Definitely not. Shall we go meet the others?"

Norna motioned at one of the servers and pointed at the bar. The woman nodded and made her way to take over bartending. Norna led us upstairs and down a hall to a room at the end. Bisbee and Dwight sat at a table inside. Surprised looks flashed across their faces when Layla entered behind us.

I took in the room with a glance. A desk with files and papers sat in a corner, and clothes hung in the closet. It was apparent they used this room regularly, so I discreetly slapped a mini-camera on the wall facing the room interior and masked it with camouflage.

Dwight spoke first. "Who's this?"

"My business partner." I sat down across from him. "She's the one I told you about yesterday."

Despite my having told them about bringing someone, they all acted as if it were new to them. It was just another bargaining tactic, often used by scammers to bend someone to their will. It wasn't going to work with me.

"Are you certain that's necessary?" Bisbee said.

I could practically see the gears turning in his and Dwight's heads as they tried to think of ways to dissuade me. "Yep," I said.

Dwight frowned and stared at Layla. "We don't know her."

"You don't know me either," I said.

Layla sat down and leaned on the table. "You'll get to know me, okay?"

"No." Dwight slapped the table. "This isn't part of the plan."

"Make it part of the plan or I'm out," I said. "I reserve the right to bring in personnel of my own if I think it'll improve our chances of success."

Bisbee held up his hands in a calming gesture. "It complicates our plans, but we can still make it work."

"Of course." I leaned back in my chair. "Why don't we get started?"

Dwight harrumphed but didn't challenge Bisbee's decision. "Before I get started, I'd like to know just how involved your partner will be."

"I'll be along for the ride," Layla said. "Where he goes, I go."

Dwight glanced at Bisbee and nodded. "The infiltration is a one-person operation. Two people increases the risk of detection, but if you're okay with that, then I'll let you adjust the plan to your liking."

Layla smirked. "Sounds good, babe. Lay it on me."

He wrinkled his nose. "Before I reveal the exact location of Deepvale, I need assurances that you'll see this through, Cain."

"I wouldn't bring my partner in on this if I didn't intend to go through with it." I clasped my hands on the table. "Shall we get to it?"

Bisbee spread a paper map of a mountainous region in Romania on the table. He took out his wand and traced a sigil on the map. A red X marked Deepvale and dotted lines traced three different routes through the cliffs surrounding it.

Layla scoffed. "Where'd you get this map, a gas station?"

"We don't exactly have photos," Dwight said.

"X marks the location of the amulet," Bisbee said. "This map is enchanted to track it."

These people were complete amateurs. I'd expected far more detail, but this was barely a general overview. How in the hell was I supposed to infiltrate the castle and steal the map when I had zero information to go on?

CHAPTER 10

"Do I have to do all the work?" I scoffed. "There's no way I can make a plan based on so little information."

Layla tapped on the X. "Do you have the internal layout?"

Dwight shook his head. "We don't have any information."

"Wow, what a great plan." Layla scoffed and looked at me. "We get to go sight unseen into dangerous territory guarded by vampires and mages to steal a map that's hopefully a hell of a lot more detailed than this piece of shit."

Norna snorted, but quickly covered her mouth.

"We're not tacticians, Cain." Bisbee folded the map and tucked it into his robes. "That's why we need someone like you."

It was enough. Doing the legwork and research for the mission was a small price to pay if it helped me free Hannah. "Looks like it's time to go to Romania. I'll try to leave tomorrow or the day after."

Bisbee looked surprised. "Just like that?"

I shrugged. "I'm not going to find what I need sitting on my ass around here, am I?"

"All of you coming along?" Layla asked.

Dwight shook his head. "There's no need for all of us to go. Norna will accompany you."

Layla looked the ogress up and down. "She's gorgeous, but she's also a foot taller than most humans. Oh, and she's green."

Norna pulled a necklace from beneath her shirt and tapped the gem. Her skin went from green to light brown. "This is what I use to mingle with nubs. I can't do much about my height, but at least my green skin tone won't stand out."

I grunted. "Good enough. You paying for your own ticket?"

She nodded.

I held out a burner phone to her. "We'll communicate with these."

Norna took it. "I'll be packed and ready to go."

"Good." I stood up and nodded at Bisbee. "I memorized the coordinates, but send the map with Norna just in case."

"I will." Bisbee smiled. "Good luck, Cain. My brother's fate is in your hands."

"I'll do my best." I started for the door and glanced at the spot where I'd hidden the camera. The illusion hiding it would last for quite some time. Layla and I left the room and made our way outside. Norna followed at a distance as if making sure we didn't stick around in the hallway to eavesdrop.

When we got into the car, I turned on my phone and watched the stream coming from the camera.

"I don't like it at all," Dwight was saying to Bisbee. "She'll make it twice as hard for us to achieve our goal."

"Hardly," Bisbee said. "Just follow the plan and neither of them will be a problem."

"Unless they figure out what we're up to." Dwight went to the mini-fridge and procured a bottle of amber liquid. "Then it'll all be for nothing."

Bisbee turned on the TV. "We'll talk about it later. Matlock is about to come on."

Dwight took a long draw from the bottle. "You realize you could binge the entire series on a streaming service, right?"

"I prefer it this way." The wizard moved from the table to the couch.

Norna came into view, presumably from the doorway. "They left. I don't think they suspect anything."

"That much is clear," Bisbee said. "Now can everyone quiet down so I can watch my show?"

I put my phone in a holder so I could keep an eye on it while I drove.

Layla pursed her lips. "I wonder what they're up to."

"They probably want all the weapons they can carry out of there," I said. "What confuses me is how Bisbee thinks neither of us will be a problem."

Layla grunted. "Overconfident?"

"He knows my reputation, and yet he doesn't seem worried." I glanced at the phone. "I've got the camera recording, so hopefully Bisbee will spill the beans sooner rather than later."

"I need to pack." Layla pointed to the parking lot of a fast food restaurant. "Drop me off here and I'll uber home."

"Uber?" I rolled my eyes. "You know where my secret lair is. About time you showed me yours."

"Nah." Layla tapped the window. "Drop me off."

"I'll just follow the uber."

"Your time to waste, babe." She smirked. "I'll lead you all over town."

"Whatever." I pulled into the parking lot. "You probably don't even have a lair. I'll bet it's something boring like a condo or a townhouse in the suburbs."

Layla got out and blew me a kiss. "Guess you'll never know." She shut the car door and waltzed inside the restaurant.

I was tempted to see if I was up to the challenge of tracking her back home, but it would be a complete waste of time. There was too much else that needed doing before the big day tomorrow. I went on a supply run, grabbing a few essentials for my utility belt, and then swung by the farmers market for groceries.

When I returned home, I found Hannah working through a complex ballet routine with a training golem. Her face was red and sweaty, but despite looking like a half-starved waif, she was nailing the moves. I couldn't help but feel proud of her. She'd been through some awful shit in her life, but she kept pushing forward no matter the odds. I had to do whatever I could to free her so she could enjoy life for once.

I clapped when the routine finished. "Looking good!"

"Thanks!" She skipped over and gave me a hug. "How'd the meeting go?"

"Wasn't much to it." I filled her in on the details as we walked upstairs. "Layla and I depart for Romania tomorrow."

Hannah looked down. "Am I not coming?"

"It's better if you don't. I had enough trouble convincing them to let Layla come." I went to the kitchen, heated up the oven, and started slicing vegetables. "Go get cleaned up while I make lunch."

"Okay." She headed into her room.

By the time she came out, I'd put all the ingredients on a homemade pizza and slid it into the oven.

"Smells great!" Hannah looked inside the oven. "That looks so yummy."

"Do you like sci-fi movies?" I asked.

She nodded. "I haven't seen many. None of my foster parents splurged on entertainment like that."

"Hopefully, you'll like this." I went old-school and slid *Star Trek: The Motion Picture* into the DVD player.

Hannah kept glancing at me during the movie as if gauging my reactions. "Do you actually like this?"

I nodded. "It's kind of slow, but good."

She grimaced. "I think it's slow and bad."

I threw up my hands and ejected it from the player. "Let's see what you think about *The Wrath of Khan*."

By the first space battle, she was leaning forward in anticipation. "Okay, now this one is good. I think Khan is my new fave hero."

I laughed. "He's the bad guy."

"Yeah, but he's awesome!"

Who am I to judge? I thought. I wasn't exactly the good guy either.

Hannah leaned against me and sighed. "This is wonderful. I really hope Khan kicks Kirk in the balls."

I really needed to get some prep work done, but gods damn, it felt good to slow down and enjoy life for a moment. When the movie was over, I got up and headed to my bedroom office. "I've got some work to do."

Hannah trailed behind me. "How long do you think you'll be gone?"

I sat down at my laptop and loaded the maps app. "I'm not sure, but it'll take a day or two minimum to recon the castle. I've got to record patrol patterns, estimate the guard complement, and find out where Horatio keeps the map that hopefully leads us to Hephaestus's original forge."

She yawned. "Sounds boring."

"All part of the job." I switched to satellite view and zoomed in on the region. I wasn't surprised when I found no trace of a castle or building of any kind in the enclosed valley. Vlad Tepes had probably hidden it beneath a veil of illusion to prevent nub technology from discovering it. That meant it'd be difficult if not impossible to spy on the castle from a distance, at least for people who didn't have an oblivion staff with a true sight scope.

Hannah peered at the map. "Isn't there supposed to be a castle there?"

"It's there, I hope." I wondered how Bisbee knew there was a castle if it was hidden.

"What if you get there and find nothing but trees?"

"Then I'll be pissed." I zoomed in as far as the image would let me but couldn't find anything to indicate a castle was hiding there somewhere.

Hannah dropped onto the edge of my bed and watched. "I still can't believe Dracula owns the castle."

"He owns a lot of stuff." I dragged the map view around the edges of the enclosed valley, confirming the mountain passes Dwight had marked actually existed.

"Is he the king of the vampires?"

I shrugged. "He's the head of the order, but that's not the same as being king." I turned around in my computer chair to face her. "There are other powerful vampires who run their own invisible empires and answer to no one."

Hannah grunted thoughtfully. "Did Dracula fight during the Human-Fae War?"

"Not that I know of," I said. "But it's not uncommon for powerful vampires to sit back while their minions fight."

She scoffed. "Most powerful people hide behind their minions. But Khan didn't."

I snorted. "Spoiler alert—that's why he died." I turned back to the computer and booked a one-way flight to Romania, then texted Norna the information with my burner phone. I reserved a business elite seat for myself and stuck Layla in coach. She wouldn't be happy, but I didn't want to deal with her for a fifteen-hour flight. The drive from the airport to the general location of the castle would take about two hours.

Flight booked, Norna texted back a few minutes later.

It was no surprise that I hadn't heard anything from Layla, so I texted her from my real cell phone and let her know when to meet us at the airport. She didn't respond.

I closed the laptop, zipped up my suitcase, and figured I'd done all I could do until I assessed the situation onsite tomorrow. I fired off a message to Aura to see how those dossiers were coming, but she didn't respond either.

"Wish I could come," Hannah said.

I didn't know if listening to her and Layla argue for hours was something I could handle. I went to the hallway closet and showed Hannah the games inside. "Up for a board game?"

She clapped her hands. "Yes!"

We whiled away the evening playing games and went to bed in the wee hours of the morning. I didn't mind. It was nice feeling alive again despite the weight of Hannah's future settling onto my shoulders.

I WENT to the airport early to catch the ten AM flight to Bucharest. Norna arrived at the gate a few minutes after me, but there was no sign of Layla.

Norna smiled. "Good morning." Her green hair and tall stature drew curious looks but not as many as I'd feared. Then again, we were at an airport and there were nubs of all kinds wandering the terminals.

"Morning." I picked up my backpack. "I'm going to get a coffee for the flight. Want anything?"

She nodded. "I'll come with you."

We went down the terminal and waited in a ridiculously long line to get our caffeine fix, then headed back to the gate a few minutes before boarding.

"I hope you don't mind that I reserved the seat across from you," Norna said.

I raised an eyebrow. "That's a seven-thousand-dollar seat."

She smiled. "For someone my height, it's worth it."

Left unsaid was that it was also a good way to keep an eye on me. I just nodded in response.

Wearing dark yoga pants and a tight top, Layla hurried into view just as the plane began to board. Her hair was tied up in a bun and wide sunglasses covered her eyes. Even though she was normal height, she drew more stares than Norna. I suspected it had to do with her muscular ass and the steady stream of curses spilling from her mouth.

Layla bared her teeth when she caught up to us. "Did you have to get the first fucking flight out, Cain?"

"Bucharest is seven hours ahead of this time zone," I said. "I want to get there when the sun is coming up so we can get to work."

"Good thing I didn't sleep last night." Layla lifted her sunglasses to rub red eyes. "I hope you don't mind listening to me snore."

I smirked. "Not at all."

She lifted the sunglasses again and glared at me. "You fucker. Did you put me next to the lavatory?"

I laughed. "No, that's Aura's special seat."

She looked at her ticket and at the zone number. "You're in first class, aren't you?"

"Business elite." I shrugged. "I wanted to stretch out."

Layla growled. "I'm going to start buying my own tickets."

"Maybe if you're sweet to the attendants, they'll upgrade you."

"Oh, I've got ways to upgrade seats all by myself." She didn't elaborate, but her gaze took in the other passengers boarding with me and Norna.

I figured it was a good thing I'd gone to bed so late since it increased my chances of sleeping on the plane. I'd brought along a sleep potion but was a little hesitant to use it. Entering a deep sleep in a plane full of strangers wasn't exactly my comfort zone.

Norna and I boarded and took our seats. Though hers was right across the aisle from me, the privacy partition and angle of the seats made it impossible for us to see each other unless we leaned around at uncomfortable angles. Our section was forward of the entry door, so we didn't even have to watch the peasants shuffling to coach.

An attendant's voice crackled over the intercom. "We will delay departure a few minutes to allow people from a connecting flight to reach us. We apologize for the inconvenience."

I didn't appreciate the delay, but the first-class attendant served mimosas and croissants to keep complaints to a minimum. We took off half an hour late, by which time I was comfortably buzzed and ready to slip into dreamland. But several inflight announcements and a crying kid from somewhere behind the curtain separating us from coach kept jerking me awake.

We were well out over the Atlantic by the time I adjusted my seat to the fully reclined position and dozed off.

I woke with a sharp intake of breath, hackles raised. The cabin was dim and the sky was dark. A shadow slid silently into view and paused next to my seat. Something metallic glinted in the dim light. I reached up and caught the wrists of the person trying to plunge a blade into my chest. The figure leaned forward, putting all their body weight behind the blade.

Death inched closer to my chest, and there was little I could do to stop it.

CHAPTER 11

My legs were wedged in the narrow space between the privacy partition and the seat. I wriggled them free, but there was no room to swing them around and shove the assailant off me. I powered the sigils on my arms, but was still barely able to keep the blade from my chest. There was no room to maneuver, no way to slide to the side and let the blade plunge into the seat.

I bent my knees and brought my legs toward my chest. There was enough momentum to swing out a foot and kick the figure in the face. The resulting grunt sounded male. He stumbled back. I used the brief reprieve to swing my legs around and get on my feet. We wrestled quietly as if, despite our desire to kill each other, we didn't want to disturb other sleepers.

He lost his footing and stumbled into Norna's seat partition. Her head poked out, but it was too dark to make out her expression. She gripped the assailant by the neck and squeezed. He gasped, flailed, and went limp.

I looked around but everyone was asleep or blinded by their bright entertainment screens. I put a finger to my lips to keep Norna from talking and slid the attacker into my seat. I turned on my reading light to see who in the hell had tried to kill me. My mouth dropped open when I saw the face.

It was the guy from yesterday and the day before. "How many brothers does this guy have?" I muttered. He even wore the same tight gray robes as the others. I lifted the shirt and found three parallel scars on his ribs. Despite being on a plane, he had no identification at all. Only a dagger and dueling wands.

"Gods almighty," Norna breathed. "Who is he?"

"I don't know, but I need to find out. This is the third time someone identical to him has tried to kill me."

"What?" She hissed. "How did he know you'd be boarding an airplane today?"

"I don't know, but he and his identical siblings keep finding me." I had a feeling there was something more to this. I wondered if the same guy was resurrecting somehow. I cast an aversion ward to keep curious eyes away from us, then summoned my staff and peeked through the scope. The assassin looked as normal as the others before him. He was a mage, not a zombie, a vampire, or other undead creature.

His body was also rapidly cooling. It seemed Norna had choked him a little too hard. Not that it mattered. This guy probably couldn't talk any better than the ones before him and I certainly didn't want him waking up for another chance at killing me. But what in the hell could we do with a dead body on an airplane?

I didn't know a lot about commercial airliners, but I knew enough. There were no hatches or ways to dump a body out of the plane. The only option would be getting into the luggage bay and stashing it there. Baggage handlers would, no doubt, find it soon after we landed, and authorities would lock down everyone as they disembarked the plane.

Then again, the solution might lie in how this guy managed to board the plane without an ID or boarding pass. I motioned Norna to wait there and went to the curtain dividing us from coach. The plane was big, a seven forty-seven. The coach seats were arranged three on each side and four in the middle.

I walked down the aisle as if going to the bathroom in the far back. There were two empty seats, but both were occupied a moment later by people returning from the lavatory. The flight attendants were dozing or looking at phones from the discomfort of their jump seats. I noticed a compartment to the side with a service cart sitting outside of it. That was when I realized how the guy had gotten onboard. He'd probably used a camouflage blind to sneak onto the plane and then hidden in the service compartment below. A service elevator brought the carts up from below. If memory served, there were sleeping compartments down there as well.

This wasn't the only service elevator. There was another one in business class. I made my way back toward my seating area and stopped at Norna's seat. "I'll be back in a moment."

She looked nervously at my seat and nodded.

I continued forward to the service area for my compartment. The attendants inside were slumped over unconscious in their jump seats, held up only by the seatbelts. I checked their necks and found pulses. The assassin must have knocked them out to slip past.

I slid open the door to the elevator and stepped inside, then pressed the down button. It descended and stopped a moment later. I opened the door into a space with a single service cart and food storage compartments. A narrow corridor took me to a pair of compact bunks. If I hadn't been trained to look for the signs of an aversion ward, I might have missed what I was looking for.

Aversion wards work in multiple ways. Some generate a great sense of unease, causing people to turn around and go away. This one was subtle, causing discomfort in my eyes so when I turned my head toward it, I felt an almost irresistible urge to blink, thus making me overlook it.

The assassin had warded the lower bunk opposite of the ones I'd looked at, layering the aversion ward over an obfuscation illusion. I forced my eyes to remain open despite the discomfort and removed a small sprayer vial from my utility belt. A fine mist of revealer highlighted the sigils traced against the side of the bunk. I dispelled the wards and my eyes began to feel better almost immediately.

I poked around inside the bunk and found what I'd expected to find—nothing. The only thing of value the assassin had given me was a place to stash his body. I went back up to the main deck and made sure my neighbors were still sleeping, then hefted the assassin with the aid of my body sigils and took him down the elevator and to his bunk.

With some effort, I arranged his body so it looked like he was asleep, and then put an aversion and obfuscation ward of my own in place that would keep anyone from discovering the body for at least twenty-four hours. By then, he'd probably be back on U.S. soil.

On the way back to my seat, I checked the attendants again to make sure they were still breathing. I noticed specks of blood and faint bruises on their necks. A quick search of the nearby trash bin turned up nothing. The assassin hadn't used potions, so he'd probably delivered electric shocks from his dueling wands. Knocking out someone like that was risky. My two-finger method delivered a mild shock straight to the nerves. This guy had used brute force.

If he'd accidentally killed the attendants, this plane would've been on lockdown for days after landing. My main concern now was that they'd wake up and realize they'd both been unconscious. I wasn't skilled at memory alteration magic. It was extremely advanced and even the experts messed up.

"What are you doing?" Norna whispered behind me.

"Thinking." I poked around the shelves and found a small locked compartment in the upper bulkhead. I picked the lock with one of my wands. Inside was a pair of tasers and a sheet with guidelines for using them. I took one and tested it to make sure it had a charge, then set it on the floor between the attendants' feet.

Norna frowned. "Are they supposed to believe it fell out of a locked compartment and shocked them on the way down?"

I nodded. "If they wake up and find no reason for having been knocked out, then they'll suspect a passenger drugged them or something. At least this way they have a seemingly rational explanation for it."

Norna's forehead wrinkled. "I guess you're right."

I stepped back and looked at the scene, then decided to put the other taser on the right side of the other attendant. It was a long shot but given the propensity for people to seek causality in an inexplicable situation, I had a feeling it'd work. They might also not say anything for fear they'd get in trouble for leaving the taser locker unsecured.

We went back to our seats. Norna leaned out of hers at an awkward angle so she could talk to me. "Who's trying to kill you?"

"That's a rather broad question." I sat with my feet in the aisle, so I didn't have to twist around the partition. "This is the third time I've killed this guy in the past three days—or his identical siblings." The strange scarring was the one thing I couldn't account for. Twins didn't share scars.

Norna blinked and shook her head. "This is the third attempt on your life in three days? My gods, how do you even sleep?"

"I sleep pretty well." I wasn't about to tell her that the tattoos on my body also acted as protection and advance warning wards. My extensive training with the Oblivion Guard had enhanced my senses, but my personal sigils provided an early alert system that saved my life on many occasions. "Thankfully, I wasn't asleep when he tried to kill me."

"How did he find you? Who else knew you were boarding a plane to Romania?"

"I don't know, but he's found me three different times." I bit the inside of my lip and wondered if someone put a tracking spell on me. "I'll be back." I went to the lavatory. It was positively enormous for an airplane, which was a good thing, because Norna followed me inside and closed the door.

"What are you doing?" she asked.

"Definitely not dropping a deuce now," I said.

She grimaced. "Sorry. I thought you were up to something else when you got that look on your face."

"I'm going to scan for trackers." I stripped off my shoes, jeans, and shirt, leaving on my underwear since I could scan through a single layer of cloth. Then I flicked my fingers through a pattern and ran my hands from head to toe down my body. The quick scan revealed nothing, but it didn't detect advanced trackers.

Norna winked suggestively. "Need help?"

It was tempting to join the mile-high club with an ogress, but my mind was elsewhere. I needed to figure out how this guy was finding me. There wasn't enough space for me to use my true sight scope and I didn't really want Norna to see me through it. My tattoos would light me up like a Christmas tree. I preferred to have Layla do it once we landed.

Warm lips touched my neck and worked up to my ear. "Watching you handle that assassin was kind of a turn-on." Norna's hand slid down to my crotch. "Let's have a little fun before going back to our seats."

I sucked in a breath as her hand went beneath my underwear. I turned around. "I want your natural skin tone."

She touched her necklace and her green hue returned. I lifted her shirt and freed her breasts. The nipples were a darker green than the skin around them. I pulled her head down for a kiss. The height difference was a little awkward, but when I slid her pants down I realized I'd have to get on my tiptoes to get my crotch high enough. Norna giggled when she saw me struggling and bent her knees slightly to give me more room. The lavatory was double the size of the one in coach, but it could barely handle two tall people at the same time.

"Are ogre males hung like horses?" I asked, a little concerned I might not have enough for her to notice if that were the case.

She snickered. "No, in fact, they have hilariously tiny dicks." Norna took mine in her large hand and stroked it. "This'll do nicely."

I kissed her again and drew in her scent. "Why do you smell like coconuts and rum?"

Instead of answering, she turned around and bent her knees. I thrust inside her and was pleased to find the proportions were just right.

After several minutes of contorting our bodies into unusual positions, and a whole lot of calisthenics, we gave each other congratulatory high-fives for our entrance into the mile-high club, and went back to our seats, flushed and tired.

Norna blew me a kiss as she settled back behind her partition and I realized she was still green. I touched the hollow of my throat and pointed at her. She activated the illusion charm and gave me a sheepish grin.

I was definitely looking forward to a round two in Romania with my She-Hulk, even if she was just doing it under orders from Bisbee.

With the chair fully reclined into bed position, I once again tried to sleep. This time I managed to remain unconscious for nearly seven hours. The sounds of first-class attendants moving about the cabin awoke me sometime later. Since they hadn't raised an alarm yet, I hoped it meant they'd accepted the staged taser scenario.

I breathed a sigh of relief when we landed a couple of hours later and the attendants bade us a cheerful farewell. I just hoped they didn't discover the assassin's body until well into their return flight.

Norna looped her arm in mine when we disembarked. Even though I was six foot two I felt like her shawty, and it was a bit disconcerting.

"Aww, isn't this sweet." Layla slapped our asses and caused us both to jump. "You lovebirds bonded on the flight?"

Norna released my arm. "I'm sorry. I should be more professional."

Layla chuckled. "What, are you kidding me? Even Cain deserves a good lay every now and then."

Norna looked back and forth between us. "I'm sorry. Do you two—"

"No," I said. "Layla doesn't like me that way."

Layla grinned lasciviously at the ogress. "But you, babe, are just my type."

A blush crept into Norna's cheeks. "Thank you. You're very sexy too."

"Oh, shit." Layla's eyes widened. "You swing both ways?"

I rolled my eyes. "Can we just get through customs without causing an international incident, please?"

Layla guffawed. "I'll do my best."

Norna smiled at Layla. "You're so full of life."

"I kill hard and live harder." Layla shrugged. "Enjoy what you have and never compromise."

"Don't ever take advice from Layla," I warned. "You'll wake up in a ditch somewhere with a sore asshole and no memory of how you got there."

"Sounds like you're speaking from experience." Layla elbowed me. "Did you ever find that purple dildo?"

Norna laughed. "I guess acting professional isn't all that important with you two." She took my hand and squeezed. "I'm going to like this trip."

I looked down at our hands and groaned. "This isn't middle school."

Norna shrugged. "Whatever that means."

I managed to free my hand when we reached customs. The border security accepted our fake passports without question, and we went to claim our baggage. I couldn't tell if Norna genuinely enjoyed our fling on the plane or if she was just an amazing actress. I leaned toward the former since she'd expressed willingness to seduce me when Bisbee asked her. But I didn't for a moment think I could turn her to our side and find out what was really going on.

I had a more pressing worry. The identical sibling assassin, or whatever he was, had found me three times. That meant whoever sent him could probably find me again no matter where I was. If I didn't figure out what was going on, I'd be dead before we even completed phase one of this mission.

CHAPTER 12

I picked up a four-wheel drive SUV from the car rental, and we headed northwest toward the mountains, during which time I told Layla about the close encounter during the flight. I pulled into the parking lot of a store that sold climbing gear, because, thanks to Bisbee's crappy map, there was no telling what we'd need when we reached the mountains.

Norna went in, and I pulled Layla aside. No one could see us around the corner of the building, so I summoned my staff, flipped up the scope, and handed it to her. "Look me over and see if you detect any tracking spells."

She backed up and scanned me up and down while I turned slowly in place. "No tracking spells," she said, "but I'd love to know what those tattoos do."

Most of my tattoos were drawn in ink that faded to near invisibility after a few days and only the scope or revealing mists and spells could reveal them. The few visible tattoos on my body weren't magical. I took back the staff and sheathed it. "We've got a real problem if another assassin shows up in the middle of reconnaissance."

"Way to avoid the subject." Layla pursed her lips. "Well, there's only one other way they could be tracking you everywhere."

I sucked in a breath between my teeth. "Blood." Tracking spells could use hair, bits of dead skin, or just about anything to locate someone. But the best results came from using fresh blood or living cells. I'd been in enough fights to lose some blood here and there, but certainly not enough to fuel so many tracking spells.

Since I didn't know for sure, I had to assume the person sending the assassins could find me anywhere. Which meant if they wanted to reach me now, they'd have to send someone to Romania. That gave me around twenty hours respite for another potential attack. Hopefully, they'd at least have the decency to wait until I returned home before trying to kill me again.

We went into the store and joined Norna in the backpacking section. Despite some complications with the language barrier, we purchased enough gear to scale Mount Everest and left the store within an hour. It took another hour and a half to reach the general area of the mountains hiding the castle. From there, we took a rugged dirt road into the forest and followed it until a fallen tree blocked our path.

I got out and surveyed the area with my scope, looking for wards or magical security. I wasn't surprised to find nothing since we were still about a mile out from the base of the cliffs and keeping a net of wards around the perimeter of the mountains would require a small army of mages to cover such a large space.

I used my brightblade to slice through the rotting tree trunk like butter, slashing it into manageable chunks that we moved out of the way. The road ended in a clearing with the remains of a firepit that hadn't seen recent use. We put on our backpacks, gathered ropes, cleats, and other climbing gear, and headed out.

Despite the cold, I shed my jacket by the time we reached the base of the mountain and shoved it in my backpack. The air was crisp and smelled of evergreens. Had we not been on an infiltration mission, I might have enjoyed a campout. But I hadn't brought graham crackers and marshmallows for s'mores, and we had too much to do to stop and smell the roses.

We located the first pass Bisbee had marked on his map, a crack in the cliff wall about a hundred yards wide. The base of the crack was at least two hundred feet up. I scanned it with my scope to make sure it wasn't boobytrapped. When I confirmed it was clear, I went to the rocky face and surveyed the best spot to start drilling anchors.

Scaling vertical surfaces without magic and surviving rough terrains had been a part of my training, so I was no stranger to rock climbing. I'd purchased a battery-powered drill and a manual hammer drill to be on the safe side. I set the guide on the powered drill to the required depth and made the first hole.

While Layla mounted the anchor bolt and hardware into that one, Norna boosted me up on her shoulders so I could start the next one.

Layla whistled. "You are one strong woman."

Norna shrugged and nearly toppled me from my perch. "Most ogresses are."

The power drill quickly bore another hole and I installed the anchor and rope. The first two anchors were the easy part. After that, I had to free climb up a little, hold on tight with one hand, then drill and hammer in the next anchor. I was exhausted by the time I hit the first hundred feet, so I sat in a loop of rope and gave myself a breather.

Layla and Norna had gathered all our equipment in the meantime. Now they sat below, talking and ignoring me entirely. I was certain Layla was propositioning the ogress, but it didn't bother me. The sex had been fun, but I had no illusions about why Norna was with us or that she'd eventually double-cross us when Bisbee gave the word. Without access to my staff, there was no way they could double cross us until we reached Oblivion. And even then, they'd be dumb to try anything until after we'd reached the armory.

I reached the bottom of the crack about an hour later, which wasn't bad considering rock climbing wasn't my forte. Ever since Hannah had freed me from the curse of Cthulhu, I'd trained hard, and it was finally paying off.

After bolting a final anchor inside the base of the crack, I climbed onto a boulder and scouted the passage with my scope. It didn't reveal any magical security, so I sheathed it. The pass ran all the way through to the other side of the mountain, albeit at a steep angle in places. Slanted cliffs rose on either side, rising hundreds of feet toward the sky.

I'd brought plenty of anchors, but I didn't know what the descent on the valley side would look like. From here, I had two options: I could hike the pass to the end and make sure a descent was feasible, or I could tell the others to start hauling up equipment and take our chances.

It'd take a good half hour or more to reach the end of the pass and I didn't want to waste daylight, so I went back to the cliff edge and dropped the equipment rope. Layla and Norna secured the netted equipment to the rope and I hauled it up using pulleys I'd bolted into place above the top anchor.

Once the equipment was secured, the women started climbing. Layla freeclimbed the rope, scurrying up it like a squirrel and reached the top in a matter of minutes. Norna was more cautious, testing the anchors as she climbed. I'd accounted for her dense muscle and used extra deep anchors in some places, so everything held just fine.

Layla peered up the pass. "Looks easy enough. Any security?"

"None that I saw." I opened the equipment net and took out my backpack. "There's a small cave about halfway up we can camp in if need be."

Layla checked the position of the sun. "It's not even noon yet. We have plenty of time."

Norna hefted the equipment net and slung it over her shoulder. "I'm ready."

We hiked up the pass and reached the end in under an hour. According to Bisbee's map, the castle sat just to the east. I perched on the rocks and looked around. The valley floor slanted inward like a crater toward a lake. It spanned miles across with mountains on all sides. The castle rose from the trees about a mile inside the sloping valley floor.

Zooming in with the scope, I was able to make out a road leading to a gate. The road itself vanished inside the mountain, suggesting a tunnel. The castle walls rose at least fifty feet and had been built to repel an army. I wondered what required such a secure structure when the mountains themselves were a fortress. Then again, human armies weren't the only enemies Vlad had faced over the centuries. Werewolves had once been mortal enemies of the vampires before the fae war united them in common cause.

Layla perched beside me. "Let me have a look."

I gave her the staff and let her have at it. While she did that, I surveyed the descent into the valley. I estimated three hundred feet to the ground, but anchoring from the top and descending would be much easier than drilling anchors up to the top.

"We'll need a closer look." Layla handed back the staff. "Too many trees in the way."

Norna looked up at the imposing cliffs to either side of us. "Doesn't look like it'd be easy to climb higher for a look."

"No need." Layla pointed to the forest. "Plenty of trees around, and it's daytime, so the vampires are stuck inside. I spotted two sentries that look like mages. It doesn't look like they're expecting company."

I nodded. "Let's get to it then. Leave the camping gear up here." I checked my utility belt to make sure it had what I needed and slipped on my backpack. Then I went to the cliff and got to work on the descent.

I drilled the top anchors, tripling them for safety, and dropped the eighty-meter rope over the side. It ended about thirty feet shy of the ground. I threaded the rope through my harness and rappelled two-thirds of the way down. From there, I drilled another anchor and attached a fifty-meter rope.

Once I moved to the other rope, Layla rappelled down. I reached the ground by the time she reached the other rope. Norna followed soon after. We paused for a snack break and then resumed hiking. I kept my staff out, scanning the area with the scope for heat signatures. The forest canopy was thick enough that vampires could roam beneath it at minimal risk, but I doubted they'd elect to take daytime guard duty when there were day-timers who could do it. I spotted birds, wolves, and a couple of bears. If large land animals were present, it hinted at a natural cave system that allowed them through, because their predecessors certainly hadn't flown inside.

The bears and wolves looked normal for the region which meant they hadn't found their way inside thousands of years ago and evolved differently than those on the outside. If a tunnel through the mountain existed, it was probably close to ground level. If things went to hell and we couldn't get back to our exfiltration point, we might be able to find the caves the animals used.

We skulked through the forest, keeping a constant lookout for bogeys, but the Combine either didn't have the manpower to put patrols in the forest, or they felt secure in their secret fortress. We found an outcropping of rock partway down the valley that offered a clear view of the castle and surroundings.

The castle perched at the edge of the lake and sprawled for hundreds of yards. The stony ground around the perimeter was clear of trees, meaning any approach could be seen by sentries in the towers or along the parapet. The walls were smooth and featureless. Vampires weren't huge fans of windows for obvious reasons.

A pair of men in a rowboat drifted on the lake, fishing poles extended out over the water. It seemed to be recreational and not out of necessity, because they weren't going to catch enough fish to feed the entire castle with just two poles.

I shifted my view to the castle towers and parapet. I spotted a total of five soldiers aimlessly wandering the rampart. They didn't have the auras of mages or vampires. The odd brass rifles they carried lead me to believe they were mechanists. I hadn't encountered their kind often, but they were an interesting folk. Their inventions were remarkable in that they looked vintage and advanced all at the same time.

My scope picked up faint energy signals emanating beneath the land around the base of the castle. I switched from thermal to astral mode on the scope, but neither could show me what lay beneath the surface. I didn't detect any wards, but the trees had been cleared for a hundred yards or more from the three sides of the castle facing the forest. It was most likely because the mechanists had planted land mines or other booby traps to protect the perimeter.

To pass through the mine field, I'd have to unearth one and study it to see if it were possible to disarm them. Then again, I might not be able to get close enough to dig without the device activating. And even if I could clear a path, I couldn't free climb the smooth castle wall, nor could I drill anchors without drawing a lot of attention.

Though there was a wide portcullis in the front of the castle, the road leading from it seemed to go only a short distance into the forest. A helicopter pad atop a wide tower seemed to be the primary method of entry and exit out of the castle and the enclosed valley.

"Guess we should've brought hang gliders," Layla said. "Because I don't see how we're getting inside."

I looked at Norna. "Did Bisbee have any idea this place is an impenetrable fortress?"

She shook her head. "We had no idea what the place looked like. Just that it exists."

"Shit." I stared at the castle and brainstormed for a way to breach the wall. During my time in the Oblivion Guard, we'd had special gloves and boots that allowed us to scale surfaces. There wasn't anything like that available on the civilian market. I knew a spell that made surfaces sticky, but probably not enough to bear my weight.

"Can you carve a hole in the castle wall with that fancy light sword of yours?" Layla said.

I shook my head. "There's a field of land mines between us and there, and a brightblade would take a long time to cut through stone that thick."

Movement on the lake caught my eye. The rowboat was on its way back to shore. How would they get back into the castle? I sheathed my staff and got up. "Let's get down to the shore. I want to see where that rowboat is going."

Layla grunted. "Let's hope there's a back door, because we're not getting inside unless we parachute from a plane."

"I'm really sorry." Norna slipped on her backpack. "Bisbee and Dwight had no idea it would be like this."

Layla scoffed. "Be glad they're not paying us for the job, or the price would've doubled."

"They're not paying because everyone has something to gain," Norna shot back. "It'll be like finding lost treasure."

"Better hope so." Layla narrowed her eyes. "If we find nothing at the end of this quest, I'm not going to be happy."

Norna stiffened. "Is that a threat?"

"Yep." Layla smirked. "Don't think being an ogress is any defense when I'm pissed."

Norna turned to me. "Is she always like this?"

I nodded. "If you keep her happy, she's a lot less likely to kill you."

Layla clapped my back. "Cain knows my deal."

I rolled my eyes and started hiking down into the valley. We circled wide of the castle, keeping to the forest. I scanned periodically for sentries, but there weren't any outside of the castle. We reached the lake in thirty minutes by which time the rowboat was already gone. That didn't surprise me. What did surprise me was that there was no dock, no back door, or any sign of the boat at all.

The lake waters lapped against the back wall of the castle. I examined the top of the wall, expecting to find a hoist of some kind that lifted the boat, but there wasn't anything, not a chain, not a rope.

I gritted my teeth and clenched my fists. There was no way in. The mission was over.

CHAPTER 13

"Where did the boat go?" Norna said.

"Now that's a neat trick." Layla peered through a pair of binoculars. "Do you think there might be an illusion hiding an entrance?"

"My scope is telling me it's a stone wall. No illusions." I zoomed in on the wall. A gray sigil pad blended in so perfectly with the stone, I nearly missed it. "There's a secret door."

"Thank the gods." Layla rubbed her hands together. "Can we get to it?"

"We'll have to swim." I lowered the staff. "Guess it's time to get wet."

"I didn't bring a bikini," Layla said.

Norna frowned. "That water is probably ice cold."

"Aw, poor baby." Layla rubbed her back. "You can wait outside and let the professionals do the rest."

I put a finger to my lips. "Voices drift across water, so keep it quiet." There weren't any sentries watching this side of the castle and the lake shore was still forested. We could probably make the long swim to the sigil pad, but it was five feet above the waterline which meant reaching it from the water would be problematic.

Layla watched me with raised eyebrows and spoke in a low voice. "What's the problem?"

"We need something to float on so I can reach the pad." I pointed to a fallen tree at the water's edge. "That might work."

As we made our way down, I regretted not buying an inflatable dinghy. It wouldn't have taken much space and would've been perfect for the job. But an aquatic infiltration hadn't even crossed my mind. Then again, I hadn't known the castle touched the lake on this side. Dwight's shitty map and a lack of information resulted in poor planning.

I scanned for sentries on the wall and wards on the surrounding area when we reached the shore and found none. I used my brightblade to lop the fallen tree into three four-foot lengths. The wood was slightly rotten, but dry, and the tree wasn't very thick, so we were able to move the pieces without much trouble. I located a fallen sapling and cut it into pieces. Using some climbing rope, I laced the pieces into a rough raft with the sapling as the crossbars to hold the thing together.

It was barely seaworthy, but it'd last long enough to use as a platform while I cracked the sigil pad.

"Never thought I'd build a raft," Norna said as she tightened the rope on the opposite end and tied it off.

"Wouldn't be the first time I've had to improvise." Layla kicked the raft to test its sturdiness. "Then again, I don't remember the last time I had to infiltrate a castle."

Castles were commonplace in Feary. Dwarves carved entire mountainsides into castles. Elves grew fortresses from living wood and combined it with stone. Goblins, trolls, and ogres built underground fortresses in massive caverns, but were also known to build them aboveground. The castles of the high fae numbered in the hundreds. The winter fae preferred ice and the summer fae used thorny vines woven together so tightly, they looked like solid wood.

This wasn't my first castle infiltration and it probably wouldn't be my last, but it was the first I remembered infiltrating with the aid of an improvised raft.

After pushing the raft to the edge of the water, I undid my utility belt and set it on top. Then I stripped naked and waded in. It was cold enough to steal the breath of most people, but training in the frigid lands of the winter fae had more than prepared me for this.

Layla wore an amused smirk on her face, but somehow refrained from poking fun at me. Norna began to remove her pants, but I shook my head and held up a hand. I could do this on my own. Layla waggled her eyebrows at Norna and motioned for her to keep disrobing.

"Keep an eye on the parapet," I whispered. "Make a bird whistle or something if you see anything."

Layla gave me a thumbs-up.

Norna pushed the raft further into the water until it began to float. Kicking my feet underwater so as not to splash, I pulled the raft after me, then positioned myself behind it and pushed. It took about five minutes to reach the sigil pad. The raft wobbled and threatened to tip when I put weight on it, but I managed to slide on top of it without too much trouble.

I took the revealer mist from my utility belt and sprayed it over the pad. A scribble of lines appeared where oil from fingers left a trail. If I'd witnessed the boaters using the pad, I could have easily figured out which sigils unlocked the slate. Deciphering the sigils from the oil trails would normally be a challenge, but in this case, the lock relied on a combination of only three.

The low level of security wasn't too surprising. The occupants relied heavily on the secrecy of the location. Failing that, they had mountains, land mines, and the tall castle wall to keep them safe.

The odds were good that the order of tracing the sigils on the pad didn't matter, but I cast a camouflage illusion over the top of the raft just in case I set off an alarm. I also didn't know how the door would open. It might make a lot of noise, or it could be quiet as a whisper. I inspected the stone and found a fine crack outlining the size and shape of the door. It was a little larger than the rowboat.

I looked at Layla and gave her a thumbs-up. She returned the gesture. Hoping there was no one waiting on the other side of the door, I began to trace the sigils. I'd just finished the first and started the second when the wall rumbled. A crack formed in the middle and began to widen as thirty-foot tall sections of the wall began to slide apart.

My butt clenched when I realized I was about to be exposed in more ways than one to whoever waited on the other side of the wall. Since I couldn't get off the raft and kick like a madman toward shore, I braced my hands against the moving wall and let it drag me and the raft to the left.

By the time the wall stopped sliding open, I was still well away from shore. The opening in the back of the castle spanned over a hundred feet wide and at least half as high. I slid into the water with the raft between me and the opening, then began kicking my feet underwater to pull the raft to shore.

Something big, bronze, and round emerged from the door. It took a moment for me to register that it was a submarine. It wasn't a small submersible or a single-occupant vessel, but a full-fledged submarine a good three hundred feet long. A large brass sphere mounted between two axes near the nose of the sub rotated slowly.

Why in the hell do the Combine have a submarine in a landlocked lake? I wondered.

A periscope rose from the top part of the submarine when it cleared the door. I kept my head low behind the raft, but the scope didn't rotate my way. The submarine continued out to the middle of the lake, turning to the right even as it sank from view. The doors began to slide shut and I was presented with a decision—did I wait until it closed, or did I try for peek inside?

Deciding on the latter, I clambered back onto the raft and pressed my hand against the door, letting it drag me back out toward the middle. Using the rough stone for purchase, I pulled the raft along the door, reaching the edge when it still had a few dozen feet left before closing. I peered around the corner and found a cavern large enough to house two submarines and several boats. I knew that because I saw another anchored submarine and a dock with not just the rowboat, but several motorized boats as well.

I counted fourteen people in and around the area, most of them loading crates onto motorized brass carts with bench seats in the front and cargo beds in the back. I could have made it through the door if I dived from the raft and swam inside, but I preferred utilizing the smaller rowboat door because I didn't want to leave all my equipment behind.

Hand-over-hand against the stone, I dragged the raft back to the sigil pad and waited until the hangar doors rumbled shut with a low boom that sent ripples across the lake. I took a moment to collect myself and to make sure the vanished submarine didn't make a sudden return, then I tried the sigils on the slate. With a barely audible click, a section of the hangar door swung inward, granting access.

Kneeling on the raft, I summoned my staff and looked inside with the scope. There were no wards to be found, but the infrared detected three more people I hadn't seen a moment ago. Even with all the activity on the docks to the right, there was plenty of room to sneak inside on the left and hide behind the stacked crates and equipment on the dock.

I tapped a finger on the sigil pad and the door shut. Then I swam back to the others. Despite years of conditioning my body to extreme temperatures, my limbs felt like lumps of ice by the time I reached shore. I let Norna drag the raft onto land while I used a heat spell to warm my frigid flesh.

We took cover in the forest on the off chance a guard happened to the ramparts on this side of the castle and spoke in hushed voices.

"Gods almighty, Cain." Layla pointed toward the middle of the lake. "What the hell are they doing with submarines?"

I turned to Norna. "Well?"

She shrugged. "I have no idea. I can't imagine what they're doing with them."

I blew out a breath. "Doesn't really matter, I guess."

Layla wore an amused grin. "This place is full-on James Bond territory, isn't it?"

I snorted. "If Horatio has a white cat and a shark tank, I'm done."

Norna frowned. "James Bond? Shark tank?"

"Guess you're not big into nub entertainment?" I said.

She scoffed. "I tried watching television, but the only thing I remotely enjoy are the soap operas."

Layla stared at my exposed crotch. "Ever think of manscaping, Cain? You're getting a little bushy."

I ignored her. "Here's the plan. Our backpacks are waterproof, so put anything you don't want getting wet inside. We're going to push the raft back out, open the boat door, and get inside."

"Are we bringing the raft inside with us?" Layla asked.

I nodded. "There's an area we can hide it. We'll probably need it to get back out again, because I don't want to steal a boat unless we're being chased."

"If we're being chased by vampires, it's game over." Layla smirked. "So, let's keep it clean, shall we?"

"On that note." I turned to Norna. "You'd better stay hidden with the raft. Layla and I will have an easier time infiltrating if it's just the two of us, and we don't have a way to easily disguise your height." An illusion would only do so much, and most experienced mages would notice the tell-tale signs.

Norna frowned but nodded. "How will we communicate?"

I patted my backpack. "I've got earbuds. I'll hand them out when we're inside."

We went back to the raft. I scanned the parapet to ensure it was still clear while the ladies stripped. We secured everything in the backpacks, put them on the raft, and cast out into the lake. With the three of us pushing the raft, it didn't take long to reach the door. When we positioned the raft beneath the sigil pad, I got on top while Layla and Norna held the raft steady.

Layla stared at my junk and shook her head. "Severe shrinkage," she whispered.

I couldn't believe she thought this was an appropriate time to joke. When the door clicked open, I slipped back into the water, glanced inside, and motioned the others to come when the coast was clear.

The right side of the docks hummed with activity. Men and women in gray unitards loaded clockwork carts with cargo. The drivers wore orange hardhats for no apparent reason. The fashion sense of these people reminded me of something from a sixties Bond flick. The grays, or as the mechanists called them, scrubs, were the lowest of the low in the order.

A pair of mechanist constables in black military-style uniforms watched the grunts work, occasionally slapping them with a whipping crop or cuffing them on the head when they thought they were moving too slowly. Those in gray never talked back or looked them in the eye.

When the constables patrolled down to the opposite end of the hangar, we slipped around the docks on the far left and used a mooring post to secure the raft. Using stacks of wooden crates for cover, we pulled ourselves onto the floating dock. I used heating spells to help us dry off quickly, then we slipped back into our clothing. I took out the earbuds and dispersed them to the others. When worn properly, they were barely visible.

Layla fitted hers into place, tapped it, and whispered, "Testing, testing."

Her voice echoed in my ear. "It's working," I said.

Norna nodded. "I hear you."

I rose into a crouch and peered around the crates. "Most people are wearing the same gray uniforms. If we can steal a pair, we'll probably have an easier time."

"An illusion disguise wouldn't work?" Layla said.

"As a temporary fix, maybe." I pointed to the far end of the dock. "Let's go. We'll figure it out when we get there."

Norna gripped my hand. "Be careful, Cain."

I nodded. "Stay put and let us know if anything changes, okay?"

"I will." She bit her bottom lip and watched us go, apprehension clear in her eyes.

Layla and I stepped off the floating dock and onto the solid pier, staying behind crates and equipment for cover. We worked our way toward the single exit. There were too many carts coming and going for us to time it right and slip out, so I traced an illusion sigil on mine and Layla's clothing. With an image of the gray uniform firmly fixed in my mind's eye, I activated the sigils and our clothes flickered to match.

We waited for a lull in traffic and then walked toward the doorway. The cart drivers paid us little heed, but one of the guys loading crates did a double take. I hurried out of the hangar and into the stone tunnel before he could put us to work. An opening in the tunnel wall led to a staircase. I had no idea where it went, but the last thing we needed was someone from the loading dock chasing us down because they thought we were shirking our duties.

The stairs ended in a corridor lined with wooden doors. I tested the handle on the nearest door. It clicked open into a small room with a bed and desk. Gray uniforms hung in a closet in the back. They were about a foot too short for me, but fit Layla fine. She slipped into one and I dispelled the disguise illusion.

I checked the next few rooms and found similar layouts inside.

Layla frowned. "Where is everyone?"

"Working the docks, I guess." I finally found a uniform long enough to suit me and put them on. With us properly disguised, I felt more confident roaming the castle. The cell signal to my phone was almost non-existent, but I'd marked the last location of the amulet in my maps app. The castle wasn't on the map, but using what little I knew of the fortress, I was able to guesstimate which direction we needed to go.

Layla stopped where another corridor crossed ours. "Horatio's quarters won't be down here." She pointed up. "He's probably got a penthouse."

"Yeah, I just don't know how to get up there." So far, the only stairs I'd found were going down not up. "I can't make heads or tails of the layout of this place."

Layla sucked in a breath. I turned around and came face-to-face with a pale-faced man. His lips parted into a half-smile, revealing sharp, yellowed fangs.

CHAPTER 14

The vampire sniffed Layla's neck. "This one's blood is hotter than the others." He spoke with a heavy Romanian accent.

Layla stiffened, but did nothing. Like me, she was evaluating the situation. Surprisingly, she went for tact first. "How may I be of service?"

The vampire sighed. "Oh, so many ways." He sniffed her neck again and groaned. "Being so near warm bloods without a taste is torturous." He turned and motioned us to follow. "There is a small matter that needs attending."

I exchanged a look with Layla, shrugged, and followed the vampire. He led us through the corridors until we reached a winding staircase leading up. We emerged in a dim room filled with row upon row of coffins, all of them closed. It didn't take me long to pinpoint the small matter he wanted us to attend to.

A shaft of sunlight shined through a crack in the far wall, catching a row of coffins directly in the crosshairs.

"The patch has failed again." The vampire hissed a breath between his teeth. "We need it permanently repaired before someone is mortally injured."

That single shaft of daylight would carve a burning hole in a vampire if it touched them for just a few seconds. There were no windows, but there was a door in the wall with the broken mortar. It seemed strange that the vampires would sleep in a chamber that could be exposed to daylight by simply opening a door.

The vampire saw my puzzlement but misinterpreted it. "Your master's experiments caused the crack, so it's your responsibility. Our lives have been extremely inconvenient for us since he displaced us from our cave."

I nodded. "Our apologies. We will fix it."

He pursed his lips and nodded as if expecting our deference. "The patching mortar is still in the storage closet."

I followed his gaze to a hallway and assumed the closet must be down there. I could tell Layla wanted to remark on the situation, but vampires had excellent hearing, so I gave her a slight shake of my head. I opened the door to the closet and found a sealed bucket of premixed mortar and a trowel inside.

We went back to the vampire in the sleeping chamber and I pointed to the door. "Is that the way out?"

He nodded. "Make it quick. The coffins keep us shielded from the light, but there is no need to risk it."

I opened the door a crack and Layla and I slipped outside and closed the door. We stood on a wide balcony about halfway up the eastern side of the castle. I counted several more balconies along the eastern wall, which seemed strange given the absence of windows. Then again, this castle could have been built before Vlad's bloodsucking days. The windows might have been sealed later, but the doors and balconies left so vampires could enjoy the night air.

The crack ended a few feet below the balcony but continued diagonally up the wall for another fifty feet. There was no sign of impact on the outside, meaning whatever caused it had happened on the inside of the wall. Mortar between the stones in this section of the wall had broken loose, leaving a gap wide enough to admit sunlight.

Layla traced the crack with a finger and spoke in a low voice. "If I was a betting woman, which I am, I'd bet that Horatio's lab is somewhere on the other end of the crack."

I nodded. "Agreed." Using the trowel, I pressed mortar into the opening, packing it into the full width. Whoever patched it the first time only slapped on an inch of the stuff.

When it was done, I took a moment to calculate which way we needed to go to reach the other end of the crack then went back inside. I packed more mortar into the gap from this side, Even though it was patched from the outside, I wanted to put on a good show for the vampire. Once done, I stood back and inspected the work. It wasn't neat, but it would hold.

"Excellent." The vampire clasped his hands together. "I pray you did a better job than the last worker."

"Part of the problem is that the crack further up the wall needs repairing from the inside," I said. "If you show me how to get there, I can patch it too and prevent more gaps from opening."

"I don't meet many warmbloods with such initiative." The vampire smiled and pointed back down the way we'd come. "Follow the spiral staircase up and take a left." His lips peeled back with distaste. "Your master's workroom is there and he is most rude to unexpected guests. Tell him Andrei requested the work and he may actually let you inside."

"Thank you." I offered a curt bow the vampire. I didn't know how old he was, but most of them adhered to formalities and appreciated it when others did the same.

Andrei's smile widened. "It's refreshing to meet a warmblood with good manners." He left us and walked to the far end of the room where a large coffin rested on a stone pedestal higher than the others. He opened it and climbed inside.

"Must be a bigwig," Layla whispered.

I didn't see any coffins larger or fancier than Andrei's which meant Dracula's sleeping chamber was elsewhere, probably in a master bedroom. It was doubtful the master of vampires was even here which was a good thing. I'd seen him in person once while negotiating with the fae, and he was no one to be trifled with.

Layla and I left the room and went down the corridor to the spiral staircase. Voices echoed from above. We crept up to the next level and peered into the corridor. The doors in the hallway were spaced further apart than below, and most of them hung open due to the nearly constant flow of people walking back and forth between the rooms.

The people on this level eschewed gray uniforms for ivory and teal Victorian-era lab coats. They looked long enough to be considered robes, with tapered hems reaching all the way to the knees. I counted nearly fifteen brass buttons fastening the left side of the coat when a simple zipper would have sufficed. Mechanists were never one to do things the easy way.

Some stood in groups, talking in low voices while they stared at complex blueprints on an easel. Others pushed carts of equipment through the hallway or jotted notes on paper.

Those in ivory were inventors, the leaders and top caste of mechanists. Those in teal, the engineers, could supposedly rise in rank to inventor if they made a marvelous discovery. Given the limited number of mechanists, I imagined upward mobility was severely limited.

I backed down the staircase until the curve hid us from the doorway. "I don't know if we'll fit in as scrubs. We might need a uniform upgrade."

Layla grunted. "Even if we did, how are we supposed to get into Horatio's lab?"

I didn't have an answer. "We'll have to try our luck." I held up the mortar bucket. "Maybe they'll ignore us if they think we're supposed to be here."

"Maybe." Layla frowned. "We can't spend too much time dallying around. In a few hours it'll be nighttime and then we'll have vampires to deal with too."

I checked the time. "At this time of year, it'll be dark in two hours. We're already inside, so we've got to make the best of it."

"Agreed." Layla pressed her lips into a thin line. "When in doubt, act like you know what you're doing. Most of the time people will ignore you."

"It's worked before." I straightened my shoulders and put on a bored look, then headed upstairs. I stepped into the corridor without pause and turned left.

The dull roar of conversation died immediately as people stopped to stare at us in confusion. A man wearing spectacles handed his notepad to the woman next to him and marched up to us. "What in the devil are you doing up here? Scrubs are to remain on the lower levels at all times, no exceptions!"

So much for acting confident, I thought.

I gulped as if nervous. "Andrei asked us to fix the crack, sir." I looked down. "It was letting in daylight and he wanted us to fix it up here too. We wouldn't have come, but he insisted."

"Bloody hell." The man threw up his hands. "All the vampires do is complain. I don't know why they don't just go somewhere else."

The woman he'd handed the notepad approached. "What's wrong, Theo?" She spoke with what sounded like a German accent while her companion sounded British.

"Andrei again." Theo bared his teeth. "He sent these grunts to fix the crack."

The woman frowned. "I don't understand. We fixed it last week."

"It broke open again and let in sunlight," Layla said in a surprisingly deferential tone. "We were afraid to refuse him."

Theo shook his head. "Horatio will throw a fit if we let them in his lab."

"He's down in the test chamber." The woman looked at us. "How long will it take you?"

"Maybe fifteen minutes," I said. "Look, if you want to tell Andrei we can't do it, that's fine. We've got a lot of work to do."

Theo rolled his eyes. "Debra, just take them in there and let them get it done. I'll deal with Horatio if there's a problem later, but if it keeps the vampires out of our hair, I'll be happy."

Debra nodded and motioned us to follow her. "This way." She looked at the bucket. "Whatever you do, don't get that on the floor or Horatio will be furious."

"Okay." I kept my head down and followed her though I never stopped scanning our environs.

Debra traced her fingers on a sigil pad outside a closed door, not even bothering to hide the combination. I memorized it in case. She motioned us in and pointed to the crack. "You've got fifteen minutes. Clean up any mess or you'll be on blood duty, okay?"

She sounded menacing with her German accent, so I acted scared and nodded without making eye contact. "We'll get it done fast."

Debra left and closed the door.

The lab was longer than it was wide. Tables lined the wall and the middle of the room. Brass gears, chains, and actuators were lined up neatly on the center table, almost like an assembly line. A partially completed sphere like the one I'd seen on the submarine sat at the end of the table. Glass vials filled with amber liquid fit in slots on the inside. Framed blueprints hung on the walls, some of them spanning several feet in length.

"What the hell is that thing?" Layla walked around the sphere.

"I don't know, but this," I tapped a finger on the glass vials, "is liquid mana converted from pixie dust. It turns that color when they extract the dust from blood."

Layla grimaced. It's a power source?"

I nodded. "But that doesn't matter right now." I made a beeline for the only desk in the room and started going through the folders and drawers. "Look for the map."

"What makes you think he keeps it in his desk?" Layla said. "If it's valuable, it's probably in a vault."

"Maybe, maybe not." I rifled through the rest of the folders, most containing rough diagrams and fantastical designs. Horatio, it seemed, wasn't a run of the mill mechanist, but an actual inventor. I wasn't terribly familiar with mechanist hierarchy, but from what little I knew, inventors were at the top.

Mechanist inventors had been high-value targets during the Human-Fae War because they conceived traps and devices that were effective at killing the fae and their allies.

I stepped back from the desk and examined the room from the perspective of an inventor. Horatio was a proud man who wanted all to witness his genius as evidenced by all the blueprints hanging from the walls. But he was also a careful man, for none of the blueprints had measurements or specifications. Someone could steal one of these blueprints but without that critical information, couldn't reproduce the device.

These blueprints represented finished inventions, but the secrets to their construction were hidden away, probably in a wall safe as Layla suggested. I knew without a doubt that a mechanist safe would be no easy feat to crack.

The diagram of a clockwork submarine hung prominently in the middle of the longest wall. I lifted the bottom edge of the blueprint and looked underneath. There was nothing there. A smaller square diagram of a spherical device hung next to it. I looked beneath and found a sigil pad next to a blank metal door.

Admittedly, I was surprised to find a sigil pad guarding a safe door. Then again, this castle didn't belong to the mechanists. This safe might have already existed before they arrived, or perhaps Dracula had his people install it. Either way, I felt like I'd caught a small break, especially since we didn't have much time.

We'd already been inside five minutes. I blew out a breath and mentally prepared myself for the challenge. "Layla, start patching the wall while I work on this."

Amazingly, she didn't argue about it. I removed the blueprint and set it aside, then sprayed revealer mist on the sigil pad. The lines left from Horatio's finger oil were so neat as to be drawn with a ruler. I also didn't recognize any of them as sigils.

That, in and of itself, wasn't terribly unusual. The patterns used to open sigil pads could be just about anything, from initials to bad drawings of cats. Most mages used sigils because they were too complicated for anyone without training to reproduce.

But Horatio wasn't a mage.

I backed up and looked around. My eyes settled on a small blueprint hanging on the side wall. I jogged over, grabbed the blueprint, and brought it with me to the sigil pad. Holding it up for comparison, I noticed a portion of the blueprint matched some of the lines on the sigil pad. I now had one part of the combination.

But there were too many crisscrossing lines to figure out how many patterns there were on the pad. I studied them and finally found a section that wasn't part of the first pattern—a spiraling line in the middle of the pad. I scanned other small blueprints in the room. My mind was well trained in patterns, but even so, I didn't spot the blueprint with a spiraling line among the many hanging from the walls.

I had five minutes until Debra returned. Layla had filled most of the crack and was smoothing out the joints. A blueprint on the wall behind her caught my eye. At first, I didn't know what made me stare at it, but then I honed in on the spiral pattern in the lower right corner of the diagram.

There wasn't much time, so I dashed over, grabbed the blueprint, and brought it with me. I couldn't differentiate any other patterns on the sigil pad. It was the moment of truth. I flexed my fingers to limber them up. The only problem now was figuring out which pattern to draw first. Sometimes order didn't matter as with the sigil pad on the hangar bay door, but I had a feeling someone as organized as Horatio would value order.

I looked over the blueprints and found the dates. The first one had been finished six months before the second. I went with a gut feeling and traced the patterns in the order of completion, praying he hadn't been tricky and reversed them. In quick, precise movements, I finished the patterns.

The metal door clicked open.

It was no surprise to find dozens of rolled up blueprints stacked inside. I took them all out and hastily examined them. All but one was labeled at the edge. I untied the string around the unlabeled one and unfurled it.

I was surprised to find that it wasn't a blueprint, but a high-resolution aerial picture of a volcano. The surrounding land was black, probably from volcanic ash during an eruption. Further down the image, the black turned to yellow sand, pockmarked with craters. White dots and lines in the sand, possibly the remains of buildings, spanned most of the land all the way to the ocean.

There were three dots marked on the map around the dead volcano, each one annotated with a series of numbers. A fourth dot was on what looked like a giant dome. The image had been taken from at least a thousand feet up, so making out details was difficult even with the high resolution.

Besides the dots and numbers, there was only one label on the image, and it was directly over the volcano: *Olympus Prime*.

I snapped several pictures, then rolled it up and put it back. What Horatio had was no ordinary map. It was an actual photo of the original Olympus on Oblivion.

And I had no idea how he'd gotten it.

CHAPTER 15

Hoping I had a few minutes to spare, I unrolled other blueprints from the vault and photographed them quickly, not taking the time to look them over. Then I put everything back in the vault the way I'd found it, shut it, and raced around the room hanging the blueprints back in place.

Norna's voice crackled in my ear. "Status update?"

I tapped the earbud. "Got pictures of the map. About to leave."

The door clicked open a moment later and Debra walked in. She looked at the patched wall and scowled. "Gods, you don't do this often, do you?"

Layla looked down. "Sorry, I did my best."

Debra grunted. "It's passable, but if Horatio complains, I'm sending him to find you."

"Please don't." Layla clasped her hands pleadingly. "I'll get it perfect if you give me more time."

"You're out of time." Debra thrust a finger into the hallway. "Get back to the docks before Horatio finds you up here."

Layla was just killing it with the acting, even though I knew she probably wanted to kill Debra. She deserved a gold star for her fridge, for once.

I suspected Debra planned to take credit for the patchwork herself since having worker bees in the lab area was a big no-no.

"What caused the crack in the first place?" I asked.

Debra frowned. "Are you new?"

"Yes." I wished I hadn't asked in the first place.

"A vampire activated the echo-sonic mapper while it was in the lab." She blew out a breath. "They're the ones who caused the crack, but of course they think we should be the ones to fix it." Debra shooed us away with her hand. "Go, now."

Layla and I headed to the staircase and headed down it. We were just passing by the vampire sleeping chamber when a group of constables raced past us in the hallway, faces tight with urgency. An overweight inventor huffed and puffed past us a moment later, barely even glancing our way. I recognized him from the picture Bisbee had shown me.

It was Horatio.

That was when I knew something was wrong. "I think we need to hurry. I think opening the vault set off an alarm."

"Shit." Layla picked up the pace. "Debra's going to rat us out."

My earbud crackled and Norna spoke. "Where are you?"

"On the way back," I said. "Be ready to go because there might be trouble."

"I can confirm trouble," Norna said. "Someone started shouting orders at the dock workers and now they're splitting up into what I think are search parties."

"Fuck." I stopped in the middle of the hallway. We were almost to the lower living quarters where the grays lived, which meant we were bound to run right into one of the search parties. "We need to find another way out."

Layla opened the nearest door and went inside a small unfurnished room. She unlatched the lock on the metal shutter and looked out the window. "Unless we sprout wings, we're not getting out this way."

I joined her at the window. It was a good fifty-foot drop to the rocky ground below. "What about the side with the lake?"

She bit her lower lip and nodded. "Might be our only chance."

We went back to the hallway, shutting the room behind us, and ran back the way we'd come, this time bypassing the spiral staircase and other intersecting corridors. We took a left at the end and entered the next room. Our hopes vanished the moment we went inside.

"Where's the fucking window?" Layla pounded a section of wall where the window had been walled over. "Can your staff cut through this?"

"Not quickly," I said. "The stone is so thick it would take thirty minutes to an hour. Besides, after cutting through it, the surface would be scalding hot, so we'd have to wait for it to cool." I went back into the hallway and looked for other options. The clop of boots and murmuring voices echoed down the hallways. The search groups had reached this floor and would be on us in seconds.

I opened door after door looking for a way out but finding only empty rooms and stone where the windows had been. I didn't know why they'd kept some windows but filled in the others. The castle had probably once been a light, airy place with sunlight reflecting off the lake and mountain breezes blowing through the corridors, but at some point, the vampires had turned it into a nearly airtight coffin.

The last room in the corner of the hallway was a bathroom with modern fixtures and plumbing. Like the other rooms, the window had been patched.

"All these rooms and just one bathroom." Layla scoffed. "I'll bet there's a long wait when they have guests."

"Most castles at the time only had a handful of bathrooms," I said. "They didn't have plumbing, so the shit literally dumped straight into the moat."

"Wonderful." She blew out a breath and cocked her head as the echoes of the search party grew louder. "We're going to die in a fucking bathroom, Cain, and it's all your fault."

"We're not dead yet." I poked my head out and saw a group of grays opening doors at the far end of the hallway. I dashed down to the next intersection and found another group methodically searching room after room. Same with the next two adjacent corridors. I went back to the bathroom. "We're cornered, but we've got options."

"Options?" Layla laughed. "Like what?"

"So far, no one I've seen has had a phone or other electronic form of communicator on them." I kept an eye on the encroaching grays. "When I opened the safe, it triggered a ward that alerted Horatio. Without a means of communicating with anyone near his office, he sent someone to organize the grays to search the floors from bottom to top, flushing out the thief."

Layla frowned. "Yeah, but he ran right past us without a second glance."

"Because he probably doesn't realize whoever opened his safe is in disguise." I peered back out at the grays. They were halfway to us. "We need to make them think we sneaked off for sex so when they burst in here, they'll ask us to join them in the search."

Layla nodded. "I think you're right. But don't think for a minute you're penetrating me just to make it look more realistic."

I feigned sadness. "Damn, you figured me out."

"Tits out." Layla slid out of her robe and began lifting the black tank top. "Cain, drop your pants and get hard. You've got to sell this."

"All this excitement already got me hard," I lied.

Someone with a commanding voice shouted from down the hallway. They were far enough away that it was hard to make out the words, so I leaned out the door for a better listen.

"Intruders are in disguise as grays," a man shouted. "A tall male with dark hair, and a chubby female with her hair tied in a top bun."

"Chubby?" Layla lunged for the doorway, bare breasts bouncing. "I'll fucking kill that asshole!"

She looked pissed enough to charge the entire squad of grays. I grabbed her and dragged her into the room.

"The sex ruse won't work." I picked up her tank top from the floor and tossed it to her. "Get dressed. We'll make our stand here."

"Fuck that." She yanked on her top like she wanted to kill it. "I'll bet Debra's the one who said I'm chubby. I'm going to ram a dagger up her ass, twist it, and make her shit blood for a week."

Just thinking about it made me wince, but it also drew my eye back to the toilet. Bathrooms in castles were located at exterior walls for a reason. A wooden shelf bearing towels and toilet paper had been built on top of a stone slab. I tugged at the shelf, but it had been secured to the stone. I summoned my staff and slashed the wood to pieces. When I swept them aside, they revealed a hole.

"Is that the old shitter?" Layla said.

I nodded and looked through the hole. There was nothing below it except a fifty-foot drop straight into the lake. But there was one problem. It had been sized for an ass to sit on, not for a person to fit through. The stone, however, was only a few inches thick, probably to ensure it didn't get caked with feces hitting the sides.

The orb on the hilt of my staff powered the brightblade. I patterned a sigil with my hand and pressed a finger to the orb, sending my own power into it. The blade glowed even brighter. I pressed the blade to the stone and hoped it was thin enough. Slowly but surely, it sliced into the hard granite.

"Can you go any faster?" Layla cracked open the door and peeked into the hallway. "They're only a few doors down."

"Going as fast as I can," I muttered through clenched teeth. It was taking everything I had to keep the power level steady in the blade. If the stone had been another inch thick, I probably couldn't have done it.

"Almost here," Layla hissed.

"Hey, do you smell burning?" someone in the hallway said.

A woman coughed. "It's coming from the bathroom."

Layla shut the door and latched it. "Time's up, Cain."

Like most castle doors this one was made of thick wood and the latch was heavy steel. It might buy us some time.

"Who's in there?" a woman shouted. "Open the door right now!"

"I'm taking a shit," Layla said. "Can't a person get some privacy around here?"

"Open up and prove it," man said. "There are intruders in the castle."

"Yeah, well this shit was intruding into my underwear." Layla repressed a laugh. "So give me a minute."

"Break it down," a grim voice said.

"With our bare hands?" the woman said.

"I'll get exo-armor," a man said.

"Hurry it up," the grim man replied.

So far, I'd only carved a single line into the stone, but it looked long enough. By the time I cut a line across the bench, I heard the rattle and stomp of heavy machinery in the hallway.

"Out of the way," the grim voice said.

More voices shouted from somewhere beyond.

"Did you find them?" and older male voice said.

"Think so, sir," the grim man replied. "They've barricaded themselves into the bathroom, but the exo should make short work of it."

"Who do you work for?" the other man shouted.

Layla raised an eyebrow. "Horatio, is that you?"

"Yes. Who are you, and who do you work for?"

Layla glanced back at me. I wiped the sweat from my eyes and mouthed the word, *Cthulhu*.

Her eyes brightened. "Cthulhu sent us."

"Dear gods," Horatio said. "How did he find out?"

Layla and I stared at each other in confusion. That wasn't the question I'd expected to hear.

Smiling mischievously, Layla said, "How do *you* think he found out, Horatio?"

I had only a few inches to go, but it was going to be close.

"It must be the echo-sonic, sir," a woman who sounded like Debra replied.

"I guess the secret is out," Horatio said in a menacing voice. "Your master can't stop us, and you won't leave here alive." He paused. "You in the exo, destroy this door and take them prisoner."

"Yes, sir!" an eager man said.

Gears whined and something struck the door with incredible force. The wood buckled and splintered.

"Fuck me sideways." Layla stood to the side of the door, blades drawn and glared at me. "Hurry up!"

Straining, I pushed the glowing blade through the last inch of stone. A wide section dropped free and plunged into the lake below.

I turned on the faucet in the sink next to the bench and splashed water over the hot stone. It steamed and sizzled.

Metal clicked and clanked, and another blow shook the door, leaving a hole through the middle that offered a view of the attacker. A man was strapped into an bronze exoskeleton that resembled a terminator. Clockwork gears spun. Actuators clicked as the man drew back the huge metal arm for another strike.

Layla didn't give him the chance. She sidestepped in front of the door and flung a dagger. It buried itself in the man's chest and pinged as it hit the metal behind him. He screamed and went limp. Gyros whirred, keeping the exo upright despite the dead load in the pilot's seat.

I splashed more water on the stone. It still steamed, but we were out of time.

"Open the door!" Horatio shrieked.

Someone dared reach an arm through the hole and fumbled with the lock.

Layla pinned the hand to the wood with another dagger. "I told you I'm taking a shit!"

A man screamed bloody murder. "She pinned my fucking hand!"

"That's what you get for calling me chubby!" Layla shouted back.

I motioned Layla over. "Get through the hole."

She looked at the opening. "My ass is never going to fit through that."

"We'll make it fit." I grabbed a bottle of liquid soap from the sink and dumped it on her backside. "Now, go!"

She looked dubiously at the long drop, then eased her legs through the hole. Her generously proportioned and solidly muscled ass was an inch too thick.

"You and your big ass!" I growled. I gripped her shoulders and put all my body weight on her. The soap did the rest.

Layla's "Whoohoo!" faded into the distance.

"Open it, open it!" Horatio screamed over and over.

I slipped through the shithole and fell through open air. I managed to keep my legs straight beneath me as my body hurtled toward the water. Even so, the blow knocked the wind out of me. I plunged beneath the surface, somehow managing not to gasp for breath by sheer reflex. I fought my way through frigid waters to the surface, the stolen uniform doing its best to hinder my limbs and drag me down.

I popped above water and drew a ragged breath. Layla bobbed a few feet from me, a maniacal grin on her face.

"Holy shit, Cain!" She looked up at the hole. "That was fun."

It was all I could do just to breathe.

Layla grabbed my uniform and pulled me close. Her cold lips pressed against mine. For a moment, I forgot just how frigid the water was as Layla's hot tongue found mine. Then she shoved me a way, a smirk on her face. "Gods be damned, that was exciting."

I blinked in confusion, then remembered we weren't out of the woods yet. I tapped the earbud. It was military grade, so it survived the water. "Norna, we're outside. I repeat, we're outside."

"What?" Norna said. "How?"

"Get the raft and get back out here," I said.

"But I don't know the combination to the door."

"Fuck!" I swam the short distance to the sigil pad, but it was too high to reach.

"Be thankful I have a muscular ass, Cain, because it's about to save yours." Layla tapped her shoulders. "Get onboard, babe."

I frowned. "You can't lift me high enough."

"Shut up and get on." She ducked underwater and came up beneath my legs.

I gripped her head for balance as she lifted me clear. Strong legs thrashing, Layla positioned herself beneath the pad. I was just high enough to reach it. Hand shaking from cold and adrenalin, I somehow managed to trace the patterns. The door swung open.

I tapped the earbud. "Norna, the door is open!"

Layla ducked and pushed me off her shoulders. Despite the adrenalin, my body felt numb with cold.

Norna and the raft were already halfway to the door. She abandoned the raft and swam faster, long limbs pumping. Norna hugged me when she reached me. "I thought you were going to die!"

"I'm fine."

Layla scoffed. "We're both fine, thanks for asking."

I slipped free of Norna's hug and started swimming. "Go, before they realize we're in the lake."

We swam as fast as possible toward the shore, not bothering to be quiet about it. The sun was already dipping behind the mountains, and soon it'd be dark enough for the vampires to join the hunt.

We were almost to shore when the hangar doors opened, and motorboats sped out in hot pursuit. Guns popped and water splashed around us. We clambered to shore and ran to our hidden gear as bullets sprayed around us, filling the air with a strange, high-pitched whine. One of the bullets lodged in a tree inches from my face. It had small fins like a rocket, one of which wiggled back and forth as if designed to steer the bullet. Smoke drifted from the wood where it struck, hinting at an incendiary payload.

If one of those struck home, it'd roast a body from the inside out.

We slung on our backpacks and raced toward the cliff where our rope hung.

"What happened?" Norna said.

I was too winded to answer, but Layla picked up the slack. "Cain and I flushed ourselves out of the castle."

"Huh?" Norna almost tripped over a fallen log.

"It can wait," I said with ragged breath.

"We jumped through a medieval shitter!" Layla shouted with glee.

Norna didn't even thread the rope through her rappelling gear when we reached the cliff and started climbing. Feet braced on the cliff and hands on the rope, she practically ran up the vertical face. I didn't complain because I was still catching my breath.

"Get your ass up the rope, Cain." Layla pushed me toward the rope. I laced it through my rappelling harness, took a deep breath, and began the climb. Norna was nearly at the top when I reached the second rope. I powered the sigils in my body for extra endurance and began running up the cliff.

"You're so slow," Layla called from behind.

I looked down and saw her catching up. I was nearly to the top when Norna leaned over the cliff and held out a hand. At first, I thought she was reaching down to help me up, but then I saw the sharp knife pressed against the rope.

The betrayal had come much sooner than expected.

CHAPTER 16

"What the fuck?" There was nothing but a hundred feet of dead air between me and the ground.

Norna's face looked troubled, but resolute. "Cain, give me the oblivion staff, and I'll let you climb down before I cut the rope."

"What good is the staff without the pictures?" I patted my pocket. My phone was gone.

Norna held it up in her other hand. "Just give the staff, please."

"Tell Bisbee to fuck himself."

"Cain, what's the holdup?" Layla called.

I looked down. "We're being betrayed."

"Bisbee has nothing to do with this," Norna said. "This is for me."

"Tell me what's going on and maybe we can come to an agreement," I said in a reasonable tone. "I promise you we can work this out."

She shook her head. "Give me the staff now, or I cut the rope. Do it,

Cain! Don't make me kill you." Tears formed in the corners of her eyes. "Please."

I didn't know what was going on, but she looked desperate enough to cut the rope. She'd never retrieve the staff without me, but I didn't feel like testing her resolve. I reached over my back and summoned the staff. "Do you even know how to use this?"

She shook her head. "No, but I know someone who does."

"Who?" I said.

"Cain, toss me the staff and start climbing down." She began counting down from ten.

I tossed it up and she caught it in her other hand. Her face went from distraught to stone cold in a heartbeat. "Torvin sends his regards."

She slashed the rope. I cast a shield at the last instant to block her blade from cutting it and then leapt back from the cliff, releasing the slack in the rappelling harness to slide down as fast as possible. Layla was already halfway down, but I didn't think we'd be fast enough.

Norna hacked at the rope again, apparently not realizing I'd shielded about a foot of it. She leaned over, extended her long arm and began sawing an unprotected length. The rope snapped. I fell. I didn't even shout. All I could do at that point was enjoy the last ride of my life.

Wind whistled in my ears. The only thought passing through my head was that Hannah would have no idea what happened to me. She'd be Cthulhu's slave until the day she died.

"Cain!" Layla leapt from the side, arms gripping me in a bear hug. I jerked to a halt. Layla cried out in pain. "Grab the fucking rope!"

I came to my senses and grabbed the free rope above her. She'd clipped her harness onto the second rope before Norna cut the first one. I took my weight out of her arms and she dangled for a moment, groaning and nursing her left shoulder.

"You caught me?" I could hardly believe it.

"Barely." She glared at me. "So much for knowing it's a trap."

"This wasn't part of Bisbee's plan." I hooked my gear onto the rope and hung. "Let's get to the ground."

Layla reached for the rope and winced. "I nearly dislocated my shoulder for that little stunt."

"I'm kind of surprised you saved me."

She shrugged and winced again. "Who else am I gonna jump into toilets with?" Then she rappelled down.

I waited until she reached the ground and came down after her. It was nearly dark enough for vampires to be out and about. I didn't dare risk drilling more anchors for another climb. Rather than remove the remaining rope, I decided to leave it. If they found it, they'd assume we escaped and cut the rope at the top. That might give us some time.

Unfortunately, the drill, most of the anchors, and spare rope were at the top of the mountain pass. My backpack held a few climbing supplies, but I had no way to drill into the rock.

That wasn't our main worry now. We had to find shelter where vampires couldn't find us.

"Cain?" Layla was watching me. "Tell me what happened."

"Norna triple-crossed everyone." I flexed my tired arms and looked up. "She put on a really good show. Cried and everything to make it look like she didn't want to hurt me. After I gave her the staff, she told me that Torvin sends his regards."

She whistled. "Gods be damned. He's been playing the long game to get you in a spot like this."

I sighed. "Now I know why he didn't come after me directly when he found out I was doing jobs for Eclipse." Torvin's methods were brutal, but he loved manipulating others into doing his dirty work for him. And Norna had played her part superbly.

Layla looked around. "We need to find cover for the night, or we'll be vampire food."

Vampires were tough to fight under any circumstance, but even more so without my staff. "I think we should circle back toward the shore. We definitely can't stay around here."

"Agreed." Layla picked up the rope Norna had cut and bundled it. "Maybe we can use it later."

Hugging the cliff wall, we walked away from the castle. After twenty minutes of fast hiking, we cut down toward the lake. It took another thirty minutes to make it to the shore opposite the castle. I hadn't removed a popup tent from my backpack, so at least we had that going for us. It was patterned with green and brown camouflage, so I found a copse of bushes and trees and set it up in the middle. After that, it was a matter of scribing sigils on all sides that would mask our body heat.

"I doubt the mechanists will hunt in the dark," Layla said. "So, all we have to do is survive the night with dozens of vampires combing the forest."

I set up some aversion wards on the trees around us. "Maybe Andrei will go easy on us since we patched the wall in the sleeping chamber."

Layla snorted. "Doubtful."

I reached for my staff and remembered I didn't have it. It was like losing an arm. I had no true sight scope to scan the night for dangers. I was blind like everyone else. I still had my dueling wands and Carnwennan, so I could put up a fight if and when they found us, but it just wasn't the same. An oblivion staff wasn't like ordinary weapons. It formed a bond with the wielder, meaning no one else could use it without consent. That bond also enabled me to summon and banish it at will.

But the bond wasn't unbreakable. In fact, within hours of holding it, my staff would start to adapt its bond to the new wielder. Before long, Torvin would be able to use the basic functions of the staff, and it made me feel a little sick inside.

My earbud crackled. "Hello, Cain." The deep voice was chilling and all-too familiar. "Norna says you somehow survived the fall."

"That somehow was me," Layla interjected. "You just fucked with the wrong person, Torvin."

"And you are?" Torvin said.

"Layla Blade, you smug piece of shit." Layla bared her teeth. "Tell Norna I've got a dagger for her asshole too."

"Guess you're pretty pleased with yourself," I said. "You won't be for long when I catch up to you."

"My honor has been sated, Cain," Torvin said. "I am willing to let the matter rest now, provided you are."

"Oh, gee, what a deal." I scoffed. "I'm not responsible for what the fae did to you, Torvin, but you sure as hell are responsible for almost killing me and my friend. So, expect a visit when you least expect it."

Layla frowned. "That's the best you could come up with?"

I shrugged. "I don't have prepared lines for this."

"If the vampires don't find you, then perhaps we will meet again," Torvin said. "But now I have your oblivion staff, and you have nothing. I suspect it won't turn out well for you."

"Yeah, we'll see." I had more to say, but the earbud crackled, and the link went dead.

"He's right about one thing," Layla said. "That staff will make him a bitch to fight."

"Maybe," I said. "Oblivion staffs aren't like ordinary weapons. They bond with the wielder, meaning he can't use it until he's held it for a day or two. If I can get close enough before then, I can take it back."

"If you can get close enough." Layla shook her head. "He's not only a former guardian, but a dark elf. He'll have a major physical advantage."

"First things first," I said. "Let's survive the night and figure a way out of this valley, then I'll worry about getting back my staff."

Layla took out a container with sandwiches and fruit. "You keep things exciting, Cain."

"I try," I said dryly. I took a sandwich and bit into it. Getting out of the valley would be a real bitch without a drill. I didn't even know what to do next.

"What do you think this is?" Layla handed me her phone and tapped on a picture. "That was on the worktable next to the wall. It looks like Horatio was drawing a map."

It looked like a misshapen bowl with a vine growing out of it. The vine branched in several places before reaching the side of another bowl. I had to look at it from different angles before I realized what it was.

I tapped on the first bowl. "This is the lake." Traced a finger to the vine. "And this is a tunnel going out to sea."

Layla frowned. "Cain, the closest body of water is the Black Sea, and it's at least three hundred kilometers away. There's no way an underwater tunnel stretches all the way from here to there."

"Could be an underwater river," I said. "Maybe that's where the submarine was going. Or maybe it connects to the Danube River to the south."

She snapped her fingers. "The echo-sonic mapper was on the other sub. They must be mapping tunnels where the submarine can fit."

"Well, whatever it is, I think that's our way out." I stared toward the castle, now a dark silhouette on the opposite shore. "We're going to steal the other sub."

Layla cackled with laughter. "Like I said, you keep it interesting."

"I admire the fact that you didn't even question the sanity of that idea." I sighed. "Guess we're both insane."

She shrugged. "I'm just too badass to scare easily."

"True." I stared into the distance. "Getting back into the hangar will be harder, and even if we make it, I've never piloted a submarine."

"It has a clockwork engine, so it's no ordinary submarine." Layla flicked through pictures on her phone and stopped at a diagram of the submarine controls. It was a good thing she'd taken pictures too, or we'd be completely out of luck. "Maybe this will help."

I studied the descriptions beneath the labels. They didn't amount to an instruction manual, but it was better than nothing. "It actually doesn't look too complicated." There was a steering wheel, a lever for acceleration, and another lever for ballast controls. "Our best chance will be to attack at the crack of dawn. The vampires will be back inside, and the mechanists won't be expecting it."

Layla pointed to pinpoints of light in the forest across the lake. "They're still next to our infiltration point. If we're lucky, they'll think we left."

It was cold, but I wasn't ready to go into the tent just yet. Thumping chopper blades echoed from the south. Moments later, a helicopter exited the pass east of the one we'd entered through and landed on the castle. I reached for my staff again and felt a pang of anxiety when it wasn't there. Moments later, the chopper rose and flew to the pass we'd used, sweeping a brilliant spotlight on the ground.

"Maybe stealing the chopper would be better," I mused.

Layla shook her head vigorously. "No, Cain, you promised me a submarine and I won't accept any less."

I snorted. "Such high expectations are why you don't have a girlfriend."

She shrugged. "Hey, a girl has to have standards."

It didn't seem there was much else to do except get a good night's rest and pray my wards kept the vampires away.

I crawled into the tent since it wasn't nearly tall enough to stand in. It wasn't insulated and I didn't dare use a heating spell. The protective wards would help against vampire night vision but conjuring a heat source was too risky. I cast a dim glow spell so we could see inside.

Layla kicked off her shoes outside and entered the tent, zipping the opening behind her. She held up a thin blanket. "Guess we're sharing."

The tent was small, so even if we lay on opposite sides, our shoulders were practically touching. I grunted. "I hope you don't fart in your sleep."

She shrugged. "No promises." Layla rolled onto her side facing me and propped her head on her hand. She spread the blanket over us and winked. "Nothing like camping in the Romanian wilderness right outside a vampire stronghold. You know how to show a girl a good time."

I grunted. "I do my best."

"I figured we'd be back to Bucharest by now." Layla huffed. "We really fucked up letting Norna climb the rope first. What in the hell were we thinking?"

"I wasn't thinking, I was running." I rolled over on my side to face her. "Norna planned well, because she was on the rope before I even thought about it."

"She fooled me," Layla said. "I never saw a triple-cross coming."

"Me either." I lay on my back. "Get some sleep, for tomorrow we plot our revenge."

"Can't wait." Layla unzipped the tent and retrieved her backpack from outside. She removed some items and tried to fashion the pack into a pillow, but it was too bulky. She put it back outside and looked at me. "You sleep on your back?"

I shrugged. "Mostly."

"Good." She snuggled up using the crook of my arm as a pillow. "Don't move your arm, even if it falls asleep. I need my beauty rest."

"Wow, so considerate." I didn't really mind having another warm body so close, but I knew from experience that my arm would be a lump of dead flesh before long.

"You can cop a feel of my ass for payment." Layla yawned without covering her mouth and blew hot breath in my face.

"I can think of better things to do," I muttered.

"Cain, we're dirty, we stink, and I've got a headache." Layla opened her eyes and glared at me. "So just accept the fact that sex isn't happening."

I scoffed. "What makes you think I was talking about sex?"

She frowned. "You weren't?"

"No. I was thinking you could just ball up the blanket and use it as a pillow, so my arm doesn't fall asleep."

"Gods, you must have no sex drive at all." Layla shook her head. "You haven't even felt my ass. Wouldn't you just love pounding me from behind?"

"What the fuck is wrong with you?" I couldn't stop myself from laughing. "You get pissed because you think I want sex, and then pissed because I don't want sex. Which is it, Layla?"

She leaned over and kissed me, pressing her tongue into my mouth. Her hand reached down and rubbed my crotch, quickly getting a reaction. I pulled her closer, reaching down and squeezing her firm ass.

Layla pushed away, grinning. "That's what I thought." She rolled up the blanket, put it under her head and rolled over onto her other side away from me.

"You're such a bitch." I laughed. "But you're my favorite bitch."

Layla stiffened for an instant then relaxed. "Shut up, Cain."

I took off my shirt and arranged it into a barely acceptable pillow. I'd slept in far worse places, thanks to Torvin and his training methods. But that didn't make me feel any better.

I dispelled the glow spell and the tent faded to darkness.

When I closed my eyes, I saw the pale, cruel face of Torvin Rayne. It had been his tactics during the war that led to me murdering a house full of women and children. His plots to defeat the humans had been ruthless, slaughtering families instead of soldiers. The fae had let him do as he pleased. They didn't care about the means, only the ends. Because of him, I'd abandoned my post. Because of him, I'd been haunted by the ghosts of those I'd murdered.

He'd chased me all over Feary, but in the end, had discovered I was more cunning and dangerous than he'd anticipated. I'd freed enslaved gryphons and other sentient beasts, fomenting a rebellion that even the fae couldn't control. The fae allowed me to leave, then stripped Torvin of his rank and disavowed him for his failure to capture me.

Torvin had nursed that grudge, planted it, and grown it into the plot that nearly saw me die today. Tomorrow, I'd plant the seeds of my own revenge. I would track down Torvin and recover my staff. Without it, I couldn't reach Oblivion, and Hannah would never be free.

CHAPTER 17

I woke to the sound of leaves cracking underfoot. Layla jerked but I couldn't see her in the pitch black of the tent. I slowly unzipped the opening and looked outside. The sky was light gray, but the dawn was hidden by the mountains.

"The vampires tracked the scent to this general vicinity," someone said in a low voice.

"You sure they didn't escape?" someone responded.

"The vampires think someone got left behind."

Leaves crackled all around us. I estimated ten people. Layla crawled out next to me. Her face was barely visible by the light of the moon, but it was hard to miss the excited grin.

"Don't kill them right away," the first voice said. "I want to torture them for information. Find out why they were here."

"Might as well make them suffer before they die," someone else said. "Set an example."

Layla bit her lower lip, tapped her chest, and pointed west. She tapped my shoulder and pointed east, making a clockwise circle with her finger.

I nodded and crept out. The ground was covered in leaves and pine straw, so I remained barefoot for maximum silence. Beams of light swept the area, but none of them crossed the copse of trees hiding our tent. The aversion wards were doing their job, it seemed. I counted ten flashlights, six to the east, and four to the west. A flashlight swept over an area, revealing another figure for an instant. For some reason, that person didn't have a flashlight.

After making sure there were no more undetected mechanists, I circled around behind the group on the eastern side of the tent. The pair I'd heard talking earlier continued their conversation, detailing the best torture methods for extracting information. I found a straggler and came up behind him. I wrapped my arm around his neck in a chokehold and put my hand over his mouth. I cast a strong shock spell. His body convulsed and went limp. I snapped his neck to be sure, then gently laid him on the ground and moved up to the next in line.

Victim number two went quietly as well. Number three turned at the last minute and nearly got off a shout before I silenced him. The last three were walking abreast which made the final approach more difficult. I had to finish them quickly before one of them turned around and noticed half their party was missing.

Unfortunately, my time ran out an instant later. The torture advocate glanced back and stopped in his tracks when he noticed his missing comrades. "Jolly? Higgs? Where the hell are you?"

"They were just there a moment ago," the other guy said.

The mechanist at the end panicked. "They're here!" He began firing blindly into the dark.

I ducked behind a tree as bullets crashed through the foliage.

Despite their brave talk about torture and killing, the other two opened fire into the darkness. I took advantage of the noise and circled behind them at a flat-out run. Drawing my dueling wands, I fired a precision strike spell at the leader. A needle of intense energy pierced his carotid artery. I used a blade of energy to slash the throat of the next guy. Both went down gurgling.

The third man ran out of ammo and stopped to reload before noticing his dying companions. He screamed and tried to run, but I grabbed his neck and slammed him to the ground. Gunfire erupted from Layla's position, but it quickly ended in screams and shouts. As daylight peeked over the mountains, Layla stepped from the shadows holding one of the mechanists' strange rifles, smoke rising from the muzzle.

Layla wore a delighted grin that faded when she saw the man wriggling in my grasp. "Why is he alive?"

"Because he's the one who panicked first." I slapped him gently on the cheek and held up a finger. "Stop resisting or I'll kill you now."

The man's eyes bulged, but he nodded. "Please let me live. I swear I won't tell anyone you're out here."

"I'll let you live, provided I'm satisfied with the information you give me." I released his neck and motioned for him to rise. I sheathed my wands to give him the illusion of safety. "What are the submarines for?"

He gulped. "We're mapping the deepways."

I frowned. "The what?"

"Deepways." He tried to stop his hands from shaking by stuffing them under his arms. "Promise you'll let me live, and I'll tell you everything."

Layla held up a hand. "Scout's honor."

I nodded. "I promise. But I will tie you up so you can't go tattle on us right away."

Tears tracked down his face. "Thank you, sir."

"Don't thank me yet." I crossed my arms and narrowed my eyes. "What's your name?"

"Kevin, sir."

I nodded. "Tell me everything about the echo-sonic mapper and what you're doing, Kevin."

His eyes flared at the mention of the device, but he started talking so fast it was almost hard to keep up with. "The deepways are a vast network of oceanic tides and tunnels originating in R'lyeh. They encircle the world and allow Cthulhu's minions quick travel to almost anywhere in the world."

"Holy shit." Layla set her stolen weapon on the ground. "You know where R'lyeh is?"

He shook his head. "We've only just started mapping. The first submarine is on its twenty-third mission. The last time it barely survived an encounter with a giant squid."

"Cthulhu probably has armies of underwater minions," I said. "I'm surprised the first sub made it back."

"They're weaponized with electrified hulls and harpoons," he said. "The second submarine is ready for launch once the next echo-sonic is completed."

Kevin's body language hinted at something left unsaid. " R'lyeh isn't the only thing you're searching for."

The mechanist gulped again. "We've charted dozens of ancient wrecks—ships that vanished at sea because they were dragged into the deepways by sea monsters. We also found that the deepways aren't limited to Gaia. Some branches lead off-world."

I wasn't surprised. "And that's how you got an aerial photo of Oblivion."

His eyes flared wider. "How do you know that?"

"I know more than I'm letting on," I said. "It's a test. If I know you're not telling me something, then the deal is off."

He shivered. "I'll tell you everything, I promise."

"How do you reach Oblivion through the deepways?" I said.

"It's hard to tell you without a map."

Layla took out her phone and showed him the picture of the partial map from Horatio's workshop. "How about now?"

He grimaced. "Nub technology."

I scoffed. "Yeah, what's wrong with that?"

"Do you have clockwork smartphones?" Layla said with a smirk.

"Show me the way to Oblivion," I said.

Kevin squinted at the phone and traced a path with his finger from the lake and down three branches, one of which had an omega symbol in the middle of it. "This branch ends in Gaia and starts in Oblivion. Once we discovered it, we began sending clockwork drones to survey the area. Inventor Horatio believes he discovered the location of the original Mount Olympus."

I nodded, giving him the opportunity to elucidate.

He cleared his throat. "The inventor believes the original armory of Hephaestus is beneath the mountain, but our drones haven't found the entrance."

"Why hasn't he sent people?" I asked.

"The atmosphere in Oblivion is hot and low in oxygen. Also, something has destroyed all the drones we sent to the mountain."

I frowned. "Dragons?"

"We don't know, sir." He shivered.

"What's the Combine's end game, Kevin?"

He spoke the next part as if it were ingrained in his head. "Nub technology and pure magic are ruining the world. We want to annihilate the nubs and the gods. Those left will see the mechanist way leads to prosperity."

"Sign me up," Layla said with a grin.

"You want weapons from the lost armory so you can achieve that goal," I said.

Kevin's fear vanished behind a scowl. "There are too many nubs ruining Gaia. They need to go."

"Someone's indoctrinated," Layla sang.

"It's the truth," Kevin said sharply.

I snapped my fingers to get his attention back on me. "You know a wizard named Bisbee or a dwarf named Dwight?"

Kevin shook his head. "I've never heard of them."

"Anything else you want to tell us?" I said.

The fear began to return to his eyes. "Count Dracula has an arrangement to control most of Europe once we're successful and has devoted vast resources to help us." He bit his lower lip, as if trying to come up with more to tell us.

"Did you walk all the way here from the other side of the lake?" I asked.

He shook his head. "We anchored about a kilometer down the shore. The other boats split up to cover the rest of the lake." He hemmed and hawed for a moment, but it looked like he'd run out of useful information.

"How many people are looking for us?" I asked.

"Almost everyone—all the grays, that is. The lab workers don't do this sort of thing."

"How many left in the castle?" I asked.

He shrugged. "I don't know. Maybe twenty grays and all the lab workers."

"That it?" Layla said.

"I can't think of anything else." Kevin shrank back. "I promise."

Layla shrugged. "Good enough for me." She plunged her dagger toward his chest.

I gripped her wrist and stopped her an inch from his heart. "Hey, we promised not to kill him."

"I'm not a fucking Boy Scout." Layla raised her eyebrows. "You really want to leave this guy alive so he can run home and tell everyone what we're up to?"

"They changed the hangar gate code," the man said suddenly. "Kill me and you'll never get in."

"We're not going to kill you." I pushed Layla's arm down. "Okay?"

She scowled, but the dagger vanished. "Fine."

"How do I open the doors to get the sub out?" I said.

"There's a sigil pad at the end of the pier, one for each submarine," Kevin said.

"You don't have problems using sigil pads, but you don't like pure magic?" Layla said.

"Sigil pads are not pure magic," Kevin said. "And they're efficient."

"What about the code for the boat door?" I asked.

"It's changed too."

I took Layla's phone and put it on the drawing app. "Put them down. If you're lying, I'll come back here and kill you myself."

"I promise it's the truth!" He drew two sets of five symbols. The lines were crooked thanks to his shaking hands, but I was able to make sense of them. They'd definitely upped security. I quickly jabbed two fingers into his neck and delivered a mild shock. Kevin slumped to the ground. Using the climbing rope Norna had cut, I sat him against a tree and secured him. He could work his way free, but it'd take some doing.

I picked up one of the mechanist weapons and examined it. The rifle was made of an alloy resembling brass, but it wasn't as heavy as it should have been. A series of gears drove an actuator that triggered the bullets. The bullets were of an irregular caliber, with spring-loaded fins that popped out once the bullet was airborne. Sigil markings on the tips of the bullets were designed to lock onto a target and steer the projectiles with movable fins. They were propelled by liquid mana, not gunpowder.

I recognized the homing spell and also knew it wasn't very accurate. It had to be right on target within fifty yards or it wouldn't lock on. It also couldn't avoid objects in its path, which was part of the reason Layla and I hadn't been hit. Had we been in the open, it might have been a different story.

Some bullets carried an incendiary payload. Those were marked red, while others were marked blue. I fired a blue one into a corpse for scientific purposes. It didn't explode or catch fire, and I considered the experiment a success since I now knew the blue bullets were ordinary slugs.

Gears in the magazines, which seemed a lot more trouble than a spring mechanism, shifted the bullets into place but mechanists often took simple solutions and made them complex.

"Gather the other weapons and ammo," I said. "We might be going in hot."

Layla rubbed her hands together. "This is going to be so much fun."

Before long, we had a pile of the mechanist rifles gathered on the ground. We shoved spare mags into our backpacks and loaded three rifles each so we wouldn't have to reload often. We took the least bloody gray uniforms from the dead mechanists and put them on, then set off for the lakeshore.

The motorboat was just under a kilometer away as Kevin promised. The storage compartment held a brass looking glass which I used to scan the horizon. The other motorboats were parked on opposite shores. The motor on our boat was, of course, of mechanist invention, powered by liquid mana. As such, it ran much quieter than its nub counterpart.

Layla stared across the placid waters at the castle. "I say we go straight in and kill anyone who gets in our way."

It wasn't my favorite plan but sneaking in wasn't an option. We'd have to get in through the boat door, open the main hangar doors, and pilot the sub out, all while under fire. It promised to be more excitement than I wanted.

But we didn't have much of a choice.

I pumped a priming lever and spun the sparker to ignite the mana fuel. The motor hummed to life. The boat's clockwork motor cover was transparent, offering a clear view of the cogs and gears driving the propeller. It seemed more artistic in design than utilitarian, but aside from a faint clicking noise, it was nearly silent.

We jetted across the lake, Layla keeping an eye on our surroundings in case the other search parties saw us and decided to intercept. No one did. If memory served, all available motorboats were parked on the shores—all but ours. I hoped Kevin's estimate of grays remaining in the hangar were right. Horatio certainly wouldn't expect us to come right back to them.

We reached the boat door in the castle wall. Kevin's code let us inside. The few dock workers inside saw and heard us, so there was no point trying to hide our approach. I parked us at the end of the floating docks. A constable hurried down the ramp from the pier toward us. I suspected he was a member of Horatio's personal security.

"Where are the others?" he shouted when he was halfway to us. "Did you find them?" He spoke with a thick Italian accent.

"Not yet," I said. "Everyone is tired and hungry. I came back to get food and supplies."

"Food?" The man threw up his hands. "You will eat when the intruders are caught!"

His gaze flicked down toward a bloody bullet hole on my uniform, and his shoulders stiffened. Without another word, he reached for the gun holstered at his waist.

The gig was up.

CHAPTER 18

A thrown blade buried itself in the hollow of his neck. He went down with hardly a sound, but the other dockworkers saw everything. They must not have been armed, because they scattered like roaches. But that didn't mean they wouldn't return fully armed in seconds.

The remaining submarine was moored between the piers to the right. The pier with the sigil pad that opened the hangar doors was on the opposite side of the submarine. Only a few crates and equipment offered cover between here and there.

"Go!" I powered my body sigils for extra speed. Layla flashed past me. She leapt atop the railing on the floating dock and jumped from it to the neighboring pier. Then she flung herself from there to the submarine and vanished on the other side. Her fae genes gave her an advantage I couldn't compete with when it came to speed, but I wasn't exactly slow myself.

I made the jump to the pier just as grays opened fire from the cover of crates at the back of the bay. I dove behind a workbench and flipped it over for cover. One of the mechanist guns in my possession had a scope, so I used it first. A worker popped his head from behind cover. I fired and bloody mist plumed from the back of his head. The next guy met a similar fate.

But the other grays spread out to flank. I wouldn't be safe here for much longer. I switched to a gun with incendiary rounds and pumped a few of them into the wooden crates they were hiding behind. The wood burst into flame and smoke filled the air, reducing their visibility to nothing. I dashed forward to more crates, shielding myself with a spell.

Bullets whined past, some pinging off my shield and leaving cracks. Before I could jump to the sub, dock workers raced into position on the right and opened fire. I ran straight ahead, toward the smoke and flames from the crates. I slid through a narrow opening between the crates and found myself face-to-face with coughing dock workers. I put a bullet in the head of the closest one, then rolled on my side and gunned down two more before they recovered.

The hangar doors began to slide open. Ducking beneath the smoke, I crawled to the end of the crates. Layla was crouched behind the pedestal with the sigil pad, pinned down by enemy fire. This group hid behind metal containers, so the incendiary rounds wouldn't do much good.

Layla produced a hooked blade shaped like a small boomerang. She flung it up at an angle. It whirled in lopsided fashion then plunged down and struck one of the dock workers in the top of his head. He screamed and went down. The other four unloaded their weapons on Layla's position.

Using the smoke as cover, I dashed to the end of the burning crates and slid across the polished concrete to the end of the metal containers. When they opened fire on Layla again, I poked around the corner and fired four shots. The workers dropped lifelessly to the floor in succession, brains and blood erupting from their temples as each bullet found their heads.

There were more attackers on the opposite side of the submarine, but they didn't have a clear shot at Layla. I fired several incendiary rounds at them, lighting as many crates on fire as I could, then ran for the sub. Layla flashed a grin at me and leapt from the pier to the sub and spun the handle that opened the hatch. I ran down the pier and across the ramp to the sub.

She slid down the ladder inside and I followed, slamming shut the hatch and twisting the handle to seal it. A lever allowed me to lock the handle from the inside so anyone left alive outside couldn't pay us a visit.

A dimly lit corridor extended forward and aft. Layla had already gone forward to the spacious bridge. The pilot chair was right near the curved nose, just as the diagram said. More chairs were bolted to the floors near other consoles, and a comfortably padded captain's chair sat in the center. Wires hung from an unfinished console, probably the one that controlled the echo-sonic mapper.

A large brass globe hung from an axis on the right side. A lever locked it in place to keep it from spinning.

We knew a lot about the layout from the diagram, but what it hadn't told us was how in the hell we were supposed to see where we were going.

I spun in a circle. "Is there a periscope somewhere?"

Layla fiddled with the controls, but they were dead. "Get back to engineering and prime the engine, Cain!"

I raced down the narrow corridor, past bunk beds and a galley, and reached engineering. A large transparent canister held a full gallon of mana—enough to power Dolores for a year without refueling. I pumped the large priming lever, then clicked the igniter. Gears clinked and the engine rumbled to life.

The sub lurched forward, and I stumbled against a railing. It saved me from falling into the giant gears turning the propeller. Holding onto the side railings, I made my way forward to the bridge.

"Where's the fucking periscope?" Layla shouted. "I'm driving this thing blind!"

I spotted a handle hanging over the captain's chair. I yanked it down and flipped open the handles. "We just cleared the hangar doors." I recollected where the other submarine had dived and hypothesized we needed to do the same. "Keep going straight."

Layla held the steering wheel steady even as it tried to jump from her hands. "This thing handles like a bathtub on wheels."

"It's a submarine, not a sports car." I noticed a faint reflection in the hull near Layla and pushed up the scope so I could investigate. I walked past her and tapped my knuckles on the curved nose. It wasn't metal, but some kind of transparent material. There were several unlabeled levers on a panel to the right of the pilot's chair. I consulted the diagram, but the levers weren't on there. I decided it was safer to test them while we were above water.

I flicked the first. Gears clicked, and the outer hull folded up, making a giant window of the entire nose.

"Holy shit!" Layla cackled with glee. "That's quite a view."

I stood next to her. "Submerge and head left when we hit the middle of the lake." I pointed to a motorboat racing from the opposite shore to intercept us. "I hope this window is bulletproof."

Layla leaned forward and rapped on it. "It's not glass, and it's surely designed to withstand pressures at depth. I doubt bullets will do anything but bounce off."

I tested another of the levers and floodlights lit the lake ahead. The next two levers opened smaller windows on the sides of the bridge. The last lever unleashed a deafening whine from a speaker somewhere outside. I quickly cut it off.

Layla grimaced. "What in the ever-loving Hades was that?"

"No idea, but my eardrums still hurt." I dug a finger into my ear as if that might help.

Layla huffed. "Don't do it again."

I monitored our position until we were at the same spot the others sub had gone down. "You can dive now and turn forty degrees left."

"Aye, captain." Layla flipped me off and pushed forward on the dive lever. Gears clanked and the sound of rushing water echoed beneath our feet as the ballast tanks flooded. Sunlight vanished and murky green waters surrounded us. The floodlights flickered but remained on, giving us an eerie underwater view.

The vessel slowed as we continued to drop lower. The lights reflected off something red. As we drew closer, I realized it was a submerged buoy. Another one was barely visible another eighty feet or so forward.

I peered through the window. "I think these buoys lead to the deepway."

"Duh." Layla altered course to head for the next buoy.

I nodded. "Hold this direction and we'll probably be there soon."

"Thanks, Captain Obvious." Layla tapped me on the back and pointed at her eyes. "Look at me. Look at me!"

I raised my eyebrows. "Uh, okay."

She nodded. "I'm the captain now."

I shrugged. "Aye, aye, sir." Then I went and sat in the captain's chair.

Layla piloted us along the line of buoys until we reached what looked like a dead end. She pulled back on the motor lever and stared at the rocky wall. "Think it's illusion?"

"Only one way to find out." I went to the window. "But take it slow in case."

"Cain, do I look like an idiot?" She rolled her eyes. "Of course, I'll take it slow."

I put up my hands. "Damn, no need to be touchy."

Layla eased forward on the accelerator and the sub drifted toward the rocky wall. She slowed us even more. With a low thud, the window bumped into solid rock.

"Well, shit." Layla backed us up. "We must be missing something."

I stared at the wall for a moment. "Why would they have buoys leading to a blank wall?"

Layla pursed her lips. "What if we need the echo-sonic mapper to find the entrance?"

I hadn't considered that but thought back to what Kevin had said. "They knew about the deepways before they had the echo-sonic." Something occurred to me. "Maybe what we're looking at is a secret doorway to the deepways. Cthulhu wouldn't want just anybody being able to use them, right? There must be a key that opens the door.

In this case, I had a feeling the key was a sound—a passphrase only underwater creatures could make.

I walked to the lever panel and pulled on the one that made the awful noise. This time a haunting echo like whale song rang out in the murky waters. Slowed and muffled by the water, it was almost beautiful. The rock wall split into four sections and opened. A vortex of water spun on the other side but didn't affect the lake water in the slightest.

"How in the hell did you figure that out?" Layla turned toward me. "I never would've connected the dots on that one."

"Probably because you haven't watched *Star Trek IV*," I said.

She snorted. "Nerd." Layla pushed forward on a lever and we moved toward the twisting maw.

"That thing looks like it'll tear us apart." I strapped myself in the captain's chair. "You'd better secure yourself."

Layla followed my example and buckled the straps over her chest. The nose of the sub touched the water. In an instant, we surged forward at incredible speed. If not for the headrest, I would've suffered severe whiplash from the drastic increase in velocity.

"Whoohoo!" Layla shouted.

We shot into darkness barely lit by the floodlights, a bullet speeding down the barrel of a rifle. Our direction abruptly changed to a downward angle, plunging us deeper beneath the earth. Moments later, the water began to glow orange. Straps bit into my chest as the vessel abruptly slowed. A great ball of energy hovered in the middle of a vast spherical chamber honeycombed by openings all around us.

I consulted the deepways map and located what I'd thought was the Black Sea. But looking at it from another angle, I realized we'd actually gone deep into the earth and were now in a transit station of sorts. The hundreds of tunnels led to different locations, or maybe even other transit stations like this one. But the map was sparse on details and labels, meaning we could end up anywhere if we weren't careful.

Layla drifted toward a cluster of tunnels. "Cain, there's writing on the wall."

I unbuckled myself and went to the window for a look. Sure enough, the Mechanists had carved numbers into the stone. It took a moment for me to realize they were map coordinates. "That must be what the globe is for." I went over to the sphere and inspected it. Longitude and latitude were precisely etched into the metal surface, even allowing for four decimal places.

I went back to the window and looked at the numbers next to the branching tunnels. Each differed by only a few degrees, meaning the destinations weren't thousands of miles apart. All we had to do was find a destination on the globe and then line it up to the coordinates on a tunnel.

"The echo-sonic must allow them to map where tunnels go before they take them," Layla said. "I wonder where the other sub went."

I shrugged. "Down one of these tunnels, I guess."

She inspected the picture of the map on her phone and tapped the omega symbol. "How are we supposed to find this tunnel?"

Looking at the map from the correct perspective, it looked like there was a tunnel leading to another chamber like this one. The omega symbol was on one of the branches leading from there. But by going there, we'd risk running into the other submarine.

"We need to get somewhere safe and regroup," I said. "Plus, we're not equipped for Oblivion."

Layla pressed her lips together. "Yeah, you're probably right. And I want to see Bisbee's face when we tell him Norna betrayed us."

"Me too." I went to the globe and put some thought our destination. I needed a place where I could moor a submarine in secret, which was a pretty tall order. The submarine didn't float too high in the water, which helped, but it was over a hundred feet long. Then again, if we kept it mostly underwater, only the sail would poke above the water. One of my backup properties had a covered dock on Lake Lanier and was far enough away from other houses that it might do the trick.

I found the coordinates for the lake on the globe and went to the window for a look. The nearest tunnel led in the opposite direction of North America, so I asked Layla to take us to the other side of the chamber. After some back and forth between there and the globe, I discovered most of the destinations were somewhere in the Atlantic, and none of them were in the U.S.

One set of coordinates lined up with where we needed to go, so I buckled in. "Let's give this one a try."

Layla steered us into the vortex, and we shot forward. We emerged in another chamber with just as many tunnels as the last. Layla took us to the opposite side, and we checked the coordinates carved in the stone. Sure enough, the next ones took us to the eastern seaboard.

"If we want to go to the surface, we'd take one of the tunnels in the top," I said. "Otherwise, we just keep going in the direction we want to go."

"On to the next one then?" Layla said.

"Looks like it." I found the coordinates on the eastern seaboard that would take us closest to our destination and located the coordinates for Lake Lanier while I was at it. Then we browsed the tunnels until settling on one that would keep us at the same latitude and longitude. The process was painstaking, but I didn't want to end up hundreds of miles off course. On the plus side, once we chose the proper vortex, it delivered us to the next chamber in a matter of minutes.

After we strapped in, Layla lined up the sub with the next tunnel and we went in. Waiting on the other side was a scene straight from a fisherman's worst nightmares.

CHAPTER 19

 squid twice as large as the submarine floated fifty feet in front of us. A giant eye regarded us as we shot from the vortex and directly at it.

"Gods damn it!" Layla steered hard left to avoid the monster.

Tentacles flailed. The submarine shuddered and stopped dead. Suckers along the bottom of a tentacle grasped at the window. They shifted aside and the squid turned a single eye to look inside. Its aquamarine eye clouded black, and I sensed the presence of Cthulhu on the other end.

"Oh, shit." I cast illusion spells on mine and Layla's faces.

The hull creaked and groaned as the tentacles tightened. I expected Cthulhu to speak through the squid, but either he didn't intend to, or he needed skin-to-skin contact for telepathy. I raced to the other control panels and found the lever that electrified the hull.

"Get ready to go," I shouted over the sound of creaking metal. "We probably need to go straight ahead to find the next coordinates." I flipped the lever. A low hum grew louder and higher in pitch. When it was high enough to hurt my ears, I hit the button beneath the lever. Electricity crackled. The water outside bubbled and boiled.

The tentacles relaxed and fell free. The giant squid drifted in the water, its eyes cloudy and gray.

"I think you killed it," Layla said.

"Better it than us."

"No complaints." Layla backed up the sub to get free of the slack tentacles. "I've never seen a sea monster like that before."

"That thing is big, but it's nothing compared to Cthulhu." I shuddered. "Let's get out of here. Cthulhu might send backup."

"Good idea." Layla thrust the vessel ahead toward the opposite side of the chamber. We located coordinates that'd put us in the southeastern part of Lake Lanier. It seemed the deepways connected with all bodies of water no matter how large or small—a frightening fact. The reach of Cthulhu was more immense than I'd imagined.

And with submarines like this one, the mechanists would be able to get anywhere on Gaia or other worlds within hours.

Layla took us into the next vortex. Moments later, we burst from the tunnel exit and into water that wasn't enclosed in one of the underwater chambers. Layla rotated the sub to see where we'd emerged. A giant hole in the rocky lakebed clamped shut, hiding the entrance to the deepways.

"Good thing that tunnel opened automatically," Layla said. "Otherwise it would've been a real short trip."

I grimaced. "Pancake city."

She took out her phone and studied it. "I've got a signal again. GPS tells me we're right where the numbers said we'd be."

"The mechanists must have been at this for a while to have marked coordinates for so many tunnels." I blew out a breath. "It's only a matter of time before they're able to reach the armory themselves."

"I have a feeling our incident at Castle Dracula probably accelerated their timeline." Layla frowned. "Which means if we're going to do this, we need to do it fast."

"Agreed." I looked at her phone and typed in the location of my nearby safe house. I almost told her to head there, but figured she'd only get irritated with me again.

Layla shifted the accelerator forward. "I didn't realize Lake Lanier was so deep."

"Most people don't." I sat in the captain's chair. "There are entire underwater towns in these waters."

She glanced back at me. "Why'd you get a safe house out here?"

"The safe house is on land once tended by a druid," I said. "He literally asked the living land to protect it from vampires, werewolves, and fae, and the land responded by infusing an acre with iron and silver deposits."

Layla nodded approvingly. "Druid magic is no joke. Not many of them around anymore."

"Because the fae ordered them exterminated during the war," I said. "The druids were making the land fight back, and even the fae can't beat Mother Earth."

"Where's that druid now?" Layla asked.

I shrugged. "Last I heard he was out west. Nevada or Arizona, I think. He stays as far from Feary portals as possible."

She frowned. "That's a hell of a life."

I knew what it was like to be hunted by the fae. "Yeah, it is." I'd struck a bargain with the high fae, so I was relatively safe. But if I'd learned anything, it was to never take chances. This safe house was a perfect backup.

It took us an hour to reach the hidden cove where my lake house was located. The water was just deep enough for the submarine to fit its front quarter under the canopy of the boathouse, hiding the sail from view. I wasn't worried about passing boats seeing it, but there was enough aerial traffic that someone might spot it from above.

I climbed out and moored the sub the best I could. The dock moors were meant to secure boats, not a submarine and I didn't have proper rope for the job, so Layla filled the ballast tanks until the sub rested on the bottom of the lake. This close to shore it was shallow enough that the sail remained above water.

It probably wasn't good for the hull, but then again, neither was a giant squid. It had survived being squeezed by massive tentacles, so the hull would probably be okay resting on the rocky lakebed for a day.

We didn't bother going into the house and went to the separate garage instead. I disabled the wards and opened the door. Inside was an old SUV that hadn't been started in months. Unlike Dolores, it ran on gas. Using a shock sigil, I gave the dead battery enough juice to crank the engine. It finally started after a couple of tries and we headed back to town.

We'd only been gone a couple of days, but it felt like weeks had passed. There was something about infiltrating a secret mountain lair, being betrayed, and hijacking a submarine that was exhausting.

"How do we play the Bisbee angle?" Layla said. "Confront him or don't even contact him?"

"Confront," I said. "We don't know for sure that he's not in cahoots with Norna and Torvin. I want to be sure." I shrugged. "Plus, he might have useful information that could lead us to Norna."

"I guarantee you she and Torvin won't waste any time heading to Oblivion." Layla bared her teeth. "They might even be there already."

"Doubtful," I said. "Oblivion staffs aren't just inanimate tools. The metallic wood, whatever it is, is actually alive. It bonds with an owner, reacting to their needs almost automatically. My staff won't start the bonding process until Torvin has held it nonstop for at least a day or two. At that point, he'll be able to use it, but it won't be as effortless as it is when fully bonded."

"Weird." Layla sighed and leaned back in her seat. "How long for a full bonding?"

"Months, depending on the skill level of the wielder." My guts twisted in knots at the thought of losing my staff. This was the first time in decades it hadn't been within arm's reach, tucked in its pocket dimension, or wherever it vanished when I sheathed it. Despite my long relationship with the staff, it still had its secrets.

Layla's eyebrows rose. "You look upset, Caine."

"The bond is two ways." I kept my face neutral. "I feel the loss like one might feel the loss of an arm. It's not pleasant."

"I wouldn't trust fae weapons anyway." She grimaced. "How do you know that staff wasn't killing you like Cthulhu's pearl?"

"It's not really a fae weapon," I said. "It was made by Hephaestus for the fae."

Layla grunted. "So it's divine?"

I shrugged. "Could be. It's made of nearly indestructible metallic wood and has active abilities of its own. It vanishes when I sheathe it, and I don't know where it goes."

"Semi-divine weapon." She grunted. "Maybe we'll find answers in the armory."

"Maybe so."

"If the staff is so important to you, why didn't you name it?" Layla cocked her head. "You named your car Dolores, for gods' sakes."

"It didn't seem appropriate. My staff wasn't uniquely mine for a long time." I shrugged. "I named Dolores because she was the first thing I really owned. It was my first act of transitioning from a member of a collective to an individual."

Layla nodded but said nothing.

I saw an opportunity to pry into her past. "What about you? Have you always been independent?"

"I've always been none of your business, Cain." She smirked. "Just because you gush about your past doesn't mean I have to."

"You told me you're half-fae, half-human." I shrugged. "That's kind of a big deal."

"It's just a fact about me," she said. "Same as saying the fae see me as an abomination."

"Wouldn't being an independent assassin be just another fact about you?" I said.

"Maybe, but I don't see a point in stating it." Layla stared at the road. "If Torvin can't reach Oblivion for at least a day, that gives us time to set up an ambush. He has no idea we can still reach Oblivion, and I'd love to see the look on his face just before we kill him and that bitch ogress."

I had mixed feelings about it. Just thinking about Torvin filled me with a sense of dread. He was sadistic, needlessly cruel to those he commanded, and even more so to those he deemed enemies. I'd sparred with him countless times and never won a bout. Though I approached most fights with confidence, that would not be the case with Torvin.

I decided not to head straight home. Shipwreck was along the way, and a quick stop would confirm whether Bisbee and Dwight knew anything.

Layla's eyes brightened when she realized where we were heading. "I want to threaten Dwight, that little runt. Maybe toss him around a bit. You can have Bisbee."

"Knock yourself out," I said. "Just remember Shipwreck is in a fae safe zone."

"Well, shit." Layla made a raspberry. "How are we supposed to get them to answer questions if we can't threaten them?"

"We'll figure it out." I parked in an empty lot just down the road. It was dark, drizzling, and cold—a miserable night for a walk, but I didn't want to leave the car inside the safe zone.

Layla grinned like an excited child as we stalked our way behind a strip mall so we could come up behind the bar and reach the door unseen. Black marks in the concrete ahead drew my eye. I stopped and knelt before a charred circular spot where one of the fae peace seals should have been.

"What the fuck?" Layla examined the mark. "Where did it go?"

I cast an illusion disguise and stepped across the line. The fae safe zone should have dispelled the illusion, but nothing happened. "The safe zone protection is gone."

"It's gone?" Layla frowned. "How in the hell is it gone?"

"No idea." I rubbed the black marks. "Only the fae can remove safe zone seals."

Layla rubbed her hands together. "Guess we can have our way with Bisbee and Dwight."

"I don't like this." I reached for my staff so I could scan the area with the scope, and grimaced when it wasn't there. "Be careful. We don't know what happened."

"I am being careful." Layla cocked her ear toward the building and narrowed her eyes. After a brief pause, she strode toward the building.

I flicked my fingers through a pattern and cupped my ear. Aside from the pitter-patter of rain and the echoes of distant traffic, I heard nothing. And that was troubling. At this time of night, the bar should have been hopping. Then again, Norna might have shut it down after we left.

Hugging the side of the building, we made our way toward the front. The hairs on the back of my neck began to rise. Layla slowed, stopped, and looked back at me.

"There's some seriously bad juju going on here," she whispered. "Someone or something is waiting inside."

"I feel it too." We had a choice to make. Either we went inside and found out what was going on, or we didn't end up dead like the curious cat.

Even Layla seemed to give it serious thought.

Shadows flickered around the perimeter of the parking lot and I realized we'd already gone past the point of no return. "We're surrounded."

Layla crouched like a panther and peered into the gloom. "Fuck me. I didn't see them."

I hadn't seen them, but I already knew who it was. "Oblivion guard." I straightened. "Let's go inside. I think someone wants to talk, or they would have attacked already."

Layla bared her teeth. "Let them attack."

"Talk first, fight later?" I have her a pleading look.

She stood and flipped off the darkness. "Hide all you want, fucking cowards."

"They're behind fae glamor. That's why we can't see them," I said. "Which means there are fae here."

"Can't you use fae glamor?" she said.

I shook my head. "Not easily. I don't have the juice to power it for long."

We strolled around the building and found the front door hanging open. We stepped inside and found what the fae wanted us to see. Bisbee and Dwight hung upside down from the rafters just inside the bar, their bodies so badly disfigured that I only knew who was who because of the height difference.

"Cute." Layla scanned the otherwise empty room. "Are you entertained?"

I couldn't see anyone, but the hairs on the back of my neck felt them watching me from in front and behind. Fae glamor not only hid them from sight but also prevented us from hearing them.

I was too busy studying the dead men to care about the fae. The wounds were consistent with blunt force trauma delivered by big, meaty fists. If I had to name a suspect, it'd be Targ. What I couldn't figure out was how he'd done it inside a safe zone, and why he'd hung the bodies instead of getting rid of them.

Bisbee and Dwight might have provided a way for us to track down Norna, so they'd been murdered and left like this as a warning. Which meant Torvin bet the odds that we'd escape. It also meant that Torvin knew how to disable a safe zone.

I ran a scenario through my head.

Torvin tells Norna that I'll probably find a way to escape. He doesn't want loose ends, so Bisbee and Dwight have to go. They return to the bar. Torvin somehow disables the safe zone. Targ knocks out Dwight and Bisbee with blows to their heads. They don't even see it coming. He brutalizes them and hangs the bodies. Torvin, Targ, and Norna leave before the fae arrive to investigate the disabled safe zone.

The removal of a safe zone seal would certainly warrant a visit from high fae and the Oblivion Guard, which meant Layla and I had just walked onto unprotected territory surrounded by people who'd love to see me dead or imprisoned.

CHAPTER 20

Since there was nowhere to go but forward, I strolled behind the bar and started mixing myself a drink. I tossed some ice in the blender, poured in rum and mango juice.

"Now that's what I'm talking about." Layla sat down. "I'll have one too, babe."

"You got it." I doubled the ingredients and started blender.

A section of the room shimmered, and an exasperated elf appeared. He put his hands on his hips and glared at me. "This is your reaction when you find a pair of corpses hanging from the ceiling?"

I stared unspeaking at him as I poured two glasses of mangorita.

Layla sipped on hers without glancing back. "Not bad, Cain. Could use a little more rum, though."

I plunked a curly straw into our drinks and took a sip of mine. It was a little too sweet, and Layla was right about the rum. I leaned my elbows on the bar and watched the elf for a moment. "I'm not interested in talking to you. The others can show themselves when they're ready for conversation."

The elf's face turned red. "How dare you take a demanding tone with me. You remain alive only at the indulgence of my masters."

"Oh, do I?" I took another sip of my drink.

Layla spun her barstool around and looked the elf up and down. "Look, we just came here for a drink. I don't know why you killed these guys, but it's none of our business."

I nodded and made a dismissive wave of my hand. "Just carry on. Don't let us interrupt."

A pale man with high cheek bones and ebony skin appeared. He was lean and muscular, his long hair worn in tight braids. "You've changed, Cain, and not for the better."

I bowed from force of habit. "Hello, Father."

"Greetings, son." His voice was deep and sonorous. Erolith and Beywin Sthyldor had adopted me after my parents were murdered. They'd led me to believe they were lesser fae and raised me as such, demanding I rise above my inferior genes and become something greater. I'd suspected for a long time they were more than what they claimed, and this only confirmed my suspicions.

"Your presence here is interesting, Father." My throat felt dry but sipping the mangorita seemed disrespectful. I hadn't seen or heard from my adoptive parents since leaving Feary over a decade ago. "I doubt a lesser fae would be sent to investigate the defilement of a safe zone."

"Your eyes and mind are keen as ever, Cain." He walked across the space between us and stopped. "What do you know about this matter?"

As usual, he wasn't one to dwell on personal connections or just how fucked up it made me feel to see the man who'd raised me after such a long time. The vulnerability I felt in his presence was a conditioned response, nothing more. I respected my adoptive parents, but love was not a factor.

I forced myself to take another sip of my drink, just to prove I could, and reined in my emotions. Erolith might be my adoptive father, but that didn't mean I was safe. "I don't know anything about this...matter." I glanced up at the bodies. "We came here for drinks and noticed the peace seal was gone. I didn't realize such a thing was possible."

Erolith watched me closely. Most fae were playful in their dealings with humans, looking for opportunities to trick them into lopsided deals. My father wasn't a typical fae, which was probably why he was High Overseer of the Oblivion Guard.

"Humans abuse truth without shame." He continued to watch me. "You did not park your vehicle in the normal place, choosing instead for a stealthy approach from the rear. I believe you were coming to see these men."

"That's quite a stretch." I drained half my drink with the next pull and wished I'd used a hell of a lot more rum. "We were sneaking here because Torvin Rayne was seen here looking for me. If you want to find the person who destroyed the seal, I'd recommend starting with him."

"Torvin Rayne." Erolith spoke the name with some reverence. "Despite his failures, he is a man of honor. Desecrating a peace seal is beneath him."

"You always were blind with admiration for him." I shook my head. "He ordered the murder of innocent woman and children. Nothing was sacred when it came to winning the war then, and nothing is sacred when it comes to exacting his revenge on me." I straightened from my slump and shook my head. "You know it to be true."

"Torvin knew what had to be done," Erolith said. "His methods won the war."

"But at what cost?" I scoffed. "Not that human life means anything to you."

"Humans of Gaia are mere shadows of their predecessors, and those shadows pale and weaken with every generation." He clasped his hands behind his back. "There are whispers that you seek a way to break bargains with the gods so you might free the demi, Hannah. Does your meeting here pertain to that quest?"

Erolith was nothing if not perceptive. He'd probably created and discarded a dozen theories already, each one successively closer to the truth. I had no plans to fill in the blanks for him.

"The only quest I'm on is finding the perfect mangorita." I finished off my drink. "If you'll excuse us, we need to get going."

He shook his head. "You will return with me to Feary and answer my questions."

"No, I won't." I scanned the room, wishing I could detect the number of guardians hiding behind glamor. The normal contingent would be six outside, six inside. Erolith went by the book. After all, he'd written it. "I reached a bargain with the queens about my past crimes. You can't force me to return to Feary."

"You're the primary suspect in new crimes, Cain." Erolith watched impassively. "I am obligated to arrest you for further investigation."

"I already told you I don't know how these men died." I walked around the bar and prepared myself for a fight. "Let us go in peace, or we will use whatever means necessary to leave."

"Just a minute." Layla set down her drink and stood. "Am I being arrested too, or just Cain?"

"Are you for real?" I threw her a nasty look. "You're going to abandon me?"

"There is no reason to detain you," Erolith told her.

Layla nodded. "That's what I needed to hear." She went behind the bar, grabbed a couple bottles of clear liquor and headed for the door. "Good luck, Cain."

I wanted to curse her, but I couldn't really blame her. The odds of defeating six guardians were low, and she didn't really have a horse in this race. Layla was along for the joyride, but even she had limits as to what she'd do for fun. So, I watched her go and said nothing. Once she was clear, I'd make my move.

Layla abruptly swung around and threw the liquor bottles to the left and right, smashing them on the floor. A pair of blades blurred from her hands, each one cleaving through the incendiary bullets she'd placed in the bottles. Flames leapt six feet into the air, leaving a narrow path to the door.

I powered my sigil tattoos and ran.

All around me, brightblades blazed to life, but the phosphorous blaze was too hot even for guardians to simply jump through. I dashed through the door right behind Layla. She cackled with glee as we ran outside. But we weren't free and clear yet.

Shadows flitted from the dark. Oblivion staffs flared to life and guardians converged on us from both sides, three in each group. I whipped out my dueling wands and cast a series of small shields on our left flank. Small and nearly invisible, they tripped up the first guardian. The second one waved his staff, smashing through the hidden obstacles.

Layla and I slipped down the right side of the building just ahead of the other three guardians. I cast another gauntlet of shields, making the pursuers veer around the obstacles. I sent more power to my tattoos, urging as much speed from my legs as possible, but the guardians, identities hidden behind their hoods and masks, were gaining.

Most guardians were elves or lesser fae, meaning they had a physical advantage over humans. Without my sigil tattoos, they'd have caught me easily. Even now, I was still at a disadvantage.

"We can't go to the car," I panted. "They'll catch us before we can start it."

"I'll go to the car, you lead them away," Layla said.

"Really? That's your plan?" Despite being in my best shape since my twenties, I couldn't run forever.

"Just keep running down the road, okay?" Layla veered off toward the car, and I began running the fastest marathon of my life down the empty street.

The guardians ignored Layla and continued after me. The other three I'd slowed earlier weren't far behind. My shadow grew larger and darker. I dodged to the side, narrowly avoiding a crackling ball of light intended to knock me out. I cast a volley of brilliant flares behind me. The guardians shielded their eyes, giving me a chance to slip down a street to the right.

One of them dropped to a knee and aimed through the scope on his staff. I dove for cover behind a big, blue mailbox. The longshot spell ripped through the metal and showered the air with burning mail. Heat washed across my body. I rolled to the side, pushed up, and ran.

He and others were already lining up another shot. I fired another round of flares to blind them and made for the corner of a closed convenience store. Three more shots streaked through the night air. One shattered a window. Another cracked into a shield I threw up at the last instant. The last blasted through a gas pump.

Gasoline ignited. Flames shot into the air from the ruins of the pump. Curiosity wanted me to wait around to see if the entire gas station exploded, but survival instinct kicked me in the ass and got me moving again.

My SUV skidded around the back of the store, nearly ramming into me. I gave Layla a dirty look and hopped into the passenger side. She spun the steering wheel, guiding the vehicle through a one-eighty, and peeled out. Another shot from a staff slammed into the side of the SUV, shearing off part of the roof and rocking the vehicle so hard it teetered on two wheels for a moment.

Layla wrestled it back onto the road and floored the accelerator. "Your daddy doesn't like you much, does he Cain?"

"I don't think he likes anything." I buckled in and grabbed the oh-shit handle as Layla took a corner and got us up on two wheels again. "His focus is on duty, not emotion."

"That's for damned sure." She checked the rearview mirror and slowed. "I think we lost them."

"Hardly," I said. "They might have tagged the car with a spell. We'll need to ditch it to be safe."

"Fake license and title?" she asked.

I nodded. "Of course. Head downtown. We'll leave it there."

Layla snorted. "Won't be anything left to find even if they do track it."

"That's the point." I looked behind us but saw no signs of pursuit. Since the guardians had chased me so far on foot, it would probably take them a few minutes to get back to their cars to continue the pursuit. Even if the SUV was tracked, we had a good lead on them.

A half hour later, we pulled off the interstate and drove through downtown Atlanta. I didn't know if we were in a high-crime area, but decided it was as good a place as any to abandon the car. We hopped out and left the keys in the ignition, then jogged through side streets and alleys until we were a good distance away.

I got my bearings and headed to a parking garage in central downtown. We probably could have called an Uber, but I didn't feel like waiting around. I punched in a code to unlock the pedestrian entrance and we climbed stairs to the second level where I pulled the cover off a motorcycle.

"Damn, Cain, I'm impressed." Layla smacked the seat of the cruiser. "You've got backups for backups."

I reconnected the positive lead to the battery and hoped it still had enough charge to start. "The problem with so many vehicles is that I can't possibly keep up with maintenance." Like the SUV, the battery was dead, so I started the bike with a jolt from my wand. I hopped on and Layla climbed on behind me.

She wrapped her arms around my chest and leaned her head on my shoulder. "This is so romantic, Cain. Can we go on a picnic?"

I snorted. "Yeah, and we'll make love, get married, and have kids."

"Sounds wonderful." She pinched my nipple hard enough to make me wince. "I hope you like it rough."

"I'm obviously a glutton for punishment since I hang out with you." I gunned the engine and drove us down the ramps and out of the parking lot. I wanted to go to the airport to retrieve Dolores, but that would have to wait until tomorrow. Instead, I headed straight home.

First thing I did when I went inside was to check on Hannah. She wasn't in her room or anywhere upstairs. I went into the basement and found her slumbering on the floor with a pile of blankets and pillows. I assumed she took up residence below because Fred didn't come down here. I didn't want to wake her, so I went back upstairs and turned on my computer.

Torvin might be devious, but he disdained nubs and their technology. I was hoping that meant the remote-control software on my phone was still active. I always loaded the app on my personal phones in case I lost one.

I logged onto a website and checked the status of the software. The GPS was disabled since I turned it off whenever I wasn't using the maps app. I turned it on. While I waited for the location, I accessed the files on my phone and downloaded the pictures I'd taken in Horatio's lab. The GPS pinged a hotel in Budapest, Hungary. Either they hadn't gone far, or they'd taken what they needed from the phone and left it behind.

Once I'd transferred all the files and texts from my phone, I wiped them. There was nothing personal on it that would lead them back to my house, so I left the operating system intact in case they still had the phone. Tracking them would certainly be useful. My phone used a simulated SIM chip, enabling it to use any cell phone system without actually paying for service. I switched the SIM information so anything else sent to that phone number wouldn't go to the stolen phone.

I activated the microphone and camera for a live feed of the surroundings. A dimly lit white ceiling with crown molding appeared on my screen. If the GPS location was correct, it was the Iberostar Grand Hotel in downtown Budapest. Aside from a few background noises, there was only silence. It was nearly three in the morning over there, six hours ahead of us. It was possible Norna and Torvin were asleep.

I set the remote software to record audio and video whenever it detected sound or motion. It would upload the clips to cloud storage so I could watch it anytime. With that set, I disconnected from the phone software so it would conserve the battery. I opened the desk drawer and pulled out another phone identical to the last. Once it turned on, I programmed the software SIM to receive calls from my usual number.

Layla hovered over my shoulder. "Nifty. If they're there, maybe we should ambush them."

"Maybe." I went through the pictures I'd downloaded and paused at the aerial view of Oblivion. I went over the options in my head and felt optimistic about our chances.

Layla raised an eyebrow. "Why are you smiling, Cain?"

"Because I know how we can get back my staff." I got up and stretched. "Get some sleep. Tomorrow is going to be a big day."

CHAPTER 21

I woke late the next morning—hardly a surprise given the lack of sleep during our time in Romania. Hannah raced upstairs, drawn by the odors of breakfast, and delivered a bone-crushing hug.

"I was so worried when I hadn't heard anything, Cain." She separated herself from me. "What happened?"

"Everything went to shit, babe." Layla sashayed out of the guest room in nothing but a t-shirt and socks. She cracked a yawn and dropped onto the couch.

I groaned. "Gods, Layla, would it kill you to not sit your bare ass on my leather couch?"

"Yeah, it would." She pulled a blanket over her lap. "I'd think you'd be grateful to see me prancing around half-naked."

"I think it's disgusting." Hannah wrinkled her nose. "I mean, you barely bathe as it is."

Layla flipped her off and smirked. "What's for breakfast?"

"The usual." I rolled the sausages in the cast-iron pan and scrambled eggs in the other cookware. "Things went great in Romania," I told Hannah. "Up to a point."

Layla guffawed. "That's one way of putting it."

Hannah grimaced. "So, something went wrong."

"Horribly wrong." Layla sighed. "But I still had fun."

Hannah rolled her eyes. "Your idea of fun is probably torturing small animals."

Layla scoffed. "I'm not a monster, babe."

"We infiltrated the castle and found the map," I said, "but Norna betrayed us during the escape. Turns out she's working for Torvin Rayne."

Hannah gasped. "That asshole who made you kill all those people?"

"The very same," I said.

Layla looked at her phone and smirked. "We've got another breakfast guest coming."

I held up a spatula threateningly. "Who?"

"Your sweet little elf." Layla cackled. "She texted me since she never got a response from you."

I checked my new phone and saw several unread texts. I'd muted notifications before going to sleep and hadn't turned back on the sound. I read through the string of messages from Aura, each one progressively using all caps and multiple exclamation points to illustrate her exasperation with me for not responding.

"Where is she?" I asked.

Layla smirked. "Almost to the gate."

"Fuck me." I motioned Hannah over. "Can you finish cooking?"

"You got it, bro." She took the spatula. "Want me to annihilate Layla while I'm at it?"

I snorted. "Nah, she comes in handy sometimes."

Layla scowled. "You talk big for a demi who can't control her powers."

"Just piss me off and see how much control I have," Hannah said.

Layla scoffed and went back to staring at her phone screen.

I went outside and drove the motorcycle to the gates at the edge of the forest. A compact car pulled onto the dirt road a moment later and Aura stepped out of the back door. She saw me and frowned. "Where's Dolores?"

"At the airport." I patted the cushy cruiser seat. "Hop on."

The Uber driver gave me a dubious look and quickly drove off when Aura closed the door.

"What happened in Romania, Cain?"

I turned off the ignition and put down the kickstand. "We got what we went for, but Norna betrayed us and stole my staff and phone."

Aura blinked. "How in the hell did neither you nor Layla see that coming, especially when you knew Bisbee and the others were plotting something?"

"Because Norna works for Torvin Rayne."

Her mouth dropped open. "How did he find you? I did everything I could—" Aura flinched as if she'd said too much.

"You blacklisted me from Eclipse and banned me from Voltaire's to keep me out of sight, out of mind from Torvin?" I chuckled. "What made you think that would work?"

"It would have if you hadn't run around town running your mouth at every bar!" Aura threw up her hands. "Torvin lured you to Shipwreck and pulled a double-con on you."

"I never saw it coming," I admitted. "I figured it was a normal con, but Norna did a great job playing all of us."

"The classic triple-cross." Aura shook her head. "Well, at least you survived so far. Tell me what happened."

I told her everything leading up to the present.

"I can't believe you're still breathing, Cain." Aura reached into her satchel and withdrew three folders. "Bisbee and Dwight are—were—con artists. I couldn't find a connection between them and Norna, but now it's clear why."

"She hired them to help her con me," I said. "That was why everything felt staged." I frowned. "What I don't get is how Torvin destroyed the fae peace seal or why he'd go through the trouble to kill Bisbee and Dwight inside Shipwreck."

"I think Bisbee and Dwight refused to leave the safe zone until they were paid," Aura said. "As for destroying a fae peace seal, it has been done before so an assassin could reach a hard target."

I blinked. "You knew it was possible?"

"I've known it for years." She shrugged. "It's a method of last resort, because you guarantee bringing down the unholy wrath of the fae when you do it."

"Tell me how it's done."

Aura shook her head. "You don't need to know, Cain."

I pressed my lips into a flat line. "Fine. Tell me about Norna."

Aura held up the thinnest of the three folders. "Her family led the slave trade in Feary. They dealt in gryphons, hippogryphs, cecrops—pretty much any sentient beasts they could get their hands on. They even ran human and elf slave rings."

"There were no fae laws prohibiting slaves," I said. "At least not until I forced their hand with the rebellion."

"The Beast Rebellion." Aura's face went cold. "It was a brilliant move, raising an army of downtrodden creatures just to save yourself."

I wanted to refute her statement, but she wasn't wrong. Something good had come out of selfish motivations, but that didn't make it admirable. "So, what you're saying is Norna is out for revenge too."

She nodded. "When the slave trade ended, some ogre tribes blamed her family for not stopping you. She and her brother, Targ, left Feary and came here. She purchased Shipwreck with the money she had left. Torvin probably identified her as an ideal ally. You've been making so much noise around town lately in your quest to free Hannah that you gave them the ideal opportunity to lure you in. So, they hired Bisbee and Dwight to concoct a plan."

"Sounds like you've got it all figured out." Admittedly, her theory was sound. "Why do you think they killed Bisbee and Dwight?"

"They probably got greedy," Aura said. "Maybe tried to blackmail them for more money or a cut of the haul from the armory."

I took the folders. "Thanks for the intel. I'll let you know when we have more." I turned back to the bike.

Aura grabbed my arm. "Hey, you're not leaving me out here."

I was about to respond when the roar of a diesel engine caught my attention. A big black truck with giant chrome bumper and a confederate license plate veered off the main road and screeched toward us. I leapt toward Aura, knocking her out of the way at the last instant. The truck plowed into my motorcycle. Metal crunched and the bike tumbled into the woods.

Wands out, I powered my tattoos and smashed the tinted windows with a spell as the truck reversed to make another pass. I blindly hurled spell after spell of crackling energy into the cab. A man screamed and leapt out the driver's door, his clothes in flames. He fell to the ground still screaming, burning, arms flailing wildly until he went still.

I recognized the gray robes. Even burnt, I knew the face all too well. I booted the still-smoking body over onto its back and scowled. "No one has this many identical siblings." I used a wand to slice open what was left of the cloth and revealed the torso. There were four scars on the ribs.

Aura stood beside me, face red. "He almost killed me!"

"Sorry." Smoke drifted from the inside of the pickup, but the leather hadn't caught fire. I opened the door and looked inside. It was a roomy crew cab—the kind people bought for looks and never used for work. A bloodied body lay on the floorboard in the back. I opened the rear passenger door for a better look. It was the body of a white male wearing a plaid shirt and jeans. He looked like a good old boy. His throat had been slashed with a knife and cauterized shut with a wand to keep bleeding to a minimum.

"Fuck this shit." I shut the door and hauled the burned body by the feet to the back of the pickup. The flesh had cooled quickly in the cold morning air, so I lowered the tailgate and tossed it into the bed. "Get in."

Aura wrinkled her nose but climbed into the smoky pickup. "Smells like burnt hair."

"Wonder why." I lowered all four windows and drove the pickup past the wreckage of my bike. I'd have to come back later to clean up the mess. I parked the truck in front of the church and opened all four doors to let it air out.

With the assassin being dead, there wasn't a lot of time to do what I needed to do. I ran inside and grabbed my utility belt.

"Cain, what's wrong?" Hannah turned off the stovetop and followed me out.

I went to the assassin's body, jammed a needle into the carotid artery, and drew blood. I found a flat spot on the ground and cleared it of leaves, then traced a sigil in the dirt. I put a spot of blood in the middle, focused my will, and powered the pattern.

It was a simple tracking spell, and it might not even work. But if I didn't try to find out where these guys were coming from, they'd eventually get lucky and kill me. I sensed a strong pulling sensation in the direction of the body, nothing else. The spell would remain active for a few hours, gradually weakening as the blood cells died, and crimson turned to black.

I drew another vial of blood and pocketed it.

Layla scoffed. "Cain, you're tracking a dead man."

Aura groaned. "Gods, Layla, put on some pants!"

Layla snorted. "Don't like what you see, babe?"

"Not in front of a kid."

Hannah pshawed. "I've seen worse, believe me."

As their banter continued, I checked the pockets of the dead redneck for an ID. His name was George Jones and his address was in Dalton, over an hour north. I checked the dead man's cell phone and found texts to a spouse. I read through them and pieced together that he worked somewhere on the southeast side of the perimeter. His last text was to a construction company about thirty minutes ago. The assassin had waylaid him sometime after that last text and driven over here to find me.

There'd been no doubt after the airplane incident that the assassins could track me whenever I was outside the protection of the fae magic that hid the church. Sooner or later, they'd narrow down where I lived. Then the entire family of identical siblings would attack the moment I left the gate.

I considered the possibility that this man worked for Torvin and immediately discounted it. The assassin brothers had been anything but subtle in their clumsy attempts to kill me. Considering how they blindly threw themselves at me, I had to assume there were more—maybe a whole brood of them. As much as I hated to do it, there was only one way to put a stop to them, and that was to use fae magic I'd learned from Torvin.

But the assassin brothers would have to remain on the backburner for now. We had to beat Torvin and Norna to Oblivion, and that meant leaving today or tomorrow at the latest. I was concerned that tomorrow would be too late. I wiped away the sigil in the dirt and the pulling sensation vanished.

Aura looked at the scars on the dead man's ribs. "I wonder what caused this."

Layla bent over the man, literally exposing her ass crack. "Looks like a scalpel cut. Maybe surgery of some kind." She produced a folded knife out of nowhere.

Hannah gagged. "Where were you hiding that?"

"Calm your tits, babe." Layla flicked out the blade and slashed open the scarred area. Thick blood welled from the wound.

Hannah turned away gagging.

Aura watched with concern and fascination. "Are you playing doctor now?"

Layla exposed the guts and poked around inside. "Looks like his appendix was removed."

"Wow, you solved the mystery!" Hannah slow clapped. "Now we just find the surgeon and we'll have the killer!"

I pursed my lips. "Everything about the attackers is identical except for this scar." I'd examined the other bodies, so I knew there weren't other scars. "Is there a way to clone people that I don't know about?"

Layla shook her head. "Never heard of a way."

"Me either," Aura said. "But the multiple scars must mean something."

I'd scanned the last guy with my true sight scope and hadn't noticed anything unusual. He had the aura of a mage, nothing more. But there was a pattern, albeit a simple one. "So far, this guy has attacked me once a day, but no more. If he has a small army of brothers, why wouldn't they all attack at once?"

Layla laughed. "Gods, you get into the weirdest shit, Cain."

"Yeah." I retrieved my shovel and dug a shallow grave next to the resting place of the last assassin.

"You going to bury the redneck here too?" Layla asked.

I shook my head. "I'll leave the truck somewhere for the nubs to find. Might as well let his family have closure."

Aura's eyebrows rose, but she said nothing.

"I think that's for the best," Hannah said. "If he just vanished without a trace, that would be torment for his loved ones."

Layla pinched my cheek. "You're so sweet, Cain." She spat on the ground and scoffed. "You're too soft. Why leave evidence that could lead them back to you?"

"Because it'll never lead back to me." I backed the pickup to the grave and rolled the assassin's body inside, then used a hose to wash the blood out of the truck bed. My stomach rumbled, reminding me that in all the excitement I still hadn't eaten.

We went inside and had breakfast, much to Layla's amusement.

"The family's all together again." She made eye contact with my and licked the tip of a sausage suggestively. "Maybe Aura will give you a pity fuck while she's here, Cain."

"Maybe you'll choke on that sausage," Hannah shot back.

I ignored them and ate my sausage in peace.

Tentacles stretched up and over the back of the couch. Fred pulled himself onto the top of the couch. His golden eyes clouded black and I felt the gaze of Cthulhu upon us.

Hannah whimpered and shrank away from the octopus even though she was sitting a distance away at the table. Layla extended a middle finger in Fred's general direction without looking up from her food.

I said nothing and let Cthulhu watch. If he had something to say, he'd say it. I just hoped he didn't know Layla and I were the ones piloting the submarine through his domain. If he decided to send an army of minions to blockade the deepways, our path to Oblivion would be cut off.

CHAPTER 22

Fred extended a tentacle toward Hannah and summoned her. She gulped, but obeyed, taking the tentacle in her hand. Her eyes glazed over, and she went still. Moments later, she blinked and wiped tears from her cheeks. Fred's eyes returned to golden once more and he retreated to his pool.

I was almost afraid to ask, but I had to know. "What did he want?"

Hannah returned to the table. "A progress report."

"You've barely been here two days."

She shrugged. "I told him I was training."

"That fucker." I finished eating. "Layla, we've got to go shopping."

She leaned back in her chair. "For what?"

"Clothing that'll hold up in Oblivion." I rinsed my plate and put it in the sink. "We'll need oxygen masks and tanks."

Layla frowned. "Gods, is it really that bad?"

"Might be worse," I said. "The world is a wasteland."

I turned to Aura. "Maybe it's time you got your hands dirty too."

She returned my stare. "I'll come."

"Can I come too?" Hannah said.

I almost said no, but there were reasons it might be good for her to ride along. When she touched her power, she sometimes saw visions of Oblivion. I wondered if a visit there might help her unlock her abilities.

I nodded. "Yeah. The whole family is going."

Hannah clapped her hands. "Yay!"

I didn't think she'd be cheering for long once we got there. "Let's hit the road. We've got a lot to do."

Once the food was put away and the table cleaned, we piled into the pickup. I put the corpse of the truck owner in the bed of the pickup and covered it with a tarp. I made Aura and Layla sit in back, much to Hannah's delight. When we were nearly at the airport, I pulled off an exit and parked the truck in the lot of a rundown shopping center.

I called an Uber and we walked a short distance to meet it. The driver arrived in a compact car even though the app said it was a full-sized sedan. I took the front seat and let the ladies squeeze into the back.

Hanna made a face shortly after we got underway. "Jesus, Layla, did you fart?"

"Smells like an elf fart to me," Layla said.

The driver snorted with mirth, then gagged as the odor reached him. He rolled down the windows without saying a word.

"Fucking elf farts," Layla said.

Aura rolled her eyes. "Elves don't fart."

Layla scoffed. "Give me a break. Elves fart all the time."

At this point, the driver didn't seem to know if we were joking or seriously deranged. He sped up and we reached the airport parking lot well ahead of schedule. I gave him an extra tip for his troubles, and we went to retrieve Dolores.

When we found her, I lovingly ran my hand down her sleek exterior and savored the smell of her vinyl interior when I slid inside.

Layla smirked. "Is that your O face, Cain?"

I nodded. "Yeah, it is."

Layla turned her smirk on Aura. "I'll bet he didn't even make that face when he boned you, did he?"

"No, it was much more intense." Aura smirked back at her. "Like he just penetrated an angel."

"Jesus, you two are nasty!" Hannah covered her ears. "Can't you talk about anything normal for once?"

I was just happy to be reunited with Dolores. I paid the parking fee and left the airport. Our first stop was a military supply store. There was nothing magical about the gear there, but it'd work just fine. There were magical ways to deal with bad environments, but the gear was hard to come by and only sold by a couple of shops. Word would probably get around our small community, gear and likely reach Torvin's ears, that the infamous Cain was purchasing environmental.

It wasn't worth taking the chance.

Getting Layla and Aura to try on jumpsuits was worse than herding cats. Layla wanted something skintight and Aura didn't want a jumpsuit at all. They were made of rugged material, slightly baggy, and meant to endure rough treatment, so they weren't the most comfortable or stylish outfits in the world, but they'd protect us from the harsh environment.

I purchased portable oxygen canisters and army-style backpacks with water storage to haul our gear. We loaded everything into Dolores and then went to the sporting goods store next. If the armory was beneath Mount Olympus, it was possible we'd need climbing and spelunking gear. I purchased several hundred feet of rope, another portable drill, and plenty of anchors.

I also snagged new camping gear and coolers. After stocking up on food at a nearby grocery store, we were ready to go.

Layla looked at the growing pile in the back of the car as we loaded it. "You don't mess around do you?"

"It's not like Oblivion is a hop, skip, and a jump away," I said. "We need to be over-prepared, because we can't just run back to the store if we need something."

"That's what scouting missions are for," Layla said.

"We don't have time to scout Oblivion," I said. "Maybe we'll get there and nothing I've purchased helps, but it's better than nothing."

We ate sandwiches on the drive up to Lake Lanier. I parked Dolores next to the dock to make for easier loading.

"Wow!" Hannah stared at the sail protruding above the water. "I can't believe we're going on a submarine ride."

"This was made by mechanists?" Aura didn't look convinced.

"Crazy, right?" Layla hauled some backpacks to the hatch and opened it. "Now, stop ogling our submarine and get to work."

Aura sighed and retrieved more supplies from the car. Once we finished loading up, I parked Dolores in the garage, kissed her hood goodbye, and headed to the submarine. Layla took the helm again and started backing us out of the dock.

"I want to name my submarine," Layla announced.

"You're really letting Layla drive?" Aura said.

Layla raised an eyebrow. "That's Captain to you, elf."

Aura groaned. "Really, Cain?"

I saluted. "Captain Layla is in control."

Hannah frowned. "I thought it was your submarine."

"We both stole it," I said. "Technically, it belongs to both of us."

"I still get to name it," Layla said.

Aura sighed. "I'm sure it'll be a perfectly tasteless name."

Layla scoffed. "Better than Dolores, that's for sure."

Hannah stood before the huge dome window in the nose, mouth hanging open as we sped through the depths of the lake. "This is so badass. I can't wait to see what the ocean looks like."

"Just pray we don't have to see another giant squid," Layla said.

I was more than a little worried about another encounter. Cthulhu knew someone had invaded his deepways, which meant he might have stationed guards in the one where we'd killed the squid. I activated the whale song when we reached the hidden entrance and the bed of the lake parted into four sections.

"Everyone strap in. You don't want to be standing when we hit that vortex." I pointed to the other seats located around the room.

Hannah and Aura buckled up.

Layla took us into the vortex and we shot forward.

"Wow!" Hannah cried out. "This is terrifying!"

Aura gripped the sides of her seat with white-knuckled intensity, jaw clenched tight.

Moments later, we emerged in the tunnel chamber off the eastern seaboard and the others breathed easy once more.

"Oh my god!" Hannah pointed at a massive creature a few hundred feet away. She unbuckled and ran to the main window.

The creature stared back with dead eyes. It was the same squid we'd killed yesterday. I looked up and around the chamber but saw no army of monsters waiting to attack. Either Cthulhu hadn't had a chance to send minions to investigate, or he simply didn't care.

I didn't know his reasons, but it was good for us. Even without an army to fight, our next step was only marginally less difficult. The deepways map lacked details. In order to chart a path to the omega symbol, I had to know which tunnels to take.

Aura looked at the map for a moment, then left us and started fiddling with the globe.

"How in the hell are we supposed to use this map?" Layla shook her head. "It's useless."

Aura grunted thoughtfully. "That's because it's just a rough sketch, not an actual map." She motioned us over and pointed to a location on the globe.

I found a tiny omega symbol near her fingertip. "I didn't notice that last time."

"Having the visual acuity of an elf helps." Aura reached under the lower axis and flipped something. Tiny pinpoints lit up all over the globe, projecting coordinates and symbols on the wall and ceiling. Aura rotated the globe, pausing each time an omega symbol projected on the wall.

"There are three of them," Layla said.

Aura nodded. "Three different ways to Oblivion." She stopped on one in the middle of the Atlantic Ocean. "The closest is this one."

Layla shrugged. "How does this help us find it?"

Aura pressed the symbol. The globe rotated with the clicking of clockwork until the omega symbol projected on a small, flat section of wall near the nose of the sub. Gears inside the globe clanked and ground to a halt.

Hannah's forehead pinched. She looked at the symbol on the wall and back at the globe. "Uh, what does that mean?"

Aura pursed her lips and approached the wall. She studied the angle of the projection and the wall for a moment, then nodded as if reaching a conclusion. "There's a tiny pinhole in the wall here. It's made of the same transparent material as the main window."

Layla stared at her. "And?"

Aura twirled a finger. "Rotate the sub a few degrees to the left and up."

Layla shifted a lever and turned the wheel. The globe clanked, rotating with the sub.

"A little more to the left." Aura held up two fingers spaced a little apart. "Up a little more."

Layla adjusted once more, and the globe rotated. A beam of light appeared in the water, pointing to one of the tunnels ahead.

Layla grinned. "The elf is useful after all."

Awesome!" Hannah pressed her face to the window. "You line up the globe and then follow the light."

I scoffed. "A GPS and computer tablet would be so much better." I almost asked Layla to engage the engines, but she whipped her gaze toward me the moment I raised my hand.

Layla held her deadpan stare on me even as she shifted the acceleration lever forward and followed the beam. After a moment, she nodded. "That's what I thought."

I rolled my eyes. "Everyone strap back in."

The target vortex took us into another chamber. We crossed it, rotated to the left a few degrees, and followed the beam of light to the next tunnel.

Hannah left the window and leaned against my chair. "Dude, this is so cool. How many people have their own submarines?"

"It's mine," Layla said. "Not his."

I pshawed. "It is pretty cool having *our* own submarine."

With the guiding light at our helm, it didn't take long to reach our destination. The tunnel leading to Oblivion was marked with a red omega symbol. I stared at it for a long time and for once, Layla seemed to be awaiting my command.

"What's wrong, Cain?" She watched me carefully.

"I have no idea what's waiting on the other side."

"Why don't we use a drone to check?" Aura said.

I blinked. "A drone?"

"Yeah." She tapped a lever. "Judging from the image engraved on the console, this thing releases a clockwork drone." Aura waggled a joystick in the center of the console. "This controls it wirelessly."

"Wireless technology?" I snorted. "I can't believe the mechanists actually use that."

Aura shrugged. "Want to give it a try?"

I nodded. "Go for it."

She pulled the lever. Something clanked above. A brass projector mounted on the ceiling above Aura's station flickered on, projecting a blank image against a screen on the bulkhead to her left. Static filled the screen and then changed to a view of the submarine's hull.

"An old-school movie projector? How quaint." Layla rolled her eyes. "These mechanists are worse than hipsters."

Aura moved the joystick and the image rotated. Using levers and the joystick, she guided the drone in front of the main window. The remote vehicle was four feet wide and two feet thick. There were two propellers mounted on the front, and two on the back. It resembled a quadcopter except it was also submersible.

I tapped a finger on my chin. "I think that's how they took the aerial shots of Oblivion."

"Let's see if it works across distances." Aura aimed the drone at the vortex and took it through. The vehicle shot forward and vanished. The projector image showed it rushing through the water, but the image filled with more and more static until there was nothing but white noise on the screen.

I sighed. "The signal can't reach that far."

"Yeah, well that's because it's on another world," Layla said. "We'll just have to go through ourselves."

"What if the mechanists haven't gone through themselves?" I bit my lower lip and stared at the vortex. "Maybe they have long-range probes for that."

"We've got no choice." Layla put her hands on her hips. "Either we go, or we chicken out and go home."

I walked to the forward window and stared out at the vortex. Surely there was water on the other side. If it was an open gateway to Oblivion, then water flowed from here to there and back. Then again, there might be an impermeable barrier that didn't allow water through and we'd be spit out onto dry land. If that happened, we'd have no way of returning without my staff.

But if we didn't reach Oblivion ahead of Torvin and Norna, we had little chance of laying a trap and retrieving my staff. So the question was, if we encountered the worst-case scenario on the other side, what were our odds of defeating Torvin and getting back home?

I met Layla's questioning gaze, moved over to Aura's impassive face, and then to Hannah's concerned frown. All of this was for her. She traded her life for mine, and that was a debt I'd repay, even if it meant losing my own life in the process. I hated to think about it, but it might be better for Hannah to die trying than returning to her life as a minion of Cthulhu.

Layla and Aura had their own agendas. They knew the risks, or they wouldn't be here.

I walked back to the captain's chair and sat down.

"We going or not?" Layla asked.

I motioned forward. "Make it so."

"Make what so?" Layla tapped on the acceleration lever. "This?"

I groaned. "You ruined the moment. Full speed ahead, Captain Layla."

And damned be the consequences.

CHAPTER 23

Everyone strapped down and prepared for the worst. Layla shifted forward the acceleration lever and we barreled toward the throat of the vortex, the thrum of the clockwork engine vibrating the floor beneath my feet.

The whirling waters grasped the hull and yanked us inside the tunnel. Like a bottle caught in the current of a raging river, we sped through darkness illuminated only by the flood lights on the submarine hull. And then our destination came into view—a disc of pitch black, radiating brilliant white rays. A black hole drawing us into the crushing void.

I gripped the armrests. "Fuck my life."

"What the hell is that?" Layla yanked the acceleration controls into reverse, but it did nothing to slow us. The vortex plunged us relentlessly onward. She threw the lever into neutral to keep the engine from burning up and bared her teeth defiantly.

"Must be the gateway." Hannah didn't look worried. If anything, she almost looked relieved. She turned to me. "Thanks for everything, Cain."

The tone in her voice told me everything I needed to know. She was okay with dying. I nodded. "You're welcome, Hannah."

She smiled. "I like it when you say my name. Makes me feel like I was worth something to at least one person in this world."

Layla scoffed. "Oh, please. At least die with dignity."

"We're not going to die." Aura scowled and pounded her fist on the console. "So will you all shut up?"

And then we plunged into darkness.

The submarine shuddered so violently my teeth rattled along with anything that wasn't firmly secured. We emerged in a swirling vortex bathed in orange light that emanated from somewhere far ahead.

"See?" Aura growled. "Still alive!"

Layla scoffed. "That remains to be seen."

Hannah smiled at me and shrugged. "Maybe next time."

I nodded. "Yeah, maybe next time."

We shot from the tunnel. Massive stone columns loomed before us. Layla hissed and pulled back on a lever. The propellers churned in reverse. We slowed gradually, coming to a stop a few feet from the nearest column. Then everyone released a collective sigh of relief.

Layla backed us away from the column and steered us around it. "My gods. What the hell is that?"

Before us stood the remains of an underwater city, its broken bones covered in seaweed and coral. The architecture resembled that of ancient Greece, with domes and Corinthian columns as far as the eye could see. But what caught Layla's eye was even more impressive than the city itself. Hovering above the city was a fiery orange ball, a miniature sun that lit the ocean depths from one end of the ruined city to the other.

"Whatever it is, I don't like the looks of it," Aura said. She went to the window and looked down at the ocean floor. "That sun probably has something to do with sinking the city."

"There's no telling." I was just as impressed by it as the others, but it wasn't why we were here. "This world was the playground of the gods for thousands of years. One of them probably tired of toying with the city and decided to destroy it on a whim. Or there could have been a war among the gods and this city is just another casualty." I shrugged. "We're going to see a lot of inexplicable things here, but we need to keep our eyes on the prize, first and foremost."

Layla grunted. "If you say so. But I don't mind doing a little sightseeing. I could use some pictures for my scrapbook."

Aura turned to face us. "The next question we should answer is where in Oblivion are we?"

"Hey, look!" Hannah pointed to the projector screen. The white noise had been replaced by a steady image of the column we'd narrowly avoided. Apparently, the drone had stopped before smashing to bits.

Aura went to the console and tested the controls. The drone rotated to face the sub. "Perfect. I'll take this up for a look." She turned to Layla. "You might want to take us to the surface, so the water won't limit the range of the wireless."

"Yeah, sure, I might." Layla yawned. "But you've got to address me properly first."

Aura groaned. "Why does everything with you have to be a chore?"

"Because I'm worth it, babe." Layla smirked.

Aura's jaw worked back and forth, but she eventually spat out what Layla wanted to hear. "Captain Layla, please take us to the surface."

Layla's smirk widened to a grin. She spun in her chair, shifted a lever, and we began our ascent. We rose until we were above the underwater sun. We continued upward for several hundred meters before light from the sky filtered down to us. The rays from the sun above weren't yellow or orange, but a bluish white that made my eyes hurt.

When we bobbed to the surface, I had to shield my eyes from the harsh rays reflecting from the water. The dials on the console in front of Hannah began spinning. One of them showed the speed of the wind in knots. The other pointed to a temperature of over one hundred five degrees Fahrenheit.

"Man, it's toasty out there," Hannah said.

Aura was too busy manipulating the drone controls to turn around and see what we were talking about. The miniature submarine poked above the surface in front of the main window a moment later. The propellers rotated until they were horizontal then began spinning faster and faster until the drone rose into the air.

It flew off into the distance and we turned to the projector screen to watch its journey. Land came into view moments later, an arid wasteland of hard-packed earth, the broken remains of buildings protruding through the ground at random angles.

"The architecture is identical to the underwater city," Aura said. The other part must have been on a peninsula that fell into the ocean."

"Yeah, because someone tossed a mini-sun on top of it," Layla said. She pushed forward on the accelerator. "I'm taking us closer to shore."

I nodded and continued to watch the feed from the drone. Aura took it higher for a better view of the ruins. The remains of the city spanned miles along the shore and further inland. Giant craters pockmarked the land, as if the civilization had been carpet bombed by meteors.

"Talk about scorched earth," Layla said. "They weren't messing around when they destroyed this place."

Hannah turned to me. "Do you know how Oblivion was destroyed, Cain?"

I shook my head. "The only history the fae allowed us to read said the world was destroyed because of the greed of the gods. That's probably as close to the truth as we'll ever get."

Aura stopped the drone and rotated it in a circle for a view of the horizon. The display crackled with frequent static, meaning there was something in the atmosphere that wasn't friendly to radio waves. The possibilities were endless, but I imagined the radiation from the blue sun probably wasn't helping anything.

"There are mountains in the distance," Aura said. "Any idea what Olympus looks like or which direction we should go?"

I took out my phone and examined the picture I'd taken of the map then compared it to the view from the drone. "Take the drone higher and point the camera down at the ground."

She pulled back on one of the levers and the view shifted from the horizon to the ground below. Another lever adjusted the altitude and the ground began to recede in the distance. Keeping the control pulled toward her, she looked from the image to me. "Just say when."

Within a few minutes, the destroyed buildings began to look like the small white dashes and dots in the picture. I held up a hand. "That's enough." The image from the drone resembled the picture of the aerial map, but there were some key elements missing, primarily the large dome with the mark next to it.

"Angle the camera out a little and look for something like this." I showed her the picture of the big dome. "It should be somewhere up or down the coast."

"I'll take it north first." Aura pressed on the joystick and the drone moved forward. After a time, static began to interfere with the image from the camera. "We need to pace behind the drone. It's getting out of range," Aura said.

Layla turned the submarine and took us in the same direction. The feed from the drone cleared up again after a few minutes.

We continued up the coast for several miles, following the trail of the seemingly endless ruins of the ancient city. The city ended at a range of steep mountains. None of them resembled the volcano, and there was no blackened earth like in the photo.

Layla huffed. "Fifty-fifty chance and we went the wrong way."

I shrugged. "Back the other way, then."

Layla reoriented the submarine and Aura turned the drone around the other way.

Aura tapped one of the gauges on the control panel. "There's a strong headwind blowing from the south. The drone is struggling to fight it."

"That explains how it was going so fast," Hannah said.

I sighed. "Bring it back to us. We'll take it back to the starting point."

That process took a good thirty minutes. Then Layla piloted the sub down several miles of coastline and back where we'd started from.

I looked to the south through the main window, but the destroyed buildings along the shoreline blocked the southern horizon and thick haze hid the land from view. "Let's keep the drone onboard and scout the coast from the water." I checked the image to confirm the volcano was next to the shoreline. "I think we'll see the volcano from the water."

Layla pushed south at top speed.

Hannah tapped the red dots on the aerial image of Olympus Prime. "I still don't understand what these markings and numbers on the map mean."

"I think we established that they're not coordinates." I zoomed to the broken dome and the mark near it so I could puzzle over the numbers and letters. An arrow ran from the dot and pointed at the center of the dome. The numbers and letters were *.9nm .5f*. Then I scrolled to one of the dots marking the volcano. The numbers and letters next to it said *s43 a 181.2*. The numbers near the other dots were higher or lower.

Layla snapped her fingers. "Hey, I see a giant dome."

Sure enough, the remains of a massive dome, cracked and leaning like a broken egg, dominated the shoreline.

I pulled out my binoculars and zoomed in on the dome. The curve of the main window distorted it a little, but the building looked like the landmark in the aerial photo. A thick red line painted on the side of the dome stood out from the off-white hue of the marble. I handed my binoculars to Layla. "Does it look like that red line was recently painted on there?"

She took a look and nodded. "I wonder if that has something to do with the line on the map."

Aura and Hannah stood next to me and peered at the image on my phone.

"Hey, I know what that symbol means," Layla said. She walked to the cluster of gauges and dials next to the pilot controls and tapped on one of them. "This has that lower-case f on it." She tapped another. "And this one has the nm on it."

There was a lever next to the gauge with the f on it. "What does this do?"

"It raises and lowers the sub in the water," Layla said.

I pointed to the lever next to the gauge with nm on it. "And that one accelerates, right?"

She nodded. "But the nm number has only gone up. The f number goes up and down."

The f gauge read zero. I racked my brain for nautical terms.

"It's fathoms," Hannah said. "It's a measure of depth, I think."

Layla snapped her fingers. "I think nm stands for nautical miles."

Aura tapped the marker off the shoreline from the dome. "We need to position the submarine point nine nautical miles from the marker on the dome and lower the sub to half a fathom."

"How in the hell are we supposed to tell how far away we are?" Layla studied the other gauges and dials. "I don't see anything there that tells us."

Hannah pointed to the handles above the captain's chair. "What about the periscope?"

I pulled down the scope, flipped out the handles, and peered through it. A pair of fine red crosshairs sat in the center of the view. In the upper left corner, I noticed two rows of numbers six digits long etched in brass. Next to them were the markings *nm, a*. There was a compass with cardinal directions and numbers marking off degrees.

A knob on one side of the periscope aimed it higher or lower. The numbers next to the *a* rose or fell in response. It had to stand for altitude. The nautical mile marker remained at zeroes across the board. There was a button on the other side of the periscope. I pressed it. Gears clanked and a loud ping echoed outside. The numbers indicating nautical miles rotated. The first number stopped at one. The next one turned to a decimal point, and the next three were two, five and four.

I pulled away from the scope and grinned. "You're a genius, Hannah. I know what the numbers mean."

Her face brightened. "Really?"

I motioned her to the scope. "Take a look."

"Me first," Layla said. "I'm the captain."

I gave her a dirty look. "Don't you dare."

Hannah scowled at her. "You might be the captain, but I'm the demi-god."

Layla groaned. "Now she's pulling rank on me?"

Hannah looked through the scope, adjusted the knob, and pushed the button to ping the distance between us and the object in the crosshairs. She backed away and clapped her hands. "All we have to do is line up with the red line on the dome, get to the correct distance, and then we look through the scope at the altitude and directional degrees, right?"

I snapped my fingers. "Bingo."

Layla took her turn and nodded. "All right. I'll orient the sub. Tell me when we're in position." She went to the pilot's seat and maneuvered us even with the red line.

Using the scope, I directed her until we were at the precise location. Then she dropped the submarine to half a fathom. I rotated the periscope toward the volcano in the distance and zoomed in. I turned until the compass matched the degrees for the first marker, and then adjusted the upward angle until the altitude matched. The crosshairs pinpointed a red slash next to a crevice leading between piles of volcanic rock.

I homed in on the next set of numbers midway up the mountain. The crosshairs found another red marker next to a narrow ledge. The numbers for the third marker led to a small cave entrance several hundred feet from the previous marker.

"There's a path leading up to a cave," I said. "That must be the entrance to the armory."

"Great!" Layla rubbed her hands together. "Let's haul ass to shore and get going."

Something near the cave entrance glittered in the harsh blue light of the sun. I angled the periscope for a better view and zoomed in. The object was the broken remains of a drone identical to ours. The side of it appeared to have been slashed with giant claws. The remains of a second drone littered the side of the mountain.

Something dangerous had savaged those drones, and it would probably do the same to any intruders.

CHAPTER 24

"Not so fast." I stepped away from the scope. "I think there's a reason the mechanists didn't mount an expedition already."

"What do you mean?" Aura peered through the scope and frowned. "Something destroyed a drone."

I nodded. "Send our drone in for a look. We need to find out what it was."

Aura went to the controls and launched the drone. "I'm going to scout the cave first. We've only got two drones, and I don't want to waste them."

"Fine." I sat back in the captain's chair. "Let's see what's in there."

Aura nodded. "Can you take us closer to the mountain, Layla?"

Layla raised an eyebrow.

Aura sighed. "Captain Layla?"

"Of course, Crewman Elf." Layla turned and piloted us south along the shore. The beach transitioned from yellow sand to black a few miles out from the volcano. It was a testament to how long ago this city had been destroyed that the volcanic rock had mostly turned to sand.

Layla slowed the sub. "There's a slope in the ocean bed. Can't get us much closer without grounding the hull." She pulled a lever and dropped anchor to keep the submarine from drifting.

Aura launched the drone and took it up and toward the volcano. She angled the camera down for a look at the crevice leading between the rocks, then climbed higher toward the cave. The ledge leading to the cave was practically hidden among the jumbled rocks and craggy bushes dotting the slope. It seemed the mechanists had selected landmarks along the path to make it easier to find when they came back.

Layla held up a hand toward Aura. "Where's the rest of the path?" She looked at me. "How are we supposed to navigate that terrain if I can't even see the path?"

"It's probably clearer when we're on the ground," I said. "The mechanists are nothing if not precise as clockwork. If we follow the markers, we'll find the path."

"It's hidden between the volcanic rocks and rubble," Aura said. "But if there's a dangerous animal living near this mountain, then finding the path is the least of our worries."

I motioned toward the projector screen. "Take the drone inside the cave."

Aura rotated the drone and flew it to the cave opening. She lined up the view with the dark entrance and activated the floodlights. The light reflected off six glowing red orbs. There was a blur and the camera feed went black.

"Gods almighty!" Layla pointed out the main window as the remains of the drone scattered in the air and fell to earth.

"What did that?" Aura said. "It happened so fast I didn't see it."

I shook my head. "I don't know."

"Uh, we've got a problem if that thing is inside the cave we need to use," Hannah said.

"No, you think?" Layla smiled grimly. "We know where the beast is. Let's just go and kill it."

I went to the projector and opened the brass door on the side. There was old-school nine-millimeter film inside. I rotated a handle next to the spool and reversed the film, then flicked a switch to start playback.

The cave appeared on the screen again. When the floodlights turned on, I put my hand on the switch. The red eyes glinted in the darkness and lunged. I stopped the film. The image was blurry, but the being behind the attack was clear. It was nothing I'd ever seen before and had no idea how to fight it. It wasn't a beast of blood and bone, but a three-headed dog made of metal.

"Gods almighty, it's Cerberus!" Layla said.

I shook my head. "No. It's even worse than that. It's an automaton, a Mecha-Cerberus."

"A clockwork droid?" Aura grimaced. "It must have been created by Hephaestus to guard the armory."

"Yeah, probably." I stared at the frozen image, but it was hard to make out many details. The film began to bubble from being in front of the light for too long, so I flicked the switch and let it go frame-by-frame to see if the details became clearer. They didn't.

Layla rapped her fingernails on the console. "Okay, plan B. We let Torvin and Norna attack the clockwork hound. Maybe they'll kill each other."

"I like that idea," Aura said. "Very little risk to us."

"Yeah, except Torvin has a much better shot of dismantling that thing with my staff." I shook my head. "Granted, it won't be easy, but between him and Norna, they could probably cut the droid to ribbons."

"Then they'd have free access to the armory," Hannah said. "Maybe we could attack them while they're fighting the clockwork droid."

I gave that plan some thought. "The footing up there is treacherous enough already without trying to fight on it. Besides, there are better ways to handle this."

Layla raised an eyebrow. "I can't wait to hear this."

I rolled my eyes. "Oh, come on. You're Layla Blade, famed assassin. Since when do you take the most direct route to kill a target?"

"Almost never unless I'm feeling plucky." She narrowed her eyes. "I see where you're going with this. Let's trick the beast instead of confronting it."

I nodded. "If we can slip past it, then not only will Torvin have to fight it when he arrives, but we'll be inside with powerful new weapons, ready to ambush him."

Hannah clapped her hands. "That's brilliant!"

Aura nodded. "That's a plan I'd expect from you."

Layla slow clapped. "Even Cain has his moments, but how are we supposed to slip past the thing without losing our heads?"

"I've got an idea about that," I said. "I just have a couple of kinks to work out first."

Layla grunted. "Well, work them out fast, because Torvin's gonna be hot on our asses in a few hours."

I rewound the film spool and reviewed the terrain up to and around the cave. After careful study, I noticed bits and pieces of another destroyed drone littering the mountainside. Apparently, the metal beast had knocked it spinning out of the air and it crashed at the base. That meant the clockwork guardian remained in the cave.

It was a testament to the craftsmanship of Hephaestus that the thing was still functional after thousands of years. I wondered if he ever returned to perform maintenance on the droid, or if he'd long-since forgotten it even existed.

The footage of the mountain wasn't conclusive, but it gave me a rough idea of what to expect and how to possibly deal with Mecha-Cerberus. I went into the hold and gathered all the supplies I'd need into a backpack, then went back to the bridge and explained my plan to the others.

Layla didn't seem impressed. "You're going to lose your head along with your guts, Cain."

"He's not the cursed old man he used to be," Hannah said. "I think he can do it."

"Provided he doesn't botch it and end up falling off the mountain," Aura said.

"You sound just like Layla when you talk like that," Hannah told her.

Aura shrugged. "Just being realistic."

"Gear up." I motioned to the rear hold.

"It's over a hundred degrees outside," Aura said. "I don't think wearing heavy clothing is the answer."

"You don't want your skin exposed to the sun," I said. "There's not much ozone to protect us from the UV rays. Besides, the suits aren't that heavy. They're designed to wick moisture while protecting your skin."

Layla clapped Aura on the back. "Just wait until you see my ass in that outfit."

Aura rolled her eyes. "Your ass is not the golden standard, Layla."

"Uh, yes, it is." Layla pinched Aura's ass. "Weak sauce, babe." Then she went back into the hold.

Aura tried to peer at her own backside. "It is not weak sauce!"

"Your ass is perfectly fine," Hannah said.

Aura's chin trembled. "It's only just fine?"

I thought she had a cute ass, but I wasn't about to comment.

I followed Layla to where I'd stowed the equipment and slipped into my jumpsuit. The material was thin, stretchy, and a little tight in the crotch, but it was rugged and allowed freedom of movement. I pulled on gloves and applied heavy sunscreen to my neck and face. I'd brought full-faced high-altitude skydiving helmets with oxygen tubes, but I didn't want to have to wear those unless absolutely necessary.

I put on wrap-around shades and pulled on a wide-brimmed straw hat for extra shade. It looked like a little funny, but the straw wouldn't absorb sweat.

Layla took one look at me and guffawed. "Is it siesta time already, Cain?"

"Laugh all you want, but you'll be happy I brought them." I tossed one to her. "Amigo."

"Cain, I've been all over the world, trained under harsh conditions, and nothing has stopped me yet." She tossed the sombrero into one of the crew bunks. "All I need are sunglasses and I'm good to go."

"The Oblivion Guard trains on Oblivion." I gave her a deadpan stare. "You think I'm wearing this for fun or because I know what to expect?"

Her grin faltered and recovered. "Fine, I'll humor you, but I won't need it."

I expected Layla to do just fine. She hadn't survived so long by being out of shape. I double-checked Hannah's equipment. She looked kind of adorable in her sombrero, but I kept the thought to myself.

She looked at me with hopeful eyes. "Am I good?"

"Suited up like a pro." I flashed a grin. "Let's step into the oven, shall we?"

Aura's forehead wrinkled with worry. "Do we need oxygen?"

I pursed my lips. "I already packed the helmets in your backpacks." I tapped the green tank on Hannah's backpack. "Strap your oxygen tanks on like this."

"Not that we'll need them," Layla muttered as she fastened the tank to her pack.

"I'll be back in a minute." I climbed the ladder to the hatch and opened it. A hot breeze swept across me when I poked my head out and nearly swept my sombrero off my head. Even with the sunglasses, the brilliant blue sunlight was almost blinding. When the ocean breeze stopped blowing, the air felt stiflingly hot as an oven. The air scorched my lungs and I felt light-headed.

Surviving Mecha-Cerberus was going to be a breeze compared to the walk up the mountain. But that was why I'd come prepared. I closed the hatch and went back below. The submarine probably had its own oxygen reclamation system and air-cooling system built in, or we would've felt the effects of the external environment already.

Layla and Aura were suited up when I returned, festive sombreros and all. I managed to keep a straight face and verified they were good to go. I checked their backpacks for skydiving helmets and oxygen tubes. Made sure the water compartments were full, and that they had enough food.

Layla sighed loudly. "You're so anal, Cain."

I zipped her backpack closed. "It's harsh out there. You'll thank me later."

"Doubt it," she said.

I led them to the hatch. "Take some time to acclimate. Don't use the oxygen unless you have to, because supplies are limited."

"Just let me go already." Layla opened the hatch and climbed out without hesitation. "Holy fuck!" She yanked her hands back from the hull. "The metal is scalding hot!"

I followed her up and found her wheezing like a smoker with emphysema.

"Gods damn this place." She sucked in another breath. "I hate it already."

I motioned Layla down the short set of stairs descending from the sail to the main hull.

Hannah emerged after me. She winced in the sunlight and slipped on sunglasses, then breathed deeply in and out. "It's not as bad as I thought."

Aura gasped the moment her head poked out of the hatch. "Gods, it's unbearable!"

"Just give it a moment." Sweat trickled down my face and my breathing was labored, but it wasn't any worse than the last time I'd been here for extreme environment training. Oddly enough, I'd fared better than most of the other races. Elves and lesser fae seemed to have a harder time adjusting despite their superior strength and speed. I suspected it was because their bodies required more oxygen to fuel their denser muscles.

We'd been sent here for wargames and solo survival. Torvin showed no mercy to those who couldn't handle the environment. Washing out in this phase of guardian training usually meant death.

"You won't survive this, human," Torvin had assured me before personally taking us to Oblivion. "The nekhbets will feast on your corpse."

I'd seen the giant vultures devour a dead elf, bones and all when he collapsed and died. They were no threat at all to the living, but there were plenty of monsters that were, and I had no doubt we'd encounter them soon enough.

I unzipped a duffel bag and removed the inflatable dinghy inside. One pull of a handle and an air canister filled it in seconds. I screwed together the compact oars and attached them to the pivots on the sides of the dinghy. I hoped the military grade material would hold up in the heat.

The submarine sat low enough in the water that launching the dinghy was no problem. I set it partially in the water and let the others board, then climbed in and pushed us off with an oar.

Layla's raspy breathing stabilized, but I could tell she wasn't enjoying it. Aura was doing only marginally better. Despite sweating as much as the rest of us, Hannah seemed to have no problem with the air at all. I attributed it to her demigod blood. If she drew power from this plane, then it also meant she shared an affinity for it.

I began rowing us to shore across a hundred yards of choppy waters and let the small waves carry us onto the black sands. Since I was wearing waterproof boots, I got out of the boat and dragged it further onto land before the others got out. Then I swapped my footwear for hiking boots and left the waterproof ones in the dinghy.

"What if Torvin passes this way and sees the sub in the water?" Hannah asked.

"There's nowhere to hide it," I said. "Besides, I think he'll enter Oblivion as close to the mountain as possible once he figures out where it is."

Layla drew a harsh breath. "And where is that, exactly?"

I pursed my lips. "The underwater gateway correlates with the Ionian Sea on Gaia, so geographically, we're somewhere off the eastern shore of Greece."

"Interesting coincidence," Layla said.

I shrugged. "I'm pretty sure they aligned the two worlds as much as possible on purpose. Everyone would probably be living on this world if they hadn't fucked it up."

Layla was too busy trying to breathe to reply. I concealed the dinghy behind some rocks just in case, and then we started our trek toward the ruins of Olympus Prime. There weren't many buildings on this stretch of beach as most seemed to have been claimed by the volcanic eruption, but there were plenty of rocks along the black-sand beach. Despite the heat and sweat, the hairs on the back of my neck began to rise only a quarter mile into the hike.

Layla and I exchanged looks. She stopped and scanned the area. Shook her head. "Something is here, but I don't see it."

"I've got that feeling too." I couldn't put a finger on what it was, though.

Aura and Hannah stopped walking and turned around.

"What is it?" Hannah asked.

The sand behind her shifted ever so slightly, but it was enough to alarm me. "Get over here, fast!"

Aura blinked. "What?"

Something big, black, and shiny erupted from the sand, giant pincers grasping. It took a moment for my brain to comprehend what it was—a dune scorpion twice as large as any I'd encountered before. The barbed stinger on the tail whipped toward Aura's back.

And there was no way for her to move in time.

CHAPTER 25

I cast a shield and the stinger cracked against the barrier.

Gasping for breath, Aura staggered toward me. I raced forward, grabbed her wrist, and flung her behind me. Hannah scrambled past me. A volley of arrows sang past my head. Most deflected off the tough carapace. Two sank into the scorpion's eyes. The creature shrieked, but it still had six more eyes to spare.

Layla dropped to her knees, sucking in a ragged breath.

"Put on your oxygen max!" I shouted.

Adrenalin kicked in and my body went into survival mode. The air scorched my lungs and provided little oxygen, but I'd endured worse and survived on less. From frigid mountaintops to desert valleys, my body had been tested and adapted. It had been years since I'd faced a dune scorpion in the hellish environs of Oblivion, but my body hadn't forgotten the lesson.

Having my staff would've been nice, but I hadn't had one during training either. I drew in a lungful of the hot, salty air, and stalked toward the dune scorpion. Its pincers clacked together. Its tail quivered, ready for the next strike. I wanted it to strike—needed it to make the first move. I slowly drew Carnwennan and paced toward the scorpion. The dagger felt like nothing compared to the four-foot stinger dripping with venom.

The dune scorpion rotated in place, watching me, instinct feeding it mixed signals. It was used to fleeing prey, not prey calmly approaching as if it had the upper hand.

"Cain, what in Hades are you doing?" Aura shouted in a ragged voice.

I feinted toward the giant arachnid. It snapped its claws. I stepped within striking range of its tail. "Come and get it, big boy."

Layla barked a gasping laugh. "Trying to have sex with it or kill it?"

I grew very still. The scorpion centered on me with its six good eyes, green ichor trailing down the front of its carapace from the arrow wounds. I waited until it was absolutely still and then flinched suddenly. That triggered its instinctual need to sting moving prey. The tail snapped toward my chest. I dodged left and swung the dagger down, severing the knobby poison gland and barb.

It shrieked and lunged, but snapping claws grasped thin air, because I rolled under them and thrust the dagger up, three feet behind the tip of its head and dead center. Carnwennan sliced through the carapace as easily as through paper and pierced the nerve cluster that served as a brain, provided the larger scorpion had the same relative anatomy as its smaller cousins.

The monster shrieked, limbs vibrating wildly. I pulled Carnwennan free and kept rolling, barely clearing the legs without getting trampled. The scorpion collapsed and sagged into a silent mound of shiny black armor.

Layla and Aura stared at me in open-mouthed shock.

Hannah clapped and rushed over to embrace me. "God, you're amazing!"

I sheathed the dagger and smiled. "I guess desert training is like riding a bicycle—you never forget."

Hannah's eyebrows rose. "You ride bicycles?"

I snorted. "Only if I'm desperate."

Aura pulled off her oxygen helmet. The hot air drew tears of pain after her first breath. She swallowed and winced, as if washing something bitter down her throat. "Thanks, Cain."

Layla smacked my ass hard. "Gods be damned, Cain, that was fucking impressive! Just when I think you've gone soft, you go and redeem your wimpy little self."

I knelt and picked up a handful of sand, letting it fall a few grains at a time as I gauged the distance to the volcano. "Dune scorpions are territorial and stake out large claims. The land turns too rocky for them further on, so we might be in the clear."

"Let's go find another one." Layla breathed easily inside the skydiving helmet. "I want to record you slaying one."

I raised an eyebrow. "How about I let you kill the next one?"

She shrugged. "It's easy now that I know where to hit them."

"Yeah, super easy, barely an inconvenience." I checked the gauges on hers and Aura's oxygen tanks. They were still almost full. "It also helps if you can breathe while you fight."

Layla pulled off the helmet and drew in a ragged breath. "I can breathe just fine."

"Yeah, sure you can." I started toward the dead volcano again. We hadn't been walking long when motion in the ocean caught my peripheral vision. A spiny ridge broke the surface of the water a few hundred meters out and vanished again. The creature it belonged to was on an intercept course.

Aura grimaced. "What lovely surprise is coming our way now, Cain?"

"Sea serpent," I said. "It's not poisonous though."

"That's good," Aura said.

Hannah blinked. "It's not?"

I shook my head. "It's a constrictor. It swallows tiny prey like us whole."

"What a relief," Aura said. "For a moment, I thought we had a problem."

Layla broke into gasping laughs.

I figured I'd stoke their worries with more facts. "It'll have no problem slithering onto shore after us unless we make it to the rocky area first."

"It doesn't like rocks?" Hannah said.

"The rocks are sharp and will cut into its belly," I said.

Layla put on her helmet and turned on the oxygen. "Let's go."

Aura wiped the tears of pain from her eyes and followed suite. "I'm ready."

We ran.

Hannah had no problems breathing the oven-hot air as if she'd grown up in it. I could breathe okay, but the heat tested me mercilessly. All of our suits were already soaked with sweat and completely saturated by the time we reached the rocky shore.

The serpent rose at the water's edge and hissed. It slithered onto the rocks and just as quickly went back into the water when it felt the rough edges digging into its belly. It measured at least fifty feet in length and was as thick as a small car. We'd hardly even be a snack for a monster that size. The spiked ridge along its spine quivered as its head rose for a better look at us.

We were only a few hundred feet in, just barely out of striking range if it decided to make a move.

Layla tugged my sleeve. "Uh, Cain, that thing looks really hungry."

Keeping my eye on the serpent, I nodded slowly. It looked gaunt and unhealthy, probably hard-pressed to find food on this dead world. The question in my mind—was it hungry enough to risk injury?

The serpent lunged toward us, launching its massive body across the rocks toward us. The webbed ridge across its back split vertically and spread into fixed wings, allowing it to glide even further.

"Holy shit!" Hannah leapt back. "It can fly!"

I'd been through some brutal tests during my training on Oblivion, but I'd never faced off against a sea serpent. A quick thrust of Carnwennan through the head wouldn't be enough to finish off a brain that size. In this case, avoiding a fight was a much better solution.

The split rocks marking the start of the trail up Olympus Prime were a hundred yards away, but the terrain was rocky and treacherous. It would be more of a hindrance to us than the serpent, but that didn't mean we had to stop and fight.

"Keep going!" I motioned toward the path. "I'll try to slow it down."

Layla nocked an arrow and arched a shot toward the serpent. It looked like it would miss, but it struck the serpent in the forehead and bounced off the armored hide. "Well, shit."

"Just go!" I pushed her in the direction we needed to run.

Her eyes narrowed in the helmet visor, but she turned and hurried after Aura and Hannah. The serpent coiled and sprang across more rocks. Blood oozed from cuts in its hide, but that didn't deter it from the easy snacks that were just out of reach.

We ran across the volcanic terrain, leaping from rock to rock, or squeezing between them. We were only yards away from the path when the serpent glided within striking range. It lunged for me since I was the closest. I couldn't cast a shield strong enough to block it, so I split from the others and ran left, away from the path.

The serpent considered this for a moment, then decided I was worth the chase. I looked for large boulders, a hole, or anywhere to take refuge, but the rocks weren't large enough to keep me safe. I had little choice but to find a decent vantage point and fight, because there was no way for me to outrun it.

"Cain!" Hannah cried out.

I clambered up a large boulder and turned to face the serpent. Hannah reached out to me across the distance, her other arm restrained by Layla. Aura stood next to Hannah, her face hidden by glare of the sun off her helmet. They were almost to the path. The tall boulders and jagged ledges would keep the serpent from following.

"Let me go!" Hannah screamed.

"Go!" I waved them onward. "I'll catch up!"

"No, you won't!" Hannah struggled against Layla. "You're going to die!"

I didn't have time to argue because the serpent was in range and coiling to strike. I ran through scenarios, plotting the moves that would potentially save my life. I was too small for it to bother constricting, so it would try to engulf me in its mouth. That was where I would have the advantage. I flicked my fingers through patterns and ran my hands along the length of my body to cover it with a thin shield that would briefly protect me against the pressure inside the mouth. Then I crouched and braced myself.

Hannah screamed my name over and over again.

I didn't have time to look her way before the serpent struck. Darkness engulfed me. The shield buckled and cracked under the pressure of the jaw snapping shut. Gravity yanked down on me as the serpent's head rose quickly into the air.

The fleshy gullet expanded around me, giving me just enough space to flex my hands even as the peristaltic motion of the throat began to swallow me. I flicked my fingers and cast a ball of light in the tight confines. It illuminated the pink flesh closing in around me. Holding Carnwennan steady, I slashed it apart like warm butter. Blood filled the gullet.

The serpent shuddered violently. My stomach lurched as gravity reversed into freefall. The shock of impact rattled my bones and shattered the already weakened shield. I felt like someone trapped in a barrel as the entire head rolled over twice and stopped. The jaws relaxed gradually, and daylight trickled into the maw.

Bracing my feet on one side of the mouth and my back against the other, I pushed the jaws open and clambered out. The odor of burning flesh filled my nostrils. Hannah's wails filled the air. I blinked in the harsh sunlight and focused on a glowing figure hovering twenty feet in the air.

Beams of white energy slashed into the charred remains of the serpent's body. The head was severed a few feet back from the mouth, and the rest had been sliced to bits.

"Hannah!" I raised a hand and waved it.

She gasped. The nimbus surrounding her body began to fade, and she drifted to earth. Eyes still glowing, she ran toward me, arms outstretched. "Cain! I thought you were dead!"

I was still stunned from the fall and trying to understand what had happened. "How in the hell?" The glow winked out and she slumped against a rock. Still woozy, I managed to jog across the space between us and took her in my arms. "Hannah?"

Hannah's eyes cracked open. "Cain?"

I nodded. "You just turned a sea serpent into chop suey, kiddo."

"Oh, that's nice," she said drunkenly. "I want to take a nap now." Then she went limp.

"Hannah!" Aura ran around a smoking mound of serpent flesh and stopped suddenly when she saw me. "Cain? You're alive?"

I nodded. "Disappointed?"

Aura took off the helmet and wiped tears from her eyes. "No."

Layla rounded the same pile of snake meat, grumbling and cursing. "It'd be nice if the girl was more reliable with her magic!" She saw me and scoffed. "At least we know how to trigger it."

I scoffed back. "By putting me in mortal danger?"

"Yep." Layla looked at the unconscious girl in my arms. "Her weakness is our strength."

"Except she's burned out for the foreseeable future," I said. "I just hope she's not out of it for long."

"She was out for hours the last time she did this," Layla said. "Maybe we should take her back to the sub."

I shook my head. "I'll carry her for now, but when we reach the cave, I'll need one of you to get her safely inside."

"I'll do it," Aura said.

Layla scoffed. "I'm stronger, elf."

Aura shrugged. "You're a better fighter. Cain might need your help."

Layla pursed her lips. "Are you patronizing me?"

"Fuck you!" Aura bared her teeth. "Can't you ever take anything I say at face value?" She gasped for air, anger overpowering her body's ability to deal with the harsh atmosphere.

Layla grinned through the visor of her helmet. "Fine. I believe you."

I cradled Hannah in my arms and made my way around the hunk of burning snake. "Let's go."

"One problem, Cain." Layla tried to pace me, but the scattered boulders forced her behind. "What happens when Torvin finds the remains of a dune scorpion and a giant sea serpent on the way to the mountain?"

"He won't find much of anything." I kept walking.

"What do you mean by that?"

"You'll see in a little while." I could have explained, but it was more satisfying making her wait.

Layla stopped talking, but I could feel her glare on the back of my neck. We reached the path opening in the boulders a few moments later. It followed a tunnel through broken rock and emerged onto a thin ledge on the southern side of the mountain before winding around and into another tunnel made of magma. It looked as if the tunnel had occurred naturally during the final eruption of the dead volcano. It also explained why much of the path wasn't visible from the ground.

Sometime later we emerged near the second mark on the map, now back on the side of the mountain facing the beach we'd traversed. I set Hannah down so I could rest my arms, stretch, and take in the view.

The submarine sail was barely visible, hidden among the rocky shoals offshore. The beach we'd crossed was no longer a wasteland of rock and sand, but alive with activity.

Scaly, yellow beasts resembling hyenas were devouring a section of sea serpent further up the shore. A pair of giant vultures, nekhbets, were fighting over the serpent's head. Smaller scavengers covered the flesh like black flies. But the ones that caused my skin to crawl were the creatures dragging themselves out of the sea to feast on the dead flesh. The leechens were the gods' first attempt to create mermaids and sirens. Though their upper halves were humanoid, there was nothing remotely beautiful about them.

Their skin was green and scaly, and giant fisheyes bugged from the sides of their faces instead of facing forward like humans. Their bottom halves were split into legs, but the feet were large and webbed, making locomotion across land awkward, but doable. Hundreds of them ambled ashore, gathering bundles of serpent flesh in nets, and dragging their full nets across the rough terrain and out to sea.

One group had already hauled off the dune scorpion. Within hours, there would be little left of our battles on the beach except dried blood and ichor. Now we faced what was hopefully the final challenge—a giant Mecha Cerberus.

CHAPTER 26

L ayla hissed when she saw the people of the sea. "What in the name of the gods are those things?"

"Leechens," I said. "Harmless to the living as far as I know. They live on decaying plants and flesh."

"There are so many of them," Aura said. "How does this world sustain so much life?"

I shrugged. "Life finds a way somehow, even when the gods have forsaken it."

Hannah stirred and groaned. Her eyes blinked open. "Cain?"

I knelt next to her. "How you feeling, kiddo?"

"Tired." She took my hand and I helped her to her feet.

"We're almost to the cave." I put my hands on her shoulders. "Can you walk?"

Hannah wiped her bleary eyes. "Did you carry me all the way up here?"

I nodded. "I can still carry you if necessary, but it'd be a lot better if you're alert when we reach the clockwork hound."

She stiffened her shoulders. "I can do it."

I nodded. "Good."

Hannah's eyes widened when she saw the beach. "Eww. What are those things?"

I repeated what I'd told Layla, let her have a few minutes to take it in, and then we started the final leg of our journey up Olympus Prime. We hadn't gone very far when Layla hissed and pointed out to sea.

The sail of a submarine protruded above the water and was quickly approaching shore. Sunlight glinted off the lens of the periscope as it scanned the activity ashore. The leechens began calling out warnings to each other with sounds not unlike dolphin calls. Their efforts to claim the remaining serpent meat became frantic. A drone lifted off from the submarine and circled above the creatures. Bright flares dropped from the underbelly probably in an attempt to frighten them off. The leechens responded by throwing rocks at it.

"I don't think the submarine has spotted us yet," I said. "Let's pick up the pace."

"What if they find our sub?" Hannah said.

"Then we'll just have to steal theirs," Layla said.

A pair of long gun barrels popped up from the hull of the submarine and began firing into the crowd of leechens. Electricity crackled and popped, the shocks scattering the creatures. We hurried up the path while the mechanists were busy clearing the beach. Layla and Aura made heavy use of their oxygen. I was tempted to use mine but concerned that we might need it for later.

"The periscope still hasn't turned this way," Layla said as we neared the cave. "But they're bound to see the giant metal dog when we fight it."

I gauged the distance between us and the cave and marked off a few paces until we were in position. "Then we'll just have to be quick about it." I knelt and examined the width of the ledge. It was perhaps four feet wide just in front of the cave—perfect for my uses. I took a moment to calm my heart and focus on the area around me.

Layla frowned. "Sure you can do it?"

I nodded.

Hannah hugged me. "Be careful. I don't want to be stuck alone with Layla and Aura."

Layla scoffed. "The feeling is mutual, kid."

I mussed her hair. "Try not to kill them, okay?"

She pursed her lips as if thinking about it. "I guess I could let them live."

"Don't go putting ideas into her head, Cain!" Layla drew one of her special arrows and nocked it in a bow. "Let's do this."

I freed myself from Hannah's hug and crept toward the cave entrance. There was no telling how long I'd have from the moment I stepped in front of the cave entrance to the attack. Judging from how quickly the clockwork Cerberus had destroyed the drone, maybe one or two seconds.

I edged along the cliff until I was just outside the cave entrance. I took a breath, and leapt in front of the cave, began waving my hands wildly. Yep, it was a great plan, all right. The ticking of clockwork echoed from the darkness. Six red eyes glowed to life. A giant metal paw emerged from the cave and swiped at me.

The claws whistled through the air barely a foot from decapitating me. I jumped back to the very edge of the path. Mecha-Cerberus growled and leapt at me, paws extended. I didn't have a great view of the cave behind him, but it was enough. I ghostwalked behind him at the last instant and cast a shield on the ground beneath his front paws.

Layla fired her explosive arrow at the same instant. It landed beneath the hound's rear end. The detonation increased the beast's momentum, and the slick shield under its front paws gave it no purchase on the ledge. With a mechanical yelp, the giant three-headed hound plunged over the ledge and tumbled. Its metal body clanked like a hundred armored knights in a mosh pit.

I cast a light pod into the cave to make sure there were no other nasty surprises inside. When I made sure it was clear, I waved the others on, and they raced inside.

Despite the long tumble down the side of the mountain, Mecha-Cerberus barely looked dented when he hit the ground. The leechens were in full retreat already, and the rest of the scavengers vanished into the ruins. Mecha-Cerberus gained his feet and looked up at us. He howled with the fury of a thousand wolves and began galloping up the steep slope back to us.

"Gods be damned!" Layla shouted. "Run for your lives!"

I was already past her by the time she said it. I cast a shield over the cave entrance. It wouldn't last long, but it might give us a few seconds. The tunnel spiraled down, down, and down some more. Metallic feet thundered from somewhere above and behind us, so we kept running.

An opening appeared a few moments later and sunlight greeted us once again. I blinked against the glare and realized we were inside the volcano right down in the bottom of the pit. Diagonally across the pit from us, perhaps two hundred yards distant, were a pair of giant metal doors.

"Fuck me," I said. "I hope they aren't locked."

"Worry about it when we get there!" Layla gasped and tapped the side of her helmet. "I think I'm running low on oxygen."

We stumbled across the uneven terrain, the dry magma undulating like frozen ocean waves. Layla's gasping grew louder. She yanked off the helmet, wheezing, and stumbled to her knees. She tried to speak but didn't have the air.

The mechanized terror burst from the tunnel exit. The three heads swiveled toward us and howled in unison. My fingers fumbled with the oxygen hose. I unscrewed it and tossed aside the depleted cannister as Mecha-Cerberus ate up the ground between us in long strides.

Hannah and Aura had stopped and turned to face us.

"Run!" I shouted. "Keep going!" I slid the other cannister into the pocket on Layla's backpack and screwed on the hose without daring to look away for an instant. I turned on the valve and air hissed into the helmet.

Layla's gasps eased, but she was too oxygen starved to simply get up and run. I energized my tattoos and hefted her over my shoulder. Her densely muscled body weighed heavy on my shoulder, and my lungs screamed in pain. I gritted my teeth and ran after the others.

Mecha-Cerberus was nearly upon us. He howled in victory, three sets of razor-sharp teeth clanking together. I decided to throw Layla ahead of me so I could turn and lead him off. It was our only choice.

The metal beast yipped and whined. It skidded to a stop twenty feet away, then backed up. He paced back and forth, growling and whining, but not coming another step closer. That worried me a lot more than his vicious pursuit a moment ago.

I ground to a halt and shouted to the others. "Stop! Don't take another step forward!"

The earth in front of them rumbled. Frozen lava shattered like glass, exploding in all directions. Aura screamed and vanished amidst the explosions. Hannah fell to her stomach. I unceremoniously dropped Layla and my shoulder practically sang with relief.

She hit the ground with a grunt and a thud. I raced through the hailstorm of falling rock fragments until I reached Hannah. The ground in front of her vanished into a pit. I dropped to my knees and saw Aura dangling from Hannah's hand inside the pit.

Aura's eyes widened with fear. I dropped to my stomach and reached out a hand. But I was too late. Aura slipped from Hannah's grasp and fell.

"No!" Hannah screamed. A beam of light speared toward Aura. It wrapped around her waist and dangled her above the dark pit. Something stirred below. Freezing air rushed past my face, refreshing my hot skin and filling me with cold fear. Hannah gasped in surprise at her feat. "What do I do now?"

"Pull her up!" I shouted over the howling wind rising from the pit.

"But how?"

"Just make it happen, Hannah!" I commanded.

She flinched but the saving light retracted toward her hand, drawing Aura up with it. I reached out and grasped Aura's hand just as the light flickered away and her body dangled free. Thankfully, the roaring air lightened the load on my arm. Bracing myself with my other hand, I slowly pulled Aura up to the ledge.

She grasped the edge with her free hand. I reached down and grabbed the waist of her suit, used it to pull her to safety. She rolled onto the rocky ground, eyes wide. Her mouth moved, but I couldn't hear her over the roaring wind.

Layla staggered over to us, teeth clenched. "What in the fuck is happening?"

I looked back and saw Mecha-Cerberus pacing forty yards away. "Something bigger and badder is about to come up here and kill us." I grabbed Aura's arm and yanked her to her feet. "I suggest we run our asses off."

No one argued. But now we had a hundred-foot wide pit to circumnavigate and the ground was still shaking under our feet. We backed well away from the side of the pit and began running around the left side. A great golden beast leapt from the pit and blocked our path. It was as big as Mecha-Cerberus, but unlike him, it was a living, breathing creature.

It was a monster I'd happily never encountered. Now was certainly not the time for firsts, but I had little choice.

It had the head and forward body of a lion. A goat's head jutted awkwardly from the back, and its hind feet were hooved. The tail was a serpent, hovering over the lion head like a scorpion's stinger, hissing and snapping.

The lion roared a twenty-foot stream of flame. It would have no problem ending our lives in seconds.

Layla drew her bow. "How many fucking challenges does it take to get to the armory?"

"Too many." Aura pulled one of the mechanist rifles from her back and popped in a magazine of incendiary rounds.

Hannah held up her hands, face screwed up in concentration, but her magic wasn't responding. "God damn it, I'm useless!" she shouted.

"Run for the door," I told them. "Get inside."

"I'm not leaving you, Cain." Hannah stepped beside me, fists clenched. "Maybe my magic will trigger again when it attacks."

I blew out an exasperated breath. "Just go. Please."

Aura stepped up beside me. "Cain, you don't have to fight it alone."

Layla nocked an arrow and laughed. "Isn't this sweet? We all get to die together."

But the chimera approached us slowly, its golden eyes methodically looking us over. The goat head bleated, seeming to speak into the lion's ear. The beast settled onto its haunches and regarded us. "Is the time of the Oblivion Codex upon us, or has yet another failed traveler come to my domain?" It spoke in the Alder tongue.

I wasn't sure if it was a rhetorical question, and I had no answer, so I said something unrelated. "I didn't know chimeras could speak."

The snake hissed and the goat bleated. The lion spoke again. "Answer this riddle and gain entrance. Fail and meet your end."

"I thought sphinxes asked riddles," Layla said. "What in Hades is going on?"

The chimera ignored her and continued speaking. "What goes on four legs at dawn, two legs at noon, and three legs in the evening?"

I blinked and shook my head, flummoxed that this was actually the riddle.

"Is he serious?" Aura whispered. "That's the oldest riddle in the book."

"It is?" Hannah looked confused. "I have no idea what it means."

Layla grunted. "Maybe they changed up the answer over the centuries."

"Maybe." I regarded the chimera for a moment. "Get ready to fight in case this is a trick."

"I'm always ready," Layla said.

Holding my place, I answered. "Man, as a baby, crawls on all fours, then walks on two legs as an adult, and uses a cane as a third leg in old age."

The goat screamed, the snake hissed, and the lion reared back its head and roared gouts of flame into the air. When it calmed down, the lion nodded. "Your wisdom grants you access to that which was locked away." It leapt over the wide pit and galloped to the giant metal doors in a frighteningly short amount of time. We wouldn't have had a chance fighting the beast. It extended a claw and pressed it into a hole in the doors.

Mecha-Cerberus howled, then turned tail and went back into the tunnel.

The chimera sat next to the door. "The time is here, traveler. Oblivion awaits."

CHAPTER 27

We were a bit leery walking so close to the chimera, but it could have pounced us at any time.

"What do you mean by that?" I asked it.

The chimera spread great webbed wings. "It is not for me to say. My time here has ended, and I have much to do before the codex is fulfilled." Its goat legs coiled, and it sprang into the sky, beating the great wings until it cleared the lip of the volcano and vanished.

"I've got a really bad feeling about this," Aura said. "An apocalyptic feeling."

Layla raised a fist and whooped. "Let's end the world, bitches."

I looked at the open metal doors and took in a deep breath. Whatever lay inside could free Hannah, end the world, or both. I had to make sure no one took anything world-ending from this place, especially Layla. She might one day destroy the world out of sheer boredom.

Layla, of course, dashed inside, heedless of any further traps that might await. When nothing exploded or sliced her to ribbons, I followed. Torches along the walls flickered to life as Layla strode past, lighting a wide staircase that led deeper underground. I didn't understand how the tunnel had survived the volcanic eruption. It had probably been protected by the power of the gods, or perhaps had been rebuilt after the last eruption.

The stairs ended in a cavern neatly carved from the rock. The stone walls were polished to a mirror gloss. Giant bellows sat against a distant wall, the equally giant forges dark and silent. Torches ignited along all the walls, illuminating racks of weapons, stone statues bearing sets of armor that sparkled as if recently cleaned, and shelves filled with a myriad of objects. There was a trumpet, a harp, several bone horns, and a collection of stones, some rough, others cut and polished.

"Ooh!" Layla hefted a silver sword. "It's so light!" She moved on to a golden bow and grunted when she pulled it from the rack. "I think this thing is made of real gold." She pulled back on the string and shook her head. "I hope this thing has good magic, because it feels like shit."

Hannah inspected the musical instruments. "How are we supposed to know what does what in this place? There aren't any labels."

Aura walked to a pedestal bearing a small golden owl. Strange geometric shapes glowed at the base of the pedestal, a sphere, a cube, and a pyramid. Aura leaned down to inspect them, then stood and looked at the owl. "This is kind of cute. Is it decoration or a deadly weapon?"

The owl's eyes blinked open with a metallic clink. Clockwork gears rotated as it spread its wings.

Aura leapt back with a startled yelp.

"Ask what you will and my answers you shall receive," the owl said in a feminine voice. Surprisingly, it spoke in English, not Alder.

Hannah jumped a foot in the air out of surprise. She dropped a white porcelain vessel on the floor, and it shattered. "Oh, god! Was that important?"

"That was a chamber pot used by those who served Hephaestus," the owl said.

Hannah's face wrinkled in disgust. "They shit in that thing?"

"Naturally," it said.

"A clockwork owl?" I regained my wits. "Is your name Bubo?"

"No."

I waited for elaboration, but it simply watched me and blinked.

"What's your name?" I asked.

"Hephaestus forged me in the fires of Olympus on Gaia as a gift to honor Athena, but she refused the gift," the owl said. "He named me Athene Noctua, or Little Owl, but referred to me as Noctua."

"That's kind of cute," Hannah said. "Can you fly?"

"Yes, but I may not leave the confines of the forge," Noctua replied.

"What's your purpose?" I asked.

Noctua's head rotated toward me. "I am a repository of knowledge."

Layla held up the golden bow. "What's this?"

"The first bow made for Apollo," Noctua said. "He deemed it clumsy and unbefitting a god though it can imbue arrows with the strength of the sun and propel them great distances."

"It's heavy," Layla said, "and I'm not a weak little woman."

The clockwork owl blinked. "It was made for a god, not a halfling of fae and human origin."

Layla's eyes flared. "You know my heritage?"

Noctua nodded. "It is obvious by your physique, just as I can tell the other woman is an elf, and the girl is the half-daughter of a god."

"Do you know who her father is?" I asked.

Noctua regarded Hannah for a moment. She opened her beak to speak, but nothing emerged. Her beak closed and she remained silent for a moment before speaking. "The information is there, but I cannot put it into words or thought. I am blocked from disseminating the information."

"Great." I sighed. "Are you familiar with Cthulhu?"

"I know of the Great Ancient One," she said.

"I need a weapon to give him that he will take in trade for the girl." I waved an arm around the room. "It needs to be powerful enough for him to want, but not powerful enough for him to destroy the world. Can you tell me which of these weapons would work?"

Noctua blinked. "You wish to supply him with a power equal to that of the girl?"

I nodded.

Noctua's eyes glowed orange. "I sense great untapped potential in her. She bears the seeds of creation and destruction within her." She tilted her head. "If her abilities are fully realized, Cthulhu will have a weapon of great power. There is only one item here that he might value greater."

I grimaced. "What is it?"

"The horn of awakening," she replied. "Cthulhu slumbers in the sunken city of R'lyeh. He is trapped in a prison of his own making, unable to wake his body. It is possible he would consider the horn a fair trade."

"Uh, wouldn't waking Cthulhu be really, really bad?" Layla said.

"It is one branch of fulfillment in the Oblivion Codex," Noctua said.

Layla glanced at Hannah. "Sorry, kid, you're stuck."

"His possession of a demigod is a competing branch of the codex," Noctua said.

"Competing branch?" I scoffed. "So there are multiple ways to fulfill the prophecy?"

"There are few prophecies with a single path," she said. "There are multiple branches leading to the fulfillment of the Oblivion Codex, one of which is this very meeting. It may be that no matter what you do, you have already started a chain reaction leading to the end days."

"Fuck my life," Layla said. "I'm too young to deal with this shit."

Aura seemed to perk up. "So, there is a high guarantee the prophecy will be fulfilled? That we will have a grand reset that removes the gods and fae from power?"

"That is one possible outcome," Noctua said. "But there are outcomes in which the gods wipe out all life and start over yet again. The branching multiverse allows them to see thousands of possibilities. One of them will be the fate of the prime."

I staggered back under the load of information she'd just dumped on me. "There are multiple universes?"

"Branches of the prime," she said. "Oracles knowingly or unconsciously gather information from the events of the multiverse, allowing them to predict events in the prime."

"So there are other versions of me running around out there?" I said.

"There were thousands," the owl said, "but they now number in the hundreds. Billions of branches have already run their course, withering from the tree of life and falling away."

Layla leaned heavily against the weapons rack. "Are those people real?"

"Every bit as real as you," Noctua said. "Different decisions, different outcomes. Some branches are vastly different from prime, having derived from decisions thousands or millions of years ago. Only recent branches from prime contain other versions of those living today."

Aura sat on a marble bench, eyes distant with contemplation. "Are there branches where the fae don't rule?"

"Yes," Noctua said. "But those branches diverged thousands of years ago."

"Are there other versions of the gods in the other universes?" I asked,

"No." Noctua shook her head. "The original gods are prime beings and exist at once across universes."

"Like Cthulhu?" I said.

Noctua shook her head again. "He is not an original god. It is his wish to transcend his being and become an original god that he might achieve power across dimensions. This requires a grand erasure and remaking by his hands."

"Okay, this is really confusing." Hannah pressed her hands to her temples. "I might cause the apocalypse and there are thousands of me in other universes?"

"Now only hundreds," the owl said. "Many perished at the hands of the Divine Council."

Hannah's mouth formed a surprised O.

"The other universes aren't important," I said. "What's important is that we get out of here with something useful." I turned to the owl. "Anything besides the horn that might suffice?"

"Nearly everything left in this armory is capable of large-scale destruction." Noctua's head rotated full circle as if taking in everything around us. "One horn can raise armies of the dead. Another extinguishes all life within range of its wail. There are swords which carry incurable plagues, and orbs which pulsate with deadly radiation when activated."

Layla grimaced. "Don't you have anything that acts on a smaller scale? Like maybe a suit of armor that allows me to fly?"

"Inventions such as those exist only in the armory of Mount Olympus on Gaia." Noctua's head rotated toward her. "There is little here which cannot destroy life en masse, though there might be something of that nature in the scrap pile."

Layla's eyes flared. "Ooh, a scrap pile?"

Hannah carefully set down an orb she'd been examining. "Did someone use those weapons to devastate Oblivion?"

"Many of these were not intended to be weapons," Noctua said. "Hephaestus believed other beings should be allowed to design their own worlds, so he built a toolkit. Some gods were outraged that he deigned to give non-divines such abilities. This sparked a war among the gods with the armory as the focal point."

"I'm just going to say it." Layla shook her head. "That toolkit was a stupid idea."

"Perhaps." Noctua blinked. "Loki and a host of fallen angels made their way into the armory. Loki took the hammer, Earthmaker, and tried to smash the furnaces."

The furnaces were a bit blackened on the outside but looked as if they had a scratch on them. "Were there more than these before?"

Noctua shook her head. "The furnaces are virtually indestructible as they were forged in the original fire of creation. Hephaestus took six orbs from the original fire and used them to light the furnaces."

"I'm really confused," Hannah said. "The gods used fire to create the universe?"

"I use the term fire loosely," Noctua replied. "It was more like a sun."

Hannah nodded. "That makes more sense. But how do you take parts of a sun?"

"It is something that comes easily to the divine," Noctua replied.

Aura motioned Noctua to continue the story. "So, Loki couldn't destroy the furnaces. What happened next?"

"His attempts freed the fires of creation from the furnaces, causing them to erupt from Olympus Prime, destroying the city of the Greek gods, and wreaking havoc on the surface of Oblivion."

Aura's mouth dropped open. "And that destroyed the entire world?"

"It laid waste to everything for hundreds of miles, casting much of the world in darkness beneath clouds of ash." Noctua's eyes glowed and projected a video on the far wall.

A beautiful city teeming with life spanned sandy white beaches. Humanoids frolicked in the blue waters alongside dolphins and other sea life. Their pointed ears indicated they were either elven or fae. The image panned upward toward the massive mountain looming in the distance. It dwarfed the dead volcano by several magnitudes, but I knew without doubt that it was Olympus Prime.

A halo of fluffy white clouds ringed the center of the mountain. Silver and gold buildings nestled on the steep slope, gathering into a great city around the sharp peak. Without warning, the peak of the mountain exploded, a distant boom that reached the denizens of the beach seconds after the event. Streaks of energy lanced through the air. Distant forms flew from the mountain, most vanishing in thin air, probably through portals. I had no doubt they were gods.

The reason for the exodus soon became apparent. The ground rumbled and fire streaked up the sides of Olympus. The people on the beach screamed, some running for chariots, others piling into ships and taking them out to sea, even as Olympus quaked.

Tremors shook the city on the beach violently. Cracks formed in the ground, swallowing crowds of people and other creatures all at once, then closing moments later. The rubble atop Olympus where the city once stood glowed orange, the dim light growing brighter by the moment. With a cataclysmic roar, half the mountaintop blew off, sending lava spraying into the air.

The point of view in the recording rose into the air for a better view.

Giant orange spheres like the miniature sun we'd seen beneath the water, soared into the air and vanished into the distance. One of them plunged into the ocean just off a peninsula. Tidal waves and tsunamis slammed into the land. A fissure formed where the peninsula joined with the mainland and the entire formation broke off and sank into the sea.

The image played faster and faster. Fire rained down and then a blanket of dark ash covered the sky and ground. What had once been a city of thousands was completely dead. Whether by land, sea, or air, I doubted anyone had escaped the carnage. Only the gods had survived that day.

The image flickered off and we turned back to Noctua.

"Can I get that on DVD?" Layla asked.

Hannah scoffed. "You're old enough to want it on VHS."

Layla flipped her off.

Aura had paled considerably. "Everyone but the gods perished?"

Noctua blinked at her. "Yes."

She leaned against the end of a weapons rack and sank to a sitting position on the floor. "But that's not what we want."

The thought of so much potential death and destruction residing in one room made my skin crawl. There was nothing in here I could safely give to Cthulhu without granting him power to end worlds.

Hannah gripped my arm and looked up at me, tears welling in her eyes. "I'm not worth it, Cain. We need to lock this place and throw away the key."

Layla stomped her feet and groaned. "Hey, owl, where's the scrap pile with the non-apocalyptic weapons?"

Noctua turned on his tiny feet to face her. "It is further back, but none of the weapons there will suffice for Cain's purposes."

I flinched. "You know my name?"

Noctua nodded. "Your names are well-known in the multiverse."

Layla pointed to a weapon on a nearby rack. "What does this trident do?"

"Tidebringer commands the seas and can level entire cities in one blow," Noctua said.

"How about that staff?" Layla asked.

Noctua fluttered her wings. "Airbender can spread pollen with a gentle breeze or destroy cities with tornadoes and hurricanes. It can be used to mix atmospheric gasses to support life or kill it."

Layla pointed to a large mallet that resembled Mjolnir. "What about that warhammer?"

Noctua blinked. "That is Earthmaker. One blow from it can move entire mountains."

"Earthmaker can literally move a mountain and not destroy it?" Hannah said.

"It is part of the toolkit designed for planet building." Noctua nodded at the other weapons next to it. "With those three tools, one could create or destroy on a massive scale."

"They're too dangerous for anyone to have," I said, "most of all, Cthulhu."

Noctua bobbed her body in a nod. "That is why they were locked away."

"Why not throw them into the depths of the earth far from the reach of everyone?" I said.

"Because there are beings who could still reach them." The owl blinked at me. "The armory was hidden and protected, at least until now."

Layla huffed. "Just take me to the scrap pile. I'm not leaving here empty-handed."

Noctua flapped her wings and glided across the chamber. The others hurried to follow her. I was about to follow when I noticed the warhammer was missing. Aura had been standing closest to the rack and must have taken it when we looked away. Rather than confront her about it, it seemed better to simply steal it from her backpack along with anything else she pilfered so she'd never know it was gone.

I strode after the others, passing row upon row of empty shelves and racks. I imagined they'd once held the weapons of lesser destruction which had been moved to Olympus in Gaia.

"What did you mean by we're well known?" Hannah asked when we reached the destination.

Noctua perched on a pedestal next to junkpile of scrap metal. "Just as Hercules was prevalent among branches in the multiverse, Achilles in another, and Jesus Christ in another, so are you prevalent among the recent branches."

Those names sent chills down my spine. "What does it mean?"

Layla barked a laugh. "It means we're famous and fucked."

Aura trailed far behind us, eyes downcast, shoulders sagging. The discovery that the gods had survived a divine war while the other inhabitants of this world perished seemed to have broken her.

Layla wasted no time digging into the pile of scraps. She dug out a metal helmet with wings on the sides. "Ooh, will this let me fly?"

"That is a helm of speed," Noctua said. "It was designed for assistants to Hermes that they might run almost as fast as him. It has the side effect of depleting the energy of the wearer, causing them to consume great amounts of food or risk death."

"Mine." Layla tucked it into her backpack. She found another metal helmet, this one carved like a skull. "And this?"

"A helm of lesser darkness," the owl said. "It allows the wearer to become invisible but only when the sun is down. It was built for minions of Hades that they might operate among mortals in secrecy."

"Any side effects?" Layla asked.

"No, but the minions of Hades were not also part human."

Layla stuffed it into her pack. "Mine too."

"Don't hog everything," Hannah said.

As if that was her cue, Layla began stuffing everything she could fit into her backpack.

An ivory orb that closely resembled the one atop my oblivion staff rolled from the pile as Layla shuffled through it. I plucked it off the floor before Layla could claim it. "What's this?"

"It was a component of the original oblivion staffs," Noctua said. "But the fae requested it be removed as it granted the bearers too much power."

"How so?" I asked.

"It increases the power of the brightblade and had other unintended side-effects." Noctua's eyes closed as if she were thinking, then opened a moment later. "There is no other information stored in my memory."

I slid it into my pocket. "Do you have other oblivion staffs here?"

Noctua pointed a wing to a thick metal vat above a dark pit. "Only the molten remains of the original staffs. They are no longer usable in any capacity."

That caught my attention. Oblivion staffs were nearly indestructible. But if they could be destroyed, that meant our next objective was clear.

We had to destroy all the weapons in the armory.

CHAPTER 28

"Can we destroy the other weapons the same way?" I asked.

"Perhaps," the owl said. "The furnaces harnessed the fires of creation and were thus capable of making or unmaking weapons of great power." Noctua's head rotated toward the dark holes where the furnaces had once burned. "But the fires were scattered. Hephaestus took some of them to Gaia to light the furnaces there. Those remaining on Oblivion are far away."

"So, there's no way to destroy the weapons in here?" I asked.

Noctua fluttered her wings as if to stretch. "I thought you wanted one for Cthulhu."

"Not anymore," I said. "We can't risk it. Unfortunately, there are others who want these weapons. I'd prefer to get rid of them altogether."

"I know the location of some of the fires," Noctua said. "One of them fell into the ocean near here and still burns. But it has lost much of its strength over the millennia, sapped by the ocean waters."

"That miniature sun is a fire of creation?" Hannah said.

Noctua nodded. "There are four others on Oblivion. But since I am unable to venture far from the forge, I cannot say if they retain the heat to melt these weapons."

"How would we know if they can?" I asked.

"The only way to know is by trying to melt a weapon." Noctua spread her wings and glided further back to a metal chest. "Inside this chest you will find forger's cloaks. They will protect your frail forms from incineration when you near the fires."

I opened the chest and found piles of silver metallic gloves. The touch and feel were similar to mithril armor, which meant it offered superior protection. But there was one major problem. I rummaged through the pile and found nothing even resembling a cloak.

"There aren't any cloaks in here." I held up a glove. "Only left-hand gloves."

Noctua blinked. "Put on the glove and make a fist five times."

I did. The cloth spread up my arm and toward my chest. I somehow kept from panicking as it spread up my neck and over my face. The world went dark for an instant and then back to normal. I looked down. I was encased from head to foot in the metallic cloth.

"Freaky." Hannah peered at my head. "It covered your face, but then it turned transparent so I can see just your face."

"Ooh, nifty." Layla smiled appreciatively. "I'll bet my ass looks good in one of those."

Hannah groaned.

"You're certain you wish to destroy the weapons?" Noctua asked.

"Positive. No one needs that kind of power." I inspected my gloved hands. "How do I get this off?"

"Clench your fist five more times."

I did so and the material flowed back from my body and into the glove. Then it was a matter of simply tugging off the glove.

Layla grabbed a handful of gloves and shoved them in her backpack. "These could be a new fashion statement."

The hairs on my neck prickled. I spun, reaching for my staff and grasped only thin air.

"A foolish perspective." Tall, broad, and muscular, silver hair flowing down the black armor covering his shoulders, Torvin Rayne watched me with cool, pale eyes. "You are a gentle soul, Cain, unworthy of such power."

Layla hissed and nocked an arrow in the golden bow. "Well, aren't you an effeminate little beauty, Torvin? I'll bet you play tough guy so the other boys don't make fun of you."

"I am beautiful." Torvin stated it as fact, not a hint of bragging in his voice. "A beautiful weapon forged and crafted to carry out the will of the fae. My strategies won the war, and yet I was discarded while Cain was rewarded."

Norna walked from behind a shelf, two huge swords sheathed diagonally across her back. Her brow pinched into a V when her eyes met mine. "Cain is a weak coward."

"Norna, that hurts." I feigned a sad face. "You're saying our mile-high club adventure meant nothing to you?"

"I used you to get what I wanted." She scowled. "Now tell us how you got here before us without your staff."

Layla guffawed. "Gods, Cain. First Aura, now this ogress. Either you don't care, or you're just stupid."

Hannah growled. "Layla, shut up!"

I shrugged. "I'm probably just stupid." I winked at Norna. "But I can't complain. It was fun."

Norna bared her teeth. "How did you get here, Cain?"

I pursed my lips and considered the question. She and Torvin must not have seen the mechanist submarine, and he didn't look as if they'd fought Mecha-Cerberus to get here. That meant they'd crossed over from Gaia in a geographical location close to the entrance to the forge. But how had Torvin known where, exactly, to cross over?

So, I made a counterproposal. "I'll tell you how we got here if you tell me how you knew where to cross over from Gaia."

"Cain used a mechanist submarine and the deepways to reach Oblivion," Torvin said.

My eyes flared with surprise.

Torvin tried to smirk, but his intense hatred turned it into a scowl. "I was the chief strategist for the fae, Cain. I knew you would find a way to get here before me. I knew you would trigger the defenses of the forge and clear a path for me or die trying. Either way, I have won."

I got my emotions under control and watched him coolly. "If you're so smart, how did you not realize I was working for Eclipse all those years?"

"I simply wasn't looking, Cain." His face remained impassive. "I learned that the fae are not the most powerful beings as they falsely claimed. Now I serve a goddess."

"Now you murder kids," I shot back.

"Demis." Torvin's cold gaze took in Hannah. "Hera wishes them dead for good reason." He turned back to me. "The anonymity of our freelancers hid you from me for quite some time. I finally discovered you were doing jobs for Eclipse almost two years ago."

I scoffed. "And you didn't come for me?"

"I considered it," he said. "But I realized you would be far more valuable to me as a tool."

I hated to admit it, but he'd completely tooled me. "Well, congrats." I shrugged. "You got me good."

Torvin managed a grim smile. "Like the clockwork machines the mechanists so love, there are too many intricate and moving parts to my manipulations to explain them all to you."

"I just think it's sad," Layla said. "All that work just to kill Cain? You could've done that anytime because he can't fight worth a shit."

I shook my head. "This isn't just about me, at least not for Torvin." It was obvious now that his multipronged plan included a lot more than just revenge on me. "He wants to destroy the fae because they dishonored him. That's why we're here right now." I smirked at him. "Eclipse has eyes and ears everywhere. He discovered the existence of the armory from his spies in the Pandora Combine. He couldn't reach Oblivion himself because the fae took his staff when they kicked him out of the guard. For a time, he saw the mechanists as his ticket here, but then he discovered me and plotted to steal my oblivion staff."

Layla blinked. "That's a lot of assumptions, Cain."

"Not really," I said. "Torvin knows we used the mechanist submarine to get here, which means he already knew about their operation."

"Impressive," Torvin said in a condescending tone. "Even a gentle deer can be perceptive just before the predator tears out its throat."

"You've obviously never been kicked by a deer," I said.

"Wow." Hannah blew out a breath. "Torvin must have been really pissed to go through all this trouble for you, Cain."

"Torvin didn't go through that much," Aura said. "We did all the work for him."

"No, you sat on your fat little elf ass and did nothing," Layla said. "Cain and I did all the work." She lowered her bow. "Which means I've got a lot of billable hours, Torvin. I expect to be paid."

"We have no quarrel with you, mercenary." Torvin shrugged. "Leave now and we will pay you whatever you ask."

Layla pursed her lips. "A billion dollars?"

Torvin nodded. "If money is what you desire, then money you shall receive."

Layla nodded. "Yeah, a billion dollars sounds right. But I don't take credit cards."

Norna spread her arms to indicate the armory. "We'll soon have all the money in the world."

Hannah growled. "Layla, if you leave us for money, I will kill you myself."

"Give up Cain and the rest of you may go free," Torvin said. "I will make his death quick and easy. But if you resist, I will torture him until he goes mad."

I hated to say it, but it sounded like a good deal. There was just one major problem. After killing me, Torvin would have the entire armory to himself, and that sadistic son of a bitch would make the worlds bow at his feet. "Torvin, I know you want to kill the fae, but by using the weapons in here, you risk destroying all of Feary, Gaia, and other planes."

"Let the worlds burn," Norna said. "We have plenty to choose from, thanks to your oblivion staff."

"The fae will pay for rejecting me and favoring you," Torvin said. "We will burn Feary to the ground and take Gaia for ourselves."

Norna's lips curled into a cruel smile. "You brought our family to ruin, Cain, but thanks to you, we will rise from the ashes and build a dynasty with the humans as our vassals."

"You really think it's worth destroying Feary just to claim revenge, Norna?" I shook my head. "Torvin tricked me into murdering a house full of innocent women and children. He commanded entire families slaughtered just to win a war the humans had no chance of winning anyway. There's no atrocity too great for him. But why destroy an entire world just because my actions ruined your family slave business?"

"You and the fae are responsible!" Norna shouted. "My father and two of my brothers died because of you!"

That was when I realized there was someone missing from this discussion. Targ was too much muscle for Torvin and Norna to leave behind. They were holding him in reserve somewhere. In fact, it was unlikely they'd come alone, and probably had considerable backup waiting for their command.

The time for discussion was nearly over. We had to act now. "Are you in or out, Layla?"

"It's a billion dollars, Cain!" She shrugged. "I've got my future to think about, you know?" Her hands moved so fast, I barely saw her draw the arrow and fire.

The arrow burst from the string like a solar flare, streaking toward Torvin. He reacted instantly, drawing my oblivion staff and deflecting the projectile with the brightblade. The projectile slammed into a furnace and exploded, leaving not so much as a scratch on it. But the explosion unleashed a scalding shockwave that burned the side of my face and singed Torvin's pretty hair.

Norna unleashed an ogre roar and multiple roars answered her back. Eleven male ogres burst around the corner, massive boots pounding the stone floor. They brandished battleaxes, clubs, and giant broadswords—enough to turn us into a fine puree of meat and crushed bone.

Torvin alone would be a handful, but this was just too much. I drew my dueling wands and began firing spells at the oncoming horde.

Noctua glided away and perched on a metal beam high above the furnaces to watch from a safe distance. I wondered if this scenario had played out in the multiverse already and she already knew what would happen.

Layla picked up something that looked like a huge ninja throwing star from the pile of discarded weapons. It had five points, each with curved blades on the ends. She flung it at Norna. The ogress ducked. The star slashed through the neck of one of the rushing ogres, decapitating him, then curved in an arc and came back at Layla.

She shouted in surprise and thrust out a hand as if to stop it. The star stopped perfectly in her palm, dripping blood. Her mouth dropped open. "I love this fucking thing!" She threw it again, but Torvin batted it from the air with my brightblade and sent it sparking across the floor.

I yanked open Aura's backpack and pulled out the first thing my hand found—the warhammer. I held it over my head. "Stop now, or I'll kill us all!"

Torvin held up a hand and the ogres stopped their charge. "You would really kill your"—his lips peeled back in disgust—"friends?"

"I'd kill all of us if it meant stopping you." I bared my teeth. "So, leave now or I'll do it."

Torvin managed a real smirk this time. "Then do it, Cain. I would see the gentle boy find his inner steel and destroy everything he holds dear. That would be vengeance enough, I think."

Norna scoffed. "He doesn't have courage."

"Do it, Cain!" Hannah shouted.

"Don't you dare!" Layla glared at me. "We can kill these idiots and get home in time for dinner."

Aura slumped. "Do it. There's nothing for us here."

Noctua had remained quiet the entire time, merely observing. I looked up at her. "Can you stop them?"

She blinked her big eyes. "I have no power to intervene."

"Really?" I gripped the warhammer tighter. "I'm about to destroy this entire mountain."

"If that is what you wish," she said. "But it is really all about control."

I was flummoxed for a moment. Then I realized what she meant. I didn't have to move the entire mountain. Maybe I could do something on a smaller scale.

"Cain, your hand is twitching," Layla said. "Do not drop the hammer!"

I imagined slamming the hammer on the floor and a great crack opening beneath the feet of our enemies. The hammer head glowed orange. "Well, it's been nice," I said.

Norna's eyes widened. "Stop him!"

I slammed the hammer on the rocky floor. The head rang like a gong. The floor shook and a crack ran from the hammer beneath the feet of Torvin and Norna, growing wider and wider by the second. They leapt aside. An ogre roared in surprise and tumbled into the fissure, his howls vanishing in the depths.

I ran to the far wall and willed the hammer to blast us a hole back up to the surface. Then I slammed it against the surface. The rock exploded upward and outward, creating a slope leading to daylight. "Run!"

Layla and Aura were already ten steps ahead of me, oxygen helmets back on. Hannah stared at me with an open mouth. I grasped her arm and shook her out of her daze. "Hannah, run!"

She flinched and took off like a shot. I ran behind her. The glare of the harsh sunlight almost blinded me when I reached the top. I stumbled into Layla and nearly knocked her over because she'd stopped moving. I quickly saw why.

Dozens of mechanists in clockwork exoskeletons were charging from the tunnel on the far side of the pit, automatic rifles aimed our way. They closed the distance rapidly and would be within range in seconds.

Torvin and Norna burst from the hole I'd made. He brandished my brightblade and she wielded a broadsword in each hand.

I slammed the ground with the hammer, sending a crack racing toward the mechanists. Their exo suits stumbled but their long mechanical legs stepped over the fissure. Rifles fired and bullets streaked through the air toward us.

"Those are homing bullets!" I shouted.

We were caught in the open with no way to protect ourselves from the onslaught.

CHAPTER 29

Smoke trailed behind the hundreds of projectiles streaking our way. I could tell by their trajectories that not only were they targeted on us, but also on Torvin and Norna. I gripped the hammer and thought about its primary purpose—building worlds. It seems such a small tool for so grand a project. But maybe it could help us in this situation.

I banged it against the rocky ground, focusing my will on what I wanted it to do. The igneous rock jutted up from the earth, forming a wall twenty feet long. The incendiary payloads of the homing bullets exploded against the barrier. Torvin and Norna were too far away to be protected, but even in the open, Torvin wasn't easy prey.

He swept my staff in an arc, sending a torrent of wind back at the bullets. They crashed into the ground, the tiny fins unable to navigate the miniature storm. I took advantage of his momentary distraction and slammed Earthmaker against the ground again. A spike of rock thrust up beneath Torvin. Only his hyper-fast reflexes allowed him to avoid being impaled.

Torvin smiled grimly and came for me.

The hammer was surprisingly light despite the large head, but I wasn't sure if it would work well in a fight against my staff. Even properly armed, I'd be hard-pressed to defeat Torvin in a one-on-one matchup.

Running was the smart move. The mechanists would be on us soon, and even if I could hold my own against Torvin, Norna could smash through all of us. But Torvin had my staff and I wanted it back. I felt it calling for me across the short distance, its bond with me still strong. But as long as Torvin held it, I couldn't simply tear it from his grasp. He had to either give it over willingly or let go by accident.

"This isn't the time to fight," Aura said. "Use the hammer to get us out of here, Cain."

"The elf is right." Layla gripped my arm. "We've got to go."

I looked at Hannah. She nodded. I slammed Earthmaker into the ground once more, and a stone wall sprang up between us and Torvin. I pointed to the nearest wall of the volcanic crater and we started running.

Despite the heat and exertion, my breaths seemed to come slightly easier than they had earlier. It seemed my body was finally acclimating. That was a good thing since Aura and Layla were going to burn through all our oxygen in no time. I glanced back. Torvin and Norna rounded the wall I'd created and were racing after us.

I reached the crater wall, reared back the hammer and smacked it. In my haste, I must not have accurately visualized what I wanted, because the entire side of the mountain—hundreds of feet high and wide—exploded outward, sending dust, rocks, and boulders flying across the beach and into the water beyond. A handful of mechanists near a dinghy at the water's edge cried out and scattered as chunks crashed all around them.

We raced through the newly formed gap. It was hundreds of yards across—big enough to march an entire army through. Thanks to me, anyone could just waltz right into the armory without problem and claim the entire inventory. The sun glinted off metal up and to my right.

Mecha-Cerberus glared angrily down at me from his perch. He reared back his head and howled bloody murder.

"Fuck my life," I panted.

The silver lining in the mess I'd created was that no one was there to stop us on the other side. If the mechanists had spotted our submarine, they hadn't taken the time to reclaim it. Even so, there was no reason for us to go back to our submarine. Another better equipped sub was a good quarter mile closer to us already, and only a handful of people guarded it. Most of those guards were scattered all over the beach, some dead, others cowering in fear.

I pointed to their submarine. "New plan, steal that one!"

"But all our gear is in the other one," Aura said.

"We'll pick it up on the way out of town!" I dodged between boulders and ran into a mechanist who was still on his feet. I slammed him with Earthmaker and he flew out over the rocks, making a nice splash in the water.

"I want that hammer," Layla said.

I ignored her, smashing rocks out of the way as easily as slapping ping-pong balls aside with a paddle. A pair of wide-eyed guards shouted in surprise when I smacked aside a boulder they'd been hiding behind. I sent one man sailing along the beach. Layla speared the other with a dagger. We hopped in the dinghy and were pleasantly surprised to see that it had a clockwork motor instead of oars.

The front window of the submarine was open, but I couldn't tell if anyone was inside. Layla revved the engine and headed out at an angle that would make it difficult for anyone in the submarine to see our approach. The periscope wasn't up, which seemed a good sign that no one was watching us.

"No!" someone howled from behind us.

I looked back and spotted Horatio standing on the beach, shaking a fist at us.

Layla burst into laughter. "Oh, that poor bastard."

We moored the dinghy to the sub, and everyone clambered aboard. Layla opened the hatch and dropped inside, ready to fight if anyone were there to meet her. But it seemed the entire crew was onshore.

Before I climbed down the ladder inside, I peered out at the beach and saw Torvin and Norna fighting mechanists in exo-suits. Despite the armaments of the exos, the trained assassin and ogress were destroying them left and right. There was little doubt that before long, Torvin would control the armory and the weapons inside.

With the oblivion staff, he could spirit them all away in no time. I had to do something—anything to slow him down. I had just the way to do it, but it meant go back ashore. I cursed myself for not thinking of it sooner, but I hadn't thought of the possibilities Earthmaker brought to the table.

I slid down the ladder and ran to the bridge. It was far more refined and finished than ours, every console fully outfitted with dials, knobs, and levers. "I've got to go back to the shore while Torvin and Norna are still fighting. Get our stuff from the other sub and I'll meet you there."

"Cain, no!" Hannah ran after me.

I gripped her shoulders. "Listen to me, Hannah, I can't let them get their hands on those weapons. I've got to do this myself."

Layla strode up behind her. "Cain can handle himself, kid. Let him do what he has to do."

"Which is what?" Aura said.

I told them my plan.

Layla whistled. "This I've got to see—from the safety of the sub, of course."

Aura's forehead pinched. "I hope it works."

I pecked a kiss on Hannah's cheek. "I'll be back." And then I climbed up and closed the hatch behind me before she could say another word.

Torvin and Norna had battled through most of the mechanists and were nearly to the trail I'd carved through the boulder-strewn beach. I untied the dinghy and angled it back toward the mountain and away from the battle. Everyone onshore was too busy fighting to notice me or do anything about it.

The clockwork engine wasn't powerful, and choppy waves slowed my progress. Torvin took note of my path and began running down the beach to head me off. I wanted to be closer to the mountain, but at this miserable pace, I'd never make it in time. There was a chance my plan would work from this far out, provided I'd visualized my goal properly.

So, I cut straight to shore and beached the dinghy.

"Cain!" Torvin roared from behind me. "Stop!"

I glanced back, extended my middle finger, and smirked. "Fuck you, Torvin." Then I filled my mind with a picture of exactly what I wanted to go down. I raised Earthmaker and pounded sand. There was no great crack of stone as the hammer hit the black sand. Just a disappointing crunching of gravel. But the effects were impressive.

The earth rumbled and quaked. The ground split into a small fissure that grew wider as it lengthened. It struck the seaside wall of the mountain. Massive cracks spread up the side of the dead volcano. The entire mountain shook. Mecha-Cerberus appeared in the distance, his metal form racing down the cliffs as his home crumbled and collapsed in on itself. I really wanted to watch everything from start to end, but with Torvin bearing down on me, I had no time.

I jumped back in the dinghy and urged it out to sea again. Our newly commandeered submarine had moved into position offshore, coming as close as the angle of the seabed allowed.

A dagger flashed past, missing me by a good margin. "Cain!" Norna shouted. "I will bathe in your blood!"

I angled toward the sub and turned back in time to dodge another thrown dagger. It was impressive that the ogress could throw them with such force over fifty yards. I didn't want to imagine what she'd do if she got her hands on me.

"I'll always treasure our memories," I shouted back at her. "Every night I'll go to sleep imagining us making sweet love all over again."

Norna shrieked like a banshee and hurled four more daggers, but they flew wide. I was about to taunt her a little more when Torvin raised an aquamarine trident that I recognized immediately. He'd taken Tidebringer from the armory.

My smirk vanished. "Oh, fuck."

Torvin reached the water's edge and stabbed it downward. The waves lapping the shore reversed course, growing larger and rolling toward me. The dinghy motor was already at full throttle, so all I could do was watch as the wave swelled higher and higher until I lost sight of shore.

Hannah and the others watched from the front window of the sub, eyes wide at the tidal wave quickly catching up to me. There was nothing they or I could do. I wasn't escaping the wave. If I continued my current course, it would upend the dinghy. Training in the Oblivion Guard had involved underwater maneuvering and survival, but none of it had prepared me for surfing a tidal wave in a rubber boat.

On the other hand, I'd binged so much television since my arrival on Gaia, that I'd watched surfing championships. The dinghy wasn't a surfboard, but the principle was the same. As the waters swelled beneath me, I angled the boat to the left, riding the wave diagonally, and allowing it to propel me forward faster without tipping. My solution might have been good except for the rocky formations rising above the waters not far away.

If I continued this course, I'd smash right into them. I looked back at the monster wave. It looked at least thirty feet high and was rapidly growing steeper. The only thing in my favor was that it hadn't begun to crest, meaning the top hadn't curled in over me. That left me with one avenue of escape.

I steered left and drove the dinghy up the wave at a wide angle. The boat skipped across the rough water and the motor strained against the tide. It was slow, but I was still going forward. The submarine was another fifty yards out, but the rock formations were only another thirty. I gripped the throttle tighter, as if that might make the dinghy go faster.

The rocks grew closer and closer. Just a few yards out, the boat crested the wave and skipped down the backside at an alarming speed. There was nothing but muddy seabed between me and the shore. Tidebringer had sucked up all the water to create the massive wave.

"Fuck me." I tried to angle the boat to slow the descent, but it was too steep. The dinghy hit a rough patch of water and flipped. I flew out and plunged into the backside of the wave for an instant before smacking solid ground. Mud splashed. Suffocating fish flopped all around me, mouths working uselessly in the open air.

The dinghy splashed upside-down in a puddle a few feet away, propeller still spinning. I pushed up to my feet. Torvin and Norna watched me from the safety of shore. Torvin moved the trident as if trying to manipulate the wave, but with no water nearby, it didn't seem to work. I took the opportunity to seek a little revenge.

I smashed the hammer down on the seabed and sent a crack chasing after my foes. They backed up slowly at first until realizing that when they changed directions, so did the crack. Torvin bared his teeth. Rather than run from the fissure, he threw Tidebringer to the ground and charged out across the mud toward me. Norna blinked in surprise. Apparently, her bloodlust wasn't as strong as his because she elected to remain onshore.

I turned the crack to intercept Torvin, widening it. He dodged aside in a blur, too fast for me to adjust the direction of the crack. I slammed the hammer down again and started another fissure, but he was almost upon me, brightblade blazing in his hand. I visualized the earth swallowing him whole. The hammer obliged and the ground sank into a pit.

Torvin's elven reflexes came to the rescue. Using the staff, he propelled himself up and over the gaping hole, nailing a perfect three-point landing ten feet away. I raised the hammer for another strike, but he intercepted it with the brightblade. I yanked it back and settled into a defensive stance.

"Nowhere to run, now, Ghostwalker." Torvin's lips curled into a sneer. "To this day, I have no idea how you became a guardian. You're nothing but a weak human, unfit to even clean the latrine of your betters."

"You're rotten to the core." I bared my teeth. "You're unnecessarily cruel in everything you do, and you couldn't strategize your way out of a paper bag unless it included killing innocent civilians." I smirked. "You're absolute shit, Torvin, and it's time to clean the latrine."

Torvin's gaze remained stony, emotionless. His response was nonverbal and perfectly in line with the kind of person he was. He swung the brightblade, going for a decapitating blow. The hammer's three-foot handle made it less than ideal for parrying, but I managed to deflect the blow with the top of the handle while keeping my fingers intact.

The brightblade blurred through attack after attack. Even after bolstering my speed and strength with magic, I was barely able to stop him from cleaving me to bits. Every time the blade came close to slicing into me, I sensed the bond between me and my staff. An old friend was being forced to murder me, but there was nothing it could do about it. Unless I dealt Torvin a lucky blow, I couldn't pry it from his iron grip.

All I could do was fend off his attacks until the inevitable death blow finally made it through my defenses.

CHAPTER 30

A massive plume of dust rose in the distance where Olympus Prime had collapsed in on itself. Those rumblings had ceased minutes ago. When the ground began vibrating beneath my feet, I wondered what fresh new hell was coming my way. When Torvin's gaze flicked from my face to something behind me, I quickly concluded that it had something to do with the tidal wave he'd created to crush me.

Under the onslaught of his attacks, I couldn't spare even a split second to look back. I managed to manipulate our positioning, rotating the fight sideways. There was nothing but muddy seabed for hundreds of yards, revealing the rock formations I'd nearly crashed against. Much of the exposed sea life had already suffocated, thousands of new casualties to add to Torvin's list.

The tidal wave had become a massive wall of water a hundred feet tall, stretching into the distance as far as the eye could see. In his first use of Tidebringer, Torvin had gone full psycho in his attempt to destroy me. But now that wall of water was starting to reverse course, tons upon tons of liquid wrath were about to crash back down and grind us into fish food.

It would almost be satisfying to keep fighting Torvin until it crushed us both. At least then I could take the cruel bastard down with me. But it was obvious that he was more than prepared to die if it meant killing me too. And I didn't want to give him the satisfaction, no matter how briefly he felt it.

My endurance was waning and Torvin's brutal strikes seemed to come faster and faster. Somehow, I had to throw him off balance. Another blow against the hammer nearly made my arm buckle. Torvin spun for another strike, this time going for my legs. And that was when I knew what I had to do.

If I botched my next move, it was over.

I'd studied Torvin's fighting methods during training. He was so fast it was almost impossible to detect the body language telegraphing his next move. But after losing to him time and time again during sparring sessions, I'd finally learned his tells well enough to hold my own against him, even if only for a short while.

I blocked the blow to my legs, parried another strike at my shoulder. And then Torvin gripped the hilt of the brightblade with both hands. There were only two maneuvers he made with a two-handed grip and either one of them played right into my gambit. His shift in stance gave me the split second I needed to time it right.

All of Torvin's attacks were vicious, but this one bore all his strength behind it. I ghostwalked as Torvin brought the staff straight down in an arc that would split a person in two. I flickered behind him as he slashed through a puff of black smoke where I'd been a moment before.

Torvin knew about my ghostwalking ability. Nearly every time I'd tried using it in a sparring match against him, he'd anticipated it and knocked me on my ass. But that was because I hadn't used it at the right time. Torvin's strike used all his weight and strength. Without me to block it, his forward momentum caused him to briefly stumble.

That was all the opening I needed. Earthmaker smacked his knuckles hard enough to break bones. Torvin cried out. His hand reflexively opened, and my staff fell. I snatched it before it hit the ground and sheathed it in one fluid motion. The towering wall of water was only a few hundred feet away. There was no way for me to outrun it, so I improvised.

Slamming Earthmaker against the seabed, I visualized what I needed. The earth rumbled. A shaft of rock twelve feet in diameter burst from the ground beneath my feet, rising into the air high and fast, carrying me skyward at a frightening velocity. The violent tremors nearly bucked me off, but somehow, I managed to hang on as the shelf of rock rumbled fifty feet higher than the tidal wave.

Torvin roared his fury at the prey now out of his reach. Then he hauled ass toward shore, slipping and sliding on the slick mud in almost comical fashion. The water pounded against the base of the rock, causing bone-rattling vibrations. As more and more water rushed past, the tremors grew stronger, making me fear my construct wasn't sturdy enough to hold up against the onslaught.

And then the main wave struck. My improvised tower swayed. Rock cracked, crumbled, and fell from the edges. I lay down flat and held on, but my grip was impeded by a thin layer of mud left by the seabed. The roar of water and cracking rock deafened me. I gritted my teeth and prepared for the sensation of freefall. If that happened, there was little I could do except try to cushion my fall with a shield.

It was unlikely it would preserve me from falling rock and pounding waters, but there really was nothing else to be done except give up and die.

At long last, the shaking stopped. The shoreline was flooded for hundreds of feet inland, but the tide was quickly sucking it back out, the water trying to once again find equilibrium. Torvin and Norna stood atop boulders, looking down at the water as it receded back to sea. Of the mechanists, I saw only corpses and broken exoskeletons. I wondered if Horatio had survived.

I wondered if Tidebringer would be washed out to sea or if Torvin would once again find it on the beach and try to kill me again. I didn't really want to wait around and find out. I gently tapped Earthmaker against the rock shaft and willed it to shrink back into the seabed. With a subdued rumble and grind of stone on stone, it descended back into the water. I stopped it about ten feet above sea level and scanned the horizon.

There was no sign of the stolen submarine. I spotted the one we'd arrived in, its broken hull cracked like an egg against the rocky shore by the tidal wave.

"Oh, shit." Had Hannah and the others survived? I turned in a full circle, searching for signs of another destroyed submarine. They could have been smashed to bits underwater, the remains now sitting on the ocean floor. My heart skipped a beat, thinking about Hannah meeting such a terrible fate. Cthulhu would no longer have his demigoddess, and I would have lost the only person in the world who actually liked me.

My fists clenched and red filled my vision. I turned the full fury of my gaze toward Torvin. There was nothing in this world to prevent me from hunting him down. I would unleash the full fury of the armory on him even if it meant destroying all of Oblivion.

Fuck existence. It was overrated.

"Cain, how in the hell did you survive?"

I flinched and spun. The submarine floated a few feet from my island of stone. Layla's torso poked from the hatch.

"Let me see him!" Hannah shouted from inside.

I swallowed the lump in my throat and wiped away the tear that burned my eye. I jumped into the water and swam to the ladder on the side of the submarine, climbed up it without a word. I didn't trust my voice to work without cracking. By the time I reached the hatch, I'd regained my composure.

"We've got to destroy the armory once and for all," I said.

Layla's brow furrowed. "Uh, what happened?"

"I'll explain." I pointed down. "Let me in."

She slid down the ladder and I joined her. Hannah embraced me in a bone-crushing hug before my feet even hit the floor.

"Cain!" Hannah looked up at me with teary eyes. "I thought you were dead."

I smiled, taking a moment to reign in my emotions, and held up Earthmaker. "I had a little help."

Aura pushed past Layla and stared at me in open-mouthed astonishment. "I can't believe it. That tidal wave was massive."

"We put the sub a full speed and barely outran it," Layla said. "Then it just stopped, a giant wall of water all up and down the coast. I took us out further, so the tide didn't drag us back. We didn't know what happened to you."

"There was nothing but mud on the other side," I said. "I fought Torvin. Then the water came back. I used Earthmaker to build a stone elevator to take me above it until it was past."

"That hammer makes you a god, Cain." Hannah smiled through her tears.

I shook my head. "No one, not even the gods, should have these weapons." I reached behind my back and drew my staff. "I also took back what was mine."

Layla whooped. "Gods be damned, Cain, you know how to make a woman sopping wet."

Hannah gagged. "No one wants to think about your stank ass getting wet, Layla."

Aura's astonished expression shifted back to neutral. "I'm glad you made it, Cain."

I raised an eyebrow. "If you say so." I squeezed water from my soaked clothes and nodded toward the back section of the sub. I'm going to look around. Hopefully, the crew has some clothes laying around. In the meantime, let's get further out to sea. We need to track down one of these fires of creation."

"And do what?" Aura said. "We can't go back for the weapons with Torvin there."

I nodded. "Maybe not. But unless he has a way to dig through tons of rock, it's going to take him some time to reach them." I went to the forward window and peered shoreward. Torvin was searching the beach, probably for Tidebringer. If it was still there, he could use the seawater to clear the rubble covering the armory, which meant he might have a way to reach the weapons after all.

"The elf has a point," Layla said. "What's the point of finding a fire of creation if we don't have the weapons with us to melt them down?"

I pursed my lips. "I think I have an idea that might kill two birds with one stone."

Something glinted in the sun. At first, I thought it was a mechanist drone, but as it came closer, I realized it wasn't that at all. I climbed the ladder and opened the hatch. The clockwork owl, Noctua, fluttered to a landing on the sail next to me.

"I thought you couldn't leave the forge," I said.

The owl blinked at me. "The magic tethering me there was destroyed when you collapsed the mountain." There was no hint of anger to her tone. "I narrowly escaped and decided to accompany you since you're the most interesting beings I've encountered in many thousands of years."

I scoffed. "That's not a good thing." I held out my hand and she stepped into my palm. Then I brought her below with me. "I'm sorry if I almost killed you."

Gears whirred softly as she turned her head toward me. "I found your decision fascinating. This was not in any of the alternate branches of the multiverse."

"Ooh, it's the owl!" Hannah clapped her hands. "I thought you were trapped in the armory."

"Destroying the mountain freed her," I said. "And I think she'll come in real handy."

Aura dropped into a seat and sighed in relief. "Well, we've survived two major disasters and a small-scale battle. Where to now?"

I looked at Noctua who now perched on a console. "Where's the closest fire that might still be strong enough to melt down the weapons?"

"The nearest one would be the Kameni Desert." Noctua's eyes glowed and projected a holographic globe in the air before me. The globe rotated, showing the landmasses of Oblivion. Oceans claimed only half the real estate, and there were no major land masses at the poles.

It was fascinating to me, because no one had ever shared an accurate map of Oblivion with us during training. I walked to the projection and jabbed a finger at the label on one of the continents. "What language is that?"

"It has no name. It was a language used by the gods, but they abandoned it in favor of Alder." The labels changed to English. "The gods created their own lands to rule over. Olympus Prime was on the continent created by the Greek gods."

The referenced land mass resembled the lower half of Europe. Other continents looked similar to those on Gaia as well. It seemed the gods hadn't deviated much from the original plan.

The image zoomed in on a black X near the western edge of a red desert. "The fragment of fire in the Kameni Desert is a day's journey on horseback from our current location."

Layla traced a finger along the coastline. "How long by submarine and foot?"

Noctua rotated her head toward her. "I don't know. I would need more information about this vessel."

"Don't you already know everything?" Hannah asked.

"I'm afraid not." Noctua's eyes clicked and the holographic image vanished. "I was once brought information from all over the worlds, but now it is difficult to come by. The Tetron at the base of my pedestal in the armory tapped into the tree of life and allowed me to gather information from the multiverse, but now it is buried beneath the mountain."

I grimaced. "Guess I really fucked up your life."

"On the contrary." Noctua's head rotated to me. "I now have an opportunity to explore on my own. Viewing events from the pedestal was impersonal."

Layla hopped in the pilot seat and rotated around to face me. "So, Cain, what's your brilliant plan to destroy the weapons?"

"I'm not sure if it'll work, but it's worth a try." I dropped into the captain's chair. "I want to use Earthmaker to knock the fire of creation back at the mountain. It should melt everything in the forge if I can land it on target."

"Good plan," Hannah said.

Layla snorted. "Crazy, but I like it."

"It sounds incredibly dangerous." Aura sighed. "But it might work."

Noctua blinked at me. "It won't work."

"Huh?" I pointed at the wake of destruction I'd left behind. "If it can level mountains, it shouldn't have a problem putting a fireball a few miles."

"The hammer only interacts with earth, not fire," Noctua said. You would also risk destroying the hammer by bringing it into contact with the fire."

I threw up my hands. "Well, what else am I supposed to do? Is there another weapon in the forge that can handle the fires of creation?"

"There are sets of tongs that can be used to move the fire, but only a god has the strength to do so," Noctua said. "In short, you would need Hephaestus himself to aid you."

I face-palmed. "What a fucking dilemma. There are a dozen different ways to end the world just lying around in that place for Torvin to steal. Why didn't those idiot gods just destroy them long ago?"

"I cannot say why." Noctua's wings fluttered. "The gods reason on levels even I cannot comprehend. Many of them are quite indifferent to the affairs of mortals and have little concern for world-ending events."

"Here's the thing." Torvin was no longer visible on the shore, but I knew he was still there somewhere. "Torvin will find Tidebringer and use the power of the ocean to move the rubble I piled on the armory. He'll eventually get to those weapons and when he does, you can be certain a world-ending event is going to bend us over and ram itself right up our asses."

Noctua blinked. "Though I don't possess an ass, I must concur with your assessment."

Unless I figured out something soon, it was game over.

CHAPTER 31

"Could Earthmaker destroy the world in one blow?" Hannah asked. "Maybe knock all the weapons into space?"

Noctua shook her head. "No, but it could be used to make the world uninhabitable with a methodical campaign of destruction."

Hannah pursed her lips. "Maybe it can't be used to directly move the fire, but could it be used to indirectly move it?"

I raised an eyebrow. "How so?"

She shrugged. "Make a big trench and let the fireball roll back to the mountain."

Noctua blinked several times. "Yes, I believe that would work." Gears whirred softy as she turned her head toward Hannah. "The mind of a demigod transcends that of mere mortals."

Layla scoffed. "The girl isn't all that, so don't inflate her ego."

Aura blew out a breath. "Shut up, Layla. I think it's a good idea."

"I'm not a mere mortal, elf, and that girl definitely isn't smarter than me." Layla huffed and crossed her arms. "How far inland will we have to walk to reach the fireball?"

Noctua closed her eyes for a moment. "Five miles. The terrain is quite difficult to traverse on foot, and it's much hotter there than here, thus the name, Kameni Desert."

Hannah frowned. "I don't understand."

"Kameni means scorched in Greek," Noctua said.

"Oh, joy." Layla blew out a breath. "Do we have enough oxygen for me to walk that far?"

I shook my head. "I think it's best if you and Aura remain on the sub. Hannah and I will handle this ourselves."

Hannah's eyes lit and her chin tilted up a little.

Layla groaned. "You're giving her a superiority complex, Cain."

I raised an eyebrow. "Like yours?"

"Mine is well-deserved." Layla rolled her eyes and spun her chair to face forward

The submarine lurched forward, careening toward a rocky outcropping.

Aura gripped her chair to keep from falling out. "What are you doing?"

"I'm not doing anything!" Layla gripped a lever and threw the submarine into full reverse. "The water's moving!"

"Son of a bitch." I looked to shore and saw Torvin thrust Tidebringer into the water. "He's already got it. We need to get out of here before he beaches us."

"On it!" Layla spun the sub around and put it to full throttle. For a moment, it seemed we were going nowhere, but we finally started to inch forward.

"Could Torvin drain the ocean with that thing?" I asked Noctua.

The owl shook her head. "Though the weapons grant godlike powers, only a true god could drain the ocean in moments. But we should put several miles between us and him to be safe."

Hannah strapped herself into a chair. "Think of how much good you could do with a weapon like that. You could bring water to the desert. You could stop a drought. It doesn't need to be used for destruction."

"They are tools and can be used for creation or destruction," Noctua said. "With great power comes great responsibility."

I raised an eyebrow. "I've heard that one before."

"Nothing with that much power should exist," Aura said. "Not even the gods."

Hannah rotated her chair toward the elf. "If the gods didn't exist, you wouldn't exist."

"Stupid elf." Layla snorted. "The gods don't mess with us that much anymore, so why worry about them?"

"The same gods who tried to kill Hannah?" Aura said. "The same gods who discarded weapons capable of destroying the world?" She thrust a finger at Hannah. "And Hannah is the vassal of Cthulhu, a god who seeks to rise above all others!"

Noctua bobbed her body back and forth in an owl nod. "Fascinating points."

"Do you agree with her?" I asked the owl in a low voice.

"I do not agree with anyone," she replied. "I gather information and evaluate it. Thanks to you, I am now among contemporary catalysts responsible for major branches of the multiverse. It will be fascinating to see how this unfolds."

"You're not worried about us ending the world?" I said.

"Worrying never solved anything," Noctua said. "I will enjoy watching this journey to whatever end may come."

"Now that's my kind of attitude." Layla guided the submarine around a shoal. "I think we're out of reach of Tidebringer. I'll head east until you say when, bird."

The tension knotting my shoulders released ever so slightly. I was exhausted. Something hard pressed against my leg through the fabric of my jumpsuit. I reached in the pocket and pulled out the ivory orb I'd found in the forge.

Holding it up to the one on my staff, it seemed there were no visual differences. "Noctua, is there a way to swap one orb for the other?"

"You must will the staff to release one orb, and accept the other," she replied.

"Make it so," I told my staff. The orb detached from the socket and fell into my open palm. I placed the other in the socket and willed the staff to accept it. It snapped into place. "Let's see what you've got." I activated the brightblade. It hummed to life, glowing a little brighter than usual. But unless I wanted to slash the submarine to pieces, testing it would have to wait.

I turned it off with a thought and wondered if it was really much of an upgrade. I turned to Noctua. "You don't know anything else about this orb?"

"Only what I told you earlier," she replied. "Hephaestus might know more."

"Yeah, well, I doubt he'll make himself available to me anytime soon."

Hannah looked worried. "It won't give him magic cancer again, will it?"

"It possesses no curses," Noctua replied. "The orb should be safe to use."

Layla shouted in alarm an instant before something slammed into the hull. "We've got problems!"

Bodies squirmed against the window, fish eyes staring at us through the fishbowl window. The water outside swarmed with leechen, and we were just plowing through them. But the sheer mass of bodies was slowing us considerably.

Layla turned to Aura. "Electrify the hull. That'll clear them out."

I held up a hand. "There's no need to boil them alive."

"Do these things talk?" Layla tapped her temple. "Do they reason like people or are they trying to kill us?"

"They don't kill for food—at least from what I know." I blew out a breath. "Slow us down and—" Whatever I was about to say ran screaming from my mind as the leechens parted. A glowing man streaked through the water toward us without moving a muscle. "Oh, fuck. Everyone hold onto something!"

Instead of smashing into us, the man came to an instant stop just outside the window. He pointed up.

Layla got the message without anyone saying a word. She pulled on a lever and the submarine began to rise. It bobbed to the surface thirty feet later. I climbed up the ladder and opened the hatch, my heart racing at what waited outside. I climbed down the sail and stood on the hull. The man flew up out of the water and landed lightly on the hull.

He was lean and muscular, with the appearance of someone in their mid-twenties. But his eyes held the experience of the ages. I steeled myself for what might come and waited for him to speak first.

"Do you know what you have done?" His voice was deep and commanding. "You have defeated the defenses of the armory and initiated the end days."

"We didn't mean to, sir." I tried to keep my composure. "Are you Poseidon?"

He watched me with sea-green eyes, and I felt certain of his identity without him saying a word. "You were warned to stop your meddling, mortal. Hermes himself came to you and asked. Now Tidebringer is free upon the world and my kingdom will be used to wreak havoc upon our creations. The horsemen will ride, and all that now stands will fall to dust."

Hannah stepped up beside me. "It's my fault. Cain did this for me."

Poseidon pursed his lips and narrowed his eyes. "It seems there are too many branches leading to the end and too few promising salvation. Perhaps this is for the best."

"You're a god," Hannah said. "Just take the trident from Torvin and help us destroy the weapons in the forge!"

He shook his head. "I cannot directly interfere, or the end of worlds will become the end of the universe itself. The original fires of creation have cooled, for reasons we know not. If all life ceases, then it will be for good."

Hannah's mouth dropped open. "But there are fires here on Oblivion that still burn."

"Fragments," Poseidon said. "Barely enough to spark a mere portion of life. Perhaps the souls of the dead will manage to live on, but even that cannot be guaranteed."

"I really don't like the sound of this," Layla said in a strained voice. I looked back and saw her and Aura regarding the god with awe in their eyes.

"So, life might end on Oblivion and Gaia, but nowhere else if you don't interfere?" Aura asked.

Poseidon nodded. "Yes, little one. Choose your paths wisely from here, for the passage to salvation is narrow and treacherous and may cost you dearly."

Aura's fists clenched and tears filled her eyes. "Perhaps it would be better if the gods killed themselves and left us in peace."

Hannah gasped.

Poseidon simply nodded. "I am sorry, little one, but that would solve nothing."

I jumped in before Aura pissed him off. "Isn't this direct interference? Surely talking to us is the same as helping us."

"Have my words aided or hindered you?" Poseidon said. "I think not. I have broken no covenant. I am simply here to visit my children, the leechens. I have not seen them in far too long."

The submarine began to move eastward even though no one was at the helm. We somehow maintained our balance despite the sudden movement.

"How lucky that a favorable tide has found you," Poseidon said. "Provided you use Earthmaker wisely, yet another tide may safely take you to one of the few burning embers of the flames that once fueled creation." He looked directly at Hannah. "Even now, Hera plots your demise. Where some see the good in our offspring, she sees only the bad."

Hannah gulped. "Isn't she directly interfering by trying to kill me?"

He shook his head. "Catspaws."

"Tools," Layla said. "If she doesn't get blood on her hands, she's not interfering."

Hope filled Hannah's eyes. "Do you know who my father is?"

Poseidon shook his head. "It is not me, that much I can say."

"Can you free her from Cthulhu?" I said.

Another headshake. "She entered a bargain freely. I cannot interfere." Poseidon's eyes met mine once more. "Thanatos bids you hello, and says he is not quite ready to ride the end days." With that, he leapt into the air, sailing across a twenty-foot arc, and vanished into the waters without even a ripple.

Pale bodies swarmed beneath the surface, following the glowing god down into the depths of the sea.

Wind whipped through Layla's hair. "We're moving fast, and the engines aren't even engaged." She gripped the ladder and looked ahead. "He has a funny way of not interfering."

I watched Poseidon's glow fade into the deep, dark depths. "What did he mean by a favorable tide if we used Earthmaker wisely?"

"It's useless on water," Aura said.

Hannah turned to her. "You want the gods to kill themselves? Maybe you should have tried to kill him yourself."

Aura turned up her nose. "As if I could do anything against him."

"You could have told him how you feel about things at the very least." Hannah trembled with delight. "It's a shame you can't appreciate such an amazing experience, Aura. How many people get to meet a god in their lifetime?"

"It's not like they're better than us." Layla tapped a finger on her lips as if in thought. "Oh wait, I'm thinking about celebrities. Gods are way better than us."

Aura shook her head. "When someone is that powerful, even a simple, thoughtless action can destroy lives. No one should have that power. No one."

"Everyone deals with shit, elf." Layla climbed up the ladder and went partway down the hatch. "Get over it, and your life will be a lot happier." She vanished below.

Hannah practically danced over to the ladder. "I like the Greek gods way better than Cthulhu. She climbed up and dropped into the hatch.

I walked toward the ladder, but Aura touched my arm gently and looked up at me with concern. "This is not the end of days I desired."

"I don't think what you want is possible, Aura." I sighed. "I don't know what happened to you to make you hate the gods so much, but there's really nothing you can do about it."

She turned out to face the sea, shoulder sagging.

I bit my lower lip and considered leaving her to sulk, but forced myself to care, just a little bit, about what she might be feeling. "Just spit it out, Aura. Tell me why you're on this impossible quest."

"I had a twin sister." She turned to me. "As did my mother, my grandmother, and all my female ancestors going back thousands of years. Even if I never mate, in two years' time, I will become pregnant and give birth to twin girls. And like all those before them, one will be sacrificed, her soul torn asunder and consumed one year after birth."

My mouth dropped open. "What in the actual fuck, Aura?"

"The gods cursed our bloodline because one of our ancestors did not see the reason for worshipping them." She shivered despite the heat. "The council elders called her to task. When she still refused, the statues of the gods came to life. One by one they pronounced her guilty. Hera handed down the judgement—that every generation of her family would bear twin females. One would be sacrificed to the gods, and the other would bear the next sacrificial child in her fortieth year."

"Okay, that's the most fucked up thing I've heard in a while." I grimaced. "Then again, Hera's the one running an assassination squad that kills kids." I looked at the dark waters. "Was Poseidon one of them?"

"Most likely." She deflated. "He didn't even seem to know or care about who I am."

"Like Noctua said, the gods don't feel or think the same way we do."

"Cain, that's why I can't afford emotional attachments." She looked back at me, tears in her eyes. "My mother tried to end the curse by killing herself before she gave birth by slashing her own throat. She woke up later in a pool of her own blood without even a scratch on her skin. She tried to kill herself in horrible ways, even leaping into an active volcano. She would always wake up somewhere else, alive once again."

"She jumped in a volcano?" I whistled. "Your mother was hardcore. That would have melted her to nothing."

"Something caught her after she leapt, and she lost consciousness." Aura sighed. "My mother became celibate after her a year before her fortieth birthday, but she still gave birth to me and my sister. When my sister was sacrificed, my mother committed suicide once again. That time, she died for good."

"Why the fortieth year?" I said. "Elves live for hundreds of years."

Aura sagged. "I have no idea."

I was astounded. If Aura was telling the truth, she couldn't die.

CHAPTER 32

"You're immortal until forty?" My forehead pinched. "That's how you survived Sigma, isn't it?" The lightning demigod had blasted her full in the face. I'd thought she was dead, but then she'd miraculously shown up at my doorstep later, claiming mithril armor had saved her.

"Yes." She looked down. "I put on the armor so you'd believe it had saved me."

"Waiting until the child is one year old is absolutely heartless." I imagined losing an infant was awful, but to know the child would be killed after a year of loving and caring for it was beyond the pale.

"My family is only one example of the cruelty of the gods." Aura wiped her eyes. "A peaceful clan refused to fight a war for Ares' entertainment, so he called down ogre hordes to slaughter them even though they didn't fight back. Zeus rained lightning on a town because a female refused his sexual advances. That once thriving community was reduced to ashes along with most of its people." She nodded out at the sea. "Poseidon called on the Kraken to devour virgins and sent tidal waves to destroy cities out of petty jealousy."

"Look, I know the gods have done some bad shit over the eons, but how can mere mortals kill them?" I waved a hand in the general direction of the armory. "Even with every weapon in that place, you couldn't kill one god."

"The Greek gods are only one example," Aura continued, as if I hadn't spoken. "The Vikings suffered greatly under the yoke of Odin. Thor helped himself freely to their women, killing any men who got in his way. The Indian pantheons were no better."

"But it's not like that these days," I countered. "Besides, how could Thor kill mortals if the gods can't interfere?"

"Oh, they can do what they want to their worshippers," Aura said. "That's the dirty little secret they don't tell you. Anyone who bows to them is theirs to do with as they please."

"It's like making a bargain." My fists clenched. "Like Hannah did with Cthulhu."

"Exactly like Hannah." Aura shook her head and wiped her eyes. "That's why I hate the gods, Cain. The goal of my faction is to hold the gods accountable for their crimes."

"They should be held accountable, but I don't know how." I almost touched her arm but refrained. "Thanks for telling me. But don't expect this to change things. I won't let you use me for Ender business. I've got one goal, and one goal only."

"To free Hannah." Aura nodded. "You're mostly a good guy, Cain." She managed a small smile. "Mostly."

I had nothing to say to that, so I started up the stairs to the sail. Aura grabbed my hand. I turned around, a question on my lips, but she quieted me with a long kiss.

She pulled away, breathing heavily, probably from the heat and low oxygen levels in the air. "We'll free Hannah."

I raised an eyebrow. "You could've told me that without the kiss."

Her forehead pinched. "You didn't like it?"

"Of course I did." I shrugged. "But I don't feel like being used again right now." I climbed the stairs and dropped down the hatch.

Layla looked back from the controls. "The tide is moving us much faster than the engines could. We'll reach the desert coast in no time."

"And then what?" I said. "I still don't understand what Poseidon meant about using the hammer wisely."

Hannah nodded. "Yeah, he can't exactly push the submarine across dry land."

"It's going to be a long, nasty walk." I blew out a long breath. "Noctua, will those forgers' cloaks give us relief from the desert heat?"

"The enchantments in the material will keep you much cooler," the owl replied. "Even so, it will be quite hot near the fire."

"Duh!" Hannah slapped her forehead. "I know what Poseidon meant."

"Yeah?" I leaned back in the captain's chair to enjoy the cool air coming from the vents. "What is it?"

She grinned. "We don't have to walk inland at all if you use Earthmaker to create a canal to the fireball."

"Accurate conclusion," Noctua said.

Layla whooped. "And Poseidon can give us a favorable tide." She turned around. "I'll give you credit for that one, girl."

Hannah scoffed. "Thanks, *woman*."

I clapped her back. "Maybe your brain is godlike."

Hannah shrugged. "I dunno. I sucked at math."

"Yeah, well the gods suck at a lot," Aura said as she closed the hatch and climbed down the ladder. "Like selflessness and mercy."

I pushed up from the chair. "I'm going to take a nap. Wake me when we reach the desert coast."

"No masturbating inside Roxy," Layla called back after me. "She's not on birth control."

I stopped. "Roxy?"

"That's my submarine's name." She beamed. "And Roxy is way better than Dolores."

My fists clenched, but I wasn't in the mood to argue over something idiotic. Dolores would kick Roxy's ass. Besides, this submarine was half mine. I flashed her a clenched-jaw grin, then resumed walking to the crew quarters.

I found a closet packed with clothes and dug out a pair of jeans and a t-shirt that fit me. There was a small shower in the lavatory, so I cleaned off the grime and enjoyed what would likely be a short-lived feeling of cleanliness. I slid into a bunk, closed my eyes, and fell asleep within seconds. It felt like I'd barely closed my eyes when Hannah woke me up.

"We're there, Cain."

I grunted. "How long was I out?"

"Three hours," she said. "Layla let me steer so she could take a nap too."

I rubbed my eyes and slid out of the narrow space. "She must have been exhausted to let you have the controls."

Hannah chuckled. "That walk to the armory wore her out. Her body doesn't much like this world."

"Yeah, I noticed." I felt well-rested and alert.

"I'll be on the bridge." Hannah looked as if she wanted to say something else but vanished down the corridor.

I sighed. It was time to go get hot and sweaty again. I decided to give a forger's cloak a test run and found Layla's backpack strapped down in a compartment near the lavatory. It bulged with all the goodies she'd taken from the armory.

A voice emerged from the bunkroom across from me. "Don't steal my stuff, Cain."

"I just need a forger's cloak," I said.

Layla grunted. "I'm watching you."

"Pervert." I unzipped her pack and items spilled out onto the floor. The cloaks, of course, were at the bottom. I took them out and jammed the various metal helmets and small bits and pieces back inside.

It felt strange referring to a glove as a cloak, especially since it magically transformed into a silver jumpsuit. But if it was good enough for Noctua, it was good enough for me. The material looked like metal but felt soft and light as gossamer.

I stripped to my underwear, then put on a glove and squeezed my fist five times. The material grew up my arm and spread across my body. Once again, I felt a moment of panic as it covered my face. It wasn't quite skintight, but it also wasn't loose. I especially liked that it didn't bunch up in the crotch.

I walked back and forth down the hallway and felt no different than being in my regular clothes. I picked up Earthmaker and went to the hatch ladder.

Aura flinched when she saw me. "Gods, you look like an alien!"

I shrugged. "Don't worry, I won't give you an anal probe."

Hannah snickered. "She might like that, Cain."

Aura ignored us. "We're anchored about forty feet from shore. Can you swim in that thing?"

"He doesn't have to." Hannah unzipped a duffel bag and pulled out tightly wrapped inflatable raft. "It doesn't have a motor like the other one, but it'll keep you dry."

"Thanks." I mussed her hair and climbed up the ladder. The usual rush of heat didn't greet me when I opened the hatch. It felt only slightly warmer than it had inside the submarine. That was a good sign. I climbed down the sail and inflated the raft, unpacked the oars, climbed in, and pushed off.

Tall, rust-red dunes guarded the beach. Gusts of wind carried clouds of red sand into the air and into whatever lay beyond. I felt like an astronaut exploring the Martian landscape. I reached shore, vigilant for dune scorpions. I hadn't been to this part of Oblivion before, but it seemed as likely a place to find the monsters as anywhere else.

When nothing leapt from the sand and tried to eat me, I decided it was safe to do my business. I formed a clear image of what I wanted in my head and pounded the beach with the hammer. The dunes split apart in a susurrus of shifting sands, forming a canal fifty yards wide and a hundred feet deep.

There was still a narrow isthmus of sand separating the submarine from the beach, so I walked until I was even with the edge of the canal and touched the hammer to the sand, visualizing the canal continuing into the sea. Massive globs of muddy sand flew apart. And just like that, we had a canal stretching as far as the eye could see. I'd willed it to be twenty miles long just to be safe.

Hannah waved at me through the front window and piloted the submarine into the canal. She pulled up to the edge. I deflated the raft and rolled it up, then hopped onto the submarine and went inside.

Thanks to the cloak, I hadn't even broken a sweat.

"That was so cool," Hannah said. "I wish I could go back to school and tell everyone I piloted a submarine after my friend blew up a mountain and made a sea canal in the desert."

I snorted. "You'd end up in a psychiatric ward in no time."

"Definitely." She pushed the lever full speed ahead and began our journey down the canal.

I looked back toward the hallway with the crew quarters. "I'm surprised Layla's still letting you drive Roxy."

"I think she got bored with it," Hannah said.

Aura wasn't on the bridge, so I assumed she'd gone to take a nap as well. "Then I guess you're the captain now."

Hannah grinned and saluted me. "I'm the captain!"

"Captains don't salute their crewmen like that," I said.

She shrugged. "Yeah, but you're my co-captain, bro."

I grinned. "I'll take the promotion."

Thanks to the favorable tide, we covered the distance in less than an hour. As dusk settled over the land, an orange glow lit the horizon. The canal passed some distance west of the fireball, so Hannah parked the submarine so we could scout the next route.

I reached into Layla's backpack and grabbed a scrap of metal that had once been a hand guard on a sword. Since it had been forged in the fires of creation, it would serve as a test subject to make sure this fireball was hot enough to melt down the weapons in the armory.

Hannah and I slipped on our forger's cloaks and went outside. Once we stood on the hull, I quickly realized that by making the canal so deep, the sand dunes were like cliffs. I tapped the warhammer against a wall of hard, red sand and it crumbled away into a set of wide stairs.

"You're getting really good with that," Hannah said. "Imagine the cool things you could do if you kept it."

"Or the utter destruction if someone else got their hands on it." I shook my head. "It's not hard to use precisely because I've had so many years of practicing magic. But someone untrained would wreak havoc." We walked up the stairs and to the desert.

With the white sun setting behind us, the glow of the fireball began to cast long shadows across the desert. After a time, we reached the edge of a crater and found the miniature sun floating in a lake of molten sand forty or so yards in diameter.

"Son of a bitch." I compared the fireball to the one we'd seen underwater. "It looks smaller than the other one."

"It looks brighter though," Hannah said. "Maybe it's more concentrated."

"Maybe." Heat rippled off the red-hot surface of the lake, and I was grateful for the protection of the cloak. I wondered how something so hot hadn't melted a hole all the way to the center of the world. The fact that it floated rather than sank was probably the only reason why. But now I had another problem. How was I supposed to cross a lake of molten silicon so I could see if the sword guard melted?

I hesitantly dipped a finger in the molten sand to test the forger's cloak. There was a noticeable rise in temperature, but not enough to scorch me. I was covered from head to toe by the cloak but wading through a pond of molten sand seemed like a risky idea.

I pressed the hammer to the red-hot silicone and willed it to solidify. Nothing happened. It seemed the hammer couldn't change the state from liquid to solid. I pressed the hammer to the brittle glasslike sand around the edges and willed the sand dunes to flow into the lake.

Nearby sand poured into the crater, coagulating the liquid and creating a solid surface. The area around the fireball began to bubble almost immediately, but this seemed my best chance. "Wait here," I told Hannah. Then I raced across the surface. The sand was soft and slippery in places where it hadn't packed as densely.

I nearly fell on my ass when I tried to stop a few feet from the fireball. The heat in the cloak began to build. It seemed cumulative exposure to a source of extreme heat gradually overpowered its protection. Up close, the fire of creation bubbled and roiled on the surface like liquid fire. It looked just like the surface of the sun and was starting to feel like it too.

It was so awesome to behold that I nearly forgot the entire reason for my coming out here. I flinched from my stupor and held out the sword guard. It sparked and turned red hot when it touched the fiery surface but held its form.

"Shit!" The fireball wasn't hot enough. The heat went from uncomfortable to mildly painful. If I stood here much longer, I'd probably start to roast in the suit. The air became stuffy, hard to breathe. I was about to back away when I noticed the tip of the sword guard bubble. A thin stream of metal dribbled from the end and the piece began to lose shape.

It's working!

I began to back away, but over the past few seconds, I'd sunk up to my ankles in melting sand. The pain factor notched up so gradually that I hadn't noticed how it had gone from one to five in seconds. I was a frog in a pot of slowly boiling water. I powered the tattoos on my body and managed to pull a foot up out of the thick lava. But it was so hard to breathe I could hardly concentrate.

I tried the other foot, but it refused to move. My muscles didn't have the oxygen to power them. I gritted my teeth and concentrated with everything I had. But it was too hot, and I was burning alive, lungs slowly scorching.

CHAPTER 33

"Cain!" Hannah slogged over to me and yanked the hammer from the sand where it had fallen from my limp fingers. She slammed the hammer to the ground and a tidal wave of fresh sand swept over us, carrying us away from the fireball and back out into the desert.

I tumbled to the ground and lay there in agony. It felt as if someone had roasted me alive.

Hannah knelt next to me. "Cain, are you okay?"

I spoke through clenched teeth. "I don't think so."

"Shit." She grimaced. "Can you move?"

The air in the suit cooled and breathing became easier. I held up a hand and wiggled the fingers. The scorched skin cried out in pain, but it wasn't the worst I'd endured. I climbed to my feet with some help from Hannah and took some deep breaths to let my head clear.

"Not my smartest move," I said. I no longer had the partially melted sword guard in my hand, but I'd seen enough. "The fire is hot enough. We can use it."

"Thank god." Hannah sighed in relief. "Now all we have to do is roll the thing back to the armory."

The notion of rolling a miniature sun like a marble through trenches in the sand was laughable. But with Earthmaker, anything was possible. The cool confines of the suit began to soothe my skin. I hoped whatever damage I'd suffered wasn't permanent. I wanted to check my skin, but that could wait until we got back to the submarine. Besides, I was feeling better by the second.

"I think I'll be okay." I started walking back toward the fireball. "Let's get this thing on the move.

"This is gonna be cool," Hannah said.

I just hoped it worked. We walked wide around the fireball to the opposite side. The sand I'd piled in was nearly all melted, once again forming a lake with the miniature sun bobbing on top. It was surreal to look at. If half of the fireball was beneath the surface, that meant it was only about twenty feet in diameter—less than half the size of the one underwater. I hoped that meant it wouldn't be too hard to move.

It also begged the question why didn't the underwater fireball float, and what kept it suspended in place?

I picked a spot near the edge of rapidly liquefying sand and oriented myself toward the armory. My angle was probably off by a few degrees, but a general direction would suffice for now. I pressed the hammer to the sand and imagined a sloped trench running straight ahead as far the eye could see. The sands parted like a giant ocean, creating gradually sloping trench. I hoped it would give the fireball enough momentum to roll for a good distance. Then we'd catch up to it and start all over again.

The only thing holding the fireball in place was a dam of sand I'd left in place. Hannah and I walked a good distance away from the crater, then I struck the barrier with the hammer and let the dam fall.

Molten sand flowed like a river, carrying the fireball with it as easily as rushing water carried a beach ball. The fireball eventually vanished in the distance, leaving a red-hot glaze of glass along the surface.

"Whoa, that was a lot easier than I thought it would be," Hannah said. "How long did you make the trench?"

"I imagined it running all the way back to the city, but I have no idea if the fireball will get that far." I held the hammer to the sand and grew a tall dune beneath us so we'd have a view across the darkening horizon. The glow of the fireball was small as a bonfire in the distance. It looked as if it had gone at least ten miles, maybe further.

"Looks like we need to catch up to it." Using the hammer, I built a canal parallel to the trench and let the ocean water flood inside. It seemed it would take a while for the water level to rise sufficiently, so I created an additional canal running back to the beach miles away to increase the water flow.

"How does it feel having godlike powers?" Hannah asked, eyes bright.

I shrugged. "It was amazing at first, but I feel like I'm relying on it so much now that it's almost an afterthought."

"That must be how the gods feel," Hannah said. "Imagine how awful they'd feel if you stripped away their powers and they suddenly had to do things with their own two hands."

"They'd probably kill themselves." I wondered if it was even possible to remove the powers from a god. They were such elemental beings, it seemed they were one and the same as their abilities.

Despite tromping around in molten sand and dirt, our forger's cloaks were perfectly clean. I checked the bottom of my feet. "This stuff is better than Teflon."

"The ultimate gimp suit," Hannah said.

I grimaced. "Oh, gods. How do you know about gimp suits?" I waved off the answer. "Never mind. I don't want to know."

Hannah ignored the request. "One of my foster families threw some interesting parties." She shrugged. "They locked me in the attic, but I made holes in the ceiling and spied on them."

I shook my head. "After everything you've been through, how are you not a complete psycho?"

She smiled. "I guess we met just in time."

"I wouldn't consider myself a good influence."

Hannah reached out and touched my arm. "What matters is you did the right thing in the end, Cain."

I wasn't so sure. Then again, if I hadn't taken Hannah with me when I did, her powers would have revealed her for what she was. Sigma might have found her sooner and killed her. There was really no telling what might have happened.

We headed back to the submarine. I removed the forger's cloak and slipped back into jeans. My skin was pink and raw, but it didn't seem to be permanently damaged or burned as I'd feared. I found Layla and Aura on the bridge, both staring out the window at the new canal stretching before us.

Layla turned to me. "How'd it go?"

"Cain almost killed himself, but everything after that went great." Hannah shrugged. "Now we've got to catch up to the fireball and make sure it hits the target."

Aura watched me with a frown but said nothing.

"What is it?" I asked her.

She nodded at the canal. "Do you still want to get rid of the hammer even though it can do that?"

I held it up. "This thing doesn't need to be in existence. Neither do the other weapons in the armory." I set it down on the floor. "Every time I use it, it feels easier, more natural. It's like it wants me to feel like a god."

"The weapons are, in a sense, alive," Noctua said. "Hephaestus used to drop by occasionally and talk to them."

Layla did a double-take. "Talk to them? How?"

"Like they were pets," Noctua said. "He would pick them up, admire and clean them, and tell them how beautiful they were."

Layla snorted. "Uh, maybe he's just fucked in the head."

Hannah grunted. "Totally fucked. That's just creepy."

"Did he talk to you?" I asked.

"Of course." Noctua bobbed her body in a nod. "He was different toward me since I can talk back. He liked to pet me and Korborus as if we were real animals."

I lifted my eyebrows. "Korborus?"

Noctua bobbed a nod. "The clockwork Cerberus."

Aura stared down the hallway behind me, as if lost in thought, or maybe staring at Layla's backpack.

I turned to the owl. "Noctua, can you identify all the items Layla put in her backpack?"

"I would be happy to," she said.

"Just let me know if anything is powerful enough to destroy the world or kill everyone on it—you know, the usual apocalyptic stuff." I turned to Layla. "You okay with that?"

She shrugged. "I don't care. I only took stuff from that junk pile anyway."

I went to the backpack, opened it, and spilled its contents onto the floor. Noctua fluttered around inspecting the pile.

"Water looks deep enough for the sub," Hannah said. "Can I drive?"

Layla shook her head. "Not now, girl. Roxy is all mine."

Hannah scowled. "Hannah."

Layla grunted.

Hannah grunted back. "Fine, half breed."

Layla's jaw tightened, but she didn't say anything. She steered the sub into the new channel, and we set sail toward the fireball.

A few moments later, Noctua finished her inspection. "The catalogue of items is non-threatening on a global scale. Most of it is nonfunctional and defensive in purpose." Her claw grasped a slender golden rod and it snapped out into the bow Apollo rejected. "This, however, offers destructive capabilities not unlike the rocket launchers used by normal humans."

"I'm keeping it," Layla said.

I bit my lower lip. "As long as she can't level a city with it."

"It will imbue normal arrows with destructive magic, but only the arrows crafted by Hephaestus grant it such firepower." Noctua flew back up to perch on a console. "Those arrows reside in the armory on Gaia."

Layla pursed her lips. "Good to know."

I shoved everything except the golden bow back in the backpack since I didn't know how to turn it into the small rod again, then stowed it in a compartment. Aura watched me carefully, as if making sure I didn't steal anything. It seemed she was worried that the godlike powers of Earthmaker might corrupt me and make me desire even more power. A part of me hoped she wasn't right, but I had no choice except to continue using the weapon until everything left in the armory was destroyed.

It was after dark when we caught up with the fireball. It hadn't reached the end of the trench, because I hadn't accounted for other irregularities in the geography once it reached the end of the desert.

The trench continued across semi-mountainous terrain and had run perpendicular to a gully. The fireball had fallen fifty feet to the bottom and had already melted the rock into a small pond of lava. I stood at the edge of the gully with the others and regarded the rolling terrain beyond. I'd have to completely wreck the landscape to get the fireball through.

There were a few trees and scrub brush, but the land was dry and arid just like it had been at the seaside city. I wouldn't be destroying forests or natural beauty. That made me feel marginally better about the destruction I was about to unleash. But first, I had to get the fireball out of the gulley.

Everyone wore forger's cloaks for protection, the shiny suits making us look like a volcanologist convention. We walked parallel to the edge of the gulley so we'd be a safe distance from the fireball when it reached the surface. I knelt and smacked the hammer on the rocky ledge. The floor of the gully began to rise with a rumble that shook the earth. Within minutes, the fireball and the bowl of bubbling lava reached the top. I upended the bowl and the stream of lava carried the fireball into the trench. I concentrated on the terrain and willed Earthmaker to tear a trench through the hills and mountains.

Massive swaths of land fell away at my whim, mountains splitting apart at the command of an ant. I felt powerful. Alive. I could use this weapon wisely. There was so much good I could do if I could rearrange the world to my liking.

I flinched and released the hammer as if it had stung me.

"Something wrong, Cain?" Hannah's concerned face regarded me through the transparent front of the hood.

"Yeah, I'm good." I retrieved the hammer and stared at the path of destruction. There was nothing pretty about it, but it did the job. The fireball continued its journey, its orange glow fading until we were in darkness.

"Question," Layla said. "What happens if the submarine hits a gully?"

"We'll fall a hundred feet and crash into the ground," Hannah said. "Broken metal will slice us to ribbons, and the rushing seawater will wash away our blood. Then the scavengers will pick our bones clean."

Layla's eyebrows rose. "Thanks for the visual, kid."

I shot Hannah a look. "I already filled in this gully. We'll just have to keep an eye out in case there are more ahead."

"A damned good eye," Layla shot back. "I don't want this trip ending with a screaming freefall into the bowels of Oblivion."

"You're so poetic," I said. Then I struck the earth with the hammer again and continued our canal parallel to the path of destruction carved for the fire of creation.

"It's dark," Aura said. "We might not see a drop off coming."

"The fireball kept going straight and didn't fall," Hannah said. "I don't think there's another gully for a while."

Layla scoffed. "Hope you're right, girl."

"I am, woman." Hannah watched the canal fill with water for a moment, then turned to me. "Do you think Torvin has gotten into the armory yet?"

I gave it some thought. "Even with the power of the ocean, he'll be hard pressed to move all that rock. It'd take him days unless there's something I don't know."

"Never underestimate the power of water," Aura said. "Enough of it can move mountains."

I sighed and nodded. "Then I guess we'd better get going."

We got back in Roxy the submarine and continued our journey.

The land eventually levelled out into the hard-packed yellow sand we'd seen in and around the ruined coastline city, making progress easier.

My angle of approach, however, took us to the ocean about two miles before we needed to get there. Thankfully, the trench guiding the fireball had stopped in the middle of the ruined city, a few hundred yards shy of carrying our prize into the ocean.

As the underwater fireball had proven, the water wouldn't put out the fire, but it might weaken it enough to make it ineffective for melting down the weapons. I couldn't risk that, especially not so close to the objective. There was no telling how far we'd have to travel to find another fireball. The brilliance of the flames in the darkness was like looking into a campfire, making us night blind. That made it difficult to pinpoint the precise location of Olympus Prime.

I decided to play it safe and directed the trench back inland toward some foothills to the north of the ruins. From that vantage point, the fireball would hopefully light up the terrain enough to show me where to aim it. After making the trench, I used the hammer to build a giant mound beneath the fireball and then let it roll down the trench where it needed to go. It still confused me how a miniature sun rolled as if it were nothing more than a flaming beach ball, but I wasn't going to complain. The fireball rolled up to the top of a hill. I used the hammer to quickly shift mounds of earth to temporarily hold it in place. The incredible heat began to melt the sand and dirt immediately. If left too long, it would form another crater with a lake of lava inside.

The flames cast orange light across the beach and ruins, reaching as far as the shattered silhouette of Olympus Prime perhaps a mile away. Something had definitely changed since leaving it hours ago. The giant mound of rubble had been reduced at least by half, and I soon saw why.

Two silhouettes stood atop the cracked dome in the ruined city. Torvin was easily identifiable by the trident he held. I summoned my staff and felt a rush of relief to feel it in my hand once again. I flipped up the scope and peered through it. I magnified the view and found Torvin staring at the fireball.

I flicked my fingers in a pattern and cupped them to my ear. The amplification spell picked up bits and pieces of Torvin's words, but the roar of water overpowered them. Judging from the concern on his and Norna's faces, they'd figured out what I was up to.

That was when I realized there were no stars visible in a large section of horizon to the southeast. The water had risen so high it was blotting out the sky and it was heading straight for the fire of creation.

CHAPTER 34

Torvin might not be able to extinguish the fireball, but that much water would certainly carry it far away, and possibly weaken its power. I couldn't take the risk, but how was I supposed to stop that much water?

"Is that a tidal wave?" Hannah shouted.

"Gods be damned." Layla smacked a fist into her palm. "That bastard is going to put out our fire!"

I held up my hands helplessly. "I don't know how to stop it."

Aura held her hand flat and raised it. "Build a wall with the hammer."

I shook my head. "I don't think a wall of sand is going to do the trick."

Hannah held out a hand. "Can I use the hammer, Cain?"

"What's she going to do, make a sandcastle?" Layla scoffed. "She's just a girl."

I hesitated a moment, then handed it over. "She's not just a girl. She's a demigoddess."

Hannah stuck out her tongue at Layla. "Yeah, bitch." Then she struck the ground with Earthmaker.

The land quaked and swallowed up a huge swath of the city. The cracked dome began to shake and fall apart. Torvin stumbled but maintained his balance. Even in the face of the ground swallowing him whole, he kept his cool. Norna's face was wide with fear. Facing down a someone with a sword was one thing, but looking down the throat of the very ground you stood on was something else.

Just as the dome fell apart, a shimmering platform of water caught Torvin and Norna, taking them up and away from danger.

"Well, it almost worked," Aura said. "Attacking the source was a brilliant idea."

The wall of water had begun falling back into the ocean, but now that Torvin was safe, it once again rose and advanced.

"You gave it your best shot," Layla said. "Maybe let the adults handle it from here."

Hannah smirked and the world was plunged into darkness. I spun around. The fireball was gone.

"What the fuck?" Layla said.

I cast a light spell over us and caught the grin spreading over Hannah's face.

"What are you doing?" I asked.

"Playing keep away," she said. "Just like those bullies used to do with my books in school. But this time I'm keeping it away from a bully."

Aura drew in a quick breath. "It's underground."

"Yep." Hannah's brow furrowed in concentration. "Wish I could see the look on Torvin's face right now."

But it was impossible to see him in the darkness. That somehow made the distant roar of water even more ominous. He might be sending it straight toward us.

The fireball exploded from the ground a quarter of a mile distant, followed by a plume of lava. It rose a hundred feet in the air, lighting up everything for miles. Torvin and Norna rode a platform of water above where the dome had been. The wall of water had stopped in place as Torvin figured out where the fireball had gone.

Then the fireball fell earthward and vanished back in the hole it had come out of.

Layla grunted. "Okay, I kind of like what she's doing. Psychological warfare against those assholes could be fun."

The roar of water grew louder. The fireball shot into the air from the peak of another hill a good distance from the previous one. When the light reached into the distance, I realized that Torvin must have spotted us, because the wall of water was now coming straight for us.

"Well, ain't this a pickle," Layla said in a passable southern accent. "I don't think the submarine will be enough to keep us safe."

"We don't need it," Hannah said.

The fireball dropped into the earth once again. Moments later, it flew skyward again. The wall of water was less than a quarter of a mile away. It spanned a mile wide and hundreds of feet tall. Unless we got in the submarine, turned it around, and hauled ass immediately, there was no escape.

Hannah cackled. "Checkmate, bitch."

"Yeah, for us," Layla said.

"Not hardly," Hannah shot back. She looked up at me. "You trust me, bro?"

I snorted. "Obviously, or I wouldn't have given you the hammer."

"A simple yes would've worked." Her forehead pinched in concentration and the fire of creation burst skyward once more, but this time it catapulted through the air, a giant orange streak traveling across the land in an arc that would land it straight atop ruins of Olympus Prime. The massive pile of rubble exploded apart, sending boulders and debris flying into the ocean, leaving barren land where it had been.

I peered through the scope on my staff and magnified. The earth had parted, revealing the armory to the night sky. Time seemed to slow as the fire of creation slammed down right in the center. Massive explosions lit the night even brighter.

"Some of the orbs in the armory were volatile," Noctua said. "I expect several more will explode when they come in contact with the fire of creation."

"Gods almighty, girl." Layla clapped Hannah on the shoulder. "Sometimes you actually impress me."

"She played Torvin," Aura said. "Made him redirect the wave to kill us and then shot the fire where it needed to go."

"How did you shoot the fireball into the air?" I asked.

"I'll answer that later," Hannah said. "Get in the submarine fast!"

The roar of the oncoming wave nearly drowned out her words. We scrambled downhill, slipping and sliding in our haste to get back to the submarine. Noctua reached it first, folding her wings and dropping neatly inside. Layla and Aura climbed down one after the other.

"Hannah, go." I waved her inside.

She shook her head. "I have to be out here."

"What?"

"To save us, I have to be out here!"

I blinked. "I'm staying with you."

She grinned. "Then hold on tight." Hannah smacked the ground. A slab of rock exploded from the earth directly beneath us and the submarine. With a massive rumble, the platform began to move, carrying us and the submarine with it.

My teeth rattled from the violent vibrations. The submarine rattled and rolled dangerously. Hannah frowned and stared at the rock beneath the vessel. Deep grooves formed to keep it upright. We traveled up into the foothills and then angled back down toward the armory. The fire of creation didn't cast enough light aboveground to see much, but the sound of rushing water faded as we outran our doom.

We came to a stop near the edge of a gaping hole where the stairs leading down into the armory had been before I collapsed the mountain. Layla and Aura climbed out of the submarine, wobbling around on unsteady feet after the rough ride. Noctua flew out behind them, no worse for wear.

"Most impressive," the owl said. "Despite your lineage, Cain, the demigoddess is superior even to you."

I shook my head. "My lineage? What do you mean?"

"No time to talk," Hannah shouted. "Put on your forger's cloaks, get down to the armory, and start tossing weapons into the fire of creation!" She created a ramp of stone with the hammer and ran down the ramp.

For once, Layla didn't talk back. She and Aura already wore their cloaks, so they followed Hannah down. I pulled mine out of my backpack and slipped it on, then went down after the others.

Water pooled in large puddles on the floor. Dead sea life lay on shelves, racks and the floor, and the odor was nearly palpable even through the cloak. Torvin had been throwing the full weight of the ocean against this place, heedless of the loss of animal life. Most of the fish were spiny with sharp teeth and looked like something out of a horror movie, so I wasn't too broken up about their deaths.

The fire of creation sat on the stone floor not far from the huge boxy furnaces. Standing a good distance away, Hannah tapped the hammer to the floor and used a stone slab to roll the fireball into the center furnace. The ground rumbled. Gravel, rubble, and water spilled from the broken ledges above. A loud hiss and thunderclap echoed through the cavern and the ancient forge burst into flame.

"A momentous occasion," Noctua said. "The forges have lain dormant for longer than humankind has existed."

Thinking about that was enough to give a person an existential crisis.

Aura and Layla watched it for a moment, a mix of concern and awe on their faces.

I clapped my hands together to snap them out of it. "We'll get gold stars for our refrigerators later." I looked around and spotted carts tucked away in a corner. "Let's use those to get the weapons to the furnace."

The carts were huge and constructed entirely of some unknown metal alloy. They looked impossible to push with mortal muscles but were surprisingly easy to maneuver. Layla and Aura took one and started at the far side of the armory. I began gathering weapons from the racks nearby and hauled the load to the furnace. The furnace seemed to contain all the heat inside, because I didn't feel a rise in temperature when I got near it. I couldn't imagine what alloy allowed the furnace to contain such incredible heat without melting.

Before I started tossing things in willy-nilly, I found Noctua to ask her an important question. "Will any of this blow up when I throw it in?"

"Only a few orbs might react in such a way," she said. "The furnace can withstand and contain the blast.

"Good to know." I carefully picked up a sword by the hilt and tossed it in the opening. There was no telling what a cut from any of these blades might do to me, and I didn't want to find out the hard way.

When I finished with the first load, Noctua fluttered over to a lever on the floor. "You will need to pull this to release the molten ore. Otherwise the furnace will overflow."

"Will it just dump it on the floor?" I said.

The owl fluttered to an area further back, landing on something hidden behind the glare coming from the furnace. I walked around and found her perched on a low metal cart with a big metal pot on the top.

She tapped a claw on the container. "Position the crucible beneath the spout, and the molten metal will pour into it. Normally it would then be poured into a cast, but Hephaestus destroyed most of them."

I pushed the cart toward the furnace and positioned the crucible beneath the spout. "Do you think everything is melted down by now?"

"You must visually inspect the inside to know," Noctua said.

I went around and peered into the bright orange light. Once my eyes adjusted, I was able to see the remains of the weapons slowly melting into slag. "They're not completely liquefied yet. Should it take this long?"

"That is normal," Noctua said.

I decided to get another cartload while waiting for the metal to melt. A distant rumble caught my ear. I ran topside and looked around, but it was too dark to see anything. Then I noticed the missing stars in the southern horizon. It had taken him time to recover, but Torvin was about to bring the full fury of the ocean down on this place.

Hannah joined me aboveground. "What is it?"

"Torvin is aiming for us. I don't know how much time we have."

She bit her lower lip. "I'll see what I can do." Before I could stop her, she struck the ground with the hammer. A slab of stone broke free and carried her across the ground toward the coast.

"Don't get yourself killed!" I shouted, feeling helpless to do anything except watch her go.

Hannah bared her teeth in a grim smile. "Better to die than go back to Cthulhu." Then she vanished into the darkness.

"Fuck!" There was nothing else I could do, so I ran back down into the armory. Layla and Aura were already dumping more weapons into the furnace. I figured the other weapons had melted enough, so I pulled back the lever Noctua had shown me. Metal grated, and a small opening appeared in the side of the furnace. Glowing hot metal poured down a chute and into the crucible.

Layla watched it with interest. "Do the weapons lose their enchantments when they're melted?"

Noctua bobbed a nod. "Yes, it destroys them completely."

Aura looked around. "Where's Hannah?"

"And what's that noise?" Layla said.

"Torvin is trying to drown us," I said. "Hannah went to stop him." The ground trembled, sending vibrations up my spine. It was probably Hannah using the hammer to divert the killer wave. "Let's keep going. I don't know how long she can hold him off."

Layla scoffed. "How reassuring to know that girl is the only thing between us and the entire ocean." She pushed another cart forward, this one overflowing with metallic boxes that had cranks on their sides.

I picked up one and examined it. "What do these do?"

"They are music boxes," Noctua said. "Hephaestus designed these for Ares so that his commanders could completely control their soldiers. Anyone hears the music is supposed to follow every command without question. But the enchantment only made the soldiers passive and compliant, which was useless in battle. So they were dumped here."

"Oh, really?" Layla made as if to turn the crank on one, but I grabbed her arm. "We don't have time to mess around. Dump them in the furnace."

She scoffed, but started tossing them in.

I grabbed a cart and wheeled it to the next rack. This one was full of metal rods shaped like lightning bolts. "What are these things?" I asked Noctua.

"Lightning pikes," she replied. "They were designed for Zeus's priests so they might call down lightning on their enemies. But the other gods complained that this was unfair, so Hephaestus stored them here."

I hefted one. It was strangely light and made my fingers tingle with electricity. After giving serious thought to keeping one, I forced myself to dump the bunch of them into the furnace. Then I moved on to the next rack.

Thankfully, the armory was mostly empty already. A place this size would've taken weeks to empty out if it had been even half full. The junk pile Layla had sorted through earlier was still there, so I dumped what I could of it into the cart, then wheeled it back to the furnace.

The crucible was nearly full, so I pushed the lever to close the door in the furnace. "Where can I pour this?" I asked Noctua.

"There are no casts, so the floor will have to do," she replied.

I pushed the cart toward a deep crack in the rock. I gripped the handle on the side of the crucible and tipped it, pouring molten metal into the ground. When it was empty, I took it back and opened the door to empty the furnace again.

Another shockwave shook the cavern. Bits and pieces of rock dropped from the ceiling. I wondered what Hannah was doing and if she'd end up killing us in the process.

Layla and Aura shoved a cart overflowing with weapons past me.

"This is everything," Layla said. "Get your shit in the furnace and let's get out of here!"

I scooped up everything else from the floor and dumped it my cart, then ran up and down the nearby aisles to make sure I hadn't missed anything. Then I pushed my cart to the furnace. The floor began to quake. The cart with the crucible rolled backward away from the open spout, and molten metal poured on the floor.

"Careful!" Aura said as Layla grabbed a sword by the blade and tossed it in. "Some of these weapons will give you the plague!"

Layla held up her gloved hand. "It isn't going to cut me through the cloak, you idiot."

"You don't know that," I said. "Some of these weapons are made to cut through anything." I didn't know that for sure, but it was better to be safe than sorry.

"Cain is correct," Noctua said. "The gloves will not protect you from all blades."

The ground buckled. Cracks ran up and down the floor. Layla held onto the cart for balance and started throwing more weapons inside the furnace. I grabbed orbs from the cart and pitched them inside.

An explosion rang the furnace like a gong. The shockwave knocked us all to the floor and the cart rolled free, straight into a crevice.

CHAPTER 35

"No!" Layla dove for the cart and caught it just before it toppled into the crack.

"Why not let the ground swallow them up?" Aura said. "We should've just used Earthmaker to send them into the middle of the world."

"Because someone could still get to them," I said. "They need to be destroyed."

Layla pulled the cart back to the furnace. "Leave it to an elf to do a half-assed job."

Aura growled. "Fuck off, Layla."

The ground heaved and shook more violently. The area immediately around the furnace remained solid, but the rest of the room began to shift and crack. The sound of grinding stone was deafening. A crack opened behind my cart and it started to roll backward. I grabbed it just before it dropped inside and pulled it up to the furnace.

Layla shoved her empty cart out of the way, and we started emptying mine.

The puddle of molten metal began to spread without a crucible to collect it. Aura backed away as it came toward her feet. Despite the shaking, we managed to empty my cart.

"Let's go!" I started running down what was left of the center aisle. Empty weapons racks toppled and crashed with deafening metallic clangs.

"That girl is trying to kill us!" Layla shouted.

Aura staggered and nearly went down. I gripped her arm and helped her stay upright. "What's wrong?"

She tapped a bulge beneath the cloak. "My oxygen tank ran out."

I helped her along. "Just take deep, measured breaths. It'll allow your lungs to get more oxygen out of the air."

She nodded and staggered forward as the ground did its best to trip us. Fissures opened and closed. Cracking and shifting rock made running treacherous. The submarine had tilted to the side, perched as it was in its deep groove on the stone slab. The ground could open and swallow it whole at any moment, but inside the submarine was probably the best place for Aura.

There was another option, but it might be just as dangerous as remaining here. My oblivion staff could take us back to Gaia, but there was no way to see what was on the other side of the portal without travelling there first. Going in blind might drop us off a cliff or we might emerge a hundred feet underwater. At least here we knew the odds, slim as they were, and had a fighting chance.

"Get in the sub." I helped Aura climb up the side. I opened the hatch and she climbed awkwardly inside.

Layla tapped the oxygen bottle beneath her cloak. "Mine's running empty too." She sighed. "How the hell can you and the girl breathe just fine, but I can't? I'm in peak physical form, Cain."

I shrugged. "If you trained here like I did, you'd probably adapt."

She grunted. "Maybe I'll get you to bring me here again. I don't like feeling weak."

"Yeah," I said. "I don't imagine you do."

Daylight peeked over the eastern horizon, giving us our first glimpse of the battlefield. A wide canyon formed a barrier between us and the ocean. The remains of stone walls ran along the coast, battered to rubble by wave after giant wave. It looked as if Torvin were emptying the entire ocean into the canyons in an attempt to drown us.

But it was too late. All the weapons had been destroyed. All except the trident and the hammer. Tidebringer and Earthmaker had to be thrown into the furnace. But I didn't see Torvin or Hannah anywhere.

Torvin had to be near the water, but there wasn't enough daylight to see clearly. The earth wasn't shaking anymore. Hannah was either done for now, or something had happened to her.

"I need to find Hannah." I slid down the side of the submarine and jogged toward the black sand beach beyond the broken remains of the mountain.

"Cain, you're our only way out of here right now." Layla joined me. "If something happens to you, I'm fucked."

"Well, better pray nothing happens to me then." I marched onward.

"My oxygen bottle is running low." She grabbed my arm. "Look, you'll be on your own."

I stopped. "I can open a portal, but it might drop you off a mountain on the other side. You want to stay here where we have a fighting chance or risk ending up dead the instant you travel through the gateway?"

Layla huffed. "I hate feeling useless."

"You're not useless." I turned back toward the beach. "I'll be back." I jogged across the jagged terrain, dodging around stranded fish and treacherous holes in the ground. It looked as if Hannah and Torvin had done their level best to remake the world in an epic battle.

A small figure in a silver forger's cloak lay on the ground further inland toward the foothills. The breath caught in my throat. "Oh, gods." I ran as hard as I could until my lungs threatened to give out. I dropped to my knees and peered through the transparent hood face.

Hannah's face was bruised, her left cheek and eye swollen. Blood trickled from a cut on her lip, and her arm was twisted at an awkward angle. I touched her neck and released a sigh of relief when I found a pulse. Earthmaker lay on the muddy ground nearby. It looked as if a wave had caught her and slammed her into the ground.

"Sending a girl to do your work, Cain?"

I spun and faced Norna. Before I could react, she snatched the warhammer off the ground and held it aloft.

Norna grinned. "Oh, Cain, you've lost."

I shook my head. "We destroyed all the other weapons. There's nothing left but the hammer and the trident."

She shrugged. "These will do just fine."

"If you think you can beat the fae or the gods with those weapons, then you're an idiot." I made a show of looking around. "Where's your master? Hiding somewhere?"

"I'm here, Cain." Torvin appeared from behind a boulder. "Just in time to watch you die."

Norna swung the hammer toward the ground. But when it struck earth, nothing happened. The hammer required focus and willpower to work. But it was hard to have either of those without a functioning brain attached to your body. It had happened so fast, Norna didn't even look surprised as her head slowly rolled off her shoulders and plopped into the wet sand.

I stood a foot behind Norna, brightblade blazing in my hand. I'd ghost-walked out of sheer reflex, the only thought in my head of protecting Hannah like she'd protected us.

Torvin blinked in surprise. "What's this?"

I slowly rotated and stepped forward, putting myself between him and Hannah. I booted the hammer behind me to keep it out of his grasp.

"Pathetic human." Torvin twirled the trident in his hand then jammed the points into the sand. He was too far from water to use it and he knew it. He grasped the hilt of a sword sheathed diagonally across his back and drew it.

I didn't remember him having a sword the last time, not that it mattered. But when the sword began to glow, I knew something was off.

"I salvaged this from the remains of the mountain." Torvin slashed a rock and the sword sliced through it like butter. "Let's see if your staff can survive a blow from this."

"Wow, a sword that cuts stuff," I said. "You really found a godlike weapon, didn't you?" I wished Noctua was nearby to identify what else it might be capable of.

"Let's put it to the test, shall we?" Torvin whirled the large sword as if it weighed nothing and dashed forward for an overhand blow. I held up my brightblade. The sword rang out against the metallic wood. Power hummed and crackled as the two energized weapons pressed against each other.

I bared my teeth. "Well, at least you can carve statues with your new toy, Torvin. I always figured you for an artist."

His knee aimed for my stomach. I pushed back and dodged it. Torvin delivered three quick strikes I narrowly parried, each time backing me up a little further. Then he swung down to the side away from me. At the last instant I realized what he was doing. I thrust out my brightblade and barely intercepted a blow that would have killed Hannah.

"You piece of shit!" I powered my sigil tattoos and flung his sword back. I attacked with a flurry of blows, knocking him off stride, back and away from her. "Gods damned child killer!" I roared.

Torvin leapt back, resetting his stance on solid ground. He blocked my next strikes easily. "You're weak, Cain. Why should the life of a child or mother matter more than any other life? Defeat your enemies by any means or you might as well lay down and die."

"Victory by any means isn't victory," I said. "It just proves you lack the wit to outthink your real opponents."

"They were terrorists," Torvin said. "Hiding like vermin and striking our forces like cowards."

"Yes, but they didn't kill civilians." My heart was pounding, but I kept my face stony. "They attacked soldiers and officials. We're the ones who stooped to killing entire families."

He sneered. "It won the war."

"No, then they attacked civilians as payback." I shook my head. "The reason we won the war was because trackers were able to trace the guerillas back to their leaders. Once they were gone, the resistance scattered. It's the little things that lead to victory, Torvin. You're just cruel because you love it."

Torvin wasn't in the mood to debate any longer. He lunged, feinted an overhead strike, and curved the blow toward my side. The brightblade glowed brighter and brighter with every strike, almost as if it were absorbing the energy. Torvin was so focused on wearing me down he didn't seem to notice.

An image flashed into my mind, of me releasing the power for a brutal strike. The only explanation for the visual was that my staff had somehow communicated with me. It had never happened like this before, but I couldn't complain. Gods only knew what Torvin's weapon would do if it touched my skin.

While brute force was Torvin's answer to everything, I had a different idea. I parried, shifted to the left, and swung my staff. Torvin blocked it. With a focus of will, I released the pent-up energy in my brightblade. But instead of attacking with it, I simply let it shine. The light flared right into Torvin's face. It wasn't enough to keep him from parrying the next blow, but it was just enough to deliver a small surprise.

Torvin hadn't seen Carnwennan in my other hand. He didn't even seem to realize I'd buried it in his rib until I yanked it up and out.

He gasped and put a hand over the long cut in his side. "What?" Fury blazed in his cold eyes.

"You're a cruel, brutal idiot, Torvin." I let his blood drip off the end of my blade and onto the ground. "You helped Hera murder demigod kids. You exterminated entire families. But all that cruelty doesn't make you a leader, and it sure as hell doesn't make you smart." I smirked. "Getting you discharged from the guard was one of the best things I ever did."

Torvin raised the sword but was too weak to hold it aloft as his life's blood poured between his fingers. "Curse you, human."

"We humans have a saying, dark elf, and I want you to hear it loud and clear." I pointed to my crotch. "Suck my dick and die."

"Bastard!" He tried to shout, but his voice was a whisper.

I didn't give him a quick death. I let him suffer and wither to a bloodless husk while I smiled down at his useless attempts to recover. For a megalomaniac like Torvin, that had to be more torturous than glass shards beneath the fingernails. Eventually, his eyes glazed over and his last breath rattled out. Then I cut off the head of Torvin, the Black Hand, and let it roll to a rest beside Norna's. I sheathed my staff and stared at the bodies for a long moment.

It was hard to believe the master who'd so tormented his pupils, who'd basted me in the poison of his scorn and tried to kill, me was finally dead. My hands trembled and I felt a palpable sense of relief settle over me. It was as if years of tension had suddenly been released. Torvin might be dead, but it didn't really mean I was safe.

Hera and the Divine Council were still out there. There might be others at Eclipse who would continue Torvin's legacy. And then there was still the matter of Hannah and Cthulhu. My plate was lighter, but it wasn't empty. I still had half a shit sandwich left to go.

I picked up the glowing sword Torvin had used and was astonished by how light it felt. I prodded a boulder with it and the blade pierced it like a baked potato. "Maybe I'll keep this one."

Yes, keep us, faint voices whispered in my head. It was as if the ghosts Thanatos had taken from me were back.

I looked around. "Who said that?"

Warm us in the blood of the living. Make us stronger and we will serve you.

"That is Pneumaliptis, or Soultaker." Noctua fluttered down and perched on a boulder. "The voices you hear belong to those who were slain by the sword."

"Gods damn it," I said. "Who thought something like this was a good idea?"

"It was made for Hades, but he rejected it, so Ares took it for a time." Noctua regarded the dead bodies. "Ares claimed many souls with it. Thanatos, however, was displeased that he could not collect the souls, so they came to an understanding. The sword was given back to Hephaestus and has remained in the armory until now."

The voices whispered in my head. I resisted the urge to drop the sword to rid myself of them. "I'll destroy it along with the trident."

Noctua blinked. "It had not occurred to me until now, but if the sword is destroyed, it will unleash an army of the dead."

"An army of souls?" I scoffed. "What are they going to do—scare us to death?"

"I am not familiar with the particulars," she said. "The wielder can also unleash this army and recall it back into the sword at any time. As you might imagine, an army like this could conquer a world."

"I can't imagine it," I said. "Ghosts can't interact with physical objects. They might scare a lot of people, but that'd be it."

"Perhaps," Noctua said. "Having never seen the army of the sword, I cannot say."

I grimaced. "Wouldn't destroying the sword free the souls forever?"

"I cannot answer that question." The owl bounced around on her feet. "I am sorry."

I blew out a breath. "I'll figure out something." I unbuckled the sword sheath from Torvin's body. It wasn't made of leather, but something with the same metallic wood of my staff. I tested the sword's edge against it and wasn't surprised that it didn't cut it. I slid the sword inside and then strapped it on my back. It was a relief to get the voices out of my head. They weren't like the ghosts that haunted me before. These spirits were violent and cruel—a perfect match for Torvin.

I hadn't seen Thanatos since he'd freed me from my ghosts, but maybe he could answer a few questions about Soultaker before I decided what to do with it. The furnace still burned in the forge, so I could always bring it back and destroy it later.

I summoned my staff and stroked the strange wood. "How did this withstand blows from Soultaker if it can cut through anything?"

"The staffs are unique in that they are made from Yggdrasil, the tree of life." Noctua rotated her head as if examining the staff. "They are imbued with a life force all their own."

"C-Cain?" Hannah sat up, pushing wet strands of hair from her face. Her eyes settled on Torvin and flared wide. "What happened?"

I knelt and hugged her. "Everything happened."

Hannah hugged me back. "Something hit me, and I don't remember anything after that." She pulled back a little. "Is everyone okay?"

I nodded. "You kept us safe. We destroyed everything except a few weapons. I came out here and fought Norna and Torvin, so here we are."

She smiled and sighed with relief. "I can't believe it. We survived!"

A nearby shaft of rock toppled over and crashed to the ground. Three massive hound heads glared down at us, mechanical growls rising in their clockwork throats.

Korborus, aka Mecha-Cerberus, was back.

CHAPTER 36

Noctua fluttered to a boulder near the clockwork hound's head. "Hello, Korborus. I imagine you are somewhat flustered by the recent turns of events."

The clockwork hound growled and softly yipped.

Noctua bobbed a nod. "That is exactly what it means. We are free."

Korborus reared back his three heads and howled.

Hannah put her hands over her ears. "Noctua, does this mean he's not here to kill us?"

"He has no reason now that you've destroyed the armory," Noctua said. "It seems Korborus and I are now free to explore on our own."

"Hey, come back with us," Hannah said brightly. "Cain's got tons of land and his house is hidden, so no one will find you."

Noctua blinked. "That is a kind offer, demigoddess, but Korborus and I would like to explore Oblivion first. I must catalogue the current state of this world, so I have as much information as possible."

Korborus yipped softly.

Hannah sighed. "I really like you, Noctua. You're smart and know everything. We could really use your knowledge."

"Is there anything we can do to free Hannah from Cthulhu?" I asked one more time.

Noctua shook her head. "Unless he agrees to dissolve the bargain, only death can free her."

All the weight that had lifted when I slew Torvin dropped right back down on my shoulders. We'd done so much to get here, but it had been for nothing. I held it all in behind a stony mask, blood boiling with rage, guts knotting with regret.

"Maybe he'll take Tidebringer in exchange," I said as calmly as I could.

Hannah shook her head. "Do you really want to give him or his minions that much power? What's the point of freeing me if Cthulhu destroys the world?"

She was right, and it made me feel even worse. The job had been a disaster. The only silver lining was that Torvin was dead. I blew out a sigh and helped Hannah to her feet. "Let's go home." I turned to Noctua. "Thanks for the help. Is there any way to contact you if we need information?"

Noctua turned to Korborus. "Of course. Take the owl-shaped whistle from his collar. When you blow on it, we can communicate."

I noticed two whistles hanging from the collar. One was shaped like a three-headed hound, and the other like a little owl. I gathered my courage and walked over to the massive hellhound. He leaned down, jagged metal teeth just feet from my arm, and allowed me to unclip the owl whistle from his collar.

I nodded at each of them. "Thank you." I picked up Tidebringer and Earthmaker, then Hannah and I headed back toward the submarine.

Noctua and Korborus watched us, then the owl perched on the hound's head and they trekked in the other direction.

"I wonder what kind of adventures they'll have," Hannah said.

I shook my head. "Gods only know."

Her shoulders slumped. "I guess it was all for nothing."

I wanted to disagree. I wanted to say something to make her feel better, but she was right. We would have been better off if I'd never taken this job. Torvin might never have reached Oblivion, and even if he had, he might not have defeated the defenses and gotten inside.

"And here I thought it was the beginning of a lovely adventure." Hannah sighed. "But really, it was just the beginning of the end."

I swallowed a lump forming in my throat. "That's depressing."

Tears sparkled in Hannah's eyes. We started walking again. Hannah had a limp and pressed her hands against her temples. "I really need an aspirin."

I rubbed the top of her head through the hood of the cloak. "We'll get you something back at the sub."

Layla and Aura saw us coming through the main window when we reached the sub. They came outside to greet us in their forger's cloaks.

"There's an oxygen dispenser for filling scuba tanks on the sub," Layla said when she came out. "Can't believe we didn't notice it before."

"Good to know, now that the adventure is over." I blew out a sigh and leaned against the submarine.

Layla looked at Hannah and grimaced. "Kid looks like she lost a boxing match."

"I feel like it," Hannah groaned.

Aura looked at the weapons I held. "What happened?"

I told them about the fight.

"The Black Hand is really dead?" Aura frowned. "That's hard to believe."

"Who's next in line to run the agency?" I asked her.

She shrugged. "I don't know. They compartmentalize everything so the right hand doesn't know what the left is doing."

I nodded. "How much pull does Hera have?"

Aura looked at me. "You want Eclipse out of the demigod hunting business, don't you?"

I nodded.

"Eclipse is the best at what it does, but it's not the only supernatural bounty hunting and assassination agency in town." Aura bit her lower lip. "Hera might have her claws in our competitors too. I'm just a handler. I have no clout whatsoever."

I grunted. "Oh well. At least Torvin in agony died thinking things would change. I guess that's good enough for me." I looked toward the ocean. The waters had calmed since Torvin's death. "Get in the sub. I want to get it to the water."

The others climbed onboard. Layla gave me a worried look before dropping down the ladder and closing the hatch. I pressed the hammer to the ground and envisioned the slab of stone carrying the submarine into the water. It rumbled to life and slid out across the beach and into the water until the submarine was able to float on its own.

Then I went down to the armory. The way down was far more treacherous thanks to all the seismic activity Hannah had unleashed. I leapt gaps and crevices, using unbroken terrain like steppingstones across bottomless crevices until I reached the furnace. A puddle of molten metal stretched around the side and front of the furnace. Silver and gold mingled with otherworldly colors, highlighting the godly origins of the destroyed weapons.

The trickle from the furnace spout was constant and probably would be for some time. We'd dumped a lot of weapons inside. I gingerly tapped a foot in the metal to test the cloak. It handled it as well as the superheated sand earlier, and when I withdrew my foot, nothing stuck to the silvery material. I quickly walked through the puddle, tossed the trident into the furnace.

When I tried to throw in the hammer, my hand refused to release the handle. Regret filled me at the mere thought of destroying so much power. Images of the destruction I'd wrought flashed through my mind. I could do so much with the hammer. I could control the very destiny of Gaia if I so chose. Worldly governments would bow down before me. People would praise me. I would be like a god.

"Fuck!" I threw the hammer into the furnace and felt instant regret. It was as if I'd just thrown a baby into a brushfire and then kicked a baby seal to death. *What have I done?* I thought. I forced myself to keep backing away despite the intense emotions twisting my guts.

As the hammer melted to slag the sensations abruptly stopped.

"Must have been an enchantment." My emotions were so raw, so exposed, I had to lean against a fallen rack just to collect my breath.

"Yes, it was." The deep voice echoed from the shadows in the far back of the broken room. "The weapons test their wielders." A boot clomped the ground followed by the sound of something dragging across the floor. The sounds repeated, clomp, drag, clomp, drag, and then a giant figure separated itself from the shadows. A beast of a man, thickly muscled and barrel-chested limped toward me, dragging a mangled foot behind him.

The broken ground closed up before him, the open wounds of the earth healing before my eyes.

My heartbeat raced when I realized who it was. *Hephaestus.*

The blacksmith of the gods towered over me even from twenty feet away where he stopped. "You destroyed everything but Soultaker," he said.

"I was told destroying it would release an army of the dead." I watched his face carefully. "Is that true?"

"It is." He looked past me at the glowing furnace. "I sensed the furnace when it came to life." Hephaestus looked around. "Everything is gone. Destroyed." He spoke in a slow, almost lumbering way. Sort of like how he walked. It seemed very strange for a god, this being the third one I'd met in almost as many days.

I had a really bad feeling about the regret I heard in his voice. "It had to be done. There were some bad people who wanted all that power, so I made sure no one could have it."

He slid a giant slab of stone to him as easily as if it were a wooden chair and sat on it. The blacksmith stared at me as if mulling over whether to smash me to a fine paste, or perhaps incinerate me in the fire of creation. Hephaestus nodded as if reaching a decision.

"I once thought the gods would destroy each other and leave behind nothing but smoking ruins. So I built tools that lesser beings could use to repair damaged worlds or create new ones." He sighed. "But in my desire to see if I could do such a thing, I never considered if I should. Mortals allied with Loki used these weapons and led to the destruction of this world. That convinced me to lock everything away."

I hesitantly interrupted him. "Why didn't you simply destroy everything?"

I thought mortals might mature in time." He shrugged his massive shoulders. "Ares enjoyed some of the weapons I'd made and asked that I keep them intact, so I did."

I grimaced. "I hate to say it, but none of the races, humans, dwarves, elves, fae, and so forth, have matured or changed much. Humans sometimes show promise, but they just as quickly throw it away."

"I have also noticed this." He pursed his lips. "This place has lain dormant for so long that perhaps it is okay to see it come to an end. Even the work of god."

I wondered if he knew that Noctua and Korborus were still functioning and decided not to ask. I didn't want him locking them up somewhere else now that they were free.

He continued to stare at me. "Soultaker, however is another matter."

I unbuckled the scabbard and held it out to him. "Take it and put it somewhere safe. I don't want it."

Hephaestus shook his head. "It is not that easy. Ares reaped many souls with it already, angering Thanatos. They took out their anger on me, as usual, and I do not desire that experience again."

"If I can't destroy it, what am I supposed to do with it? I said. "Can I drop it down a deep hole and hope no one finds it?"

"The magic protecting this place until today prevented the weapons from calling out to those who would wield them." Hephaestus massaged his mangled foot. "So long as you claim it, it will not call out to others."

"Can't you just enchant this place again?" I asked.

"I am not the one responsible for the original enchantment," he said. "That was done by Athena, and she has not been heard of for quite some time."

"But you're a god," I said.

"I am a god of some things, but not all." Hephaestus shrugged. "Do you think I would have a mangled foot if I was the god of healing?"

"Asclepius can't patch it up?"

He sighed. "Perhaps. But I believe my unique deformity also shapes my art. It allows me to create beautiful things even though I am the ugliest of gods."

I didn't know if he was fishing for compliments, so I managed a lame response. "Oh, you're not that bad looking."

Hephaestus blinked in confusion, as if I'd just voiced something unheard of. "Even my own wife will not lie with me."

I had no response to that. It was hard to believe he was still married to Aphrodite even after all this time. "Is there anything else you can tell me about Soultaker? Is there a way to free the souls without unleashing an army of the dead?"

He put a hand to his chin in thought. "Perhaps Thanatos would know. When summoned, the army of the dead can take a partially physical form. They would be nearly unstoppable by mortal means."

"That's not what I wanted to hear." I sighed. "Damned if I do, damned if I don't. I really hate having this much responsibility."

He nodded gravely. "So much weight cannot rest easy on mortal shoulders. You will not be the first or the last to bear it."

"Can't you take the sword?" I said. "Find someone else with more free time on their hands?"

Booming laughter filled the chamber. Hephaestus slapped his knee and shook his head. "I am sorry, but it seems to me you are the best person to guard the sword for now." He stood up and started limping back into the shadows.

"Wait!" I held out a hand. "What makes me the best person? Maybe another god or a fae could do it better."

He turned back to look at me, an amused grin on his face. "You don't want power, Cain. And that makes you perfect to guard it or wield it as you see fit."

"What about Hannah?" I said. "Do you have a way to free her from Cthulhu?"

Hephaestus pursed his lips and shook his head. "He is an outsider. The only thing he wants is to upset the balance and gain power. I have nothing I wish to offer him except that he continues to slumber." He turned and limped toward the shadows. Before I could stop him, he seemed to fade away into the darkness. I cast a ball of light where he'd gone. It revealed nothing but emptiness. Except for the marks left in the rubble by his bad foot, it was as if he'd never been there.

I groaned. "Fuck my life." I looked around, half-expecting another godly visitor, but saw nothing. "Thanatos, you there? Can we talk?"

Death didn't reply. It seemed that once I'd shed my ghosts, he'd lost interest in me. And here I thought we'd become friends. Silly me, the gods didn't have friends. Just curiosities and interests. And that was all I was to them.

It was a tenuous position no one reasonable would want to be in. But it looked like I was stuck with it. And despite everything, I'd failed to find a way to free Hannah. All I had to look forward to was training her for the rest of the month. And then she'd return to Cthulhu. If she was good enough, he'd let her live and then use her for his purposes.

There was only one way out of this, and I hated to consider it, but I owed it to Hannah to give her the choice. Cthulhu might kill me for it, but at this point, I'd probably be fine with that. I almost wished I'd kept the trident and hammer if only to track down R'lyeh and destroy the ever-living fuck out of it.

But that chance was gone. I was back to being plain old me. At least, aside from a sword with an army of the dead inside it.

All that was left to do now was go home.

CHAPTER 37

I had to swim out to the submarine.

The task was somewhat more frightening now that I knew what kind of monstrous fish roamed the dark waters. I could have sworn something brushed past my legs several times, but the anticipated stab of sharp teeth through my flesh never came. A leechen popped to the surface when I was nearly to the submarine. He looked at me curiously for a moment, then vanished beneath the surface.

I wondered if they'd been protecting me at the behest of Poseidon. I wondered if the appearance of so many gods recently signaled something momentous that I hadn't picked up on yet. It was nice having a little divine help, but when the gods took notice of someone, that usually didn't bode well. Perseus and Hercules knew that all too well. As did the many men and women who made the gods jealous. Medusa came to mind.

The best course of action from here on out was going back home and laying low until it was time for Hannah to return to Cthulhu. I considered the sword at my back and wondered if an army of the dead was enough to overcome the minions of old Octopus Head.

Perhaps it was time to threaten instead of bargain with the ancient bastard.

Back on the sub, I took a shower and changed into an ill-fitting uniform I found in one of the bunkrooms. Layla had already set course for the deepways and we were just passing the underwater city and its miniature sun when I went to the bridge.

"You were in the armory for a while," Layla said. "What took so long?"

"I had a visitor." I told them about Hephaestus.

Aura grimaced. "If I didn't know better, I'd think you've been chosen as a hero of the gods, Cain."

Layla chuckled. "That's exactly what's happened. There's a feud among the gods, and Cain is the one who gets to sort it out."

I shook my head vehemently. "Not gonna happen. They can settle their own differences."

"Hermes was a messenger for Hera," Aura said. "I suspect Poseidon and Hephaestus are on the other side of the dispute."

"I think it's even bigger than that," Layla said. "I think they want Cain to deal with Cthulhu for them."

"Hermes told me not to," I said. "He didn't want me finding a way to break a bargain with a god."

"Hera has never liked it when mortal heroes challenge the gods." Aura sighed. "Not even when the gods in question are outsiders like Cthulhu. So in addition to him, you have Hera to worry about."

"Nothing new there," I said.

"I'm sorry I brought all this down on you, Cain." Hannah slumped in her chair. "You probably had a nice quiet life before me."

I nodded. "Yeah, but it didn't have meaning." I put a hand on her head. "At least now, I've got something to fight for."

Layla groaned. "Famous last words."

Aura's forehead pinched. "You're not the same Cain I met years ago."

I shrugged. "You're not the cute friendly elf I thought you were years ago. The more you get to know someone, the more they disappoint you."

Layla scoffed. "Say what you want about the elf, but I don't disappoint."

I chuckled. "Yeah, you've always been an amazing asshole."

"Damned right," Layla said.

Our new submarine was much more advanced than the one we'd stolen before. Once a destination was marked on the globe of Gaia, it was able to navigate us straight to the proper channels without all the guesswork. I expected to meet an army of Cthulhu's minions during the journey back through the deepways, but only the corpse of the giant squid lurked in the underwater waystations.

We traversed from the oceans of Oblivion back to Lake Lanier within a few hours. After we gathered our belongings from the submarine and stepped onto the dock, it was hard to believe we'd ever left Gaia and fought apocalyptic battles over a devastated world.

I drew in a deep breath of fresh air and sighed in contentment. My lungs rejoiced at the rich concentration of oxygen and nitrogen. It was damned good to be back on a non-apocalyptic plane. Back to nature and a world at peace.

Layla waved goodbye to the submarine. "See you soon, Roxy."

Then we turned and headed toward land.

"Stop!" A desperate voice called out behind us. "I'll kill you all where you stand."

I set down my backpack, then raised my arms and turned slowly. A very battered and bruised Horatio brandished a mechanist machine gun. A red stripe on the magazine clip told me it held incendiary rounds.

"How in the fuck?" Layla shook her head. "Am I losing it, or did he somehow sneak past us onto the sub and hide without any of us detecting him?"

"Where are the weapons?" Horatio said. "Give them to me and I will let you live."

"We destroyed them all." I studied the tremble in his hands. He was weak, tired, and scared. "No one deserves that kind of power."

Horatio shook his head. "No, you're lying. No one would forego the chance to become a god."

"That's exactly what we did," Hannah said. "We don't want idiots like you destroying the world."

The realization that we were telling the truth sank into his mind, and his eyes widened in horror. "No!" Horatio's lips trembled. "All those decades of work, wasted!" Tears trickled down his cheeks. "How could you be so monstrous?"

"What you accomplished is no mean feat," I said. "You've mapped the deepways and enabled travel to other worlds without portals. Why not put your genius to good use and start cataloguing what's out there instead of seeking weapons to destroy it?"

"No!" Horatio pulled the trigger.

I summoned my staff and the brightblade hummed to life. I deflected three rounds into the water and cast shields to block another volley. I ghostwalked to his side and slashed down across the barrel of the rifle, turning it to scrap.

Horatio yelped in surprise, dropping the weapon and jumping back. He tripped over his own feet and nearly toppled into the water. I gripped him by the front of his lab coat and yanked him upright. A solid right hook sent him to dreamland.

Layla slow clapped. "Good job beating down an old man, Cain."

I flipped her off.

"What will we do with him?" Aura said. "We can't just leave him here."

"I think killing him is for the best," Hannah said. "Even though I don't feel good about it."

I pursed my lips. "We'll haul him back to my place until I figure out what to do with him." I slung Horatio over a shoulder and grabbed my backpack with a free hand. Then we headed for the garage. I was so happy to see Dolores that I almost cried. "Hey, baby," I whispered as I stroked her glossy black paint.

Layla snorted. "I heard that."

I didn't care. We slid our stuff into the back. I used some climbing rope to secure Horatio and gagged him with a shirt tied around his mouth. Then I backed out and drove along the gravel road through the woods. We were nearly to the main road when a blue compact car screeched to a halt ahead, blocking the route. A rusty old SUV skidded to a stop right behind it.

A man in gray robes hopped out of the compact car. His identical twin leapt from the SUV. They warily regarded each other for a moment, as if neither expected to find the other right here, right now. And that surprised the hell out of me because they were the same identical siblings who'd been trying to kill me for the past few days.

I'd almost forgotten about this particular threat. Apparently, they hadn't been able to find me during my time in Oblivion, but once I'd returned here, they'd been able to track me once again.

Layla groaned. "These jerkoffs again?"

I put Dolores into park and got out. Strode down the gravel road toward the twins. They drew dueling wands and stalked toward me, hatred burning in their eyes.

"Can either of you talk?" I said. "It'd be great if you could tell me what in the hell is going on."

The one on the left shouted gibberish at me. The one on the right blinked, as if startled by the nonsense spewing from the other's mouth. He tried to talk to his twin—tried to, anyway. His incoherent sounds drew a surprised look from the other one. They started making noises at each other, visibly alarmed because they didn't seem to understand each other any better than I did.

"Who are you people?" I said. "Where did you come from?"

They turned to me again, the hatred burning away their confusion and narrowing their focus down to the objective. They flicked their dueling wands, mirroring each other almost perfectly, and stalked toward their prey. Seeing me seemed to override their higher reasoning and caused them to ignore everything else. And yet they were definitely not automatons or golems. They charged me, wands flaring to life.

I drew my staff and flicked on the brightblade. I deflected their spells into trees. The odor of charred wood filled the air. They whirled through identical patterns and fired more spells simultaneously. It was as if they were wired exactly the same with no deviance.

They were so focused on me they didn't seem to realize how they mirrored each other.

Hannah got out of the car and hid behind a tree. "How can I help?"

I held up my hand to halt her. "By staying out of the way."

Layla took cover behind another tree, two arrows nocked in her normal bow. She flicked from cover and fired. Invisible shields blocked the arrows just feet from piercing the eyes of the attackers. She ran sideways, strafing them with arrows. I took the opportunity to switch my staff to longshot mode. I flicked up the scope, took aim, and sent a surge of power through the staff. Aimed again and released another energy projectile.

The first should have seared a hole through the head of the man on the right, but both projectiles cracked into an invisible barrier. Yellow energy crackled up and down the length, briefly revealing it.

"Where the hell did that come from?" I said.

Aura stood next to me, eyes wide as she looked skyward.

The crisp, cold air abruptly warmed and shadows danced all around us. I followed Aura's gaze and saw a dark-haired girl floating on wings of golden sunlight above the trees. Eyes gleaming with anger, jaw set in fury, Daphne, the demigoddess of the sun, threw glowing yellow orbs toward us.

"It's the Firsters!" Layla shouted from somewhere to my left.

I threw up a shield, but the golden orbs smashed through it like paper. Someone grabbed me and threw me bodily through the air. I caught a glimpse of Aura as superheated energy blasted her, charring clothes and flesh.

She screamed in horrific agony, limbs thrashing as she burned and died. I tumbled through the leaves and back into cold air. A volley of arrows sang through the air toward Daphne but turned to ash before coming close.

Aura's body went still, smoking amid a pile of burnt leaves. I turned in a circle, looking everywhere for Hannah. Where had she gone? I spotted movement and saw her crouched behind a tree, gaze locked on Aura's still form, eyes wide with horror. Body trembling, she looked up at Daphne.

I wanted to call out to her not to do anything stupid but didn't want to give away my position. The demigoddess floated above, rotating slowly as she searched for targets. The assassin twins, no longer defending against Layla's arrows, reset their position directly beneath Daphne.

Rustling branches and crackling leaves drew my attention away from the most immediate threat and out into the forest. At first, I didn't see anything, but then I noticed the slight blurs in the air. I peered through the true sight scope on my staff. It penetrated the camouflage illusions hiding over a dozen mages as they tried to sneak into position around us.

A black van parked behind the other two cars blocking the end of the road and a dozen figures in black military gear piled out, followed by a man in gray robes. The man looked identical to the twin assassins, but there was something much different about his bearing. He was calm, collected, and seemingly in charge.

Hannah looked away from Aura and locked eyes with me. I pointed toward the hidden mages sneaking in from the direction of the road, but she didn't seem to understand. Layla had vanished to gods knew where, and I couldn't blame her. There was no way to get back to Dolores without drawing fire from Daphne, which meant we had to retreat on foot back toward the lake.

I pointed at Hannah and then back the way we'd come from. She nodded. I didn't have the range to cast an illusion blind to hide her, which meant I'd need to provide a distraction. I held up three fingers and counted down. Three. Two. One. I made a fist and urgently pointed toward the lake. At the same time, I burst from cover, brightblade glowing in my hand.

"What do you want?" I shouted at the gray mage.

Daphne and the mage twins turned all their attention on me. I stomped around in the leaves, covering the sounds of Hannah's retreat as she dashed toward the lake. I didn't know if anyone saw her, but since the camouflaged mages hadn't burst from cover to chase her, it seemed my ploy had worked.

The assassin twins whirled their wands and prepared to attack, but a gesture from the gray mage stopped them. He walked between his doppelgangers and stopped just in front of them, eyes narrowed at me.

"You know what we want, Cain." He spoke in a low voice. "You killed three of our leaders and ruined years of preparation to destroy the Human-Fae Alliance."

"Oh, is that all?" I shrugged. "That's just a fun night on the town for me."

He didn't crack a smile. "Mead, Digby, and Ingram founded the Humans

First movement and worked tirelessly all their lives to overthrow our fae overlords." He shook his head. "They gladly gave their lives for the cause."

"Well, it's good to know they died doing what they loved." I whirled my brightblade. "What I'd like to know is who you are and how many identical brothers you've got."

His doppelgangers burst into excited chatter, all of it gibberish.

He held up a hand to quiet them. "I am Keenan, among the first to survive the demigod serum. Once per day, I am able to create a shadow copy of myself and have it do my bidding."

"Do you know how many household chores you could get done with clones of yourself?" I whistled. "You're in the wrong business, friend."

"They fade away after a few days, I'm afraid." Keenan put a hand on the shoulders of his shadow copies. "And they are unable to speak properly. But they are single-minded about the tasks I send them to do. Fearless."

"What about the scars?" I said. "They multiply with each one."

He nodded. "Scars do that for some strange reason, but only if I continue to copy myself daily. If I wait for a few days, the next shadow will only have the one scar."

At long last, I knew the truth. But now it seemed the truth was here to kill me for good. Running for the lake was no longer an option. Even if I had the strength to ghostwalk until I was miles away the flying demigoddess above would turn me to a charred corpse like Aura.

There was only one way out.

CHAPTER 38

I turned off my brightblade and lowered the staff. "Look, I was only a hired gun. I don't know who commissioned the job, but they're the real people you need to deal with." I knew all too well it had been a unicorn who wanted them dead. "So, what do you say we just shake hands and go our separate ways?"

Keenan's brow furrowed briefly, a miniscule crack in his stony exterior. "We know you are merely an assassin, a tool used to kill our leadership. We want you dead for personal reasons, but also because you have someone that we want. The demigoddess named Hannah."

I sighed. I'd known my offer wouldn't work. No one would go through this much trouble to kill me and just walk away. Wanting me dead for personal reasons and wanting to conscript Hannah into their organization were reasons enough to mobilize a small army to come take me.

"How have your shadows been tracking me?" I said.

"We have some of your blood, neatly preserved," Keenan said.

My hand tightened around my staff. Even if we escaped, that was going to be quite a problem. Then again, that worked both ways. I just hoped my preparations with the blood I'd taken from a dead clone paid off. "Your shadows are exact copies, yes?"

The shadow copies tilted their heads like curious dogs. Keenan did the same, but to a much lesser degree. "Down to every last hair."

"That's good." I reached into my utility belt and pulled out a little side project I'd been working on in my spare time. I held up a tiny crimson prism and let the golden rays from Daphne make it sparkle. "How willing are you to die for the cause, Keenan?"

He blinked twice, clearly not expecting the question. "Whatever that weapon is, it won't work against our combined power. Give up the girl, and we will end you quickly."

"You know, you're not the first person to make me that offer in the past twenty-four hours." I pinched my chin and grunted as if seriously thinking about it. "It's really tempting. If you throw in a mangorita, I might just take you up on it."

The doppelgangers shouted angrily.

Keenan hushed them again. "You will die in agony like your friend, Cain."

I looked down at Aura's charred corpse and prayed to the gods she hadn't been lying about her curse. "Hey, at least she died warm." I held up the prism again. "This isn't a conventional weapon, Keenan. In fact, it's quite specific in purpose."

"I don't know what you mean," he replied.

"I took some of your shadow's blood," I said. "And with it, I wove a neat little fae enchantment that will turn your blood into acid."

Kennan scoffed. "The words of a desperate man."

I scoffed back. "Do you wish to test me?"

He shook his head. "Even if it were true—"

I interrupted. "I'm not close enough to use it on you?" I said. "See, that's the neat thing about fae magic. I don't need to touch you. All I have to do is activate the curse, and it's a done deal." What I hadn't mentioned was one small item—I really did need to be about fifty feet from him for it to work, and right now, I was a good thirty feet too far.

Keenan must have thought I was bluffing if his next words were anything to go on. He pursed his lips. "Kill him."

My brightblade hummed to life. "Hey, Keenan, prepare to die in agony."

Aside from floating in the air on gossamer wings of sunlight, Daphne looked like a cute little teeny bopper who should be clothes shopping with her besties. But the malicious grin that formed on her face when Keenan gave the kill order told me she'd been programmed into a killing machine.

Killing the demigod kid, Sigma, hadn't been pleasant, but it had been necessary. Ironically, killing a kid had cured me of my ghost problem. I hoped killing Daphne wouldn't start that all nastiness over again because it was nice to be alone inside my head again after all these years.

Shields didn't do the trick against Daphne's magic. My only hope was the untested theory that my upgraded staff might help me fight fire with fire. Or in this case, sunlight with sunlight. After all, the staff withstood the might of Soultaker, so surely it could take on godlike powers.

The demigoddess flung a golden orb of sunlight toward me. It flew so fast I barely had enough time to dodge to the side. I thrust out my brightblade and swatted it. Either this would work, or they'd be naming a crater after me. Most normal spells deflected easily, but magic of this magnitude usually wouldn't. I'd found that out the hard way with Sigma. Then again, I was nowhere near fast enough to deflect lightning bolts.

The blade crackled, hummed, and sent the golden orb flying straight back at Keenan and his shadows. Eyes wide, they dove out of the way and the orb smashed into the armed personnel behind him. People screamed and died as they burned in agony. The first row of their formation took the brunt of the attack and the others scattered behind cover.

Arrows sprouted from the eyes of two men as they ran. Another volley streaked past and ended two more lives. The armed men shouted and began firing into the trees as additional arrows claimed souls.

Daphne thrust out her hands and fired a solid beam of energy at me. A little more confident, I blocked it with an overhead parry and angled my brightblade to deflect it to the right. The beam sliced through trees. Camouflaged mages screamed and flickered into view as their own demigoddess mowed them down.

She screamed but refused to relent. The brightblade crackled louder. The hilt grew hotter and hotter until it threatened to scorch my flesh. I dove away as Daphne raked the beams toward me. There was only one safe place to go, and it wasn't left, right, or back. So, I ghostwalked straight ahead.

I could only manage to go about ten or fifteen feet in a single try. And unless I wanted to burn through my endurance fast, I couldn't afford to do it several times in a row. But my sudden vanishing in a puff of black smoke and appearing a dozen feet away was enough to throw most people off their stride. Daphne was no exception.

She stopped her attack, confused and searching. And in that brief instance, I ran straight for Keenan, uttering the final words of the curse in Alder. Keenan was a hair faster than his shadows, drawing his dueling wands and firing. His shadows mimicked him almost exactly. But it was too late. I finished the curse and flicked the prism of his blood at him.

I didn't really need to do that, but it felt good seeing the surprise on the bastard's face, mirrored perfectly by his shadows. Then I dove to the ground, barely dodging the hurled energy from their wands. One of the armed men aimed at me. An arrow pierced his throat before he pulled the trigger.

The hilt of my staff was still uncomfortably hot, but I had no choice but to wield it anyway. I rolled to my feet and swung it in an arc to fend of the bullets from another man's gun. Flicking my fingers though a pattern, I thrust them forward and sent a gust of energy at the attacker. He grunted and flew backward a couple of feet, landing on his back.

I ghostwalked forward, slashed down, and sent his head rolling. The next man spun toward me, rifle already spraying bullets. I slashed off the barrel, ducked, and whipped the brightblade sideways. His torso slid off his legs, and sizzling guts splashed onto the ground. The next man lost his arms, and two more went down with arrows in their eyes or necks. Then Layla blurred from cover, daggers flying. People screamed and died.

Daphne screeched, but didn't dare unleash her power with so many of her people in her vicinity. Keenan roared and rushed me. Surprise lit his face as crimson-speckled foam bubbled from his mouth. His wands fell from limp fingers and he dropped to the ground. His skin bubbled. He convulsed like a dying fish, flopping uncontrollably on the ground. Blood dribbled from every pore in his skin as it turned to acid and ate its way through soft organs and flesh.

"Cain!" Hannah screamed. Beams of white light slashed down a dozen trees at once.

Mages dropped their camouflage illusions and scattered to the wind as the furious demigoddess unleashed her wrath.

Daphne shrieked in fury and fired down at Hannah.

"Hannah!" I shouted.

Concentrated sunlight exploded against the earth. Hannah flew through the air and was lost to sight. Daphne grinned maliciously at me. Layla loosed more arrows, but they burned up before reaching the girl.

"Die, you pre-pubescent little bitch!" Layla hurled daggers.

The demigoddess tried to stop them, but the metal didn't melt fast enough. She thrust out her hands and a burst of energy deflected the blades. But Layla had more at the ready. The girl looked toward the fleeing mages and flew after them. Layla's daggers flashed through empty air where she'd been.

I ran toward Hannah's last position. Smoke from burning leaves filled the air. I heard someone groaning and found her lying behind a thick pine tree that had taken the brunt of Daphne's wrath. I dashed through the burning leaves and scooped her up.

Her face was black with soot, but she looked otherwise okay.

Hannah's eyes blinked open. "Ship out of danger?"

"What?"

A small smile lit her face. "Don't grieve, admiral. The needs of the many outweigh the needs of the few or the one."

"You nearly died and you're quoting Spock's last words to me?" I growled. "I told you to run, not come back and die!"

"I couldn't leave you, Cain." A tear cleaned the soot from her cheek. "You're the only family I have."

"Can you walk?" I said perhaps a bit too gruffly.

She nodded, so I set her down. Hannah winced, but started walking. I scanned the area with my true sight scope and made sure it was clear of enemies. The Firsters had fled, but with the fires and exploding cars, this place was sure to be crawling with authorities in minutes.

"We need to go." I hurried back to the car.

Layla stood over Aura's body, brow furrowed.

Hannah looked down and fresh tears gathered in her eyes. "She was a bitch, but she saved you."

"Stupid elf." Layla sighed and looked at me. "Just so we're clear, Cain, I wouldn't have done the same."

"Yeah, I know." I knelt next to the still-smoking corpse and winced at the odor. The flesh was warm, but not too hot. Flesh and muscle were still intact beneath the charred exterior, making it a nasty sight indeed. I activated a sigil on Dolores and the trunk opened.

Horatio was awake and squirming like a worm inside. A gray amulet on a chain of cogs had spilled from beneath his lab coat and twisted around his neck. I yanked it free so he wouldn't choke.

His eyes widened when I brought Aura's corpse to the back, and he started screaming through his gag when I laid her curled form on a blanket next to him. Then I knocked him out again and closed the back door.

"Let's go." I climbed into the driver's seat and the others hopped in the back. I gunned the car forward. Thankfully, there was just enough room to squeeze by the bloody puddles of flesh and bone that had once been Keenan and his twins. I dodged between the rest of the bodies and navigated through the remains of the burning cars on the main gravel road.

I turned opposite of the way back toward the main highway because I didn't want to be seen coming from the scene of the fire. This road would take us around the lake and eventually back to the highway where we could blend in with other traffic.

"I can't believe she's dead," Hannah said.

Layla sighed. "Gonna cry, little girl?"

Hannah bared her teeth at Layla. "I'll make you cry, asshole!"

I groaned. "Can you two behave for the ride home? I'm fucking tired!"

Layla burst into laughter, but it sounded forced. "Yes, Dad."

I sighed and shook my head.

We made it home without many more outbursts. I dumped Horatio in a cell in my basement and put Aura's body in another room on a blanket. Then I went upstairs, made myself a sandwich and a stiff drink, and sat down to relax.

Layla plopped down on the couch next to me and patted my leg. "You okay, Cain?" For once, she sounded serious.

"I'm fine."

"I seriously thought you'd be way more broken up about Aura." She pursed her lips. "I mean, she didn't like you, but you had a thing for her."

"I'm over her," I said. I hadn't even considered telling her or Hannah about Aura's curse. Partially because it was none of my business to tell the others, but also because I wanted to see the looks on their faces when she came back to life.

"Damn, you're harder than I thought." Layla sighed. "That's good, I guess."

I nodded. "Yeah."

"I thought the girl made you too soft. But I'm glad to see you have what it takes."

I took another bite of sandwich and grunted. "You don't sound happy."

Layla swallowed hard and wiped her eyes. "I'm happy as a fucking lark." Then she got up and made herself something to eat.

"Don't you have an orgy or something to attend?" I asked her.

Hand blurring, she cut a tomato into perfect slices. "I'm not in that kind of mood tonight."

"What kind of mood are you in?" I said.

Layla shrugged. "Hell if I know." She finished making her sandwich and vanished into the guest bedroom with it and a bottle of my good tequila.

"You're a terrible guest," I shouted after her.

"I know," she shouted back and then shut the door.

Hannah emerged from her room, freshly showered and wearing a black onesie. She curled up next to me and leaned on my shoulder. Her eyes were red from crying. "I can't stop thinking about Aura."

I set down my sandwich and put an arm on her shoulder. "Everything will be okay." I wrestled with telling her. After all, Aura would have to explain things when she came back to life, right? I hadn't expected it to affect Hannah so much, and it seemed cruel to cause her unnecessary pain.

She looked up at me. "Why can't I use my powers when I want to, Cain? I could have killed Daphne and saved everyone."

"First of all, don't worry about Aura." I leaned forward and whispered in her ear. "Whatever you do, don't tell Layla, but Aura is alive."

Hannah gasped and clamped a hand over her mouth. She leaned closer and whispered back. "How?"

"It's not for me to say. But don't breathe another word about it, okay?"

"Doesn't she need a healer?" Hannah whispered.

I put a finger to my lips. Shook my head. "Go get something to eat and get a good night's rest. We'll start training again in the morning."

"Can we watch another classic *Star Trek*?" she asked.

I smiled. Nodded. "Yeah. But be prepared for disappointment. *The Wrath of Khan* was the best of the bunch."

She smiled and wiped away her tears. "Thanks, Cain. For everything."

"You're welcome, Hannah." Even though our mission had failed miserably, everything suddenly seemed worth it. All because I made Hannah just a little bit happier. Layla was right, I was going soft. But for some reason, I really didn't mind.

I made some popcorn, put on the third *Star Trek* movie, and settled in. It was hard to believe everything we'd been through in the past few days. Unfortunately, we weren't through the worst of it yet.

CHAPTER 39

After the movie, Hannah went to bed. I took my laptop down to the basement room where I'd placed Aura. Her corpse still looked the same, but the blood was blacker, and the body had stiffened. The room served as a storage space for old furniture I didn't use anymore. I sat down on a red leather couch that had been there for five years and turned on my laptop.

Now that I had a moment, it was time to deal with the next big issue. I couldn't let Humans First keep tracking me with my blood. While I was within the confines of the silver circle around the church, they couldn't track me, but eventually, they'd triangulate my coordinates on a map and figure out where I lived. I only hoped they weren't tracking my locations too closely already.

I went to the dark web and navigated to a site run by someone who could probably help. I hadn't talked to him in a long while, but that was mainly because he moved around a lot to avoid the fae. I'd never gotten the full story from him, mainly because I didn't think it was any of my business. The silver lining for his predicament was that he'd come up with ways to stay off the radar even with people actively searching for him. In fact, he was the druid who'd protected the land around my lake house.

A quick email through his secure link gave him the number to my burner phone. Then I shut down the laptop, leaned back, and rested my eyes.

I jerked awake not much later to loud moans. I check the time—midnight, right on the nose. Ragged groans and moans emerged from Aura's still form. Her body convulsed. Burnt clothing hair, and skin sloughed off like a shedding snake. She sucked in a breath and her body convulsed again. The rest of her charred skin fell away, revealing undamaged pink flesh beneath.

Aura shrieked and jerked upright, hands shielding her face as if facing the wrath of Daphne again. She blinked, looked around at the room, and spotted me on the couch. "Cain." Shivering and naked, she stood, even as new hair grew to cover her bald scalp and private parts.

I picked up a folded blanket and wrapped it around her shoulders, then sat back down. Aura sat in my lap and burrowed her face into my shoulder, sobbing gently.

"Thank you," she said.

"For what?" I said. "You saved my life."

"For being here when I resurrected." Aura kissed my cheek. "For the blanket and warmth."

I patted her back. "Uh, sure. Least I could do."

Then she scooted off my lap and lay down, using my lap as a pillow. Despite having been dead for several hours, Aura went peacefully to sleep. It was a little awkward, because I didn't want to spend the rest of my night sitting on the couch. I slipped out from beneath her, then lifted her and carried her upstairs.

I set her down on the couch in the den and put another blanket over her.

Fred perched on the lip of his pool, golden eyes watching me. I needed to have a conversation with Cthulhu, but now was not the time. I waved at him. "Talk soon." Then I went to bed.

"Gods almighty!" Layla's shout of surprise yanked me from slumber at three in the morning. "Why aren't you dead?"

I stumbled out into the den and enjoyed the shocked look on Layla's face as she stared in horror at a bleary-eyed Aura.

"Can you shut up and let me sleep?" Aura said. "Being dead is tiring."

Layla looked up at me. "I'm not dreaming right? The elf is alive?"

I nodded. "Yep."

"How?"

I sighed. "It's not my place to say."

Layla looked down at Aura. "How are you alive?"

"Will you go away, or do I need to kill myself again to get a good night's rest?" Aura said.

Layla bared her teeth. "You realize this makes you a zombie, right?"

Aura scoffed. "Exactly."

"Don't come looking to eat my brain." Layla spun on her heel and went back toward her bedroom.

I frowned. "Did you come out here for some reason?"

"No!" Layla shut the door behind her.

Aura rubbed her eyes and looked up at me with a faint smile. "You enjoyed that, didn't you?"

"Yep." Then I went back to my room and tried to go back to sleep.

I jerked awake not much later as the hairs on my neck prickled. My bedroom door clicked softly open and closed. I knew from the scent of leather and lavender who'd just entered. The other side of the bed shifted slightly as she climbed in next to me.

I blew out a breath. "What are you doing, Layla?"

She sidled up to me, arm across my chest. "I couldn't sleep." The odor of alcohol was heavy on her breath.

"You were up earlier for a booty call?" I said.

"You should be a detective, Cain."

I snorted. "Yeah." A yawn stole my next words.

Layla's lips touched my ear, my cheek. "Do you ever think about that night in the tent?"

"When you got me wet and left me hanging?" I blew out a breath. "Not really."

Her hand went down to my stomach. "Liar."

"Why are you doing this, Layla? You don't even like me that way, as you've reminded me so many times." I gripped her wrist and kept it from going lower. "I don't appreciate being tortured."

She sighed. "Fuck it. This is stupid." She got up.

I flicked on the lamp and grabbed her arm as she tried to leave. She wore nothing but one of my t-shirts she'd stolen the last time here. Her small breasts pressed tantalizingly against the fabric. My hand went up the back of her neck and gently gripped her hair close to the scalp. I leaned forward and kissed her.

Layla's body pressed against mine. Her hand grabbed my ass and squeezed. I bit her neck, her ears, and then shoved her against the wall for another deep kiss. She writhed and moaned.

Then I opened the bedroom door and shoved her outside. Closed it and locked it.

"Are you fucking serious?" Layla pounded on the door. "Cain, I'm going to rip off your nuts!"

Aura burst into laughter. "Gods, Layla, that was pathetic."

"I'll kill you again if you don't shut up, elf." Layla pounded on my door again. "Gods damn you, Cain!"

"They already have," I said. "They already have."

Layla's angry muttering faded as she retreated to her room, and Aura's laughter died back down. With the house once more silent, I went back to bed and fell asleep with a grin on my face.

There was a text on my burner phone the next morning.

He can help you when he gets back. Major problem with the Norse gods right now.

I frowned. *Who's this?*

His associate. He'll try to have something for you by the end of the week.

I texted back. *Thanks. I don't know if the Firsters are still tracking me. It's urgent.*

Understood. Will let you know soon.

It wasn't what I'd hoped for, but it was something. My druid acquaintance was the only one who had the kind of magic to block blood tracking.

I pocketed my phone and went into the kitchen to make breakfast. This time I put some extra finishing touches on the pancakes and hastily scrawled a sign.

Hannah gasped behind me.

I turned just in time for her to ram into my midriff with a bone-crushing hug. She looked up at me, tears in her eyes. "Thanks, Cain."

Aura yawned and sat up. She saw the sign and shook her head in amazement. "You never cease to surprise me, Cain." She turned to Hannah. "Happy birthday, Hannah."

Hannah frowned before managing a small smile. "Thanks. But don't think you dying makes me trust you."

"Can I still have some of your birthday pancakes?" Aura asked.

Hannah nodded. "Sure."

Layla marched into the dining area a moment later and shook her head when she saw what I'd written. "Gods, Cain. You're too damned soft."

I shrugged. "Deal with it."

"Yeah, deal with it!" Hannah said.

Layla dropped into a seat and looked at the frosted pancakes with the candles on top. "Well, girl, can you blow out the candles so we can eat?"

Hannah grinned and skipped over to the pancakes.

I lit the candles with a spell. "Make a wish."

She wiped a tear from her cheeks. "It's already been granted." Hannah stood on tiptoe and kissed my cheek.

"Kill me now," Layla groaned.

I started singing "Happy Birthday to You." Aura joined in immediately. Layla groaned, but begrudgingly joined. When the song was done, Hannah blew out the candles in one go.

She took a stack of pancakes for herself, and Layla snatched the next few.

I sat down and watched in amusement as the hastily arranged birthday party went off with relatively little bitching from Layla.

Layla licked frosting from her lips. "Okay, I'll admit these are some damned good pancakes."

"They're amazing," Hannah said.

Hannah might not have made a wish, but I had, despite knowing all too well such things came with steep prices. I'd wished for her to be free from Cthulhu's grasp. There was no genie available to grant my request, but I would do everything in my power to make that wish come true.

Copyright © 2020 by John Corwin.

Paperback Edition ISBN 978-1-942453-20-8

All rights reserved. Except as permitted under the U.S. Copyright Act of 1976, no part of this publication may be reproduced, distributed, or transmitted in any form or by any means, or stored in a database or retrieval system, without the prior written permission of the publisher.

The characters and events in this book are fictitious. Any similarity to real persons, living or dead, is coincidental and not intended by the author.

LICENSE NOTES:

The ebook format is licensed for your personal enjoyment only. The ebook may not be re-sold or given away to other people unless expressly permitted by the author. If you would like to share this book with another person, please purchase an additional copy for each recipient. If you're reading this book and did not purchase it, or it was not purchased for your use only, then please go to a digital ebook retailer and purchase your own copy. Thank you for respecting the hard work of this author.

❦ Created with Vellum

ABOUT THE AUTHOR

John Corwin is the bestselling author of the Overworld Chronicles. He enjoys long walks on the beach and is a firm believer in puppies and kittens.

After years of getting into trouble thanks to his overactive imagination, John abandoned his male modeling career to write books.

He resides in Atlanta.

Connect with John Corwin online:
Facebook: http://www.facebook.com/johnhcorwinauthor
Website: http://www.johncorwin.net
Twitter: http://twitter.com/#!/John_Corwin

Made in the USA
Monee, IL
23 May 2020